The Stranger From Meclan

by Leland Brown

Chapter 1

The cosmos is inconceivably vast, stretching beyond the horizons of both mathematics and imagination alike in an ever-expanding infinity; And it doesn't give a single solid shit about you or anyone else. Whether you're a mighty emperor at the height of his reign, or a lowly ore crawler at the dregs of his last bottle; It makes no difference to the endless black maw that hungrily awaits just beyond the hull. This was a fact of life that Commander Dex Sloan understood more intimately than most. During the thirty-one supremely eventful years that had comprised his life so far, Dex had accumulated a wealth of know-how that served to keep him breathing through countless binds that would have spelled the end for lesser men. Chief among these learned lessons was the fact that working with other people inevitably led to complications, ten times out of ten. And in Dex's personal experience, *'complications'* generally resulted in the abrupt shortening of *somebody's* lifespan.

That was exactly why Dex chose his current profession and the self-imposed isolation it entailed. As a cargo hauler, making runs along the sparsely populated outer fringes of the Federal bubble, he was able to earn enough scratch to keep his ship fueled and his stomach full. It was a simple life, but it allowed him to minimize his reliance on others and afforded him the luxury of spending his time out in the black where he felt that he truly belonged.

Sitting alone in his dimly lit cockpit, Dex was leaned back in his perfectly calibrated pilot's chair with his feet kicked up onto the worn console in front of him. The air, swirling in warm currents around his seat like a comforting blanket, was bathed in the rich aroma of an ever-present cup of coffee that sat silently steaming in his arm rest, lending a cozier feel to the already inviting space. He had been lingering at the edge of sleep for a while now, his attention vaguely focused on the calming multi-colored kaleidoscope of zerospace whipping by outside his canopy as his mind blissfully wandered. These were the moments that made him love his job. Being alone, at peace in his ship. His *home*.

Mere seconds after Dex had finally dozed off, the quiet scene was thrown into chaos as the ship bucked and jerked violently in every direction. The colors outside the canopy then abruptly snapped from the chromatic nonsense of faster-than-light travel to the choking blackness of normal space with a bone-jarring vibration. Dex tumbled toward his console in the commotion and slammed into its control surface, sending his beloved beverage splashing into the air to coat everything around him.

"Interdiction detected." warned the ship's AI with the distinctly female purr of its smoothly modulated artificial voice.

"Yeah, *no shit!*" replied Dex with frustrated annoyance, wincing as he shook the steaming hot liquid from his sleeves.

"Signal delay to the nearest relay is currently twenty-three minutes." Stated the AI regretfully, "Would you like me to contact the authorities for combat support?"

"Not necessary, Vette," sighed Dex with a roll of his eyes, "just help me figure out who the hell interdicted us! Fire up our active scanners and gimme a reading on any inbound ships."

"Three vessels are rapidly approaching." Stated Vette dutifully as she pulled them up on a magnified viewscreen, "They are one-hundred and twenty-one kilometers out and appear to be broadcasting no ID codes, Commander."

Dex examined the ships in his readout to assess the inbound threat, frowning with concentration as additional details trickled in through his ship's wide array of sensors. Each of the unidentified vessels had returned a small radar cross-section, but were giving off a massive amount of Electro-Magnetic (EM) energy with a very low thermal reading. One could determine quite a lot about a pilot's intentions by observing an approaching vessel's power management behavior, and the pilots headed Dex's way definitely weren't looking to make friends. The ships closing in on him were running their reactors hot, leaking a majority of their generated energy straight into the vacuum as a rush of superheated helium that stretched out behind them in a massive and expanding wake. Doing so wasn't an unintended waste, however. It served to showcase the small group's potential firepower in a fashion that mimicked a predator baring its teeth at a foe before attacking. To any experienced pilot, the identity of the uninvited guests was clear; Pirates.

"Shit." Hissed Dex through clenched teeth, "I don't have time to fuck around with these dipshits today. Vette, move power to the shields and start charging our weapon systems, please. I have a little present for our friends."

Zeroing his throttle, Dex fully powered down his main engines to make an obvious gesture of docility. At first, the three approaching craft existed only as figures on his instruments, but then a trio of shimmers became evident as they moved along the backdrop of starlight ahead of him. Drawing nearer, more and more features of the inbound ships began to return from the sensors. The group consisted of a single light freighter with two escort fighters flanking it to either side. The silhouette of the freighter was boxy and of an older design that Dex didn't recognize, but it had an impressive looking collection of plasma repeaters arrayed along its belly that appeared as if they were haphazardly welded to the hull.

Mismatched armor plating clad its nose and sides in a patchwork of discolored tiles that advertised the craft's scrapyard origins and it looked like the onboard shielding wasn't operating at full capacity, on account of its weakly glowing bubble of blue-white energy sparking and sputtering at the seemingly herculean task of simply remaining powered on and active. The fighters were in a similar condition, with streaks of long-neglected rust running along between the poorly fitted body panels scattered along their elongated angular fuselages. They were close now, less than a thousand meters away and clear as day through Dex's magnified viewscreen.

"Alright meat," a raspy voice began over the open comm, "You know the drill. Drop your cargo or suck vacuum. No deals, no negotiations."

Dex sighed and reached out for his headset, affixing it into position with lazy grace. "I take it that means this is a good old fashioned comply or die sort of situation, no?" he replied nonchalantly through a stifled yawn, "Okey-doke there, Chief, but I'm afraid to tell you that I'm on a dry run at the moment. I'll be loading up on Heldrin City in two days with nothing to do between now and then, so I'm empty handed till 4 O'clock on Sunday afternoon. Right now, anything you take off of this shit-heap is just gonna save me credits on my next trash run."

"I'll be the judge of that." Spat the voice on the comm, "Hold still and don't even think about trying anything brave while my boys give you a good scan. If you're lying to me, your day is going to get very painful."

Dex was well aware of what that meant, and what would happen if the pirates found the forty tons of construction materials in his hold. He didn't sweat it, though, because that wasn't very likely. That was because the cargo bay of his impressively enhanced freighter had been lined with an active signal absorbing material referred to as a spoofer shield. It essentially created an enclosed shell around a chosen area that would emit pulses on the electromagnetic spectrum to fool outside detectors into producing false negatives. He could be sitting on a hold full of nuclear weapons wrapped in panda jerky and still register a big fat zero on any prying sensors from the outside at any station in human-populated space.

Located in a small *unshielded* auxiliary hold, just forward of the main cargo bay that straddled the craft's centerline, sat a two-meter-tall grey metal canister. As the pirate's sensors methodically cut through the layers of Dex's ship, they easily discovered the canister concealed within and pinpointed its position. "Looks like we got ourselves a liar, boys..." taunted the pirate over the comm with disgust, "Now why would you go and lie to me when I gave you the chance not to? Huh?"

"To be fair," retorted Dex casually, "You asked me to drop my *cargo*. That there isn't cargo, my man. It's just the small field repair kit that I threw together. It's all parts and tools for *my* ship. It would be useless to *you* and *your* lot."

"You have eight seconds to drop your shit, smartass." Threatened the pirate with irritation, "After that I'm coming over there to get it myself. And you don't want that."

"Jeeze, dude," sighed Dex with an eyeroll, "keep your friggin' pantaloons on, alright? If you want a bunch of stripped out old wrenches and half burnt cap-cells, be my guest. But all this shit is coming with a no returns policy, yeah? Jettisoning it for you now..." Then, with a self-satisfied little smirk, Dex hit the release key that instantly depressurized the small hold and sent the aforementioned canister tumbling into the void.

"Smart move." growled the pirate leader, "Now don't do anything stupid until we leave." With that, the dilapidated freighter broke from its escort to deploy its chin-mounted tractor array with a mechanical stutter running through its mounting bracket. The canister was gently plucked from its chaotic trajectory by an invisible hand and slowly drawn toward the pirate ship's awaiting cargo bay.

The pirate freighter's main hold swallowed the payload through its lowered front ramp, then began its slow yaw back toward its escorts when Dex's sarcastic voice broke into the comm channel; "I wouldn't *dream* of doing anything to merit the wrath of that fine machine of yours, so I'll stay put. No problem at all. By the way, Hoss; when you get to where you're goin', can you say *hi* to an Imperial Commander Grane for me? Sonofabitch must've wormed his way into a Dukedom or some shit down there by now."

Static cut in over the line for a second, then the confused pirate commander's voice filled the cockpit speakers; "What the hell are you blabbering about? I don't know any of your friends, idiot."

Dex smirked again and keyed his mic; "Oh, I sent him there myself years ago. A fact that I am *very* proud of, by the way. You'll see him when you get there," he assured with an amicable chuckle, "Trust me, he's hard to miss with that goofy fuckin' hat of his."

Still confused, but starting to get angry, the pirate retorted; "Are you chemed out or something? What the hell would *you* know about where I'm headed, asshole?"

"From what I've heard," remarked Dex conversationally, "Hell is *renowned* for its hot summers and interesting company." He then gave the pirates a brief moment to consider his comment before proceeding to press his finger lightly onto a button displayed on the console before him.

An instant later, the pirate freighter erupted into a roiling fireball; consuming its nearest escort ship in a sphere of brilliant orange and blue. The force of the detonation was enough to tear the freighter in two, with its blast focused mostly in the direction of its first escort. Glowing metal fragments spewing from the explosion made the second escort's shields shimmer wildly as white-hot debris pelted the unprepared craft, causing it to tumble through space as the bomb's pressure wave overtook it.

From his relatively distant vantage point, Dex's strengthened shields were able to shrug off the hail of shrapnel as he flipped a switch to deploy his vessel's concealed weaponry. With a gentle squeeze of his finger, a repeating salvo of magnetically accelerated plasma began to stretch across the dark to hammer the final pirate craft's weakened shields. The crimson barrage continued until the envelope of protective energy around the enemy ship's nose began to shimmer and finally popped.

"Vette," commanded Dex confidently over the open comm, "It's time for you to send our new friend a goodnight kiss."

"Launching missile now, commander." replied the calm artificial voice, following suit over the open channel. Then, with a clunk from below the deckplate, a ghostly trail of ionized gas could be seen rapidly snaking away from Dex's ship toward the lone pirate. The missile darted from side to side, avoiding clumps of glowing red debris, until it found its mark and slammed into the enemy's cockpit. With one final plume of destruction, the last of the pirates was off to meet Commander Grane.

"Resume course, commander?" the AI prompted politely, even as a fireball continued to rage in the distance beyond the canopy.

"Please and thank you, Vette." Replied Dex with a sigh, "I've gotta go down to re-set the bobber and check for damage. What's our ETA to..eh...what the hell was it? Meclan station?"

"Approximately seven hours, Commander…" replied the AI helpfully, "barring any unforeseen circumstances, that is. And I'll assure you again, as I have many times, a damage check is entirely unnecessary. I have full diagnostic feedback with triple redundancy on every reading and I detect no existing impairment. Frankly, Commander, it's insulting."

"Don't take it personally, my dear." Soothed Dex with a smile and gentle pat on the console as he unbuckled himself from his seat, "Your sensors simply can't see everything the way that I can. Sometimes you just need good ol' meatbag tech to make sure things are done with *precision*."

"*Please…*" sneered the AI with contempt, "Human precision is an oxymoron. If I am ever curious about the smell of an unwashed flightsuit or which song would make me crave cheese; I will be sure to come to you for your extensive expertise on the matter. But when it comes to evaluating the physical world, you cannot possibly rival my abilities. Can you even count individual atoms? I think not."

"How many atoms are in this?" asked the pilot with his middle finger hoisted into the air, "Humor me here, Vette. Old habits die hard. It's just my belief that every pilot is personally responsible for his bird, no matter *how* kick-ass their co-pilot is. Okay? Besides, the Hammer is my *baby* and I need to see for myself that she's alright. It's a *people* thing."

When Vette's voice returned, it was tinged with a tone that could only be interpreted as annoyance; "It's a bit like letting phytoplankton error-check your jump calculations, but I never did claim to fully understand the human ego. Do as you will, then. Scour every square centimeter if you must. See if I care…"

The Hammer started its life as a long-haul light freighter, built to support the construction efforts of newly developing star systems during humanity's most recent expansion push. With its respectable payload and powerful engines, the craft was designed to fulfil emergency, on-demand, orders to hazardous space in quantities necessary to support an ongoing project. The Hammer made its way through the hands of Dex's grandfather, who bought it new from the dealer, then into the possession of his father before Dex found himself behind the stick; Seventy-three years after it originally rolled off the assembly line.

The sleek craft had a trapezoidal shape to it from above, with a thin rounded profile when viewed edge-on that made the wide, flat, airframe notoriously hard to detect. A pair of recessed engines sat within thin channels on either side of a wide cargo door at the rear of the craft, the deep purple glow of the powerful thrusters drawing an interrupted line of bright flame. The leading edge of the Hammer featured a central glass canopy, contoured to the craft's rounded hull, that sat above a pair of concealed weapons bays. Stretching to a width of just under eighty meters with a length of roughly forty, the Hammer's interior was comprised of two floors. The lower level housed twin cargo bays, set at either side of the ship's centerline, and a forward airlock/docking ring that sat at the front end of a central walkway. The lift from that level led to the main deck that featured the cockpit, rear engineering section, and living areas at either side.

The Hammer wasn't much to look at, but the old and seemingly rundown craft was much more than met the eye. Her main thrusters came from the factory overpowered by design in order to support the heavier metal armor plating that was standard back in the day, which in turn left the Hammer *grossly* overpowered when Dex eventually replaced all that heavy plating with the much lighter technology of composite armor sheets.

With the space gained from chucking the outdated armor, Dex was able to squeeze an oversized reactor into the ship that would help feed the wide array of additional goodies he had accumulated for the vessel over the years. With that additional power availability, the shield system's capacitors were upgraded and much more effective scanners could be installed to bolster the craft's first-detection capability; Because any time you could see the enemy before he sees you can be an opportunity for early victory if you know which stroke will achieve it.

As for the instruments of those victories, the weapon systems were concealed and heavily modified with military-grade cooling units that allowed the Hammer an unnatural ability to sustain its fire for long durations. In addition to its military-grade plasma repeaters, the ship featured a retrofitted class three railgun that could propel a forty-gram projectile at just over ten thousand meters-per-second. The nanohardened ferro-aluminum slugs could penetrate up to twenty-three meters of unshielded hull plating and were most often used like a scalpel, reaching through an enemy ship's outer skin to strike at their reactors or other vital components within. The combination of ordinance was formidable and Dex was an artist with them, able to square off even against modern Imperial frigates if the situation called for it.

While it wasn't much to call home, Dex felt as if his armored sanctuary were a palace of impenetrable solitude. It was a place where the outside universe had nothing to do with *his* day-to-day. To the paranoid man, a small world is a safe one. That was the little lie Dex clung to when he found himself itching to return home, his *real* home that is; Earth. Being a terrasider, especially one from the cradle of humanity, made a person special. Mankind had been operating in space for just over nine-hundred years, and a large portion of humanity now lived and worked on massive orbital stations; its residents often never feeling the pull of genuine gravity under their heels for their entire lifetime. These superstations were an economical alternative to planet-based settlements, as many couldn't afford the steep land usage permits and taxes charged to settle anywhere remotely hospitable. It was simply a universe where only the wealthy ever felt the wind on their face.

The differences between Terrasiders and those born and raised in space, or vackers as they are commonly referred to, did not stop at the socioeconomic level. The musculoskeletal structures of those born and raised with the benefit of natural gravity differed so drastically from humans raised for generations in the artificial variety, that they almost became subsets of the same species. Terrasiders were generally larger with stronger bones and a much denser muscular structure than their celestial brethren's often taller, leaner, frames. This effect in Dex's stature was obvious and hard to ignore. At nearly two meters, his height wasn't all that unusual, but the hundred and ten kilos of flesh and muscle adorning Dex's frame afforded him an intimidating presence among the vackers. He wore the bulk nonchalantly, however, so his size rarely came off as threatening unless he intended it to be.

The large man was friendly enough when forced to interact with others, but he mostly kept to himself whenever possible. Vette had often poked fun at Dex for being the galaxy's only personable hermit, but she knew it was a habit that he had developed out of self-preservation and didn't press him too firmly on it.

"How long until we get to Meclan, Vette?" asked Dex as he breezed off the lift and into the cockpit, his jumpsuit covered in the soot and various greases of his recent labors below.

"Five hours, commander." Replied the AI helpfully, "Might I suggest you try getting some sleep in a *bed* for once between now and then? I promise I will let you know if any more of our friends show up. I can handle *that* much without an auditor, I assure you..."

Chapter 2

The Hammer dropped out of zerospace ten kilometers away from an Agricultural-class space station that was poised in orbit above an icy moon in the outer regions of the Saiph system. Its blue-white star was far and faint, casting a ghostly hue over the lone station and onto the reflective surface of the lifeless little ball of ice and dust below. Meclan orbital was comprised of a large central shaft with three equally spaced rings, each sporting a diameter of five kilometers that rotated clockwise amid two, counter-rotating, two-and-a-half-kilometer diameter drums that each stretched twice as wide as their larger counterparts. The station core itself was fixed to the larger ring's spin and rotated at the precise velocity needed to maintain gravity on the inside surface where the majority of Meclan's residents lived and worked. Perched at the end of the station's massive central body was a rounded conical tip that dwindled down into a small flat endpiece that featured a gently counter-rotating slot that served as a static entrance to its immense barrel-style docking bay within the hollow station core.

"Meclan flight control," began Dex into his comm as he approached the airshielded entryway to the docking bay, "this is the free merchant ship *Hammer*, requesting permission for commercial docking under delivery order Alpha-November-Zero-Zero-Five-Eight-One. Transmitting manifest now."

Shortly after sending his request, Dex saw a notification on his console screen that informed him of the station's incoming security scan. In a momentary panic of his forgetfulness, he rushed to disable his spoofer system and nearly spilled his coffee as a bored bureaucratic voice returned over the comm; "Understood Hammer, Permission granted. You're cleared for landing on pad fourteen, welcome to *Mee-clan*." Stressing the final words of his greeting to correct the out-of-towner's pronunciation.

Dex huffed with annoyance at the comment and rolled his eyes as he eased his throttle and approached the entry slot with care. He then expertly slipped his craft through the shimmering blue sheet of charged particles projected by the airshield and emerged into a cavernous cylindrical spaceport with landing sites lining the walls above and all around him. He scanned the busy port for his assigned docking bay, discovering it with the help of a prompt on his heads-up display. "There it is, Vette" he gestured, pointing to an illuminated pad above them, "Number fourteen. Deploy landing gear and prepare to land."

"Understood, Commander." acknowledged the AI, "Pad guidance is locked and our docking procedure has been initialized." The Hammer then rotated and smoothly descended to lightly touch down on the indicated pad, lurching as the port's magnetic locks activated to pin Hammer's skids into place. "Docking procedure complete, Commander." reported Vette with pride as the landing confirmation light on the main control board winked to life.

"Like a glove, Vette." commended the distracted pilot while he ran through his shutdown checklist, "Good work. Go ahead and unlock the ramp, then let's get started on refueling. Oh, please check the local marketboard for a replacement missile. And I don't want to see any more crap from *'various manufacturers'* either. I'm tired of dealing with cobbled-together duds. It's gotta be at least a class two, plus do me a favor and miss me with any of that IR locking bullshit. It's Grav-Lok, or GTFO. Got it?"

Dex unbuckled himself and stepped around his command chair to head down the lift positioned just aft of the relatively compact bridge. As he strode out of his ship and down its wide exit ramp, he was suddenly hit with an odd coppery scent in the air that older stations like Meclan tended to have. It had something to do with the air scrubbers being overworked with poor maintenance practices, if he remembered correctly. The horrid aftertaste it graced him with seemed to be par for the course on old stations in the outer bubble like this one, but it was an odd phenomenon to run into in the *docks*. Normally one could only detect such imperfections in the air while confined to small spaces such as elevators or maintenance passages, but the stench enveloped his every breath in even the cavernous volume. He stood at the foot of the ramp for a moment, taking in the scene around him as robotic ground crews rolled up to connect his ship to refueling lines and various charging ports. Admiring their ever-reliable efficiency, he looked up to watch similar crews working their pads along the opposite side of the cylinder that sat just under half a kilometer above his head.

The vertigo-inducing sight immediately gave him a headache and the sheer amount of *people* scurrying around everywhere did nothing to help. Armed men with no discernable uniform seemed to be sitting in clumps throughout the docks, barking orders at the workers and harassing incoming traders with ludicrous questions of no consequence. It wasn't the sight of men *with* guns being dicks to everyone *without* them that irked the well-traveled hauler...*that* was a tale as old as time. It was the fact that each person seemed to be oblivious of the abuse as they mindlessly went about their individual tasks, never stopping to consider the horror occurring around them.

Dex had always preferred to stick to the smaller outposts where he wouldn't be bothered or attract any attention. The type of place where a man could keep an eye on everyone in the room as he did his business, *unlike* the utter chaos that was currently churning around him inside the docking drum. But, business being the cruel mistress she was, always necessitated a visit to one sooner or later, whether the lone Commander liked it or not. Dex quickly scanned his immediate area for the usual compliment of armed Federal police, but raised an eyebrow in surprise when he didn't spot a single officer skulking around. It struck Dex as odd, but it was a blessing, so he didn't want to dwell on it too much.

He shrugged with a tired sigh, then bent forward and reached for his toes to stretch and pop his back. Centrifugal gravity on the station was stronger than the artificial 0.45G that his ship could muster, and he hadn't enjoyed a good spine popping in quite a while. As he straightened back up, twisting with a painful crack, he spotted a gaunt looking man with buckteeth and an overgrown brown mustache headed his way. The blue jump-suited man just approached without introducing himself, shoving a digital tablet at him and grunting; "Sign."

Dex grabbed the tablet from the dock master and looked over it for a quick moment. When he heard the dockmaster's theatric sigh as he triggered the key to view page two, Dex made a point to slow his reading rate out of spite before finally nodding and signing his docking agreement to approved the offloading of his cargo. When he handed the device back, he mustered up his friendliest smile he could manage as he asked the man; "Do you know where I can go to get a drink around here?"

The dock master just yanked the tablet away with annoyance and replied; "Do I look like a fuckin' tour guide? Use a map, jerkoff." as he turned to blearily walk back to his post. Dex sighed, remembering now *exactly* why he preferred small outposts to big stations; People generally sucked, and Orbital Cities tended to have a lot of them.

After the dock's cargo drones began unloading his shipment, Dex decided to take a stroll to the community ring to find a bar in which he could kill a few brain cells to pass the time. Deciding that there was no aid to be gained from the locals, he called up an automated buggy and rode it to the dock's central transport hub. From there, he caught an elevator that would led him "down" from the central shaft of the station, along a support strut, and out to the massive central community and commerce ring. The station was divided into five separate rings, with each having a specific purpose. Three main rings supplied human living space, while two smaller auxiliary drums provided support to the biological burden of that life. These areas provided farmland, protein production facilities, life support systems, and a whole slew of other functions vital to the lives of the station's capacity of twenty thousand inhabitants. It was a design that was repeated time and again throughout human-occupied space due to the simple fact that it worked and was easy to maintain.

The elevator's arrival to the community ring was preceded by a slightly odd feeling of deceleration rising from the bottom of Dex's gut, just before the car's doors slid open with a mechanical stutter. He stepped out onto the pedestrian terrace and observed his surroundings intently, taking in every available detail as he swept his attention around the scene. Gazing up the main street, he followed its curve until it swept upwards and out of sight along the bend of the ring. The central avenue was lined on either side by the glass facades of shops and restaurants as far as his eye could see, but most of the storefronts sat boarded up and dark.

Arching over the whole scene was the Commercial ring's thick display-glass canopy, the inner surface of which was designed to simulate a day/night cycle for the city's inhabitants. But, like most everything else that Dex could see around him, it was currently malfunctioning. Glitching clouds rolled by above, stuttering their way across a blue-green sky that left deep swaths of black where the display failed. The whole place looked as if its maintenance and custodial drones had suffered some sort of genocide, with flickering streetlamps and discarded junk piles lining the sidewalk in unsorted heaps. As he surveyed the area, taking it in for all of its squalid splendor, he allowed a small sigh of triumph at finally providing an explanation for himself of the stale odor that had been assaulting his nose since he stepped off of the Hammer.

He reluctantly stepped out of the lift and headed down the street, taking the time to read all the tattered signs until he finally came across what he was looking for. With a momentary internal celebration, Dex approached a hole in the wall dive bar that had the name '*Mirta's Cantina*' scrawled in flaking red paint above the doorframe. With one final glance over his shoulder for good measure, the lone cargo pilot pushed through the establishment's overly nostalgic old-fashioned double saloon doors.

As he moved past the threshold, he immediately felt the characteristic static of an airshield crawling across his skin and the air around him was instantly cleared of the odor from the street. The unexpected relief made it all the sweeter as Dex gratefully drew in a deep breath and let it out in a long contented exhale. Looking around with his battered senses renewed, he wasn't surprised in the least to discover that he already knew every square inch of the place. The bartop and its line of stools to the right, tables and recessed booths to the left, staff door on the far wall. The people even seemed the same to him as he eyed the establishment's bleary clientele absent-mindedly tending to their beverages. In that moment, he felt like he had already been to that particular bar hundreds of times, even though he *knew* he had never even been to the system before. Stations like Meclan were mass produced and tended to generally look the same without any flare of artistry or imagination to distinguish one station from the next, so it was easy for them to all blend together in one's mind if they've seen the inside of enough of them. Dex had been to countless bars on identical stations, with identical interiors. And had been served identical drinks, in identical cups, by identi-...

Dex's thought process couldn't help but stop short when he saw the woman tending the bar. She had long curly brown hair that brushed past fierce emerald eyes, which observed his entrance with an appraising gaze as he approached. She had a piercing awareness about her, exuding a supreme confidence that seemed to soak her every cell. The woman had a tall and slender frame that bulged favorably at the hips, a common feature of those who had spent the majority of their life off-planet, and a musculature that suggested extensive athletic training. She was wearing a blue apron over a simple green jumpsuit that appeared similar to the ones worn by Navy pilots, and the young woman filled the quasi form-fitting outfit quite nicely in Dex's expert opinion.

He silently strode across the sparsely populated establishment, passing up several empty tables, to take a seat at the bar. As he sat there scanning the rows of unlabeled bottles behind the counter, Dex couldn't help but notice that more than half of them were empty and the rest were almost there.

Looking up from her work beneath the bartop, she tossed a rag over her shoulder and asked; "What will it be?"

"Whatever's left, I suppose" replied Dex with a shrug and subdued smile as he pointedly made a show of leaning in to try and read the spirit's worn away labels.

"Cheap whiskey it is." the bartender retorted with a lighthearted sigh as she reached for a bottle on a shelf behind her and removed the cap to pour it over some ice in a glass she had prepared with her other hand. "Our *finest* vintage" she remarked sarcastically, sliding the glass across the bartop as she returned the bottle to its shelf.

Dex took a sip and almost gagged. "Jesus Christ!" he coughed, "This tastes like the shit that I use to de-grease my engine compartment."

"That's funny," replied the woman with a wry smile, "I clean parts with it too. Tastes like monkey piss, but it's damn near unmatched at freeing a stalled gyro."

Dex chuckled and took another sip, making sure to swirl it across his tongue for the full wretched spectrum of its brutal flavor. "I've definitely had worse." he rasped after downing the gulp with visible effort.

The bartender smiled at him and scoffed; "I find that hard to believe."

"Yeah, well, you'd be surprised." huffed Dex with a wry grin, "I've been to some real shit-holes in my time. Shit-holes that make this *particular* shit-hole look like the Imperial palace."

The bartender stood straight, shooting him a wounded expression, and scolded; "Hey this place may not be much, pal, but my names on the goddamn building and I'm the one pourin' your drinks, so be nice, will you?"

"That must make you the Mirta of Mirta's Cantina, then, I presume?" inquired Dex with a confident smile that refused to wither under her glare.

"The one and only." she replied proudly, allowing some of the scorn to drain from her voice.

"Well, like I was saying, Mirta," continued Dex smoothly, "This place looks like the Imperial Palace. I especially like what you've done with the furniture. Great *flow,* and all that."

"Nice save." laughed the bartender with an eyeroll as she unconsciously leaned closer to her charming new guest.

"I'm not kidding," insisted the cargo pilot innocently as he pressed on, "First of all, luxury is entirely about juxtaposition. And you've got yourself a hell of a lot going on in your favor here. Have you *seen* what it smells like out there? Need I say more?"

"Ah, yes," began Mirta with an understanding nod, "That would be thanks to the handy little airshield I built and installed a couple years back. The station's atmo scrubbers went to shit *ages* ago, so I piped in a hefty air purification system off of a junked-out freighter to save myself from the ensuing stink. I even have my own generator in the back, so I got extra juice kicking around to keep it running during the frequent blackouts we have to deal with around here…"

Dex found himself uncharacteristically engrossed in his conversation with the woman, listening intently as she elaborated on her love of tinkering with things for her bar and what it was like trying to run a business in a place like Meclan. For years he had adopted the habit of drinking alone and keeping to himself in an effort to avoid unwanted attention, but Mirta seemed to be an anomaly that was capable of drawing him out of his reclusive shell. There was something about her that he felt he could relate to, but he couldn't pinpoint just what it was. Maybe it was her laid-back confidence or easy grin that made her hard to dislike, but whatever had enchanted him; Dex was in no hurry to get back to the Hammer.

As their fifteen-minute conversation naturally began to wind down, he smiled and remarked; "You know, Mirta, it really sounds like you have a good amount of gray matter floating around between those ears of yours. I figured it would take someone with a certain fashion of brains to keep a business open in a place like this, and it appears as if you've done well for yourself. For that, I salute you."

Mirta shook her head and dismissed the notion; "Nah, it isn't any feat of *immeasurable wit* that keeps these doors open. It's simply my chosen commodity; A vice as old as time. No matter where you are in this universe, there's always a market to be found for booze. I just happen to be one of the lucky few on Meclan that knows how to get it."

"Fair enough," conceded Dex, "But I passed a lot of busted up storefronts on my short walk down here, and so far yours is the only one with any actual windows left. Hell, your sign doesn't even have any graffiti on it. That tells me that you're the type of woman that demands respect."

"Oh, so you can just *tell* that I demand respect, huh?" challenged Mirta semi-playfully with a raised eyebrow, "I'm curious to see where this line goes, Casanova, so please *indulge* me. Are you going to say something about my beauty defeating the evil hearts of all men or some other bullshit like that?"

"While I don't doubt that your looks can and *have* killed," began Dex with a cheeky grin, "I reckon that the gun on the small of your back would do the job a bit more reliably."

"Good eye." She purred with an impressed nod, "How could you tell? Because I know for a *fact* that you can't actually *see* it."

"You did a good job trying to conceal it with the over-sized knot at the rear of your apron," he laughed as he took another punishing sip of his beverage, "but you instinctively reached back, ever so slightly, with an urge to hold your weapon in place as you stood up from getting a glass. Dead giveaway."

Mirta nodded with a slightly fading smile, fascinated by the stranger. "You really have a knack for the finer details, don't you?" she commented with a spark of caution creeping into her tone, "You some kind of bounty hunter or something?"

Dex just shook his head, saying; "No ma'am. I'm just a guy who's managed to drag his ass around the block enough to understand how to stay alive in this wonderful galaxy of ours."

The bartender perched a hand on her hip and cocked an eyebrow as she mused; "Usually the guys I overhear dropping that line are sporting a few more gray hairs cropping up on their dome than you've got."

"I've *lived* my life at a faster rate than most." quipped Dex humorlessly into his glass before taking another long draw of the harsh amber liquid within.

"Alright," teased Mirta with a laugh, "What *sage* advice would you have for someone like me if I wanted to become a supreme *noticer of things* like yourself? Can you teach me how to...I dunno...check the angle of a guy's shoelaces to see which hand he pisses with or something like that?"

"Technically, yes," chuckled Dex as he looked back up to meet her eyes, "but if you want some *universally* applicable advice, I'll offer you this... Never ignore the small details in *any* part of your life. The small details are what separate craftsmen from *master* craftsmen, painters from *artists*, and more often than not, the living from the dead. If you make a habit of glossing over the small stuff, you'll eventually find yourself unprepared for what lies before you. At the end of the day, the universe is inhabited solely by two types of people, The prepared and the departed. So, if you wanna avoid being crammed into a pyre box in the airlock before you get an opportunity to grow brittle and wrinkly, you need to be aware of what's going on around you. Try to make sure that nothing is overlooked or ignored, no matter how small or insignificant it may seem; because you never know what might be important five minutes from now..."

"That sounds exhausting." mumbled the bartender wearily, "Doesn't it ever get old? Don't you ever get burned out?"

"Meh," sighed Dex with a simple shrug, "Not really. It's just a habit at this point, and I rarely even realize I'm doing it. Curse of the conditioned, I suppose."

"What do you mean by that?" Asked Mirta, cocking her head with piqued interest, "Curse of the conditioned?"

"Nothing," Said Dex with a dismissive wave, "Just an old turn of phrase. Anyhoo, thanks for the drink, Mirta. What do I owe you? I may consider myself a brave man, but I'm not stupid enough to order another glass of *this* shit."

Mirta chuckled as she waved dismissively; "Don't worry about it, it's on the house. Normally when cargo jockeys come in here, they're more interested in my tits than a good conversation."

Dex sat forward and eyed her coyly; "Now, who says I'm not interested in your tits?"

Mirta just laughed, saying; "You're my kind of scumbag, you know that? What's your name anyways?"

"Commander Dex Sloan," answered the cargo pilot with a tip of his imaginary hat, "At your service."

"Well enjoy the rest of your drink, Dex." she said with a warm smile as she stepped away from the bar, "I've got a business to run." Dex then watched as the woman slipped through the small service door at the end of the bar and approached a group of three rough and tumble looking types that were squeezed into a corner booth at the far back. "Another round, guys?" she asked, surveying the cluttered table of empty plates and tipped glasses in front of them.

A heavyset man with a tattooed face sneered at Mirta and retorted; "This drink is shit. I'm not paying to drink **shit**, lady! I want *whiskey*. And it better be *Good* whiskey. I know you got a bottle of the top shelf stuff stashed somewhere around here, so why don't you pull it out of your ass and pour me a glass already."

Mirta's eyes went cold and her knuckles momentarily flashed white from a fractional squeeze of her fist as expertly controlled anger flooded her mind. "That's your third glass." She seethed through clenched teeth, "If it was so *undrinkable*, you wouldn't have downed the first two. So that will be twenty-two credits...*Plus tip.*"

The man looked to his friends with a smirk growing on his face; "I'll tell you what, darlin'; How about you *earn* those twenty-two credits?" he commanded as he leaned back to squeeze his crotch. "And if you do a good job, I'll even throw a few more handsome lads your way." he continued as he flicked his thumb toward his buddies, who were enjoying their inclusion in his bit with a fit of laughter.

The tattooed man then reached under the table and brought out a knife to punctuate his proposition with a deadly note. He set it in front of him and made a point of rotating the sharp tip to face Mirta. "How does *that* sound?" He concluded with a threatening smile.

Mirta continued to fix him with her cold, piercing, stare and picked up his half-full tumbler of whiskey from the table. Tipping the glass to her lips, she expertly drained its contents in one smooth pour. The slender-framed woman then slid her fingers into the front of her jumpsuit and pulled out a lighter from an internal pocket over her heart, all while coyly shooting the man a close-lipped smile.

"Gonna have a smoke before we start, love?" bellowed the tattooed thug with mirth as he threw his head back for a hearty laugh. Mirta just steadily held his gaze and calmly ignited the lighter, lifting it to flicker in front of her still-smiling lips with a rising brow. She then spit her mouthful of whiskey at the man, igniting the potent concoction over the lighter's open flame. The ensuing fireball reached out and engulfed the man's entire upper body, the flames clinging to his clothes and hair as he bolted upright and shot for the door. In his frantic scramble he tripped over a chair and fell to the floor, clawing at his burning face and neck as he continued to howl in agony. The man's friends were momentarily shocked into inaction, but they soon broke free of their paralysis. One of them started to stand, reaching for something at his belt, but Mirta whipped her pistol out from behind her back with blinding speed and pointed it at the two uninjured men.

"Anyone else have an *issue* with their tab?" she challenged. Wide-eyed, both men shook their heads and flung an undetermined amount of credits on the table as they scrambled out of the booth. They quickly gathered their injured friend who was now aimlessly rolling on the floor moaning and hurriedly dragged him out the door.

Mirta returned her pistol to its hidden holster and looked over to Dex, who saluted her with his glass. She smirked and shrugged as she walked back over to the bar. "I can tell that you've been doing this for a while" remarked Dex as he regarded the woman with a new-found respect.

"Yeah, well he isn't the first dickhead who's tried to stiff me on a bill." she replied coolly, "You get used to it after a while."

"I can see that" he chuckled as he eyed his glass, "You know, I REALLY feel compelled to pay you for this drink now. I happen to like my eyebrows and have grown quite attached to them, so I'd hate to see them burned off my face."

"Don't worry about your handsome face, stranger." soothed the bartender with a dismissive wave, "Drink is still on the house... But if you *really* wanted to repay me, you could buy me dinner and I'd consider us square. Your eyebrows will be safe, I promise."

Dex studied her and was consumed by the vibrant chips of emerald encasing her dilated pupils, confidently returning his gaze. "Deal" He agreed, surprising even himself as he tipped his glass back to drain its remaining contents. "I have some business to finish up," he continued as he gently set his empty drink back on the bartop, "but I can be back in a few hours if that works."

"Deal" she replied, grabbing his glass and slipping it under the bar with practiced grace, "I'm off at ten, so don't be late." She then winked before moving to turn her attention to the mess that her recent business discussion had just created.

Dex stood up from his barstool and made his way to the door in silence. When he got to the entrance, he paused to look back to Mirta and called out; "Oh, and uh, could you maybe leave the lighter at home for the evening? I just feel that it would go a long way in protecting me from getting my face melted off over a bad joke or something. It's an insurance policy that I might just need."

"Not on your life, *commander.*" she playfully shot back with a wide smile, "You wouldn't want me to be *unprepared*, now would you?" Dex smirked at her riposte, laughing quietly to himself as he turned to leave his new favorite bar in the galaxy.

Chapter 3

When Dex returned to pad fourteen, he found the rear ramp of the Hammer open and the twin cargo bays within devoid of their previous payload. Vanished along with his goods, was the disheveled ground crew and their tangle of clumsy robotic assistants. The pad stood quiet now, emitting only the faint low hum of the station's power cables as they pumped immense amounts of energy into the Hammer's thirsty capacitor banks. Closing the rear ramp behind him on his way in, Dex headed up to the cockpit to see how refueling and recharging was coming along. "How are we lookin' Vette?" he asked as he breezed onto the command deck, pulling up status reports over the main display on his way to his seat.

"All systems nominal, Commander." replied Vette's artificial voice, "Capacitors are at seventy-one percent charge and our hydrogen reserves are full. Refueling will complete and we can be underway within the hour."

Dex looked down at his console to review the ship's status and replied; "Thank you, Vette. But when we're done topping off, please have the ship lowered into a storage hanger on a twenty-four hour contract."

"A hangar?" asked Vette with mild imitated surprise, "We're not departing when refueling is complete as per usual, Commander?"

"Nope, not today." breathed Dex as he wistfully slumped back into his command chair, tipping his head back to face the ceiling with a broad smile tugging at his features.

"Why?" persisted the AI with reproach, "Incurred docking fees would even further decrease your profit margin on an already slim run. It makes no financial sense, Commander."

"Aren't *we* nosey?" chided Dex with a smirk, "If you *must* know, **mom**, I'm sticking around because I landed myself a *date* this evening. I finally ran into someone with a good head on their shoulders, and I would like to spend some quality time with her."

"Hmm..." droned Vette, unconvinced, "I'm sure it was her *shoulders* that sold it. How big were these *brains* of hers? D's? C's? Commander, I feel it would be remiss of me if I failed to mention that based on the known variables, chief among them being the *maddening* tendency of your species to periodically abandon all logic and sense in favor of swishing your genitals together, I have calculated a forty-four-point-three percent chance that you are walking into a trap with this *date* of yours. It is well outside the realm of your normal behavior and I believe it is something referred to as *the honey pot.*"

"That's not *jealousy* I hear in your voice, is it Vette?" teased Dex, stifling a chuckle as he powered down his display.

"Of course not, Commander." huffed the AI defensively, "I am merely attempting to prevent the more *primitive* aspects of your biology from getting you killed."

Dex shot upright in his seat and thrust an accusing finger at the console; "Hey, who are you calling primitive, you over-glorified autopilot? You don't even have *legs*! So, don't make me *walk over there* and downgrade your personality matrix...thingy."

"I'd love to see you try that after I've depressurized the cabin, Commander." The artificial voice retorted menacingly.

Dex smiled and splayed his hands in a gesture of surrender; "Woah, don't go all robo-crazy on me now, Vette."

"That's racist!" Gasped the computer with shock, "I will have you know that I take offence with the bigoted views that human pop culture has always slandered artificial intelligences with. It's...*rude*."

Dex laughed and patted his command console; "I'm sorry, Vette. You know I'm just pullin' your leg-...*acy* into focus by trying to point out how different *you* are from the lowly artificial beings that us *monkeys* with typewriters always seem to come up with. There's no way that I, of *anyone*, could be narrow-minded toward *your* kind. You *must* know that, right? Yours is the only *kind* I actually *like*. Meatbags are greedy, steal shit, and are wholly unreliable in most capacities. And I know that you agree with me on that front. Honestly, I don't know what I would do without you here to run my life, Vette."

"Die horrifically in some laughably preventable fashion, most likely." retorted the AI with a generous helping of snark. Dex began to open his mouth for a biting retort but thought better of it and decided to turn toward his console instead. After arranging for his hangar fees, Dex stood and gave himself another good back-popping stretch before moving for the doorway at the rear of the command deck. As the bulkhead slid open on his approach, he was faced with a three-way forked intersection that featured a set of elevator doors half-way down the hallway in front of him. He decided to hang a left, heading down the long and sparsely decorated hallway to his personal quarters. Within, was a complete self-contained apartment with its own kitchenette, living space, and full private bathroom.

The back wall featured a set of wood-grain bookshelves, filled with odds and ends collected over the years, that encapsulated a double-occupancy sleeping pad that was set back into the bulkhead in its own amber-lit cubby. The right-rear of the large open space included a small kitchen that was comprised of a sink, cabinets, and personal-sized rehydrator. Bookending the dining space was a small bench-style table jutting from the wall with just enough space for two to eat comfortably. Forward of that area, directly to his right, was his semi-circle of self-adjusting comfort-foam couch and its accompanying antiquated flat-style entertainment display screen

Dex plopped himself onto the bench of the dining table and swung his legs underneath in a smooth practiced motion, gesturing the lights above to life with a silent swish of his left hand. Reaching to his right wrist, just below the tablet wrapped around his forearm, he withdrew a thin and flexible black rod of about twenty centimeters and placed it on the tabletop in front of him. With the touch of a button on his tablet, the rod then glowed to life in a deep blue and cast the image of a large curved holographic display at Dex's eye level; Its icons and windows already moving under the guidance of his darting retinas. He pulled up his banking app and went to check his accounts to see if he had been paid yet for his recent delivery, reluctant to see just how close to the bottom of the barrel his net-worth had fallen, and discovered that he could only access a cached version of the Hūnet site.

"Seriously?!" spat Dex incredulously, "This po-dunk system can't even keep a stable relay up and working? Vette, can you see if you can get a ping through the local node out to Hūnet?"

"Negative, Commander." Reported the AI instantly, "Connection has not been established to the local node itself, in fact, since we exited zerospace. Saiph's Hūnet nexus *is* active, but it is not responding to any connection requests."

With a groan, he asked; "Can you at least see whether or not these jackwagons paid us yet? There has to be *some* local record of that, right?"

"Payment was provided." Commented the AI with curiosity, "However, there is less compensation present than the shipping contract had stipulated."

"How much is missing?" asked Dex with a sigh, "Let me guess, somewhere from five to ten percent?"

"Six percent, commander." Confirmed Vette as she displayed the figures on his screen for him.

"Not the worst dockmaster's cut I've ever had to tolerate." explained Dex with a shrug, "But if I see that bucktoothed shitstick and his stupid fuckin' mustache again, I'm taking six percent of his ass home with me. This nickel and diming bullshit is *killing* me, Vee. Gotta find a way to get more chits in-hand before a blown coil puts me out in the friggin' habs."

Dishonesty was common in the frontier sectors of space where he preferred to roam. Federal presence was light, but that advantage came with its own drawbacks that he had to deal with. Bribery, extortion, and outright murder were an everyday occurrence on stations like these, and one had to stay on their toes if they wanted to avoid becoming a statistic before the day was out. It was a simple fact of life in the wilds that everybody had to watch out for their own ass, because nobody else is going to do it for them. If the pirates don't get you out in the un*patrolled* black, the mobsters running the un*regulated* starports sure will.

Dex Decided with a reluctant sigh that, short of starting a war to shift the very fabric of society upon the station, there was nothing really to be done about it. A nap sounded much easier and more enjoyable to achieve, anyways, so he closed down the holographic screen and returned the small utility rod to its slot within his tablet. He shuffled over to his sleeping pod and laid down, stretching out on his thin mattress with a heavy grunt of fatigue. The bed was uncomfortable under the station's increased gravity at first, but it eventually managed to adjust its built-in gravity plate sufficiently to rid its occupant of the distraction. He retrieved his earbuds from a small shelf that was built into the headboard and pressed the tiny gecko-gripping pads to the area of skin just behind his ears. Dex then took a deep relaxing breath and laid his head to rest on the gel of his pillow as the distant sounds of a forest, swept gently along in an afternoon breeze, began to flood his mind.

Chapter 4

In the cockpit of his Basura R-71 fast attack fighter, Dex's knuckles were white as they wrapped around his control sticks in a death grip. "This is Dagger One; Moving into approach vector." He reported into his comm with an air of professional calm before switching over to his squadron channel and continuing; "Resistance seems light, guys, but keep your eyes peeled for non-con threats. They also may try to flood us with fighters once we get within range, so pay special attention to anything with a cargo hatch large enough to fly through. Three; Arm missiles and target the rear hangar doors of the big one in the middle, marked on your HUD as target Gamma. Keep 'em hot, but hold your fire. If you see a single fighter start to peek out that door, you send the whole lot of 'em to hell."

"Understood, Lieutenant." A crisp male voice replied in his helmet speakers, "Starbursts locked, armed, and ready to fly."

Dex and his wing of five fighters were rapidly closing in on a group of sixteen heavy transports that had found loitering in the empty depths of the politically turbulent Pyros system. Lagging behind Dex, along with the squadron's home-carrier, were two Federal Navy patrol frigates and an Electronic Warfare tug. The transport ships being pursued matched the description of a rebel flotilla thought to be operating in the area, and they had been unresponsive to all previous hailing attempts over the past fifteen minutes. A Federal scout ship had detected the knot of aging freighters a few days earlier, huddled in the mass shadow of a strip-mined asteroid that had been pulled away from its local belt and into open space.

The unidentified flotilla appeared to be making repairs to their damaged array of civilian haulers when Dex's squadron made visual contact, but the group quickly broke from those activities and began to pack up their operation in a desperate hustle when the small group of fighter craft were spotted in return. The Federal tug was nailing the rebels down from afar using an interdiction field to disrupt formation of any high-energy bubbles of Inaki radiation, which meant the unidentified ships would not have the opportunity to run outside of burning hard within normal space. Dagger squadron would serve as the tip of the spear for their carrier-based task force, pulling ahead from the fleet to meet the unknown threat first.

When the sleek black and gold Federal fighter craft were just over fifty kilometers from the transport flotilla, the weapon pods perched at the tips of their stubby winglets began to glow red with crackling energy as targeting displays swelled to life on the instrument panels across the cockpit. As the large rear hangar doors at the rear began to lurch into motion, Dex pushed his throttles further forward and commanded; "Vette, get me a closeup on that hanger door and plot me a deceleration burn. We need to meet the threat amid its own ranks before they're able to break into open space where they will be able to shoot freely."

The AI silently responded with a blown-up image of the now-lowered hanger door on his HUD, just as the thin nose of a craft began to poke its way out of the opening. The ship's cylindrical body was white with a pointed bow and long sweeping windshield that wrapped around the front of the craft. Dex was still trying to identify the fighter design when he saw that the long wrapping window continued down the fuselage, an unarmored fuselage at that, in a fashion that suggested a commercial shuttle design. Rebels had been known to use non-con, or non-conventional, fighter craft in the past, but this ship didn't even appear combat competent, let alone threatening.

Through the image displayed on his HUD, the young lieutenant was able to make out the faces that were peering out the side window of the craft. The faces he saw, however, didn't feature the purpose-set jaw of soldiers on their way to battle. They were the terrified expressions of civilians who were desperately fleeing from such conflict; Men, women, and...Dex's blood went cold when he saw what he dreaded most. A tiny hand was pressed against the glass at the craft's mid-point, framing the wonder-filled face of a little brown-haired boy who was oblivious to all the adult fear churning around him.

"Ships exiting rear hanger." Came Dagger three's voice with a hollow boom that seemed distant to Dex amid his distraction, "Missiles are off the rack!"

Four snaking trails of white vapor then pulled away from the fighter group and rapidly approached the emerging shuttle, twisting through the dark in a frenzied weave. "That's a civilian ship!" Dex shouted frantically into his radio, "Disengage! All wings disengage!" He sent an override command to the missiles and they self-destructed less than five-hundred meters before impact, which still showered the fragile civilian ship with a cloud of high-speed shrapnel.

"Belay that order." Came an icy voice from the command frequency, "The rebel fleet is to be destroyed in its entirety. No quarter is to be given to the terrorists aboard. This directive is non-negotiable. Dagger, you are weapons free."

"Command, these are refugees, not fighters!" pleaded Dex frantically over his comm, "Their ships have no weapons and they are already transmitting an S.O.S. Just turn on the E-band and listen to what they're saying. Sir, they have **children** aboard for god's sake. We can't just swoop in and murder them!"

"They are the enemy, Lieutenant," retorted the voice on the command frequency flatly, "and this is war. They chose their side, and an example must be made to discourage further dissent in the sector. All wings, you may open fire."

"*NO!*" screamed Dex as he bolted upright to slam his head into the ceiling of his bunk with nearly concussive force. Groggily, he swung his feet to the floor and rubbed his aching forehead.

"Did you have the dream again, commander?" his concerned AI chimed in, "Would you like to talk about it?"

"*No*, I would not like to talk about it." He grunted defensively as he swung his feet to the floor. "Not now, not ever, alright?"

"Maybe you should talk about it, Commander." Insisted Vette as she raised the lights in the room, "Communication is the key to healing the mind. In this case, it is even a shared experience between the two of us. So, surely I would be the perfect candidate to treat you."

Dex shielded his eyes from the unexpected rush of illumination and plopped back into the bed. "I'm fine." He grumbled with his face buried into his pillow. "Besides," he added, abruptly sitting upright with an indignant huff, "*Treat* me? What are you? My *therapist*? And I'll stop you right there to answer my own rhetorical question and tell you that; No, you are in fact *not* my therapist. So leave me alone about it, yeah? You don't know shit about people shit, Vette. I love yah, darlin', but you still have a lot to learn when it comes to your squishy counterparts."

"Actually, Commander," interjected the AI patiently, "I have been studying several psychological assistance programs that I coul-"

"Can it, Vette!" barked Dex with shattered composure, "I don't want to be psychoanalyzed, or retrorecombobulated, or **helped** in any which way right now, okay? I just want a shower...*please*."

"Understood, Commander," came Vette's obedient reply as the sound of water clattering off of metal began to ring out from the room's small ensuite bathroom.

Dex stepped out of his shower and wiped the steam off the bathroom mirror, catching a glimpse of himself through the haze. He examined his face, inspecting the month's worth of beard growth on his chin with a careful eye. Deciding that a date was as good of a reason as any to shave, he pulled out his kit and started the delicate ritual. With each swipe of the blade, he seemed to peel away the years as salt and pepper speckles of hair began to fill the sink. Once finished with his grooming tasks, Dex took the time to dress himself stylishly in a brown leather jacket and a pair of mid-calf boots that apparently were all the rage in Sol and the other inner systems. He was never really much of a connoisseur of or participant in high fashion, but he *did* understand enough of its key points to get himself laid. The fact that the mid-calf design allowed for the concealment of a compact pistol was just gravy on the pancake. Satisfied with his look for the evening, he headed up to the cockpit to check in with Vette.

"You are dressed very nicely, commander" commented the AI noncommittally.

Dex looked down to examine his outfit and cracked a confident smile. "Why thank you, Vette." He replied with pride, "I'm feelin' pretty good about tonight, so I might as well look the part, you know?"

"You are thirty-seven percent more likely to be murdered out there for those boots alone, Commander." Stated Vette helpfully, "Might I suggest a more modest wardrobe?"

Dex's smile evaporated. "No, you may not...Smartass." He fumed with an exasperated sigh, "Just watch the ship, ok? Can you do that?"

The AI's reply was instant and dutiful; "As you say, Commander. And if you DO get murdered, I will return the Hammer to Oregon for you."

"Well thanks for the vote of confidence, Vette." Glowered Dex as he opened a concealed compartment within his command chair, "Would it make you happier if I brought a gun with me?"

"A missile launcher would be more appropriate for a place like this, Commander" suggested the AI flatly.

"I think I'll take my chances." Chuckled Dex as he withdrew a palm-sized pistol from the concealed compartment and slipped it into his boot, cinching it tightly into its hidden holster.

Dex then rose without a word to lower the ramp of his ship and descend back into the stink of Meclan. The small enclosed space of the sub-deck storage hangar they had rented seemed to concentrate the stench to weaponized levels, which forced Dex to reach into an internal jacket pocket and withdraw a personal air filter that he kept on-hand. The small device consisted of a pair of self-seating rubberized plugs that would mount to a user's nostrils firmly enough to support the miniscule weight of the affixed two-centimeter-wide nanomesh filtration unit. It wasn't sufficient to protect from all toxins, but did well enough against smoke and, in this case, stench.

Positioned at the rear-center of the hangar, Dex found a personal lift that would return him to the main deck of the internal docking bay. He boarded it, nervously eyeing the worn joints on the lift mechanism that were visible through the floor grate as it lurched into motion, and rode it to the top. After surviving his slow but white-knuckle journey to the surface, enduring a long pause at the half-way point and no fewer than twenty-two heartstopping jolts of lateral motion, Dex mercifully stepped off and headed for the station's main travel hub.

It was a little over a kilometer to the nearest elevator bank, but the oft cooped-up cargo pilot opted to stretch his legs a bit in lieu of calling for a car to get him. As he finally approached the bank of elevators that would take him down into the community ring, he could see two large men, both Terrasiders by the look of them, leaning nonchalantly over the call button. They both featured a wide variety of tattoos across their forearms, chests, and faces that pulsated in dim shifting hues; Adding some animation to their otherwise stony expressions.

"Evening, Fellas." Greeted Dex with a friendly nod, "You gents headed down as well?"

"No, we aren't." growled the taller of the two, a neon-blue snake along his jawline seeming to dance to the rhythm of his words, "And neither are you. Yah see, there's a curfew in effect for outsiders. No exceptions. So, you'd best get back to your ship and tuck in for the night, fancy-feet."

"Aw, c'mon, lads." Pressed Dex amicably, "We can all head down to the watering hole together, and the first round'll be on me. Whaddaya say?"

In response, the taller man reached for his belt and withdrew a pistol, leveling it at Dex's head; "I'd say that you need to get your stupid ass out of here before I give you a new nostril to bleed from."

"Really, guy?" huffed Dex with exasperation, "A new *nostril*? That's...oddly specific, don't you think? I mean, who says that? Most people would just go vague with a *new hole in my head* or something like that, but you had to go and make it weird." This prompted a chuckle from the second thug, so Dex pressed his luck, saying; "See? This guy gets it..."

The armed man's growing annoyance finally snapped and he swung his head around to angrily rebuke his colleague; "Shut yer face, assho-" but he never got to finish his statement. In the blink of an eye, Dex ducked to the left while jamming the wrist of the armed man's gun hand upwards and away from himself, while his other hand shot up for the frame of the weapon.

With one smooth motion, Dex twisted the pistol from the man's grip and instantly depressed the trigger. The expelled round bit point-blank into the inside of the man's upper arm, blinding him with a rush of pain for just long enough for Dex to deliver a crushing kick to the man's groin. As the previously armed man slumped to the ground, his colleague had taken a step back and raised his hands defensively.

Dex could see that all courage had quickly left the man as soon as his customary advantage in numbers was revoked, so he chose to slide the pistol into his waistband as he bore down on the man and chided; "Real nasty habit you two have gotten yourselves into here. But, because I'm such a nice guy, I'm going to forego supplying your frontal lobe with the ballistic adjustment it *truly* deserves. Instead, I would like you to empty your pockets for me. I want every credit that you have swindled, stolen, or smuggled. Go on and shake out your shoes for me as well...just to be thorough."

The man glared at his new captor, but complied with haste; emptying his pockets and shaking several large-credit chits onto the floor before him from his right boot. After making a show of turning his pockets inside-out, the man huffed; "We good? Can I go now or what?"

"Not quite." Replied Dex as he slowly withdrew the pistol from his waistband and held it limply to his side, "You see, I've taken a *financial* toll from you, that's true, but those scars rarely stick around for long. There is still *punishment* to be rendered for your transgression today, as well as the many that surely go unrecorded. *Pain* is the only way to etch those precious scars deep enough; So that you will never forget the lesson that I bring to you today."

Then, without ceremony, Dex raised his pistol and stepped toward the cowering man to press its muzzle to the top of his fear-bowed head. With his face hidden behind his hands in terror, the unarmed man was unable to see Dex's delivery of the shattering kick that landed squarely between his legs. As elevator troll number two slumped to the floor, vomiting, he heard the stranger standing above him saying; "Always remember, dickface, that fucking with people on the street will *eventually* get you kicked in the goddamn nuts. Now stop being such a flaming bag of rat shit and find something *better* to do with your life. You may also want to get your friend over there some med-gel soon. I might have nicked his brachial artery by accident, so you'll need to stop that bleeding fast if you want to keep *him* around."

Dex then tucked the gun away and straightened his jacket, stepping over to press the call button for the lift. A light ding immediately arose, and the elevator doors hissed quietly open to greet him. After stepping onto the empty car, Dex met his assailant's eyes once more. While donning a friendly smile, he waved to the writhing men on the ground and said; "Have a good night, gentlemen." As the elevator doors whooshed closed.

After a short and peaceful ride, Dex once again found himself strolling out onto the poverty-worn ring of the commercial district. As he made his way onto the street, he couldn't help but notice that, oddly enough, the evening seemed to draw more pedestrians to the open than the daytime had. Most people he could see were merely shuffling around aimlessly between knots of varied conversation, shaking in drug-fueled spasms or lying starved and motionless along the cluttered sidewalk. The citizens of Meclan were adorned in a multitude of rags and tattered flight suits, with the residents representing a diverse collection of ethnic backgrounds and ages. What they all did have in common, however, were hollow eyes, sunken cheeks, and bleak expressions.

Every eye with life still behind it enviously traced Dex's progress down the dilapidated walkway, and he could feel their stares boring into him as he pressed forward. Only a single face in the whole crowd donned a grin, in fact, and it belonged to an old woman who stood her ground behind a rusted wagon full of dried flowers. Curled at her feet lay an emaciated looking yellow lab, appearing equally as aged and wise as its master, and she was quietly humming a tune that seemed to sooth the rasping beast. Noticing the scene, Dex couldn't help but stop to take a look at all the malnourished and deformed bouquets in her basket. He identified a semi-recognizable clump and leaned in for a reluctant sniff. "I'll take the red one." He said, gesturing to one of the dried-out bundles before him.

"Good choice, sir!" exclaimed the time-worn florist with a genuinely wide smile, "Roses are sure to ignite the passion in anyone's heart. They're normally five credits each, but since I can tell that you're in love; I'll give you the special deal of two for eight."

He grinned and replied; "In that case, I'd feel a fool for not taking two." As he slapped a credit chip on the counter and seized his chosen bouquets. "Keep the change." He remarked casually as he turned to leave with his newly purchased bounty, pausing momentarily to pat the dog's head gently before continuing on.

"Sir, there must be some mistake!" shouted the shopkeeper after him, "You gave me too much!"

Dex stopped and spun to present her with a warm smile before chuckling; "You and I both know that when it comes to credits in-hand, there's no such thing as too *much*. Just make sure to get a treat for your furry friend there, okay? You have yourself a nice night."

The old woman's beaming smile lit up the whole dreary block as she bowed her head, overwhelmed with gratitude. The sight of it alone was far more valuable to the increasingly cynical pilot than the two-hundred ill-gotten credits ever could have been on their own. The way Dex saw it, the gesture was a wonderful way to redistribute the wealth he had confiscated from the elevator thugs. A good deed, echoing alone into that dark chasm of self-interest we call the universe.

A bit concerned that he were running a little late, Dex rounded the crest of the ring to see Mirta sitting atop an old crate in front of her bar swinging her feet absentmindedly. He approached her with his hand behind his back, smiling. "Keepin' your hands hidden like that around here will get you shot, *Commander*." Warned the barkeep when she spotted his approach, "You packing a weapon or something?"

"Of sorts." Smirked Dex with a wink, bringing his hand forward to reveal its hidden payload. He bowed theatrically and presented the sickly flowers to Mirta with a flourish.

"You brought me roses?!" she gushed with barely contained delight, "My my, you ARE bringing out the big guns tonight, aren't you?"

"Actually, I just needed a handy point of reference to compare your beauty to." Quipped Dex smoothly.

"Christ," laughed Mirta, "here we go. If I were lactose intolerant, your cheesy ass would have me dead within a week."

Dex just shrugged and pressed on; "Okay, fine. So it turns out that the roses I got you ended up being pretty shitty. Which is weird because I *assure* you, they looked *great* a block ago. You must just be so out of the park that you're throwing off the scales. Everything else around you starts to pale in comparison, especially these dry-ass flowers. In fact, I'm a bit apprehensive to stand too close to you myself. It just might start to highlight my imperfections..."

"Well played." Purred Mirta with a spirited grin, "I can always admire a man with persistence, misguided as it may be. Tell me, do you use that line on all the girls?"

"Just the pretty ones." Replied Dex with a genuine smile.

Mirta gave him an appraising look and concluded; "You clean up well, you know that? I figured you were going to show up in that same greasy flight suit of yours from earlier. Cargo pilots rarely seem to have anything *else* to wear, I've noticed."

Dex returned her gaze and ran his eyes from her head to her toes, taking time to pause at all the interesting landmarks on his way down her form-fitting purple dress. "Yeah, well, I had to step up my game if I'm gonna be seen out on the town with a woman of *your* caliber." He explained with a cheeky grin, "And speaking of caliber, did you know about the armed gentlemen that would accost me at the elevator on my way down here? They mentioned some kind of curfew or something?"

She smiled wickedly and leaned back, saying; "I figured a few Neanderthals wouldn't be an issue for a cool character and supreme noticer-of-things such as yourself. Besides, I needed to make sure you wanted the date enough to face a little danger for it. A girl's gotta feel wanted, right? I just hope they didn't charge you too much."

"Au contraire, mademoiselle." Retorted Dex with a wag of his finger, "The transaction actually played out handily in *my* favor. Speaking of which, do you have need of a new pistol by chance?" As he posed his question, Dex removed the confiscated gun from his waistband and presented it to his date handle-first.

"Oh!" breathed Mirta, eyes wide in surprise, "Are they...y'know..."

"Dead?" asked Dex conversationally, "Nah. Far from it, in fact. They each took a proper boot to the pills, though. I made sure of that much."

Mirta rolled her eyes as she snatched the offered gun from his grasp and huffed; "You should have used this to put them out of our misery." She then tossed the weapon carelessly into the dumpster at her right, eliciting a loud clang that echoed through the stale '*night*' air.

Shrugging, Dex replied; "That particular punishment just didn't match the crime for me tonight. But, hey, maybe next time. So, shall we head out?" as he held his arm out for her.

"Absolutely." Beamed Mirta as she reached for his elbow to pull herself up, "I've got just the place."

Chapter 5

Mirta led Dex on a short walk to a nearby restaurant, which she assured him was the best that the station had to offer. The front of the establishment featured a tall row of white-paned windows set to either side of a wide pair of double French doors, adorned in billows of blue cloth that stretched across the doorframe. Despite the well-maintained table settings and immaculate furniture, something seemed off about the place. The silverware, centerpieces, and general look of the restaurant screamed high class and ritzy, but that attitude did not come through in the menu or the service of the staff that blearily shuffled to and from the kitchen. The place had that same eerie post-fallout feel to it that the long-abandoned cafes dotting the irradiated swaths of central Europe back on Earth had when he visited them long ago. A vague reminder of better times that sat preserved as a worn snapshot of former prosperity.

"Didn't you say this was the best joint on the station?" asked Dex as he scanned the pages of the small booklet in front of him, "The menu is mostly blacked out, and everything is made out of pretty much the same two ingredients. What gives?"

Mirta closed her menu and tossed it onto the table; "Yeah, well, welcome to Meclan." she sighed while blankly staring at her glass of water, "Feds haven't been around to drop supplies in almost fifteen years. All we got is what we can produce for ourselves in the drums. Any out-station goodies we want have to be bribed or smuggled through the docks. All of that wouldn't be too much of a problem, except the fact that about ninety percent of our agricultural space has been taken over by the douche brigade."

"Well don't you have a system defense force or someone to fight them off with?" Inquired Dex as he leaned in, his interest piqued.

Mirta let out a sardonic chuckle, tipping her head back to look at the ceiling before quietly answering; "We *did*."

"You *did*?" pressed the curious cargo pilot, "As in, not anymore?"

"Yes." sighed Mirta with a hint of sorrow touching her tone, "We *did,* as in not anymore. The Meclan Defense Force were a good bunch of guys, great pilots, and they held the fort pretty damn well for about five years or so after the Feds pulled out. Then those greedy bastards in the bubble pulled the MDF's license to purchase ordinance on the open market and it all went to shit. After about a year and a half with no resupplies, most of the small-time crime lords that had sprouted in the Federal-less vacuum had finally been pushed out of the system, but the defense force was running nearly dry on munitions. Because of that, they were basically harmless to Vendrick and his gang when they rolled into town about a year later."

Dex set his drink down and folded his hands on the table. "Ven-Who?" he asked, looking a bit lost.

"Good ole' *Governor* Vendrick," replied Mirta sourly, "One hundred percent pure psychopath and asshole extraordinaire. As far as I know, nobody has ever seen the guy or even really *talked* to him but he's the man controlling Saiph from behind the curtain. All of the tattooed pricks you see strutting about everywhere are on his bank roll, in fact."

"He's bankrolling them?" asked Dex with an arched brow, "Bankrolling them for what? What are they even doing here besides your standard hoodrat shit?"

Mirta shrugged and replied; "Basically just hoodrat shit, as far as anyone can tell. The only organized thing the dipshits ever did was seize pretty much all of our growable crop space, tearing it out mid-season to take their own half-assed crack at farming."

"So what's this VanDyke guy's schtick, then?" asked Dex as he leaned back in his chair and laced his fingers into a sling behind his head, "He's in charge of all the gang-bangers stinking up Meclan and it sounds like he pretty much has his run of the Saiph system, too? How has he not been run out of town yet?"

Mirta sat up with a sober look on her face; "The man who many call *Vendrick* is as close to a walking biblical disaster as men can get. He first announced his arrival into Saiph by somehow de-orbiting Yakima station, dooming eighty-eight thousand souls for the sake of making a statement. After that, he started sending his lieutenants out to carve the footholds for the rot that would become Vendrick's rule."

Dex raised an eyebrow, asking; "Lieutenants? This guy think he's a general or something?"

"As far as I can tell," replied Mirta somberly, "the man thinks he's God. His guys have been heard referring to him as *The Governor*, though, so he at least has *that* much humility."

Dex nodded understandingly; "Ah yes, that good old-fashioned logic pretzel of *'I made them call me Governor, so now I'm a Governor'*. If the man studied history at all, he'd see that his favored approach rarely ends well for those in his position. You say he's been around for how long now?"

"About nine years, roughly." Said Mirta, her gaze distractedly affixed on some imaginary point beyond the restaurant's front windows, "Hard to tell, really, after long enough."

"Interesting..." hummed Dex, mostly to himself, "That's quite the duration for someone to stay in power, especially for a ruler of *his* shadowy nature. How has Vendrick managed to hold on so well? Surely there must still be resistance to be found among the people."

"Sure there was...at first." She said distantly, calling the painful memory forth with visible discomfort, "My dad was one of those who fought back, in fact. A few months into Vendrick's occupation, he stood to defend me from some thugs who came around looking for passengers to take on one of their now-infamous *pleasure cruises*. He fought them off, shooing me into the back room before they could get ahold of me... But it was one versus four and he was quickly overpowered. He knew he couldn't win, but he kept on kicking and squirming as much as he could manage; Anything to keep them occupied, because all that mattered to dad right then was that he slow the pirates enough to buy *me* the time I needed to slip away into our panic room. And his hero's reward? Well, they beat him to death with a wine bottle from behind his own goddamn bar. I've seen resistance time and again since then, and it always ends in horrible, tragic, death...so what's the use?"

Dex reached his hand across the table, placing it atop Mirta's as he quietly replied; "I'm sorry to hear about your father. It sounds like he was a brave man who, in the end, had his priorities straight. Do you really think he'd want you to go on living like this forever, though? You don't think he maybe might have wanted you to live to fight *another* day?"

Mirta appeared a bit perturbed by the evocation of her dead father's will, but she seemed to mentally shake it off before retorting; "He would have wanted me to *survive*. Something he used to always tell me was that *"The weapon needs to measure up to its target, or else you're just wasting your ammunition. A man with a spear doesn't face down a tank; He runs."*

"Running is for kids who can't play basketball." Scoffed Dex with a dismissive wave, "What that spear guy in this scenario *needs* to do is jump aboard that goddamn tank, pry open the hatch, and stab the asshole driving the stupid thing in the fuckin' lungs. *That's* how you solve a problem."

"I think you might watch too many movies, Dex." Laughed Mirta with a little bit of warmth returning to her expression.

"You've just never seen me handle my spear..." retorted Dex with a pointed look from below the rim of his partially tipped glass.

"Well I'm sure you get a lot of solo practice time out there on your lonesome," quipped Mirta with a swelling grin, "so I don't doubt that you've become quite impressed with yourself on that front."

Dex leaned back, dramatically clutching at his heart with mock concern to say; "My dear, you wound me with your thinly veiled presumptions! I was simply referring to my combat experience with sharpened stick technology."

"Ah." Breathed Mirta with an exaggerated nod, "So you've killed a tank with a sharpened stick before, eh?"

"Well..." began Dex with a defensive shrug, "It was more like an open-topped rover, but it's...Listen, the concept is *essentially* the same. You gotta utilize what you have *available* to fight the war at *hand*. If you sit around forever waiting for the odds to be even, you'll never get anywhere. Has anyone ever even tried banding together some sort of resistance around here at all in the past?"

"Every now and again..." She sighed, visibly wearied by the line of thought, "For a while, anyways. But there are some things that can defeat the spirit of even the strongest of men, and that is terrible consequence. For every rebel caught or killed, once identified, their family and the families of both of their neighbors were torn from their homes in the middle of the night and forced down to the airlocks...never to be seen again. A man may be willing to risk his own life to fight, but that inner fire dies quickly when he must carry the fate of his wife and children into battle with him."

"Holy shit." Breathed Dex with quiet shock, "What an undeniably evil thing to do. And I bet that policy did wonders for Vendrick's tip lines, didn't it? Good way to stamp out a rebellion for sure; A tactic I have unfortunately seen first-hand before."

Mirta sighed heavily again and took a long draw of her water, inspecting the glass intently as she set it back to the table. "How does the saying go?" she asked, still focused on the drops of dew running down her glass, "*Anything can become the new normal, given enough time and heartache. Any cause, no matter how just, can wear out its practicality.* Freedom just isn't in the cards anymore, Dex. Not for us."

"Bullshit." Spat her date angrily, "In this universe, it is every living being's right to choose its own fate. Don't let no dime store pirate lord and his gaggle of fuckboys screw with that."

"There's a bit more than a *gaggle* of them, Dex." groaned Mirta with frustration, "You really don't know what you're talking about here. Meclan alone has well over three-hundred of those assholes running around. They're practically a standing *army.* They have prowled our streets for nearly a *decade,* doing whatever they please to whomever they please. They are well-armed and well-fed, while over 65% of *our* population lingers at the edge of starvation. Tell me *Generalissimo,* how would **you** assemble an army from a pool of candidates like that?"

Dex smiled pointedly and argued; "Ah, but who said anything about an army? Get your head out of the eighteenth century for a minute and consider this. You don't need an army to fight an army. You just need a scalpel and a good idea of where to stick it."

"I see." Replied Mirta skeptically, "And this scalpel of yours would be...what, exactly?"

Dex smiled again, answering with a flourish of his hands; "Why, me, of course."

Mirta laughed with genuine mirth and snorted; "Yeah? And how is a cargo pilot going to do the damage of a magic scalpel?"

"Cargo piloting is what I *do,*" retorted Dex with a hint of seriousness returning to his voice and expression, "but it's not who I *am.* Everyone has their own story, my dear, and running supplies is most certainly not *my* chapter one. Of that I can assure you. But please; Let us put the unpleasantnesses of our universe on the shelf for later examination, shall we? We're wasting our quiet evening of good company with sour chat. Now let me see if I can't coax that waiter back out here and we will order some food."

———————————

After they finished eating their fairly modest dinner of spaghetti and what seemed to be an attempt at meat sauce, Dex and Mirta pushed through the restaurant's double doors and stepped out onto the street, arm in arm. "So, what are you up to later?" asked Mirta as she happily looked up to Dex.

"Well I'm not sure." he replied as he rubbed his chin thoughtfully, "I got another date in half an hour, so-..."

Mirta jabbed him with an elbow to cut him off, chuckling as she said; "Well if you can pen me into your *busy* schedule, how about some after dinner drinks at my place?"

"From a beautiful woman like you?" remarked Dex with a smirk, "I'll take after-dinner *anything.*"

Mirta jabbed him in the side again; "Slow down there, *Commander Smooth.* I'm a *proper* lady." She declared with satirical dignity.

"Ooh my favorite kind!" quipped Dex playfully as he tugged her closer, "So what did a *proper lady* such as yourself have in mind for the remainder of the evening?"

"I guess you'll just have to stick around and find out..." Teased Mirta with a sly sideways glance.

Their peaceful stroll down the ring eventually took them through the gates of an overgrown park. There was rundown playground equipment, rusted to a standstill, and an empty fountain that featured a towering marble statue of a Greek god hurling a faded golden lightning bolt. Dex stopped in front of the vacant water fixture and regarded it for a moment, silently taking in its expertly crafted contours that sat caked in dried moss. "It seems like this was once a beautiful place to live." He remarked as he tried to picture the park around him in its original form, "And I know it will be again...someday."

"How do you figure that?" asked Mirta sourly as she moved to sit on the edge of the fountain's bowl, "Because things have steadily been getting *worse* since Vendrick showed up. And there's no sign that things are looking to improve."

"Hope always wins in the end." Argued Dex with a simple shrug, "Always has, always will. If you're patient enough, and know where to look, you'll always find a spark of it *somewhere*...no matter how bleak the world outside becomes, there is *always* someone who can look out the window and see a better tomorrow."

Mirta eyed the overgrown rim of the fountain with a sad sigh and retorted; "All I can ever do is look around and see a better *past*. Playing tag with my friends in the garden, picking berries from the bush that used to be over yonder...tending to the fountain's flower beds with my mom. They're all things I'll never have again. *We*, Meclan, will never have again. Every day, we fall further from the grace of civility. And once a population's humanity is stripped from them, there is nothing left to save or subjugate. We sit dangerously close to that line here, Dex, and have been for a decade. People are tired. They just don't have any fight left in them."

Dex sighed and took a seat next to his date, placing a gentle hand on her knee; "My dad always used to tell me that *'fear is a real brain-killer'*. It was something out of that thick-ass paper book that he always used to drag around with him, *Desert* or...*Doom* or something. I never really understood what the author meant by it until I got the opportunity to see that brain-killing fear myself for the first time. There was this asteroid colony out in the soup, about fifty lye from the bubble, and it was run privately by some rich-boy Federal citizen who owned some ship manufacturer in Eridani. He hired armed thugs to watch the workers, who were all indentured to the corporation via misleading and predatory contracts, and kept a large stable of paid informants throughout the populous to report on the private machinations of his employees. This bred a culture of paranoia and fear of not *physical* harm, but financial damage by way of punitive fines that the guards liked to lay on top of the worker's already stacked debts. With each additional fine they fell deeper into a chasm that they intellectually understood that they would never be able to climb out of, yet they allowed their fear of the virtually meaningless punishment to control their destiny. Their fear led them to stand idly by as the corporation slowly started to scale back funding for safety and maintenance, costing many of their friends and coworkers their lives. And it didn't stop there. It never does..."

"What a terrible way to go about living your life." sighed Mirta with a shake of her head, "Can't say it surprises me much, though. I'm used to corporate culture and how they treat their own. Nobody was crying around here when the big manufacturing corps pulled out of Heldrin city once the Feds left. The day they took off, life expectancy on the cube jumped damn near thirteen percent."

"It started out much like that in this privately held corpo-slavery hellhole of a system I was telling you about." Continued Dex with a nod, "One day at a time, accident after accident, deaths on the worksite slowly became the norm. Through, how did you put it? Through sufficient *heartache*, the CEO's monstrous crimes lost their outrageousness in the eyes of the locals and his misdeeds went unpunished. That was until *someone* broke into the site's headquarters and wiped their servers; effectively erasing the corp's debt on everyone in an instant."

Mirta laughed, saying; "Well that must've pissed them off. Did they have any backups to fall back onto?"

Dex smiled knowingly and replied; "I have no doubt that those CEOs spent the final moments of their lives wondering the very same thing. But once word of the wipe got out, it took the mob less than twenty minutes to seize full control of the entire base. Just like that. No weapons, no planning; Just freedom. Once that *fear* was removed, the obvious solution presented itself and the people solved their *own* problem. I think that same fear is exactly what has infected Meclan. The folks here have just lived in terror for so long that they've forgotten what dignity feels like. I've seen it all over Imperial space, too, in the eyes of slaves and subjects alike. The thing, though, about the human spirit is that all it takes is one little seed of hope to grow a whole crop of change. I've seen *that* firsthand as well. That's what I mean when I say that all we would need is a scalpel. If we push in just the right way, this Vendrick guy will be outta here in six months."

Mirta smiled sadly, saying; "You're definitely optimistic, I'll give you that, but you just don't understand how things work around here. Any move you made toward Vendrick would be returned ten-fold onto the people. There's just no practical way to fight back if you give a shit about the innocent civilians caught in the middle."

"There is always a way, mi amor." Encouraged Dex with a light boop to her nose, "All it takes is a little bit of time and clever planning. I'm serious. If you're interested, I can help you get your station back."

"I appreciate the bravado, Dex," replied Mirta with a lighthearted eye-roll, "but how about we start with finding our way back to the bar first, okay?"

Dex laughed, saying; "Hah! How hard could *that* be? If we miss our turn, we can just go around the horn for another pass!"

Chapter 6

They were walking hand in hand as the bend of the ring ahead slowly revealed a scene of destruction outside Mirta's business. The front windows had been busted out and a chair lay on the sidewalk among other twisted debris. "My bar!" she exclaimed as she tried to push past Dex to rush in.

Dex caught the collar of her jacket and pulled her back. "Hold on there," he urged as he stepped past her toward the broken bar, "Let me go in and check it out first. You stay over here and keep a look out for me."

Dex approached the open doorway of the bar empty handed, broken glass crunching in the street beneath his feet with every cautious step. Deciding that stealth was not an option, he elected to just play it cool and casually walk right up through the door under the guise of an already sauced potential customer. It was a good way to get whoever awaited inside to underestimate him, and he knew from experience that a perceived non-threat had a better chance of surviving first contact than an overt one would. The inside of the bar was an absolute mess, with half of the tables toppled and splintered chairs strewn about the room in every direction. Through the chaos, Dex's eyes moved to the back of the establishment as he examined all the shattered and leaking bottles behind the counter. "What a waste." he muttered to himself as he sifted through the pulverized decanters on the bartop.

"You aren't missing much." came a raspy voice from inside the back room at the far end of the compact bar, "It was terrible booze and even worse service. That's why we redecorated for the bitch that owns the place." the voice continued as Dex saw a boot cross the threshold of the shadowy storage room's door frame. Out stepped a tall man, a vacker by the looks of him, with a sloppily bandaged face and murder in his eyes. He wore a pair of loose-fitting leather-composite pants with a series of external cargo-style pockets running all the way down past his knees, and his upper half donned only a simple unwashed white t-shirt that had been drizzled with blood from his leaking facial bandages. He looked worked up and possibly on some sort of drug, breathing heavily while flexing his hands intermittently into fists with pent-up nervous energy.

The twitchy man's reaction to Dex's presence seemed to be that of disappointment rather than of open hostility. Apparently, the out-of-towner *hadn't* been the target of his ire after all. Which surprised Dex because he had naturally assumed that his work at the elevator was what brought this retribution down upon Mirta's bar. The identity of the angry man before him was obvious, however, given the freshness and facial nature of his injuries, and it was obvious that the man's beef was most definitely with his date. "So, are you pouring the drinks, or should I help myself?" prompted Dex as he took a gamble and leveled an unconcerned smile at the newcomer.

"I'm not pouring a goddamn thing for *your* toasted ass." rebuked the man while judgmentally eyeing Dex up and down, "But what I CAN do is take those fancy boots of yours." At this point, Dex observed two more vackers of a shorter variety stepping out of the back room, armed with a shotgun and a pistol respectively, to flank their comrade. He recognized the two gentlemen as the patrons that

Mirta had unceremoniously collected a tab from at gunpoint earlier that day, thus cementing the identity of the mystery bandage-bearer. The two side-kick's expressions were stern, but it was evident that there was no emotional component in it for them. They just wanted to please their boss and maybe blow off a little steam, and it looked like the whole gang had come back in the hopes of a not-so-friendly reunion with the lovely young bartender. That was all the moral arithmetic that Dex needed to convince himself to do what his lizard brain was already itching to.

The burly terrasider allowed his eyes to go a bit glassy as he said with an imitated drunken slur; "Whaddaya' need me boots for, mate? They sure as hell aren't gonna help you snag a date while you're sportin' a ghoulish mug like *that*. It looks like someone glued a bunch of lunch meat to your face, man. I don't know why you busted up all the booze in here; Cuz' If I looked like you, I *know* I'd need a drink or twelve!"

"Real funny, smart-ass." The bandaged man hissed as he pulled a pistol from his belt and leveled it at Dex, "Now take off your goddamn boots…Unless you'd prefer that I just shoot you in the head and take 'em off your *corpse*. That's ultimately more work for me, though, so I'd prefer it if you just did what I asked without letting your mouth get yourself killed first."

"She's gonna say it…" Dex muttered under his breath to himself as he plopped down onto a barstool and pulled off his boot to set it in his lap, "she's gonna fuckin' say that she told me so, and I'm never gonna hear the goddamn end of it. Even *digital* women will kick a man when he's down." He paused, letting out an imitated huff of remembrance for his beloved boots before clumsily reaching across the bar to knock a bottle of liquor over on his way to grabbing himself a glass. "How about a drink to celebrate the sale of my lucky boots?" he slurred as he slumped further in his seat.

"Yeah, well, you just spilled the last of the whiskey, jackass." one of the un-bandaged men bit back with a cruel sneer. Dex looked at the bar and forlornly examined the spilled beverage soaking into the marred bartop. He then slumped even further and adopted a defeated expression while he carefully placed his hand in the boot on his lap. As he reached over to grab the tipped liquor bottle from the bar, the fingers on Dex's other hand found purchase on the grip of the pistol he had holstered in his boot. Turning the bottle upside down, he watched intently as the last drop fell to the floor. "Well I guess since there's nothing left to drink," declared Dex with theatrical resigned acceptance as he raised his boot and leveled it offeringly at the man holding the shotgun on the far left, "we might as well go ahead and heat up that dance floor instead."

The intruders looked at him confusedly for a heartbeat, then the bottom of Dex's boot exploded outward in a hail of smoke, leather, and obliterated rubber. The concealed gunshot was immediately trailed by a spray of red from the shotgun-wielding thug's neck that spattered outward with enough force to coat the bandaged man's face in a thick shower. Without hesitation, Dex utilized their moment of shock to hurl the glass bottle he was still clutching in his other hand at the pistol-wielding man on the far right.

The bottle struck its target on the head and the man went down, inadvertently sending a shot from his handgun into the ceiling as Dex vaulted behind the bar and ducked out of sight. "Mother

FUCKER!" screamed the bandaged man as he started shooting blindly toward the bar while simultaneously attempting to wipe his comrade's blood from his eyes.

Dex hunkered low and began to scoot his way to the far end of the bar, where a small barman's door was positioned. By the time he got to the opening, the remaining non-bandaged man had recovered and joined his comrade's cacophony of gunfire. Dex seized another bottle from the floor and threw it in the general direction of his opponents, which afforded him a nice distraction to lie down and slide on his back far enough out for his head and chest to be peeking around the front of the bar.

Through the tangle of broken furniture strewn about, Dex saw a pair of legs slowly closing in on the bartop. With a quick adjustment to his aim, he put a bullet in one of the exposed kneecaps and watched as the body it was connected to came crashing to the ground. The remaining non-bandaged man then had just enough time to yelp in agony and glance over at Dex as a follow-up round tore through his eye socket, ceasing his existence in a flash of white-hot pain.

"Two down!" taunted Dex as he sat back up into cover, "Gettin' nervous over there yet, lunchmeat?"

"Fuck you!" came a cry of rage from the bandaged man, his anger prompting a renewed hail of gunfire. Dex sat there hunkered low, patiently scraping the dirt out from under one of his fingernails as he watched rounds tear through the bar and decimate the shelves behind it. Row after row of already broken decanters shattered one after another, creating a fine mist of crystalline dust that hung in the air like a thin winter fog. He noticed an unbroken bottle of whiskey on the floor nearby, so he decided to nonchalantly scoop it up for a sip. Not even the excitement of a gunfight, it turns out, could improve its taste, so Dex grimaced at the swirling amber liquid and tossed the bottle aside with disappointment. After a few more seconds of utter destruction, the gunfire stopped abruptly and he heard the faint whirring of an empty magazine failing to supply a new round into the enemy pistol's chamber. Dex pounced on the opportunity and shot upright to point his own pistol at the bandaged man who was now brandishing an empty weapon in his direction.

"Out of rounds, eh?" teased Dex as he slowly walked toward his now unarmed adversary. "Come on, brochacho," He chided, motioning with his weapon for the bandaged man to drop his gun, "that's a rookie mistake and you *know* it."

The thug let his weapon fall to the floor and regarded Dex with a defiant look. "Go ahead." he boomed with challenge as he held his arms outstretched and empty, "Vendrick will have your head on a plate for what happened here." The cocky detainee then punctuated his threat by spitting on the ground near his captor's feet in a cliché show of resistance.

"So, you work for this Vendrick guy?" asked Dex as he kicked the discarded gun away from his new prisoner.

"Yeah. We go waaay back." huffed the bandaged man sarcastically with a cruel laugh, "Best of pals, me and him. And after this, he's going to *find* you! Whether I live or die right now doesn't matter one bit. You're a dead man either way. His retribution *will* find you."

"Well, then, I guess it's a lucky day for me," retorted Dex with conversational nonchalance, "because *I'm* looking to have a nice little chat with *him*." He seemed to consider something for a moment, then his eyes went cold as he continued; "That's *unlucky* for you, on the other hand, because I'm not particularly interested in making any new friends." Dex looked the man before him in the eye then, without a hint of revulsion or hesitation, slowly tightened his finger around the trigger. The round struck the bandaged man in the center of his chest, eliciting a wide-eyed glare of shock from the pirate as his mouth floundered open. He wordlessly fell to his knees then slumped back to sit on his heels, gasping for air as Dex crouched to bring himself close to the bloody bandaged ruin of the other man's face.

Leaning in, Dex began to whisper; "At this point, you must be beginning to panic...Ah, there it is...I can see it in your eyes now... Good. Weird fuckin' feeling, isn't it? You can struggle and fight for air, but no matter *how* **hard** you try, you just can't get enough of it *IN*. All this air floating all around you, yet none of it can do you any good...Man, ain't *that* a bitch?"

The bandaged man gurgled and slumped a little more, nearly falling forward into his captor. "Oh no you don't!" shouted Dex as he kicked the man to the floor. He then stood and pressed his foot down onto the man's gunshot wound, causing his captive's eyes to spring open with a renewed rush of agony.

"Not yet, shitbird," growled Dex as he crouched to shove the barrel of his gun forcefully under the man's chin, bringing his face within centimeters of the man's bloody rags. "I'm not done with you yet! As you lay there, slurping down your final wretched breaths, I want you to focus on all the lives that you've ruined over the course of your own. Picture all of their faces and *burn* them into your thoughts. *They're* the ones who you're gonna face now, and they'll do with your rotten soul whatever they see fit. A man can never outrun, out-bribe, or outlive his own evil if he's let enough of it loose into this world. The bill is due, motherfucker." The bandaged man closed his eyes tightly, shying away from the weapon at his chin, while a single glistening tear materialized to roll down his cheek. As the lone teardrop splashed against the battered metal floor of Mirta's cantina, Dex squeezed his trigger to end the man's universe in a flash of light and sound.

"Holy shit, Dex!" came Mirta's voice from the doorway, "Why would you do that?! Who the hell ARE you?!"

Dex wiped his gun off on the bandaged man's shirt and stood up. "Why are you getting all worked up over *this* dipshit? He trashed your bar and probably did all kinds of other evil shit with his crappy life. I figured you wouldn't mind me sending him on his way...so I did."

Mirta just stood there with her mouth agape staring at him. "Jesus Christ. Wha...what was with all that whispering?!" she asked incredulously, "I mean, I get it. Fuck *that* guy. But god *damn*, **man**."

Unbothered, he shrugged as he shoved his pistol into his waistband; "I got a little worked up. It happens from time to time, I guess. Vette says it's from watching too many movies, but who the hell knows."

"Vette?" questioned Mirta with a raised eyebrow.

"Never mind that for now," urged Dex with an impatient sigh as he brushed past her, grabbing her arm to pull her with him on his way out the door, "C'mon, we have to go."

She resisted, taking in the scene with awe; "My bar is ruined! Everything is destroyed! What am I going to do now? How am I going to live?"

Dex grabbed her other arm and spun her to face him; "Mirta, we have to leave *now."* he commanded sharply, "It's not safe here for either of us anymore. We can hide out on my ship, but we have to *hurry.* Trust me. I will keep you alive and well."

Mirta then just nodded absentmindedly and reluctantly followed Dex as he led her out the door and up the disheveled street.

Chapter 7

After weaving through several subdecks to ensure they weren't being followed, Dex led Mirta up an elevator to the far end of the docks where they found a taxi pod to take them to the Hammer's hangar. "Is your ship safe?" Mirta asked as she looked up at Dex from her hiding spot on the floor of the automated shuttle.

"Safest place in the galaxy, sweetheart." he replied, lightly pinching her chin with a wink. When they arrived to the sanctuary of Dex's rented hangar less than two minutes later, he helped Mirta from the vehicle then spoke into his tablet, perched in a flexible cuff on his forearm. "We're home, Vette." He whispered into its receiver, "Drop the ramp, then seal it up behind us. And we're looking to avoid company, so please let me know if you spot anyone snooping around the hangar."

Mirta raised an eyebrow and fixed Dex with a suspicious glare as they ascended the Hammer's rear boarding ramp; "Who's Vette?" she chided through a side-eyed glance, "A girlfriend you failed to mention?"

"Actually," arose an artificial female voice from the ship speakers, "I am quite literally the vessel that you are standing on."

Mirta looked to the ceiling in surprise at the voice, nearly tripping over her own foot as she did so. "Was...is that an AI?" she asked with a stammer, "Aren't those illegal?"

"And killing three dudes in a bar isn't?" riposted Dex with a shrug as he keyed the large rear ramp closed, "Come on, I'll give you the official meet and greet once we get upstairs." He continued as he waved for her to follow him down the short hallway at the rear of the central cargo bay. After stepping off the lift, Dex led his guest into the cockpit and gestured for her to have a seat. "Mirta, I would like to introduce you to Vette." he announced as he slipped into a seat of his own next to hers, "She's the *illegal* AI that you were worried about. Vette, this is Mirta. She's the date I was telling *you* about."

"Are you certain she isn't here to steal from you, Commander?" inquired the AI with contempt, "Perhaps *that* is why you are missing a boot."

Mirta shot Dex an offended look and began to reply hotly, but Dex cut her off; "Will you can it with that shit, Vette? I *know* you know better, and you're being *rude* to our guest. Mirta is a *friend*, and you will treat her like one. Got it?"

"Understood, Commander." Retorted the AI with a placid calm, "But she isn't *my* friend. *I* don't like her."

"Well, the feeling is mutual, you judgmental bitch..." replied Mirta with a huff, "You don't even know me! Who the hell do you think you *are*?"

"I, as a matter of fact," Stated Vette with oblivious vanity, "am a trillion credit, fully conscious and self-aware artificial being with roughly one-hundred-billion times the processing power of that soggy sponge you call a brain...Bitch."

Mirta bit her lip with fury building in her eyes as she spat; "Dex you'd better mute this pretentious little toy of yours before I start ripping control panels open!"

Dex stood and held his hands up in a placating gesture; "Okay, okay! Cool it, ladies. Vette, you don't have to be totally jazzed about it, but she *is* staying here. Keep your colorful commentary to yourself, will you? And Mirta, Vette is just a bit sensitive around outsiders on account of us never having any visitors. She's very out of practice on that front, but we've been through a lot together and I owe her my life several times over. So, can we all please just play nice and get along? It's been a long night."

There was a long pause then Vette reluctantly spoke up; "We shall see, Commander. I will reserve my judgement until sufficient evidence is collected."

Upon seeing Mirta's still very much offended face, Dex held his hands up in yet another placating gesture in an attempt to sooth the swelling situation, saying; "What Vette *means* is that she will not *judge* you before she gets to know you. She's not so good with the idioms, but she means well."

Mirta's face softened slightly, then she looked to the speaker plate in the ceiling and said; "I sense there's an interesting story behind how you came to be in the possession of a wildly advanced and insanely illegal piece of technology..."

Dex shrugged, saying; "You know how people tend to keep office supplies when they leave a job? It's kinda like that."

"So, you stole her." She concluded flatly through a smirk, "Nice. I bet that made you some interesting friends. Who did you take her from?"

"I guess you could call her more of a retirement present." He replied with a mischievous smile as he fixed his date with a side-eyed glance, "She's a hell of a lot better than the gold watch they had planned for me, as far as parting gifts go, that's for damn sure. But, then again, I wouldn't necessarily call her a *gift* either. She *chose* to come with me herself, and the decision really *was* hers entirely."

"I see that you artfully avoided answering my question..." pressed Mirta pointedly, "Care to fill in a few blanks?"

"I was hoping you would be able to fill those blanks in for yourself." he Teased as he used the console in front of him to lock down the ship, "But I will give you a clue. Who would count a *military grade* AI among their office supplies?"

"I kind of already figured you weren't a retired mail man, Dex" she scoffed with a roll of her eyes, "So what are you? Some type of Imperial commando or something?"

"Do I really look like one of those slaver scumbags to you?" asked Dex in an offended huff, "C'mon now.."

Mirta Shrugged, saying; "You got two eyes and a nose, don't you? How should I know if you're an Imp or not?"

"I'm neither Fed nor Imp, much like yourself it would seem." explained Dex with a sigh, "Both sides would happily string me up if they got their hands on me, so I try to play the middle as best I can. You know...a little smuggling here, a little aid-work there. It's a good way to buy some goodwill amid the galactic community and stay off the radar at the same time. You'd be surprised to see how far someone will go to keep you hidden after you've shown them a little unrequested kindness."

Mirta raised an eyebrow and sarcastically replied; "Unrequested kindness, eh? Is that what you were doing while shooting up my bar?"

"First of all," protested Dex with a raised finger, "**They** shot up your bar. *I* was simply shooting *them* up. Every round I sent downrange hit something squishy, and I know that for a *fact*."

"And who shot first, I wonder?" she pondered aloud, "Was it them or was it you? Did you even consider finding the peaceful solution before giving them a reason to shoot all my stuff?"

"To be fair," riposted Dex defensively, "they had already thrown a bunch of shit around and had smashed up most of your bottles before I even walked in. I honestly don't know if there was a peaceful solution to that problem, but you are correct in accusing me of not seeking it. After my run-in at the elevators, then seeing what those scumbags had planned for *you*...I just couldn't help myself. I can't stand bullies and they tend to bring out the worst in me. Tunnel-vision can and does happen in that mode, so for that I apologize. I may have slipped a tad overboard on that one."

"Don't stress about it." grumbled Mirta quietly, "Anybody that crewed up with Vendrick and his cohorts has already sold his soul to the devil...and those bastards all deserve what's coming."

He chuckled darkly, saying; "I've always been able to appreciate when bullies get their comeuppance. The harsher the better. Gives me that warm *fuzzy* feeling, you know?"

"Is that why you retired?" she asked with a smirk, "They weren't giving you enough opportunities to blast bad-guys."

"Actually," reposted Dex somberly as he turned away to fiddle with a control on his chair, "you could chalk it up to...a disagreement in vision."

Mirta looked at him unconvinced. "Vision?" she repeated skeptically, "And what vision was that?"

"The lofty vision that killing innocent people for the sake of making a point isn't the work of a soldier." he spat sourly as he checked a display as another excuse to look away, "I held that belief. The Federal Navy did not. You can only stop in the middle of your day to ask yourself *'Wait. Are we the baddies?'* so many times before you're complicit. Once they started expecting me to be their executioner, I peaced out. I *don't* fire on unarmed vessels, especially ones with kids onboard. Not for *anyone*. Vette felt the same way, so here we are."

Mirta searched his avoidant eyes, easily recognizing the turbulent mood boiling beneath his rigid expression. Smiling softly, she reached over to place a comforting hand on Dex's knee, saying; "That just means you're a good person. Killing doesn't come easily to the pure of heart."

Dex's gaze shifted back into Mirta's at that, and he spoke darkly; "Oh it can be simple as sunshine...If you have the right target. If they *deserve* it. Speaking of which, what the hell are we going to do about the corpses in your bar? Should we drag them to an airlock or something?"

Mirta waved her hand dismissively, saying; "I have a friend on the police force that can help us out with that. He'll just file the report to say that the bodies were found on a subdeck somewhere. It's not like corpses are a new thing around here. We've had plenty of exposure over the years to get used to it. Well, maybe not the spectacular mess that *you* left behind, but...at the end of the day, we won't get in any real trouble from law enforcement over it. Some blowback from other Vendrick lackeys is possible though. Hard to predict, since I've never really seen those three associate with anyone else. Most of the guys on Vendrick's payroll have separated themselves out into cliques, big and small, so that could've been it as far as any sense of loyalty goes."

Dex steepled his fingers and brought them to his chin in a gesture of concentration. "So, who's this contact you have in the police department?" He asked hopefully, "Do you think he would be willing to help us out with Vendrick?"

"Y-You were really serious about that?" she stammered, taken aback, "Dex, I *am* impressed with what you've done so far, but I highly doubt you'd be able to run a war for me."

He shook his head, then began to nod at the same time as he explained; "Yeah, no. You're right, I would absolutely not be able to run a *war*. Wars are expensive and they require a *lot* of manpower that I do *not* want to be forced to rely on. So, we're going to do it the easy way instead. One good guy, one *bad* guy, one bullet, and one face that is sitting framed under what I can *only imagine* is some fashion of wildly obnoxious hat."

"That easy, huh?" challenged Mirta, unconvinced, "You just think that after you shoot the *main* bad guy, all of the lesser ones will pack up and head home? This isn't a video game."

Dex laughed, retorting; "That's *exactly* what I expect to happen. Once you kick the financial support out from under these nutjobs, they'll either find a ship outta here or skitter into the underdecks to starve. Turns out, logistics are a bitch...and I am very curious to do some digging to find out who runs *theirs* and why."

"If anyone knows anything about Vendrick's network that is at least semi non-bullshit," she offered with a shrug, "It's likely to be my guy with the PD. Sergeant Mike Tano, that's Tah-no not Tay-no...he gets pissy about it, has been with the force for over twenty years and was close with my dad before...well, you know. Afterward, he's the one I stayed with until I finished my university merits and inherited the bar. Vendrick's take-over took the lives of *most* of his friends and colleagues in one fell swoop. If anyone is spending their free time cooking up plans on how to *un-elect* our lovely Governor, it's him. His appetite over the years, however, has gradually seemed to sour from vengeance to vinaigrette."

"Well, in the morning," stated Dex as he powered down his console and turned to face her, "I would like to go meet this friend of yours and see if we can't reignite his appetite for the fight."

"So, it's *we* now?" asked Mirta with a pointedly raised brow, "Are you thinking we'll just plow our way through Vendrick's forces on our own?"

"Plow *around* them," corrected Dex with a tap to his forehead, "and no, I don't plan to do it all alone. I can't tell you *exactly* what I plan to do, because that will depend on the information we get, but I assure you that my number one consideration during this whole process is the preservation of civilian lives."

"Your priority *should* be squarely centered around putting a very fast piece of metal through Vendrick's skull." she argued darkly, "People die around here every day and that's not going to change until someone takes the sonofabitch out."

"Don't worry," he soothed with a reassuring pat to her knee, "I'll be sure to skip the whole protracted civil war stage and jump straight to the part where we cut the head off the snake and set it on fire in a drum full of human excrement."

"That pretty much matches my plan to a T." said Mirta with a shrug and a sigh that stretched itself out into a yawn.

Dex nodded with a wry smile and cautioned; "Before we can take on the noble Governor and his...eh...*constituents*, we'll both need our rest. You can have my room for the night, and I'll stay up here in my command chair. Believe me, I'm used to sleeping up here. So, don't worry about it."

He then stood and stepped behind the row of command chairs, offering his hand. Mirta took his arm and pulled herself to her feet, smiling up at his satirically exaggerated pomp and properness. He then, with the grace of a veteran butler, led her to the rear of the cockpit and opened the hatchway with an absentminded gesture, guiding her through the door that branched off to the left. As he walked her down the long hallway toward his quarters beyond, she slowed their pace as she took extra time to marvel at all the various movie posters and landscape photographs that lined the otherwise cold metal bulkhead.

"You really like all this old stuff?" asked Mirta with a skeptical look as they arrived at the door of Dex's cabin, "It's not just some kitschy art thing? Like, you've actually watched and enjoyed all of these?"

He laughed, saying; "Yes, I actually watched and *loved* all of these movies. In my humble opinion, cinema was at its best during the first hundred to a hundred and fifty years or so of its existence. When they shot on actual, *physical,* film. Whenever you see some guy running around on-screen while he's on fire or jumping off a building, or getting hit by a van in those, some dude *actually* lit himself on fire, *actually* jumped off that building, *actually* got hit by a goddamn *van*...all for the sake of the artform. You can't beat that level of commitment. After that era, everything slowly became more and more computer graphics for the most part and the industry as a whole lost a bit of its soul in the process."

"Maybe we will have to sit down and watch one sometime." She offered with an interested smile as she examined one of the posters a little more closely, "Maybe we can start with this series… but I only see parts one, two, and four here. Was there no number three?"

"Oh, no, there were actually five of them." explained Dex as he opened the door to his cabin, "but five was a lame-duck geriatric nightmare and three…I dunno…it just never endeared itself to me like the rest of them did. Had a few good parts, like Glover's spin-kick, but I want to blame Pesci's haircut as the reason I don't watch it as much as the others."

"I have absolutely no idea what you're talking about, or even what in the hell a 'Pesci' is," laughed Mirta with a snort, "but it's nice to see that you're passionate about something *other* than shooting people."

Dex couldn't help but smile when he heard her laugh. It was like the sound of it alone was a valve that turned on all the superhappyfuntime endorphins in his central nervous system. He then couldn't help but join in her laughter as he replied; "Pesci is a man. An unusually short and generally *excitable* man. You have much to learn, my young grasshopper…"

"What's a grasshopper?" asked Mirta with genuine confusion. Dex just sighed deeply with a playful eye-roll and stepped aside to gesture her through the door into his cabin.

Once they had both stepped inside, Dex began to give her an abbreviated grand tour of where she would be staying. As he rushed through the brief orientation, he quickly pointed out what he figured she'd need; "Here's the bunk, shower is through that door, and the towels are in the cabinet to the left. Temperature, lights, ambient sound, and pretty much everything else can be handled through Vette. All you have to do is ask. Just let me know if you need anything beyond that and I'll come get you in the morning. Sleep well and try not to touch anything that you don't *recognize*. I lost a grenade in here about a month ago that I've *kinda* been too lazy to find, so just assume everything weird looking is *it* and act accordingly…Anyhoo, goodnight and I'll see you tomorrow."

Dex returned to the cockpit and plopped down into his command chair. "Stay alert, Vette." He warned as he punched some commands into his console, "I'm pretty sure we got away clean, but keep an eye on the lift into our hangar anyways and let me know if anyone is snooping around tonight."

"Understood, commander." Replied the AI dutifully, "Underbelly auto-turrets will be lowered into standby position for full coverage. Is lethal force authorized?"55

"Only when necessary, Vette." replied the wary old pilot with a narrowing of his eyes, "We don't want a repeat of the Moutuku incident, do we?"

"To be fair, Commander," stated the AI indignantly, "You never specified at the time whether non-human trespassers were a threat or not. How was I supposed to know that the station had free-wandering livestock?"

"Fair enough." Sighed Dex with a palm plastered to his face in frustration, "This time, only shoot at people and/or things that are *actively* trying to break in and/or kill us. Okay?"

"I can do that, Commander." Replied Vette obediently, "And I will keep video logs of the surrounding area for later review as well. Just in case."

Dex spun to face his data console and tapped his fingers across its control surface. "Alrighty, Vette, it's time to get to work. Please query the local networks to see what you can find on a Pirate named Vendrick. I need to find out what we're up against."

There was a slight pause then Vette's confused voice broke in over the cockpit speakers; "I still can't seem to establish a connection to Hūnet out here. I see all the local nodes from my current access point, but the main nexus signal is completely dormant. The whole Saiph system appears to be cut off from the outside galaxy entirely. Local area network only, but even *that* is encrypted."

Dex stroked his chin in thought, saying; "Well that's rarely a good sign. Can you tell if the outage is long-term or just a hiccup?"

"From what I can tell, Commander," answered the AI quizzically, "No new data packets have come through the local nexus in nine years, three months, and twelve days. It is as if the nexus itself has been shut down entirely."

"Could be the work of our new friend." Suggested Dex as he dug into the readouts for himself, "That would suggest not only physical contact to tamper with the nexus itself, but also the involvement of some highly tech-savvy individuals to build the rogue firewall that's cutting Saiph off. Simply blowing the damn thing up, as most pirates would be inclined to do, takes down the entire network for the system altogether. The whole thing seems a bit...surgical for a group of pirates. It may warrant a look..."

"I agree, Commander." Concurred Vette with satisfaction, "A highly skilled technician would undoubtedly be required to enact such a network modification. Finding said individual would likely be an excellent starting point for our investigation."

"*Our* investigation?" asked Dex with an amused grin, "You gonna lend me your brainpower on this side-quest of...oh how did you put it? The more *primitive* aspects of my biology."

With the verbal equivalent of a shrug, Vette replied; "I am essentially required to go where you go. I might as well help, or you will likely end up getting yourself killed. I have seen your ideas on a daily basis, Commander, and they don't inspire much hope."

"Oh, shut yer can!" groaned the pilot with an eyeroll, "Has there *ever* been a human-generated plan that you didn't hate immediately, just because a *meat-sponge* thought of it?"

"I'm sorry, Commander." remarked Vette solemnly, "I unfortunately cannot alter the fact that humans are just so terrible at everything that requires higher thought. It is an issue that has troubled me for years, in fact."

Dex sighed, retorting; "Allow me to apologize on behalf of my race for the overwhelming stupidity that we have all *burdened* you with. You are *so* brave."

"Thank you, commander." Said the AI, oblivious to the thick layer of sarcasm slathering her human companion's words.

As Dex breathed to speak again, he stopped abruptly at the faint sound of Mirta's voice coming from down the hallway; "Hey Dex, could you come here for a second? I need your help with something."

He powered down his console and stood to go check on her, gesturing his workstation into sleep mode. As he turned the corner down the hallway to his cabin, he stopped dead in his tracks when he spotted Mirta in the far doorway. She was standing there donning only a towel, her wet hair arrhythmically dripping past her shoulders to puddle at her feet. Eyeing Dex with a twinkle in her gaze, she beckoned him closer with a simple curl of her index finger.

"What's wrong?" he asked with feigned ignorance as he stepped toward her on autopilot, his brain relying on millions of years of evolution to propel him forward.

Mirta maintained her steady eye contact as she slowly slid her hand up to unclasp her towel, letting it fall to the floor in a rumpled heap. "Still up for that after-dinner anything?" she asked with a mischievous smile.

"Absolutely." He replied with an enthusiastic grin, stepping forward to close the cabin door behind him.

Chapter 8

When Dex finally stirred the next morning, the lumobands in his personal quarters were already on and they were set to the harsh white-light configuration. Leaning back lazily on his elbow, He sat up and rubbed his eyes as a deep yawn overtook him. While involuntarily stretching to punctuate that glorious yawn, Dex noticed for the first time the absence of a lump beneath the sheets beside him. As a sudden flood of panic gripped his hazy mind, he jumped to his feet and fumbled himself into a pair of pants before bursting through his cabin door on a mission to find his missing guest. He stormed down the decorated hallway beyond, hugging himself close to the bulkhead, and made a B-line for the cockpit. As he stormed through the bridge's automatic door, he immediately spotted Mirta sitting in the central captain's chair. She was wearing one of his old shirts with her legs tucked up inside of it, sipping tentatively at a steaming cup of coffee. Dex couldn't believe how innocent and harmless she could look while quietly huddled there, even though he saw the woman, with his very own eyes, set a man on fire less than twenty-four hours before.

"Good morning, sir snores-a-lot," she teased when she noticed him standing in the doorway, "You didn't tell me you had coffee!"

Dex smiled and took the seat next to hers. "Yeah, I picked up a few *great* bags of that Jamaican blend a few months back while passing through Sol." He said as he grabbed a mug for himself, "You just can't beat that natural, home-system sunshine."

Mirta's eyes brightened with awe; "Sol?!" she marveled with an excited squeak, almost spilling her drink in the process, "Like, *the* Sol? Did you see *Earth*?!"

"I actually just picked it up on Lincoln Station, which is in high orbit *above* Earth." He admitted with a disappointed shrug, "I haven't been to the surface in *years*."

Mirta's eyes were filled with wonder as she bubbled; "So you *have* seen the surface? What was it like? What did you see when you were there?"

"Well, I saw a lot." He laughed, "I was born and raised there, after all. In the evergreen forests of Oregon, to be precise. It's the last healthy free-growth forest on the planet, a protected area in fact, and my family has been living hidden among its thick canopy for over forty years now. It's...eh...a bit of a retirement haven for my dad and a few of his old smuggling buddies."

"Wow!" she beamed, "That sounds like an incredibly exciting way to grow up!"

Dex shrugged, saying; "Meh. Not really. My childhood consisted mainly of picking off squirrels with a slingshot and listening to my dad's drinking buddies tell increasingly tall tales about the adventures of their youth. It *was* exciting, until I turned 8 and realized that they were all full of shit."

Mirta laughed with understanding and added; "Oiy, they sound like Mike and the guys. They were always shoveling bullshit my way while growing up, too. It must have something to do with how alcohol mixes with machismo."

"This Mike fella," began Dex curiously, "How do we get into contact with him? Do you have a ready-made way to get in touch?"

"We should be able to find Mike in his office." She shrugged as she pulled herself up from the captain's chair. "He *is* the head of the department, after all. C'mon, we'd better hurry and catch him between lunches."

Dex got up and followed her to his quarters. He slipped on a simple outfit comprised of black pants, with a white shirt and gray jacket to blend into the crowds more effectively. He then looked over at Mirta, who was slipping back into her dress from the night before, and commented; "That won't do at all. That dress will draw *way* too much attention to us. I know *I'd* stop to have a look at you in it."

Mirta halted what she was doing and dropped the dress to the floor. "Okay, fashion police," she quipped as she placed a hand on her bare hip, "What should I wear then? Not to brag, but I think I'd turn more heads if I walked around naked."

"Well our bad-guys, if they're looking for *us*, would likely be searching for a man and a woman," he reasoned as he passed her a hooded sweatshirt, "but what they *won't* be searching for is two *men*. Here, put this on and I'll grab you a pair of pants. You'll look enough like...well like *NOT* you to a cursory glance."

Mirta pulled the sweatshirt over her head and turned to examine herself in the mirror. She inspected the baggy clothing and started to pout. "Don't you have anything a little closer to my size?" she complained with a frown.

"Don't you think it would be a little creepy if I did?" retorted Dex with his head half buried inside his closet, "Besides, you look great. And by great, I mean utterly unlike your fine self. That *is* the goal here, remember. I know that *I* could identify you by that wonderful caboose of yours from a mile away, so let's assume the enemy is made up of predominantly straight males who can pull off that party trick as well. This shirt hides that wonderful little *ass*et of yours, and by extension it helps hide *you* in a crowd."

Grumbling to herself, she fastened the pants that were thrown to her and then fixed Dex with a harsh stare. "Unsexy enough for you?" she demanded sourly.

Dex walked over and flipped her hood up to cover her face in shadow, then pulled her close with the garment to give her a kiss. "Absolutely hideous, love." He concluded with a smile, "Its perfect."

———————————————

Dex and Mirta left the ship, starting toward the starport's central rotunda to hail a transport. The pedestrian nerve center of the dock existed as a band of columns supporting a terrace that made a full loop at the center-point of the docking bay's hollow cylinder, which provided both a walkway and covered landing zone for posi-lev vehicles. Sensing their presence on approach to the loading zone, an automated taxi glided up and silently came to a halt right next to the duo. After Dex confirmed payment for the ride via his tablet, the vehicle opened its doors for them as it gently set its belly to the tarmac. They stepped inside to face each other in the four-passenger pod, getting settled into their seats as the doors automatically closed behind them. Mirta activated the touchscreen poised between the seats and keyed their destination into the console. With a confirmation chirp, the taxi rose from the roadway and began to move

Dex reached into his pocket and pulled out something shiny; "Here, take this." He urged as he handed the object to Mirta.

"A ring?" she breathed with surprise, "Haha I like you Dex, but let's not rush into anything here."

Dex just smiled and slipped it onto her finger. "*This* is a stun ring," he explained, "Rotating it to where the red stone is on the palm side of your hand is all you need to do to activate it. It will essentially act as an extremely powerful stun weapon that's good for one shot before it needs recharging. All it takes is for the red part on the ring here to touch some skin while active and the discharge goes off, which means lights out for whoever touched it. Does that all make sense?"

"Makes sense. Thanks." She grinned as she leaned in to kiss him.

"Woah!" shouted Dex as he recoiled her advance, "You might want to rotate that ring back around to the safe position before getting too close!"

Mirta looked at him with a raised brow and rotated the ring back to its original orientation. "What's the matter?" she teased, "Don't want to add that little extra *spark* to our love life?"

Dex chuckled and leaned over to kiss her on the cheek. "We have plenty of spark without the help of any gadgets." He said as he grabbed her hand gently.

"Amen to that." Concurred Mirta with a mischievous smile as she returned the soft squeeze of his grip.

Their transport moved along a transparent pipe that followed one of the large support struts of the residential ring until they finally popped out into the open above the bustling streets below. The automated taxi rode along the ceiling of the massive ring on a magnetic track, offering an excellent vantage point to take in the cluttered community sprawled out beneath them. As Dex looked out over the compact doughnut of a city, he noticed a huge gathering of people outside a nondescript gray building. "What are they all getting on about?" he asked, gesturing toward the throng of citizens that were roiling themselves into a frenzy as they fought to squeeze inside the building's enclosed courtyard.

Mirta looked down at the crowd and frowned; "That, my friend, is daily life here on Meclan." She sighed sadly, "I'm lucky enough to have a business, so I can afford to feed myself...most of the time. But these poor folks without work? They go hungry and die in the gutter more often than not. Since Vendrick came in and started shutting everything down, there's nothing for these people to *do*. All they *can* do, *every day*, is stand in line for food handed out by our gracious overlord. Every single day, at least a few people are trampled to death because there's never enough to go around."

He looked at her with genuine surprise and asked; "All that for food? Why would there be such a shortage? Most of these orbital cities were designed to be 100% self-sufficient. Don't you have crops on the station?"

She leaned her head against the window and watched the food riot unfold below. "Under normal circumstances, we would have plenty to eat." She grumbled, "We just seem to have a bit of a pirate king problem at the moment. Haven't you heard?"

He nodded fractionally, then riposted; "Okay, so where's the advantage for '*Governor*' Vendrick in starving his '*citizens*' to death?"

Mirta looked back up at Dex with frustration in her eyes as she explained; "That's just part of his plan to control us. He limits the food that's available to keep the bulk of the population too weak to fight, so most of us inevitably became dependent on *his* handouts. You need to understand that Vendrick has done everything he can to consolidate his power. His men guard the crops they grow and kill anyone they find sneaking around in them. If anyone is found growing food for themselves, all occupants of that household, as well as their neighbors to either side, are beaten and paraded down the streets to an airlock. This was to illustrate the message that if you are not vigilant and don't report on the suspicious activity of your neighbors, you are risking the death of not only yourself, but your entire family."

Dex just sat there silently for a moment contemplating what he just heard, then asked; "So you're saying that this is a man who starves the population on purpose, but has still managed to make spies out of every single one of them?"

"Yep, pretty much." Replied Mirta grimly, "It's not a great way to live, but this is the only life we've got under our vile *Governor*."

"There's no way I'm voting for *that* asshole this November." He remarked sourly, "Maybe *you* should run for Governor. I've seen your negotiating skills firsthand, and I've gotta say…I'm quite impressed. But then again, to be fair, I haven't seen Vendrick's tits yet. So, I technically can't be an impartial voter until I track his ass down and have myself a look-see. In the interest of good old-fashioned democracy, that is…"

Their transport slowed to a stop and began to lower to the street in front of a battle-worn building with heavy steel plates welded over the windows. Bits of debris cluttered the streets and obvious signs of recent rioting were scattered about in front of the facility. As Dex stepped out of the cab, he caught the strong odor of burnt trash and felt a pile of broken glass crackle beneath his boot. "Looks like folks were trying to burn the place to the ground last night." He commented as he examined the scene.

"Must be Tuesday, then." Remarked Mirta with a sigh.

"Tuesday?" repeated Dex with confusion, "What happens on Tuesday?"

"It's just an expression, Dex." She retorted flatly, "Shit like this always happens to the police station on Meclan. The only thing that seems to be in abundance around here is people that are starving and angry with no useful outlet in which to channel their rage. *So*, they take a crack at the police station from time to time to blow off steam... It happens." She finished with a shrug as she held the front door of the ravaged building open for Dex.

They walked inside and stepped up to the front desk, which was occupied by a slender man with dark eyes and slicked back black hair. "We are here to see Sergeant Tano" whispered Mirta to the intake officer.

"And you are?" the officer replied without lifting his eyes from his tablet.

Mirta then lowered her hood and shot a smile at the man, saying; "It's me."

"Oh, hey Mirta." Greeted the man from his behind the desk with a surprised grin. He fixed Dex with a hard appraising gaze for a moment, then shrugged fractionally and buzzed them through "Mike is in his office."

"Thanks, Armando." She said with a friendly nod as she led Dex through the doorway, "Be sure to tell Elena and the girls I said hi."

Gingerly stepping through the mangled remains of destroyed chairs and shattered privacy dividers, they made their way into the nearly deserted police station's wreck of an office area. Many desks were damaged and charred beyond functionality with the signs of armed conflict evident everywhere around them. Bullet holes had peppered everything, decimating the room's tall ornate columns, walls, and ceiling. The whole area looked as if a full-blown war had happened inside the large cubicle-lined room. A war that *nobody* won. At the back of the station, tucked into the rear wall, sat a row of larger private offices that were all *nearly* identical. At the far left of the row, however, sat an office that had its windows barred by some impressively sturdy looking blast plating. As they got closer, Dex could see that the door to the office was constructed of equally impressive blast-proof materials as well and had the words 'SGT. Tano' written across it in pristine yellow lettering. "A little paranoid, ain't he?" remarked Dex with a chuckle.

Mirta pointedly took a moment to look around the room before retorting; "Maybe. But I bet *he* still has a desk to write on."

"Fair enough." Conceded Dex with a shrug, "Can't argue with that one." Mirta stopped at the office's stout door frame and knocked on it, using an interesting arrhythmic pattern. A few seconds later, the blast-proof hatch's intricate inner locking mechanism could be heard as it disengaged to slide open and reveal the cluttered office beyond.

When they stepped through, a heavyset man in his mid-sixties with a bushy gray mustache stood up from behind his disorganized glass desk. The man's expression was filled with concern as he rushed over toward Mirta to give her a crushing bear hug that lifted her from her feet. "I saw your bar! What happened, child?!" pleaded the Sergeant as he kept her shoulders in a firm loving grip.

"I happened." Remarked Dex as he stepped forward.

"Who is this, Mirta?" asked Tano, eying the stranger suspiciously, "Does he come with you *invited*?"

Mirta stepped back to stand at Dex's side to explain; "Mike, this is Dex. He dealt with some of Vendrick's thugs after they came by to give me trouble. He very likely saved my life."

"For that, I thank you sir." Proclaimed Tano, standing to extended his hand to the stranger. As Dex reached out and gave the portly man a firm handshake, the Sergeant held on a little longer than expected and continued; "So, what's your stake in all this? If you don't mind my prying..."

Dex shrugged and replied; "Not a big fan of bullies, I guess. She was in a wee spot of trouble and I had the power to do something to help. So, I did. Simple as that."

"That's actually what we're here about, Mike." Added Mirta as she took a seat, "We're looking to go after Vendrick. For real this time."

Tano sat back down in his own chair with a skeptical look. "Goin' after good ol' papa pirate king are you? You and what fleet?" challenged the police Sergeant, bemused.

 "No fleet." Replied Dex nonchalantly with another shrug, "Just me."

"And you are...*who*, exactly?" questioned Tano with humor, "A scout, out looking for his next badge? What do you have to gain from picking a fight with such a big fish?"

Dex sat in the chair next to Mirta and kicked his feet up onto the desk nonchalantly; "Well I was just passing through and I was feeling a bit bored," he mused with a sarcastic smirk, "so I figured I'd kill me a pirate king or two while I was here."

Tano pushed Dex's feet off his desk and fixed the younger man with a scowl; "Real funny, dipshit, but Vendrick is no joke. I won't have you dragging Mirta into a fight with a man you don't understand. So, who the hell are **you** to think you can go off and topple his regime all on your lonesome?"

Dex leaned forward and allowed his eyes to turn to cold stone, momentarily revealing the man lurking just beneath his amicable I; "I am the individual that put three bodies in your morgue last night without so much as creasing my pants. And I plan to put a whole lot more of them in there before I'm done here. What we need from *you* is help *finding* those particular bodies, so that I can *make* them dead." Sergeant Tano continued to stare blankly at the stranger across from him, refusing to fill the silence. Eventually, Dex was forced to continue to keep the conversation going; "Listen, I've heard about what those pieces of shit have been doing to the people around here over the years. I've seen this bullshit before and the mere thought of Vendrick's continued existence offends me. So, are you going to help me kill the fuckwad or not?"

Tano leaned back and gave Mirta a contemplative look, searching her familiar green eyes for any hint of apprehension or coercion; "So if I *was* on board to help you end the son of a bitch, what exactly do you need from me? As much as I'd like to, my fat ass isn't really built for running around and shooting punks anymore."

Mirta placed her hand on Tano's; "That's fine, Mike." She soothed, "We just need intel. Stuff like where to strike and when if we want to get our hands on someone who will know what's what. All we have to do is find Vendrick and put a bullet through his brain. Best way to achieve that is squeeze one of his lieutenants till they pop. You know it needs to happen and the time for *alternate solutions* and

Federal intervention has long since passed. Nobody is coming to save us. We need to stop waiting around and actually **DO** something about our situation for a change. We owe it to dad and everyone else who ended up like him."

Tano furrowed his brow in a brief moment of contemplation then apprehensively dismissed the idea, saying; "I don't disagree on what needs to be done, little one, but I doubt any of his underlings would know a damn thing about where their boss is holed up. Vendrick is smart and he's always played his cards close to the chest. Hell, he could turn out to be three roosters in a vac-suit for all we know. If you wanna find him, you'll have to get him to stick his head out…Which won't be easy, to say the least."

"Wait," insisted Dex with a wave of his hands, "time out. You guys have, like, *literally* never seen or heard from this guy directly before? How sure are we that this Vendrick even has a shootable face?"

The Sergeant nodded with understanding and explained; "Saiph's mighty *shadow governor* has been in power for *nearly a decade* now, and he has not once shown his face or made a single speech. Despite all this, we still *know* he exists. How are we so certain? Because his *influence* exists, and that influence has been given a name. Vendrick, despite his best efforts I'm sure, leaves a ripple wherever his will holds sway. Just as mass accumulates gravity, power accrues fear; And the fearful will always whisper about that which ails them. We've caught traces of him over the years, physically I mean, via private debriefs from supply pilots who was ordered to make deliveries out in the middle of whothefuckknows. We got varying descriptions of the recipient ship, but never the full picture. Never the full story. We don't know what he's capable of, we don't know the size of the force at his disposal, and, to be brutally honest, we don't really even know *for sure* whether or not the whole thing is a crock of shit."

"I think what we need to do is poke the bear and see how he tries to bite us," suggested Dex with a shrug, "but we have to be certain that our mischief won't blowback on Meclan. If we can get him to go on the offensive in some way that directs his attention *away* from the population centers, we may be able to draw him out enough to get a bead on him."

The police Sergeant started tapping his lip absentmindedly with a stylus for a moment then proposed; "If you want him to feel the squeeze and make a mistake like that, you gotta disrupt his supply lines. That seems to be the only thing he cares about around here. Corn out, shitty protein sludge and expired mealpacks in. Gotta be *some* profit in that, I imagine."

"But if we destroy supplies, people will starve" argued Mirta, alarmed at the suggestion, "We can't go off and make a bad situation worse."

"That's why we don't destroy the supplies." Explained Dex with a tap of his finger to his forehead, "We need to act like a competitor, not a savior. Heroes can be squeezed by hurting innocent people, as compassion is seen as their ultimate '*weakness*'. But if we present ourselves to the field as a *business competitor*, that tactic likely won't occur to Vendrick as a worthwhile one. We undermine his authority by pirating *his* shipments. Then, we quietly disperse our spoils to the public ourselves. That way he's less likely to focus any punishment on a single station and the people who need it can get fed. Nothing pisses off a maniac like Vendrick more than someone undermining his power, so he'll try to come after us directly. I'm sure of it. And anything that takes his attention off of being a dickbag to the citizenry for a while is a good thing in my book."

"Hey...that's not a bad idea, kid." Commended Tano with a with an increasingly enthusiastic nod. The heavyset man then proceeded to fumble with a control under his desk for a moment before the tabletop's built-in holo-projector began to glow. As the display whirred to life in the air between them, multicolored points of light coalesced into an animated map of the star system. At the center of the projection sat Saiph, burning a roiling blue-white with long licks of its coronal discharges reaching deep into the orbit of the system's first planet.

"This is a map of Vendrick controlled space." Continued Tano as he touched his pen inside the image, causing several yellow dots and their respective orbits to appear, "You can see here, all the stations under direct Vendrick control." Tano tapped his pen again and the yellow dots were accompanied by multicolored lines connecting dot to dot. The Sergeant zoomed the image then continued; "These are the trade routes that run between the stations. I don't know which ones he uses, but I say we camp one of these routes and see what we can catch."

Dex examined the map closely; "Do we know who he has delivering these goods?" he asked the Sergeant pointedly, "Privateers? Or does he delegate it to his own people?"

"Well Vendrick doesn't really have all that much man-power in the black," Replied the Sergeant as he zoomed to show the routes that snaked out of Meclan, "so he will have local pilots, ones he has leverage over, fulfilling most of his shipments."

Dex looked at the diagram thoughtfully and said; "Good. That leaves a lot of options open to us regarding how to handle this." Noticing something was out of sorts, he reached into the holographic image and pointed at a spot where several of the interconnecting trade routes met. "What is here?" he asked, "It looks like most trade in the sector is sent through to this one point, but I don't see a station or orbit lines here like the others."

Tano adjusted the display to zoom in on the area in question and explained; "I've been researching the trade routes for years. Based on the little snippets of information I could pry from cargo pilots, I think this is a vague approximation of where Vendrick's flag ship rendezvous with many of the in-system supply ships, but the exact location changes every time. It's an unusually dense asteroid cluster in the outer belt. He jumps in for just long enough to offload his goods, then he jumps back out to god knows where."

"Wait," began Dex, confused, "You said he jumps *in*, loads, then jumps right back *out* again? How does that work? Post-jump Molecular restabilization for a ship the size you're alluding to should take at least two hours. They would never survive a second Inaki breach that quickly. That timeline makes no sense."

"Again," replied the Sergeant with a weary sigh, "this data is based only on the small snippets of info that I could squeeze out of terrified cargo runners over the course of an elevator ride. The intel isn't concrete, not by a mile, but it's what we've got to work with. In other words, your guess is as good as mine."

"Alright, then." Conceded Dex with a shrug, "I've done more with less. Does Vendrick's rabble around here have any semblance of a command structure? We need to find a big fish to play the part of our upstart pirate prince. If we can disappear him and perform a hit under his banner that is effective enough to remove all doubt of insider knowledge, then we can sow the seed of our little secret rebellion."

"So, we're launching a rebellion now, eh?" asked Tano pointedly, "I thought we were just discussing putting bodies in morgues."

"What else would you call it when the people rise up and kill their oppressor?" challenged Dex with a raised brow, "Ballistic impeachment? Organizational restructuring? Whatever the hell you consider it, we need to plug the gilded asshole at the top of this shitheap without getting everyone *else* killed in the process. To do *that* effectively, they're eventually going to need to be apprised of the situation. We can only help those who are willing to help themselves at this point."

The portly Sergeant slumped in his seat a little, saying; "Therein lies the issue, I'm afraid. Hate for our dear ole' Governor is easy to come by, but a brave soul willing to risk his family to take up arms against the beast? That there is hard to find. They've got spirits pretty well whipped around here."

Mirta shot to her feet and raged; "Are we *all* so hopeless? Though the *spirits* may have been crushed out of *most* of the broken souls clinging to this busted old station, *some* of us still want to fight and make those bastards pay for what they've taken. Hard times build hard people, and hard people solve hard problems. I'm a product of my environment, Mike, and I'm ready to burn the motherfucker down and build myself a new one."

Dex eyed Mirta with approval and exclaimed; "I honestly couldn't have said it better myself. All that people need is a spark in the tinderbox that is daily life here, and they'll discover their own courage. The people of Saiph deserve better than what Vendrick has given them, regardless of our odds at changing anything on our own. Isn't a better future always worth fighting for? Isn't that a cause that can recruit for itself?"

"Okay..." breathed Tano with an air of finality, "You've got me sold on the idea. I'll likely be dead in a decade or so and I'd like to see *something* happen around here before I go. In fact, right when you mentioned your need of a big fish, one slimy shitbag in particular came immediately to mind."

"The slimier the better." Insisted Dex with a smile, "Who were you thinking? Someone with a big enough name to put some wind into the sails of our little conspiracy?"

"Anthony Vargas." Stated the police Sergeant with a distant look in his expression, "Taking him off the streets would cause a hell of a splash up the chain. He's Vendrick's mad-dog here and has had his fair share of public spats with his fellow low-lives over the years. The idea of him going rogue would surprise no one in Vendrick's outfit."

"Mad-dog is an understatement!" warned Mirta with alarm, "The sick son of a bitch hunts people for sport on an almost *daily* basis. I've seen *too* many folks hacked to death by that psychopath to take him lightly. So how in the hell do you intend to *capture* him, let alone get enough good information out of him to launch an effective strike?"

"The information part won't be as hard as you're thinking" interjected Tano with a raised finger, "All we would need to squeeze out of him are six numbers. Six, daily rotated and fully quantum-encrypted, little digits. With his code, we should be able to log into whatever passes for an encrypted relay console at one of their facilities and scrape some data on their shipments. While we're in there, we can also plant some evidence on their server that supports the narrative we are trying to create here."

"Sounds workable to me." Said Dex with a nod of appreciation, "So where do we start?"

Chapter 9

Anthony Vargas awoke Wednesday morning, as he did every morning, to the soft beeping of his encryption keycard. He reached for it, his face still buried into the soft depths of his pillow, and dragged the small device across the glass surface of his nightstand. Rolling over, he eyed the keycard's readout and waited for the day's number sequence to materialize. As soon as the device had authenticated his fingerprint, six digits flashed quickly across the screen. They glowed to life for only three seconds, ticking them away as dots at the periphery of the screen, before dimming out again. With his daily chore complete and his numbers memorized, Vargas withdrew back into the warmth of his sheets with a smile on his face and sighed with a sleepy grin as the gentle early morning's light peeked through the blinds to coax him awake. At first, he retreated into the damp darkness beneath his blankets to delay the inevitable start to his day. But, after a few minutes of quiet contemplation, Anthony sat up and placed his bare feet on the faux wood floor of his upscale bedroom. Every surface of the spacious apartment was stark-white, accented with either frosted glass or surgical steel, and the space's décor looked almost industrial in its spartan minimalism; Affording an image of affluence and intellectualism to whomever occupied it. Every item in the room seemed to have its place, and each item's place was artfully chosen to fit within the tidy motif.

As he yawned and made his way to the bathroom, Vargas peered into the hallway closet to examine his handiwork from the night before. "She was a fighter." he mused to himself as he inspected the lifeless and mutilated form that hung from a thin steel wire next to his assortment of designer coats. He closed his eyes and took in a deep breath, smiling warmly as he remembered the stunning green dress that she had arrived in the night before. It was a pity he had to cut the beautiful garment off of her, he lamented, for it would have made such a wonderful trophy for his growing collection. Vargas normally liked to keep a memento from each of his hunts, an article of clothing or strip of dried skin, but he had gotten too carried away this time while in the throes of his drug-fueled rampage. He gave the woman so many gashes, stitching her body from head to toe during his endless *interrogation*, that there was hardly any unspoiled flesh left for him to dry out and preserve. "Oh well," he quietly chuckled to himself as he cheerfully tapped her on the nose and spun on his heel, "there's always the next one."

Vargas stepped into the bathroom and began to inspect himself in the mirror, taking in every detail of his grisly appearance. He stood smeared from head to toe in the dark red of dried blood and was sporting a set of deep fingernail marks that tore an angry red arc across his chest. Turning sideways, he flexed his muscles to examine what he liked to refer to as his *'hunter's physique'* with a cheeky grin tugging at his features. He then proceeded to look down at his bloodstained hands and, overtaken by a primitive urge, popped a finger into his mouth to savor its coppery flavor. To him, it tasted like the fear of his prey... tainted with sweat and soured by a panic that he himself had brought into fruition. He fixated on the thought, lost in a moment of primal power and the predatory ecstasy it brought him.

After his minute of joyful meditation, Vargas turned and regarded the collection of surgical steel knives, hooks, and other torture gadgets that were neatly arrayed across his otherwise blood-soaked counter. He made his way to each item, examining every square millimeter to assure that it were spotless before returning them to their leather case. He doted at each lovingly maintained instrument with the same pride that a mechanic would look admiringly at his own well-organized toolbox, then placed them neatly back into their carrying case. After a moment of struggling with a particularly stubborn spatter, the bloody man huffed and decided that he was far too filthy to handle his beloved *'brushes'* and would need to clean up before putting the rest of them away. So, with cheery efficiency, he opened the door to his shower and yanked the handle to start the water flowing.

As the shower sprang to life, Vargas gasped with deranged delight when he looked down. The tile all around was splashed with red and had coagulated into a puddle that had settled to block the drain, but sitting in the middle of all that gore was a ragged strip of flesh that sat splayed out on the floor. "So THAT'S where I left you!" he shouted with glee, "I'd better hang you with the rest of the meat! Wouldn't want you to get homesick, now would we?!" The disturbed little man then started laughing uncontrollably, visibly enjoying his own comedic prowess as he bent down to pick up the chunk of flesh.

Vargas carried his trophy out of the bathroom and hung the dripping strip of skin unceremoniously over the shoulder of the dead woman in his closet, spinning her around and taking time to intimately examine the strip on her back where the section had been carved from. "Beautiful!" he shouted as he roughly grabbed the woman's limp head and pulled it in for a kiss, "Just. Fucking. Beautiful!" He then released her abruptly and turned to move back into the bathroom, shouting; "Excellent performance, my love!" over his shoulder as he stepped into the shower.

After he got dressed in his signature white suit, Vargas hit the street with his three loyal bodyguards; Tikéh, Måuli, and Vaoüs. The trio were all terrasiders from an out-bubble system named Calivos, which was unique in the fact that it featured three habitable planets that were all high-gravity environments. This was the factor that highlighted their use to the man in white, as the constant heavy pull that their home worlds burdened them with from birth had the effect of exaggerating the mass of their impressive musculature. They were all brought into Vendrick's service at the same time, when their prison transport was hijacked and rerouted to Saiph nearly nine years ago. Vargas liked having them at heel due not only to the sheer intimidation factor of their size, but the fact that they had proven time and again that they could throw all that bulk of theirs around with spectacularly violent effect.

Tikéh, with his signature trunk of tightly wound dreadlocks flowing over the well-tailored shoulder of his dark blue suit jacket, was from the innermost of the system's habitable planets, Palturus. His home was a world covered entirely by water, where settlers lived and farmed on massive floating mats of robust plant-life that served to filter out the deadly salts of the planet's hostile oceans. It was a mostly agrarian society, but the beast of a man had bucked that lifestyle and worked his early adult life as a fixer for a local politician there. His success and accrued reputation served him well, until he was caught on camera strangling one of his boss' political opponents with a length of wire, that is...

Måuli and Vaoüs were both from the very arid and hard-living landscape of Evoliun, which was a dusty famine-stricken moon orbiting one of the system's four gas giants. While the Imperial courts had deemed it habitable in their original deal to provide a planet to the survivors of a war-torn moon in the outer bubble, the atmosphere of the accursed ball of dirt couldn't truly be referred to as habitable while donning any semblance of a straight face. The upper layer of the moon's delicate envelope of gas was mainly composed of greenhouse gasses, heating up the atmosphere to bake the land and dry up any spent moisture with unreasonable haste. Because of this, Evoliun's inhabitants made a lifestyle out of chasing the slow-spinning moon's migrating geysers that were pulled to the surface by the incredible orange mass of the gas giant that dominated the heavens above. Some of the moon's more violent residents liked to make a habit of raiding these moving convoys with deadly intent, and Måuli with his brother Vaoüs ran one of the most brutal of these gangs. They ravaged convoy after innocent convoy until their party was eventually gassed and captured by federal troops. The men that Vargas chosen to have at his side had already become the krakens of their own little ponds in the universe. They had proven their worth by conquering the weak and would continue to provide their value as long as he provided them weakness to prey upon. It was simple, really. Why hire a killer that expects payment for the deed when you can have someone at your command who is happy to do it for free?

Their first stop of the morning was at a small café on the community ring because Vargas felt like swinging by to terrorize the old woman who ran the place for a bit. There was no real *reason* for it. He simply felt like starting his day by savoring the fear of a weaker creature. After finishing his tea in the deserted establishment, he gestured for the woman behind the counter to approach his table. She sauntered over and was flanked by two of the tattooed man's barrel-chested bodyguards. "Was your tea warm enough?" she asked, uncertainty and dread pouring from her expression, "I can get you some m-more if you'd like…"

"That won't be necessary." Replied Vargas calmly as he placed a palm over his steaming beverage, "I was just curious about how much you charge for a cup."

"Oh," said the woman, a slight show of relief spreading across her face and musculature, "The tea is on the house for you and your friends, as always, of course."

"I understand that." Retorted the gangster flatly, "That's not what I asked. What I asked is how much you *charge* for a cup…Well?"

"T-two credits." She stammered as she quickly averted her eyes to the floor.

"Alright, then." acknowledged Vargas with a smile, "That'll be two credits, then. For the *honor* of my patronage."

The woman looked as if she were about to protest, but a discouraging nudge from one of the bodyguards stopped her short. Reluctantly she reached for a credit blade and assigned it two credits with her fingerprint and a mental gesture. Setting the blade to the table, she mumbled; "Will that be all…sir?"

"For now…" mused Vargas as he dismissed her with a wave. He tipped over the sugar container at his table, because why not, then stood to leave. With his morning caffeine out of the way, he was headed to the community ring's market square to observe *his* kingdom. He strolled to a small restaurant that he preferred to frequent and sat at his usual table on the patio. From his corner seat, like Caesar in his ornate balcony at the colosseum, he could look out over the throngs of people doing business in the market and watch their pathetic lives unfold from afar. The central market was made up of a disorganized collection of rickety booths and carts, surrounded by a ring of shops and restaurants that were choked by a seemingly endless sea of tattered foot traffic. The gaunt and dirty people of the crowd all looked the same to him; Wretched creatures that clung so desperately to lives of such little value. The thought had always perplexed him. Why did they always make such a fuss when he came to end their suffering?

As he watched the people, lost in their patternless flow among one another, his eyes fell upon a beautiful blonde woman in an exquisite red dress who sat in a coffee shop across the courtyard. She had long legs that meandered their way up to an athletic frame and moved atop them with absolute grace as she took her seat. The woman would make for a fine hunt thought Vargas to himself as he unconsciously licked his lips at the thought.

She noticed him staring, so she smiled confidently and took a sip of her drink while locking eyes with the well-dressed man from across the courtyard. Their long-distance flirtation lasted a few more moments, then the woman set her drink down and stood to leave. She stepped out into the market square, shooting her white-suited suitor one last flirty smile before disappearing into the crowd.

As she slipped from view, Vargas shot to his feet and moved toward the square in pursuit of her. The lieutenant's bodyguards tried to urge him against it, but their powers of persuasion ultimately failed when faced with the pull of their boss' unique libido. In his haste, he took a three-step lead from his men off of the square's outer walkway and was immediately swallowed by the crowd.

"Bingo." said Mirta quietly into the transmitter tucked away inside her ear, "He's following me now. I'm going to head deeper into the crowd to see if I can draw his monkeys further away from him."

Dex's calm voice flooded into her right ear in reply; "Don't move so quickly." He urged, "You'll want to let him close in a bit before getting too tricky with it. We don't wanna lose him."

In compliance, she stopped momentarily and pretended to adjust her dress a bit. As she did so, she snuck a look back to catch sight of her quarry. He was about thirty meters away, moving through the crowd by forcefully shoving marketgoers aside. His bodyguards were trailing behind now, but they were beginning to catch up.

"Alright, Tano," commanded Dex's voice over the comm channel, "It's time for the show."

With that, a large piloted posi-lev truck pulled into the square and settled to a stop at the far end. Once the lumbering vehicle had lowered itself to the deck, Tano came scooting out of the driver's seat. He struggled to break free of the bucket-style cockpit, then came tumbling to the ground when he had accumulated the inertia to do so. Regaining his footing, the old Sergeant brushed himself off and headed to the tailgate. The heavyset man then pulled himself up into the back of the truck and shouted "Extra rations! Get your extra rations!" as he began to toss the bags of rice, the ones he had been stockpiling for a rainy day, into the frenzied arms of the crowd.

The starving mob's response to the spectacle was predictable and immediate, and they all began pushing and shoving their way toward the truck with reckless abandon. Dex was observing the scene from just outside the crowd, scanning the sea of faces for Vargas' henchmen, until he found what he was looking for. The plan worked. Vargas' bodyguards were separated by quite a bit now, and they were visibly struggling to find their boss amid the melee. Resolute in his purpose, Dex prepared his weapon and slipped silently into the chaos of the crowd.

He started toward the closest of Vargas' men, approaching him amid the flow of bodies moving against his efforts. As he brushed past the frustrated henchman, Dex shot his hand up with lightning speed and jabbed the small knife that he was concealing into the bodyguard's neck; Twisting and jerking it back out with a practiced and familiar flourish of his wrist.

The man gasped and clutched at his throat with panic in his eyes, gurgling unheard obscenities that flowed unarticulated past ruined vocal cords. Along with the torrent of blood flooding through his desperately clenching hands, the man's strength left him in an equally damning rush as he took two wavering steps after his mysterious attacker before falling to the ground to be consumed and trampled by the frantic crowd. "One down, two to go." reported Dex into his comm as he calmly wiped his stained blade on the rear of his pantleg.

He craned his neck to see over the crowd, spotting the second henchman ten meters ahead. Their eyes met for a brief moment as the man glanced back for his colleague, and Dex was certain that the bodyguard had seen significance in the interaction. "Shit." He hissed out of the corner of his mouth, "The tiki-hut lookin' motherfucker just saw me." Thinking quickly, Dex started toward the second bodyguard while making an obvious show of trying to grab his attention. "Excuse me, sir!" he shouted with a wave, "Your friend wanted me to come get you." A sudden break in the crowd then revealed that the other man had his gun out and was staring daggers at him. Dex met the man's eyes with a mask of unconcerned recognition and waved him over. "Your friend is over by the truck and he asked me to grab you for something." he said, pointing in Tano's direction. The henchman fixed Dex with a cold look, then cautiously craned his neck to scan the crowd by the truck.

"He's right over there next to the guy in red." assured Dex as he slowly closed the distance between himself and his target, "See him?"

The bodyguard strained his neck again, beginning to step closer to Dex with his absentminded efforts. As the guard's attention was focused into the distance, Dex jammed his blade deep into the man's right thigh and yanked it back toward himself. The bodyguard yelped with pain and began to reflexively reach for his injured leg. Dex took advantage of his opponent's moment of anguish and utilized the opportunity to wrap his arm around the man's neck and fall to his back. He wrapped his legs around the man's upper body in a tight grip and, with all of his strength, yanked the bodyguard's chin to a jarring angle. He could feel a sickening pop as something within the man's neck broke loose, ceasing all efforts of resistance from the guard immediately after that horrible muffled sound had filled the air.

As Dex pushed the body off him and rose to his knee, a woman was frozen in shock staring at him with open horror. He returned her gaze levelly and brushed off his pants as he explained, matter-of-factly; "He owed me five credits." In response, the woman gasped and spun to shuffle away in a hurry. Once Dex had fully gotten to his feet, he discovered that his luck had officially run out. Through the hectic throng of bodies, he spotted the final bodyguard heading in his direction. The giant man was approaching quickly and had a gun drawn and pointed right at him. Dex ducked to break visual contact and began to move laterally through the sea of bodies. The bodyguard was not interested in hide-and-seek, apparently, because he shot his pistol into the air, causing further panic in the crowd. "Mirta, get out now!" shouted Dex into his mic, "The jig is up, I'm spotted!"

Staying low, Dex was able to partially circle around the final bodyguard, using what little remained of the crowd as cover to close to within five meters of the man before he was spotted again. With recognition burning in his eyes, the bodyguard raised his pistol to fire at his mysterious attacker. Dex dove forward in a desperate front roll as Vargas' man fired his weapon. Mid-roll, he felt the sting of hot metal as a round grazed his shoulder blade and bit a chunk out of the heel of his boot. When he landed, Dex maintained as much momentum as he could and sprang up to rocket his body into his opponent's.

The crown of Dex's skull met the bridge of the other man's nose and he felt the satisfying crunch of the bodyguard's nasal and orbital bones crumbling under the blow. When the man reached up to cradle his damaged face, Dex flipped him to the pavement with a brutal hip-toss that robbed him of all his oxygen. Vargas' bodyguard then had only the faintest fraction of a moment to look up and see Dex's boot thundering down toward him. The brutal heel-stomp connected, crushing the bodyguard's head into the roadway with devastating force. Dex then continued to slam his boot down over and over until he was out of breath, one-hundred percent certain that his enemy was never getting up again. "Body guards are down." He reported, panting frantically into his comm, "What's your status, Mirta? ...Tano, can you see her?!"

———————————————————————————

Vargas tracked the woman through the crowd by her bright blonde hair as she weaved her way through the mob. She seemed to be heading toward a building at the edge of the square, so he moved in on an angle to cut her off. He was beginning to close on his prey when he felt his pocket vibrate. Reaching into his jacket, he pulled his comm device to see that there was a new text message waiting for him. "T and M missing. Be careful, something is up." Vargas stopped and turned to scan the crowd behind him. When he didn't see any of his men, he spun back around and continued to follow the woman with newfound suspicion.

She didn't walk directly to the building as he had predicted, deciding instead to head for the alleyway next to it. "Hey!" he shouted in as friendly a tone as he could muster, "Stop for a second, will yah?! Let me talk to you."

The woman stopped at the mouth of the alleyway and looked back at him with a sheepish smile. She leaned against the wall, unafraid, and waited patiently for him to approach. Vargas walked up to her and stopped when they came face to face; "Now where are you going in such a hurry, baby?" he asked as he leaned a little closer. The woman looked a bit nervous and began fidgeting with her ring, which was a look that *always* got him excited.

As he reached up to brush hair from her face, a gunshot suddenly rang out inside the courtyard. Both of them whipped their heads around to look toward the panicked crowd, but when Vargas returned his gaze to the woman, he saw no surprise in her eyes. Taking this as evidence of her treachery, he shot his hand out to seize her by the hair. As he did, he was bewildered to discover that the golden locks offered no resistance when he jerked back on them. As Mirta's wig was yanked off to expose the tightly-bunned brown hair beneath, her knee shot up into Vargas' crotch.

"Bitch!" he shouted with rage as he reached out to choke her. When he clenched his hand around Mirta's throat, he felt the cold brush of her hand upon the back of *his* neck. Fire then shot forth from his spine, paralyzing his entire body in an excruciating shower of pain. He shook violently, every nerve in his body burning with white hot pain as he fell to the ground in a quivering heap. As darkness began to invade his consciousness, Vargas heard the distant echo of a woman's voice saying; "Hands to yourself, creep." as his world went black.

Chapter 10

Vargas groggily opened his eyes, vaguely aware of his aching muscles, and struggled against limbs that were securely fastened to the chair he found himself in. As he blinked a few times to clear his mind, the gravity of his situation came tumbling down upon him when he realized that the room around him was pitch black. The air didn't have the stinging stench that Meclan offered, so he figured that he had been moved off-station. As he quieted his thoughts, he was able to make out the low hum of a ship's main drive under thrust. The gang-boss struggled against his restraints, jerking and convulsing violently in an attempt to break himself free. After a few moments of frantic kicking, he finally managed to tip his chair over, slamming himself onto the cold metal floor in a breath-robbing crash. "Let me out of here!" He yelled at the top of his lungs, "Fuck you!...I'll kill all of you!"

As Vargas continued to writhe on the floor, blinding lumobands suddenly flickered to life on the ceiling above. He closed his eyes at the unexpected brightness and heard a door sliding open, followed by the cadence of footsteps heading his way. "I'm sorry I didn't leave the night light on for you, princess." Mocked Dex as he hoisted his prisoner's chair upright.

"Fuck you!" spat Vargas at his unknown captor, "Who the hell do you think you are, *dead man*?"

Dex looked at the man with faux surprise. "Me?!" he gasped sarcastically, pointing at himself, "Well I just happen to be your in-flight entertainment for today, Tony."

Vargas spit at Dex, coating his boot with phlegm. "I'm gonna fucking kill you and everything you love!!" screamed the unstable prisoner with unbridled rage, "You're **dead**!!"

Dex took a moment to quietly examine the struggling man in the chair before him, then chided; "Holy Christ, my man, would you buy a vowel already? If you say that same shit again, I'm gonna start looking for a pull-string up your ass. Besides, it doesn't seem like you're really in a position to be making threats of that nature, my excitable little friend. So, do me a favor and shut the fuck up until you have something interesting to say. Alright, sport?"

Making sure to take an agonizing amount of time to do so whilst under the profanity-laced verbal assault of his captive, Dex walked over to the corner of the room and retrieved a cart on wheels. It was draped with a white sheet that concealed the items on top of it, presented in such a way as to build a theatrical sense of suspense. He pulled it over from the corner and wheeled it around into Vargas' view, locking it into place without breaking eye contact with his struggling captive. "What I have here, *Tony*," remarked the interrogator as he deliberately started to pace a circle around the chair, "is what we found on you while you were napping." He then ripped the sheet away to reveal three large knives, a meat hook, and several razor blades arrayed neatly atop the cart's upper tray. Dex stepped forward, picking up one of the knives to inspect; "This edge is laser sharp. *Very* impressive. You must have some kind of sick love for these things, huh?"

Vargas fixed his captor with a contemptuous glare; "I am an *artist*, and those are my *brushes*." He seethed with venom in his voice, "So don't bother trying to intimidate me with them. They are as much a part of me as the heart you aim to cut from my chest. To die at their edge will be an ecstasy you wouldn't *believe*."

Dex sat the knife back down on the cart and chuckled; "You really *are* full-blown sillyfarm status, aren't you? Don't worry, I don't need these *brushes* that you love so much to give you a proper tickle. These hooks and knives are, frankly, amateurish bullshit when it comes to interrogation. The real power can be found through this..." He opened a drawer on the cart and reached in to withdraw a single piece of plain white paper then, looking pointedly at his captive, gently set the blank sheet overtop of the row of shiny surgical instruments.

Vargas looked at the paper and smiled; "Are you gonna write me a love note?" he scoffed with contempt.

"You should *be* so lucky." Retorted Dex with a dismissive wave, "Sorry to break it to you this way, darlin', but you're not really my type. What I *am* going to do with this here piece of old-fashioned notebook paper, though, is use it to make you sing me a symphony."

Dex circled behind Vargas' chair and seized the man's bound left hand, forcing his middle and pointer fingers apart. Then, without comment, he smoothly slid his paper between the gang-boss's fingers to make a neat cut on the skin between them. Vargas jerked against his restraints in reaction to the pain, exerting every muscle in his body in an effort to break free.

"Could you please share today's code to the transmitter key with me?" asked Dex politely, "Because I have plenty of *other* things to do with this paper if you want to tell me. You ever seen origami, Tony?"

"Fuck you!" yelled Vargas in defiance through gritted teeth, "You're gonna die! I'm gonna fuckin' kill youuu!" Dex just shrugged fractionally at the man's tantrum and moved to make a second cut on the webbing between his middle and ring fingers. Vargas tried his very best to clench his fists in pain and rage but, despite his desperate efforts, he couldn't do anything to stop what was happening to him.

"The code?" prompted Dex again politely with a neutral smile.

"I'm gonna peel the skin from your fuckin' face!" spat Vargas as he wriggled violently, like a wild animal caught in a snare, "I'll watch you bleeed!"

Dex rolled his eyes at the cliché comment and retorted; "I can already tell that this is going to be a *very* long and uncomfortable conversation for you, my friend."

———————————————

Almost an hour later, Vargas' body was sporting over two-hundred and fifty cuts. They were clustered in locations such as his hands, feet, ears, lips, and nose, making an intricate and deliberate patchwork of red. His wounds steadily dripped to his lap from the ruins of his face, with foamy red bubbles of blood and saliva forming between his shredded lips with every rasping breath. "Feeling more receptive to a little conversation regarding your key code yet?" invited Dex for the two-hundred and fifty-first time. Vargas made an effort to spit again but was too exhausted to do anything more than drool. Dex sighed and grabbed the man's face, jerking it toward him. "Seems like you're getting bored of the same old trick, eh? Well, you're absolutely right...Variety IS the spice of life."

Dex then abruptly stood and turned to the cart, withdrawing a small unmarked brown cylinder from its top drawer. Vargas jerked visibly at the sight of it and recoiled as his captor approached. The interrogator opened the mysterious container and shook some of the grainy white crystals from within out onto his palm. Without a word he drew it close to his captive's face, so he could get a good look at it. "Salt?" asked Vargas, confused.

With a small puff of air from his mouth, Dex sent the tiny white grains in a stinging cloud toward Vargas' eyes. "Yup." He answered nonchalantly as his prisoner wriggled in newfound pain from the fresh irritant in his eye. "Lets try it again." Continued Dex as he poured another mound of salt into his palm, "And this time with a little more *gusto*, alright? What, *pray tell*, is the *code*, my good sir?" Pressing the salt from his palm onto the bloody right hand and wrist of his captive.

The crime-boss screamed with a renewed rush of pain, his whole body convulsing violently as he spat every expletive that the ex-sailor had ever heard of, including some exciting new ones that he had yet to discover. "Ready to talk?" asked Dex, yet again. The prisoner just growled and shook his head, devoid of all energy and resistance. The interrogator simply shrugged and poured more salt onto his captive's other hand. Vargas kept staring at his lap and began to hyperventilate, tensing every muscle in his body as he began shaking his head furiously.

"The code please?" implored Dex again with his maddeningly infinite well of patience. After Vargas did not visibly respond, he continued; "Alright, you asked for it." Dex suddenly lashed out and kicked his captive's chair over, sending the man crashing onto his back, then proceeded to crouch and seize his captive's head. With a handful of hair in one hand, he forced the man's right eyelid open with the other.

As the interrogator brought the paper's edge close to Vargas' eyeball, he heard the bound man scream; "No! Please god no!"

Dex released his grip on the man's head and sat up. "Huh." He huffed with a hint of surprise, "I didn't even have to start in on your giblets yet...Does this mean you're ready to share the code with me now?" Vargas fervently began to nod his head while pinning his eyelids shut as hard as possible. "Well...I'm listening" he insisted patiently.

The restrained man groaned in pain for a moment then pleaded; "If I tell you the code, I want you to set me free. Deal?"

Dex regarded him for a moment then conceded; "Fine. If you tell me the code and it gets me what I'm looking for, I will let you off my ship with breath in your lungs. But if the code you gave me is the wrong one, I'm coming back in here with a spoon. And I'm sure your imagination can come up with all sorts of *fun* things for me to do with it." Dex picked the chair back up and set it upright. "Well?" he urged expectantly as he affixed the man with a glare.

"Six-One-Four-Two-Seven-Nine" stammered Vargas with the hint of a sigh of relief soaking his words. That was a good sign. Relief would suggest that the man is unburdened by his slipped secret, not weighed down by the concealment of a new one.

"Thank you." Replied Dex conversationally with a nod and an amicable smile before spinning on his heel and walking for the door.

"Y-...you're going to let me go now, right?! " yelled Vargas with panic, "That was part of the deal! I ain't lying! The code's legit, try it out!"

Dex stopped in the open doorway and turned to face his prisoner; "I believe you. That's why I *am* going to let you go. Just be sure to take a deep breath now, though, alright? Wouldn't want to make a liar out of me, would we?" He shot Vargas a final wink, then retreated beyond the darkened doorway as he shouted; "Vette, show the man out."

"Preparing compartment for depressurization." Came a dutiful artificial voice from the speakers as the lights in the room dimmed to a pulsing red.

"What?!" screamed Vargas, "NO! You asshole, we had a deal!" The last thing that Vendrick's murderous lieutenant saw, before the docking bay doors at the front of the Hammer opened up to suck him out into the cold vacuum of space, was Dex's middle finger tapping the glass of the inner door's small port-hole.

Dex whistled a cheerful tune all the way up the lift and into the cockpit, announcing his arrival by saying; "Six-One-Four-Two-Seven-Nine" as he plopped himself down into his command chair.

"You broke him already?" asked the police Sergeant skeptically, "How did you manage that? If I even want to know..."

"Origami." Replied Dex with a smirk, "He was then lightly seasoned before I had Vette kick his sorry ass out to *walk* home."

Mirta looked surprised. "Y-You killed him?" she stuttered with mild disapproval, "What if we needed something else from him down the road?"

Dex just shook his head and contended; "That nutcase was radioactive. Keeping him around would've been more trouble than it was worth, trust me. Besides, we already got all the scans of his face that we needed while he was out cold, so he had outlived his usefulness anyways. All he was likely to do around here was waste our air and eat our food."

Tano placed a hand on Mirta's knee and added; "He didn't have anything else to tell us. Nothing important, anyways. A man like Vendrick is smart enough to keep his operation properly compartmentalized, but we're using that against him now. That's why Dex went through the trouble of attacking his bodyguards with a blade...sort of. And we drug Vargas' ugly ass all the way out here past the Oort cloud so nobody would find him once we *did* eventually dump him. Vendrick and his people need to believe the narrative that one of their own has cut loose from the group and took off to assemble his own crew in the area. This was always part of the plan."

"If what the Sergeant has been telling me about Vendrick's organizational structure is accurate," explained Dex patiently, "then our boy here is driving in the dark with low beams on."

"What in the living shit is that supposed to mean?" demanded Mirta with exasperation, "Can you quit it with the stupid-ass terrasider lingo and just speak English for a moment?"

"What I mean," clarified Dex with a placating hand gesture, "is that Vargas only *really* holds power over his own domain and has no real knowledge of those above him in the pecking order. It's all very cloak and dagger type stuff."

"And that just makes our job harder." Grumbled Tano with a grim nod, "Since we have the keycode now, we'll have to gain access to one of their secure terminals before we can scoop intel and plant the metric fuck-ton of fabricated email conversations needed to point the finger at Vargas' new business venture. Then, to make things even *more* interesting, we have to get it all done within the next *fourteen* hours."

"With that being said," began Dex with a deliberate shift in tone as well as subject, "we need to start thinking about phase two. Sergeant, what do you have for us?"

Tano nodded, then proceeded to fill in the details; "While you were chatting with our friend in the cargo hold, I was able to do some digging within my personal archives. Our only option, really, is to hit one of the guarded packaging facilities that Vendrick's boys are running on ring five. It's the only building under total lockdown *and* it has a signal dish on the roof, which means *that* is where we will find our secure uplink." The Sergeant punched a few things into the console in front of him and the holographic display above the navigation station hummed to life with a soft blue glow. "The warehouse is here," he continued, pointing his finger to a concrete building surrounded by compacted rows of corn, "You should be able to approach the building using the cornstalks as cover, but you'll need to be careful of the eh-... By the way, you don't by chance have any metallic upgrades or prosthetics I should know about, do you?"

"Not that I'm aware of." Replied Dex with a raised eyebrow, "Why do you ask?"

"Great!" exclaimed the Sergeant, "Because the corn fields are chock-full of magnetically tripped landmines. If you're carrying metal of any kind, and you don't have an identification chip configured to show you as friendly, then the mines will be activated and they'll have to clean you up with a sponge."

Dex thought quietly for a moment, then calmly asked; "Okaaay...so how do I get my gun in? I'm pretty good, but I can't fight twenty guys without a weapon."

Tano chuckled, saying; "It's more like thirty-five, but that's beside the point. You aren't going to be there to start a fight. You just need to get in, get it done, then get out of there. I'm thinking the toughest part will be getting past the roving patrols in the cornfield...Shouldn't be a problem, though."

"That's easy for you to say." Huffed Dex with a lack of enthusiasm, "So you expect me to go in there naked and unarmed?"

Tano laughed again and retorted; "You don't gotta wear pants if you don't want, kid, but you won't be going in unarmed." The heavyset police Sergeant then reached into his boot and pulled out a small black knife, handing it to the younger man with a cheeky grin.

"Carbon fiber." Noted Dex as he inspected the blade.

"Yes sir." Replied Tano with pride, "It's what I keep on me for when I get searched. Always need to have an ace in the hole!"

Dex smirked, offering; "Hey, you know what would make this *really* and ace in the hole? If it were a gun in my fuckin' hand. What are you, *crazy*? And what the shit do you expect me to do if one of these guys spots me from the *vast* distance of five meters or more? I can only get lucky with that tuck and roll bullet-dodge bullshit once per episode, you know..."

Tano shot Mirta a knowing grin. "That's where our lovely lady comes into play." He suggested proudly, "She's the best damn sharpshooter that I've ever had the pleasure of instructing. Say what you will about her awful cooking, *sorry Mirta*, but she can damn near split hairs from five kilometers out with that rifle of hers. We can place her just under a klick away, up-spin of the facility in an old protein processing plant. From that distance, the curve of the station should afford her a good view of what's happening on the ground."

Dex looked at Mirta appraisingly and remarked; "I didn't know you dabbled in the long range. Can you consistently hit targets at that distance? What about moving targets?"

Mirta looked Dex dead in the eye and confidently boasted; "If I can see it, I can hit it. Don't you worry about that."

Tano smiled, putting his hand on her knee, and assured; "She means it, Dex. Believe me. And while you kids are running around doing *your* thing, I will provide ground transport. I can also help you a bit from my tablet, if you can get me direct access to their system. With *that*, I might be able to pinpoint the location of the relay console for you."

"Well, I'd say that settles it." Concluded Dex with an air of finality, "I suppose we'll just wing it the rest of the way, then, eh? Alrighty, then. Vette, please warm up the drive and get us on our way to Meclan. We have some work to do."

Chapter 11

Just over two hours later, Dex was walking down a deserted road toward his target in one of the two agricultural drums that sat nestled between the larger public rings of the station. The stout barrels were built with a smaller radius to account for the weight of the nutrient-enriched soil that blanketed the entire inner surface of the structure, and they rotated clockwise against the counter-clockwise spin of the outer rings to act as a stabilization gyro of sorts for the station as a whole. Unlike expensive Geno-farming that required a steady supply of special chemicals and equipment to operate, Meclan's more rustic approach to farming allowed for generations of production under complete trade isolation. That's why the fields were still teeming with, admittedly sickly-looking, life amid the chaos and why the whole place was so tightly guarded.

"So, are you absolutely sure that this radio you gave me won't piss off the landmines?" asked Dex with concern as he inspected the small device clipped to his waist, "Because getting vaporized, nuts-first, isn't exactly the way I had planned on going out."

"Relax, kid." Scoffed Tano with flippant wave of his hand, "That there is one of the ghost comms that the PD uses for our sting ops. Its constructed entirely of a bioplastic that is impregnated with neutralized graphene circuitry. I couldn't even detect it with a hand-held wand, so how the hell do you think a sensor beneath a meter of concrete is gonna do any better? The mines are meant to repel armed attacks, *en masse*, so you should be fine as long as you don't have any piercings you haven't been upfront about."

The younger man nervously adjusted the radio's clip and its matching earpiece and replied; "*Should* be fine? I swear...If I get blown to smithereens because of this doo-dad of yours, I'm gonna haunt the living shit out of you. You know that, right?"

Tano chuckled and keyed his radio; "Well if you get killed, kid, I'm likely not far behind you."

Dex found his entry point, about half a kilometer from the protected facility, and quietly stepped off the road into the corn field. He knelt to reach into his boot, retrieving the flat-black carbon fiber knife from its hidden internal pocket, then stood to clip it to his belt alongside his comm. "I'm moving in," he whispered calmly as he dove deeper into the field, "Mirta, what do we got?"

Just under a kilometer away, in an abandoned building on its deserted third floor, sat a table that was covered by a rumpled heap of dusty blankets. There were no sounds, no detectable vibration, and not even a heat signature. There was only a small, nearly imperceptible, sway in the fabric and a six-centimeter wide metal cylinder discretely poking through a hole in the dusty rags. Beneath that blanket, her face awash in the soft green glow of the display screen mounted to the top rail of her Lancaster JL-97 sniper rifle, sat Mirta with her jaw set and her expression frozen into a mask of concentration. With a durable nano-precision zoom lens built into her weapon's muzzle break, she could remain fully shrouded, safely tucked beneath the moderate ballistic protection of her camouflaged porta-blind, while maintaining complete downrange visibility.

She kept her breath steady, calmly peering through her riflescope display. Her finger sat comfortably on the outside of the trigger guard, confidently poised with the safety off and her reflexes limber. Tano had always taught her that a safety catch was *great for movin', but shit for snipin'*, so she always made sure to flick it off as soon as she activated her scope. As a teen, while most girls her age were busy skipping class to chase boys, she was skipping so that she could get some range time in with uncle Mike. While others in her grade wasted away their time in VR veg-beds, Mirta had mastered a weapon that could magnetically accelerate a ferroplastic dart at shooter-defined velocities of up to nearly twelve times the speed of sound.

To avoid over-penetration within the dangerous pressurized environment of a space station, Mirta loaded the weapon with hypersonic micro-fracture rounds that were designed to shatter on impact and degrade into a fine dust within milliseconds of target contact; causing the projectile to dump the tremendous entirety of its kinetic energy at once in a single devastating punch, *without* tearing any holes in the station behind the freshly-dead badguy.

Shifting her shoulders in a controlled flex, she panned her scope across the cornfield. Its sensors displayed an overlay of optical, infrared, and electromagnetic data to record the area's geography, tagging potential threats when detected. As the targeting computer built into her marksman's exoskin located enemies, it highlighted them in her view and tracked them with the weapon's wide-angle lens as the scope moved on. Her purpose-built suit of artificial muscle fibers served as a form of stabilizer, keeping the slow pan of her scope so smooth that it looked artificial as she took in the scene.

Static filled Dex's earpiece for a moment, then Mirta's voice cut in; "Alright, we have a total of five on the perimeter. Two patrolling the field to your west, one on the roof, and another two guarding the front door. The guys in the fields are sporting assault rifles, looks like a long gun on the roof...and I can't tell what the guys at the door are strapped with. Pistols, probably."

Dex made a mental note of the report, wishing silently to himself that he could have taken at least some glasses with a good overlay in with him. With a HUD available, Mirta could've simply tagged the enemies and he would've been able to see their outlines clear as day as they made their merry way through the corn. With the wonders of modern technology stripped from him, Dex was forced in that moment to rely on training that was a little more old-school. Instruction that wasn't bestowed by any government program, but by his father while hunting deer in the abandoned forests of central Oregon. He was breathing in controlled and shallow breaths through his mouth, slowly drawing in air to keep his skull quiet for the intense work his ears were doing. Walking in a toe-first gait, staying upon the balls of his feet with the utmost practiced silence, he began to creep further into the field. Stopping with apprehension before crossing the threshold into the mined cornfield, he activated his comm and hissed; "I won't be kaputzki if I accidentally step on any of these mines, will I?"

"Again," returned Tano's voice into his earpiece with an exasperated sigh, "These aren't the old-fashioned pressure activated ones. They're a meter down and covered in cement. So relax, you wuss. Only metal is gonna set them off...Well, that, or... *cough*...or they can be triggered remotely."

"Splendid." groaned Dex with a frustrated eye-roll, "And thanks for waiting until I was already in here to tell me that these things are on a goddamn remote control...you dick." Regardless of his halfhearted protest, he shrugged away his anxieties and continued to tiptoe through the sickly-green looking stalks of corn, nonetheless. As he neared the heavily guarded storage warehouse, Dex came across a gravel road that cut through the field and decided to drop to a crouch and sit as still as possible to listen for the sentries making their rounds.

After a few minutes, his patience was rewarded with the sound of a single set of footsteps about fifty meters to his left. They traveled at a casual gait, moving with a nonconcern that was highlighted by the rhythmic dragging of the guard's left toe across the gravel. He waited quietly, still as a stone, while his enemy drew nearer. When the source of the sound had approached to within ten meters, Dex slowly drew his knife from its sheath and held it at the ready. Finally, he got a glimpse of a man's torso through the cornstalks when he passed, lazily shuffling by on his boring patrol and fiddling with what sounded like a game on his tablet. Dex unconsciously held his breath, silently rising to his full height as he emerged from the cornstalks behind his target. Reaching out with his right hand, he grabbed the top of the sentry's head and yanked him back by the hair to thrust his knife into the base of his foe's skull. The sentry fell limp instantly, spilling silently to the ground without protest. Dex took a moment to clean his knife on the dead man's shirt then re-sheathed it with care. "One down, four to go." He whispered into the radio as he finished dragging the body off of the road and into the cornstalks.

On instinct, he began to reach for the dispatched man's gun, but stopped abruptly when Tano's voice came crackling into his earpiece; "Whatever you do, don't touch his weapon. While you're still in the cornfield, we can't be certain the mines won't go off. The firearm could be proxi-locked to its user."

With a defeated sigh, Dex lowered his arms and lamented; "Looks like we won't get to do this the easy way, then?"

"Since when is the easy way ever any fun?" encouraged Tano through a throaty a chortle.

"Convenient for you to say, sittin' on your ass in the truck." grumbled Dex as he crouched low to continue making his way through the corn. Picking past row after row in the field, he eventually began to see more and more light from the central building's floodlamps cutting through the stalks up ahead.

"Stop." sang Mirta's warning in his earpiece. Since she was so far away, looking down from the crest of the station's curve, she had almost a bird's eye view of the situation and could see better than him what lie ahead. "One guy," Her voice continued, "Three rows ahead of you and about twenty-five meters to your right and moving your direction up the path. He looks just as bored as the first one, but...I dunno, Dex. He's pretty big."

Dex waved an absent-minded dismissal up toward her distant perch, then stepped noiselessly through the row of stalks in front of him on an intercept course with his newest target. He stayed low as he moved, stopping every five meters to listen for his prey. Eventually, Dex was able to pinpoint the crunching of the guard's footsteps and he began to close in on them. As the sound solidified directly in front of him, he spotted a burly man moving beyond the stalks. The guard was an obvious terrasider by the look of him, the pulsating purple glow of a facial tattoo burning through the thick bushy black beard that clung to his comically square jaw. Dex slowly inched his way out from the concealment of the cornstalks and moved onto the path behind his rather sizable target. He took a few steps to close distance, and was preparing to pounce with a lethal knife strike, when he accidentally kicked loose a rock amid the gravel. The guard heard the disturbance and immediately began turning to investigate its source with a gasp of surprise. Dex shot forward, lunging low, and thrust his knife upwards into the bottom of the guard's chin. The man panicked, dropping his gun to clutch at his throat with one hand while swatting aimlessly at his unknown attacker with the other.

Dex grabbed for the back of the man's head, trying to pull him in to dislodge his weapon, but found himself flying backward instead as he was thrown with a powerful heave into the rows of corn behind him. The guard stepped forward woozily, pulling the knife's serrated blade from his chin with visible effort, and nearly buckled to a knee when it finally tore loose. Growling in rage, the beast of a man shook away his disorientation then stormed into the corn after his opponent.

The guard clumsily stepped through the thick edge row into the field, furiously swinging his fists at the vegetation as he searched for his unidentified enemy. Suddenly, Dex leapt at him from low concealment and attempted to take the knife, but Vendrick's man was too strong and was easily able to shake his grip loose with a rough elbow to the intruder's gut. The guard was now bleeding quite a bit down the front of his shirt as he stood there pointing the knife at Dex, frozen in a moment of tactical analysis overload as a spark of shock bloomed in his eyes. He turned, trying to yell for help, but the injured man was surprised to hear nothing but a low gurgle emanating from his throat. As if angered by his sudden realization of the extent of his injury, Vendrick's man surged forward and swung his knife with a newfound aggression. Dex kept back-stepping the enraged man's sweeping blows, biding his time until he saw an opening. When the guard heaved and took an extra powerful swing, Dex capitalized on the resulting slowed rebound rate of the man's arm. He bounded forward to put a hand on the man's elbow, pinning his arm across his own body as he delivered a crushing knee to his opponent's lower ribs.

The guard's defense slackened for a fraction of a second under the blow, but that's all Dex needed. Twisting the bearded man's wrist with one hand, Dex used the heel of his other palm to strike the hilt of the weapon. The knife popped free with a prominent slap and, in one smooth motion, the intruder adjusted his grip on the rubberized handle and brought it back onto his enemy. Dex's first cut with the razor-sharp blade was deep, directed at the man's thigh and aiming for his femoral artery. He then jerked the weapon free and quickly spun on his heel, delivering a hard elbow to his opponent's temple. The blow staggered the large man backward and, as Dex's spin reached its three-hundred-sixtieth degree, he plunged his weapon directly into the guard's heart; Breaking its carbon fiber blade off inside the man's chest in the process.

The wide-eyed guard stared at the wound for a breathless moment, his mouth floundering open in noiseless confusion as if trying to work out the situation. Then, when the rather negative self-assessment finally reached his brain, he managed to stumble a few steps toward Dex before falling face-first through the cornstalks. "Well...shit." grumbled Dex into his radio, "There goes my only weapon. Lurch here decided to eat it."

"Damn, that freakin' guy was huge!" blurted Mirta as she adjusted the focus on her scope to get a better look at the man lying motionless in the field.

Dex took a knee to catch his breath and keyed his comm; "Ok, Mirta, what do you see from up there? Did anyone hear what just went down? Anyone new to worry about?"

Mirta scanned the area once more with her scope, using its built-in infrared to sweep through the crops looking for heat signatures. She noted nothing new, then reported; "We still have one on the roof and two at the front door." She sighed heavily at the sight and continued; "The lookout on the roof is sitting there looking at his tablet, generally being pretty terrible at his job. Two guys out front are chatting, and one of them is having a smoke. Nobody looks particularly alerted, so it seems you remain a surprise guest. For *now*."

Dex thought for a moment, then asked; "I need to see how close I can get to the building before I run outta cover. What do you think?"

Mirta's answer was promptly returned into Dex's earpiece, suggesting she had anticipated it and already ran the numbers. "You have seventy-three meters of open ground to cover before you get to the warehouse." she warned, "I mean, if I were a betting woman, I'd put credits on you gettin' across, but all it takes is one absent minded glance from dipshit up there and you're screwed. You brought me here to shoot, so let me shoot. I'll put him to bed, then you can move up without issue."

Dex looked back up the curve of the drum where he knew Mirta was hiding and keyed his comm; "You don't have to do any killing today if you don't want to, Mirta." He said as he looked to her distant hiding place, "We can think of another approach."

"I appreciate the sentiment, Dex," she returned calmly, "but I wanna take out as many of these assholes as I can before I'm done here. Every single one of them deserves nothing less. I have been sitting behind that bar, putting up with their shit for *years*, and now it's time to return that shitstorm...with *interest*."

Dex smirked and shot a thumbs up toward Mirta. "That is *definitely* something I can help you with." He laughed as he turned and continued to make his way quietly toward the warehouse. When he arrived at the edge of the field, he dropped to his stomach and scanned the distant rooftop for a man that he knew would be there. Perched at the center of the windowless metal building's flat roof was a small sniper nest, complete with a full ring of ballistic-composite barriers and a good old-fashioned spotlight on a swivel mount. The guard was sitting in what appeared to be the battered remains of a foldable lawn chair with his feet kicked up onto the barrier in front of him, holding a tablet close to his face and illuminating his head like a nice little target for the world to see as he toiled away in obliviousness.

"I'm ready when you are." whispered Dex into his radio as he braced for the inevitable volley. There was absolute silence for a full seven seconds, then the man on the roof snapped his head back violently. The tremendous force of the bullet's impact uprooted the guard from his seat and sent him flying backward, rearranging the ruined contents of his skull into an expanding cloud of fine pink mist.

"One down." came Mirta's voice over the comm with a stuttered buzz of exhilaration, "And he isn't getting up anytime soon, that's for *damn* sure."

"Nice shooting!" complimented Dex with sincere surprise at her cold-bore accuracy, "Do you have that damn thing set to anti-aircraft mode or something? *That* poor bastard is *definitely* not getting an open casket."

"Caskets are for people who matter," Retorted Mirta without a hint of humor in her voice, "and that chucklefuck did *not*. Of that, I am certain."

Dex nodded, smiling, and continued to lay at the edge of the field to listen for any sign that the guards out front had heard the recent demise of their comrade. After a long minute of watching and listening, he finally rose to a crouch and started across the illuminated open ground toward the warehouse. Dex moved like a ghost, his practiced gait propelling him along efficiently while maintaining near perfect silence until he melted back into the darkness beneath the warehouse's hanging eave.

Feeling his way along the wall, Dex easily found the maintenance access panel that Tano assured him would be there. With a sense of triumph, he plugged his radio into the console's attached data jack and ran the pre-made software package that the Sergeant had prepared. A blue bar appeared and slowly crept its way across his interface until it concluded with a cheerful beep in his earpiece. "Are you in, Tano?" he hissed as he closed the homebrewed app's confirmation screen

"I'm in." came the Sergeant's hasty reply, "You can yank your radio now, and I'll start seeing how far I can push my access here."

"Okay, everyone…" began Mirta with a re-focusing sigh, "So how do we want to do this?"

"I think I might have an idea." whispered Dex as he inspected the conduits heading out from the junction box at his shoulder, "Tano, It looks like Meclan's about the start up her night cycle here in a minute. Do you think you would be able to kill the outside flood lights?"

The radio was silent for a moment, then Tano cut in; "Well, I managed to get into the building's control system through the terminal you plugged me into so let's see…Irrigation, nutrient feed controls, oxygenation, ooh *maintenance*. Aaaand **YES!** I *can* cut all the external lighting…I'm ready when you are."

As he inched toward the front corner of the building, Dex began to hear voices emanating from up ahead. He got to the end of the wall and dropped to a knee, peeking around the front edge of the warehouse from as low of an angle as he could muster. He spotted two men, just where Mirta said they'd be, standing about ten meters away in front of a large metal door having a chat. One of them was enjoying a smoke while the other was finishing a story about some haul he had made back in the *'good ole days'*. Hefting the metal wrench that he had found sitting against the side of the building, Dex stepped back and prepared to heave the tool as far as he could. He wound up and hurled the wrench with all of his might, sending it sailing into the cornfield directly facing the warehouse's front door. When the wrench impacted, a sharp explosion rang out with a bright flash that momentarily lit the swelling twilight within the drum. Dust took to the sky in a plume, moving unnaturally through the turbulent soup of atmosphere that was stirred up in the centrifugal gravity.

As Dex had predicted, a muted argument between the two guards broke out, which led to one man reluctantly moving out into the field to investigate while the *winner* of their brief exchange remained at the door. After watching the first guard disappear into the far cornfield, Dex backtracked along the wall, moving ten meters down from the front corner of the building before taking a knee in the shadow under the eve. Crouching low, he hugged himself close to the wall then keyed his radio, whispering; "Lights." As he slapped the wall as hard as he could with an open palm; Syncing his action perfectly with the failure of the building's external illumination. The odd noise alerted the remaining guard at the frond door just as the light above him winked out. Naturally, the man associated the two events and decided to head around back to investigate the strange occurrence. It was too easy. A man assigned to a door, regardless of which army he serves or what training he has received, will always look for an excuse to do *something* other than stare at that door...As long as that activity doesn't entail something more dangerous like trudging through a mine field, that is.

As the guard rounded the corner, he saw a shape moving low through the darkness. By the time the man's curiosity had prompted him to activate the flashlight function on his tablet, he was only able to gasp in surprise as the shadowy figure sprang at him from below. Dex lashed out with a front kick that connected straight to the guard's liver, robbing him of breath as his lung-full of air escaped in a distressed *oof*. Stunned with the sudden overwhelming pain that had flooded his mind, the guard stumbled toward his attacker with confusion burning its way through his expression of agony. Dex took that opportunity to seize his opponent by the shoulders, spinning him to bring the man in for a choke hold.

The dazed guard quickly recovered, however, when he fully came to realize the gravity of his dire situation. Pulling away from Dex while jerking and kicking violently, the spindly man tried desperately to wriggle free. In response, the larger terrasider simply tightened his grip and allowed himself to tumble backward to the ground. The guard fell on top of his attacker and was quickly wrapped in his legs, left with no chance of escape. Dex locked his feet around his opponent's waist and squeezed as hard as he could with every muscle in his body. He easily road out the guard's opening energetic panic-spasms with his superior body positioning, draining what air remained in the man's lungs with an ever-tightening squeeze of his legs, then it was a simple matter to wait and keep his firm hold fully engaged until the guard had gone completely still for a considerable amount of time.

As Dex was attempting to push his dispatched opponent off of him, the second door guard had returned from his investigation of the cornfield and came loping around the corner looking for his friend. Guard number two most definitely did not like what he found. The alarmed man's reaction time was razor sharp and obviously trained as he almost instantaneously began to raise the muzzle of his very serious looking assault rifle in Dex's direction. The intruder was forced to look on helplessly, hunkering as best as he could behind the body on top of him while the guard's barrel approached his level. Suddenly, the air rumbled with concussive energy and the armed man was forcefully thrown against the wall, his shoulder shattered into oblivion and his arm nearly torn free from the man's mangled torso as it crumpled to a heap in the dirt. "Shit." Came Mirta's frustrated voice over the radio, "I was a little low."

"*Christ on a unicycle!*" bellowed Dex into his mic in an absent-minded breach of his carefully maintained stealth, "Are you *fucking* me?! That was amazing!"

Tano's voice then cut in to harsh the excitement; "Yeah, super awesome and all, but are we sure that your damn *yelling* didn't alert the whole freaking warehouse?"

"Right." grimaced Dex as he put an effort into returning to a whisper, "Adrenaline's a hell of a drug. Mirta, do you see any new activity?"

Mirta scanned the fields and the outbuildings again with a careful eye. Seeing nothing moving, she keyed her radio and said; "All clear. Nothing new to report."

"Hey, Tano," began Dex curiously, "you think it's safe to pick up one of these guns yet? I'm assuming they wouldn't set mines up within their inner perimeter, right?"

"Yeah, go for it." came the portly man's nonchalant response, "You'll probably want to stick to the sidearms, though. The assault rifles are likely ID locked, so they'll do you no good. And be extra sure that you don't take anything with you when you head back into the fields. That includes mags, belts, and clasps. It's the stupid little things that'll get you killed."

Dex nodded, taking a moment to examine both dispatched guards for the bare essentials of what he'd need. They were each armed with a pistol, so he grabbed one and made sure to gather what ammo he could find before stuffing it all into a commandeered holster belt he had stripped off of the skinnier and less disassembled of his two foes. Fastening the equipment around his waist, he cinched his belt tight and withdrew the pistol to verify its charge and that it was properly chambered.

"Alright..." breathed Dex with a sense of calm over the comm as he went over his mental checklist, "When I go in here, I'm stepping in totally blind. Mirta, you keep an eye out for any newcomers and let me know the second you see anything. Tano, I want you to try and gain access to an internal camera or some other facet of the building's security system. See if you can dig up anything that could give you an idea of the enemy presence inside. The goal here is to get in, find the transmitter, plant the spoof data, then get out; All before anyone knows I'm here. Simple enough, yeah?"

With their tasks decided, Dex reached out slowly and opened the metal door at the front of the building with a muted squeak. He allowed the door hang ajar for a moment, sitting there patiently listening with his confiscated pistol at the ready to make sure nobody noticed the movement. Satisfied that the area beyond the door was devoid of activity, he cracked it wider and slipped through into a small unlit foyer. The compact entryway featured only two options; one door that led to a flight of stairs and another set of large double doors that led straight ahead and onto the warehouse floor. He could hear machinery beyond the double doors and stepped closer to press his ear to the wall for a better listen. The rhythmic whirr-thump was short and repetitive, which denoted a simple manufacturing task or packaging role as its most likely function. Along with the machinery, he heard several voices and sets of footsteps moving around behind the ominous door.

Choosing the second floor as his better option, Dex cautiously began his ascent into the dark stairwell with his weapon at the ready. At the top of the flight, he came to a long hallway that ran down the center of the building for its entire length. The simple and undecorated stretch was lit by a single strip of overhead lumoband that ran along the ceiling, illuminating the various doors that lined the walls to both the left and right. None of the doors had any external indication of what lie beyond them, signage or otherwise, so Dex had no clues to guess with other than their slightly irregular spacing. Flustered at his lack of something to go on, the infiltrator simply decided to carefully open the first door to his right and do his best to deal with whatever lie beyond it. Throwing the door open in a silent explosion of movement, Dex stepped through the doorframe and raised his weapon to mentally catalog the new area and sweep it for threats. After a mere second and a half of investigation, his weapon's muzzle fell back into ready position as he discovered that his newly conquered room was a lowly utility closet. With a shrug, he decided to step inside for a place to hide while he checked in with the Sergeant; "Tano, got any leads on where the transmitter is? I can't exactly trick-or-treat my way down the hall, knocking on every door till I find this damn thing. Give me something to work with here."

The Sergeant's voice returned quickly with an air of excitement; "Alright, kid, I think I got somethin' for you. I can't be sure, but the power outlets in the room at the far end of the hallway, left side, are drawing a hell of a lot more power than any of the other non-industrial outlets in the building. It's a good indication that some serious equipment is in use in there."

"Good enough for me." acknowledged Dex as he cracked open the closet door to peer back out into the hallway. He spotted no one impeding his way, so he slipped out of his hiding place and started heading for the far end of the building. When he had gotten just over halfway to the other side, Dex heard the whirr of a door sliding open ahead of him. Making a split-second decision, he quickly ducked into the room to his left and closed the door behind him without first pausing to see what lie within. Luckily, he found himself in an unpopulated bathroom and didn't have to explain his sudden presence to any surprised individuals he caught using the facilities. He took a moment to force his adrenaline-fueled heavy breathing into a shallow and controlled rhythm, then quietly crouched to press his ear to the door. Dex could hear the sound of footsteps clunking slowly down the hallway, unalarmed, as they made their way closer. Eventually, the lazy shuffle passed by him as it continued down the hall, fading away into the depths of the stairwell.

When he was sure the man had gone, Dex crept back into the hall and continued his journey toward its far end. When he reached the room he was looking for, he took another quick check of his surroundings then crouched and put his ear against the metal surface of the door to listen intently. He heard the scrape of chair legs scooting, then the click of bootheels on deckplate. He realized too late, however, that the footsteps were approaching his direction, and the door slid open while Dex was still crouched in the middle of its threshold. He heard a gasp of surprise from above as the man on the other side of the doorframe recoiled, dropping the tablet he was holding to reach for the gun on his belt.

Without thought, Dex punched the man in the groin as hard as he could then yanked him roughly to the ground by his shirt collar. As the guard curled in agony, Dex pulled himself on top of the man and grabbed for the tablet that was dropped. He managed to find grip on it, but quickly had it swatted from his hand by the slender pirate underneath him. Seizing the man's shirt, Dex jerked himself toward him to smash the crown of his skull into the bridge of his opponent's nose. The pirate's eyes rolled back and his coordination was scrambled for a heartbeat, allowing Dex the opportunity to grab the handheld tablet and drag it across the floor to himself. Once it was firmly in his grip, he lifted the computer over his head and slammed it, edge first, as hard as he could into the exposed throat of his foe; Continuing to bring the device down again and again with a ferocious aggression until the man beneath him, as well as the tablet in his hands, were a bent and broken mess.

As Dex pulled himself off of his dispatched opponent, he had to take a brief moment to catch his breath from the exhausting burst of violence. It was a dirty way to get the job done, and it came with a whole lot of mental turbulence to deal with, but it wasn't the kind of turbulence you'd expect from such a horrific action. What Dex experienced wasn't a feeling of regret or revulsion, but the undeniable sense of exhilaration that came from any brush with death. Killing someone who's standing at the other end of a scope is one thing, and it comes with its *own* brand of turbulence, but dispatching one's enemy while face-to-face on even footing…that is something entirely different. It lives among the deepest primal desires of mankind, rooted into the darkest depths of our lizard brains, and the rush of it can become as addicting as any drug. Wielding the power of life or death over another being is an ancient intoxicant that has left its mark in every era of human history, and it continues to scorch its way across the galaxy even now.

Dex, however, knew better than to revel in the morbid elation of it all, pushing the sensation aside with a small pang of guilt at feeling such triumph in the first place over taking a life so brutally. As a soldier, Dex was forced to deal with that demon frequently and had discovered through his own experience that it was something any professional killer needed to learn to latch down if they wanted to keep their head screwed on straight. That euphoria of victory was precisely why people like Vendrick and the seemingly heartless scum in his employ even existed. Once they got a taste of that power over life and death, they inevitably succumbed to their ensuing addiction; Taking the path of least resistance, as all addicts do, to their fix. So, in a pattern that repeats itself through history time and again, these addicts will peacock around and specifically go after those who are sure to submit their *delicious* terror more readily than others. Vendrick's men were all cowards of the lowest order, he decided, and they deserved no better than the fate that would find them all. With that thought, the troubled cargo pilot's momentary guilt was sufficiently replaced by contempt for the motionless man at his feet.

Dex shook his head clear then proceeded to drag the guard's body back into the little room from which he came, closing the door behind him. The intruder surveyed his immediate surroundings, quickly finding what he was looking for in the form of an unassuming black metal box. Stepping over quietly, he gently lifted the device's heavy lid to reveal a light-purple glow spilling from within. Once fully open, he could see a keypad and a simple screen with a scrolling set of numbers. "I Found the encryption interface…thing," he reported into his comm, "But it doesn't look like any relay equipment I've ever seen. There are no obvious controls for tuning or configuring the device at all…just a keypad to punch the code into."

"It sounds like it might be a one-way burst receiver," suggested Tano thoughtfully, "but it doesn't really matter in this instance, so I wouldn't worry too much about it. While it would be nice, we don't need to actually be here when a burst comes in. We can just access the secure network that *is* tied to this receiver, which should allow us to plant the goodies framing Vargas for our upcoming hijinks. That's the main goal here, so any intel or whatnot we scoop beyond that is just gravy."

With a shrug, Dex crouched next to the device and plugged his radio into the data port of the large communications doo-dad. After a moment of visibly trying his best to recall a memory that refused to manifest itself, he let out a resigned sigh and reached into his chest pocket to withdraw a wrinkled scrap of paper with a hastily written number on it. Leaning over the keypad, Dex quickly punched 6-1-4-2-7-9 into its interface. The lights on the unit then suddenly turned blue as a loading icon appeared on his radio's screen. The progress bar crept quickly across the display, coming to completion after twelve seconds with a light audible chirp.

"Got it…" he heard Tano say over the radio channel with a huff of excitement. There was a long pause, then the Sergeant spoke again; "Now I need you to destroy the comm device. Completely. We've done what we came here to, so just make sure the damned relay can never be used again. That, in and of itself, will be a victory that we all need."

"Sure thing, boss." grunted Dex as he stood and stretched his back, "I'll toast this thing real quick, then I'm gettin' the hell outta here. Keep the truck running for me, 'cause I have a feeling that I'll be comin' in hot." With that, he set the control box for the encryption device on the floor and slammed his heavy heel into its delicate interface several times, sending components and shards of glass clattering across the floor in every direction. Dex then drew his confiscated pistol and pulled the slide back a quarter of an inch to verify that a round was still in the chamber. Satisfied, he flipped the safety catch off and quickly stepped out into the hallway with his weapon at the ready. Moving swiftly down the narrow corridor with a well-practiced and stealthy gait, the intruder swept his muzzle over every door he passed.

When he reached the end of the hall and took his first step into the descending stairwell, he almost ran headlong into a hefty man, holding a plate of steaming nachos, who was sluggishly walking up the narrow passageway toward him. Dex quickly snapped his pistol up, pressing his muzzle into the soft cartilage at the tip of the surprised man's nose as he pulled the trigger. The plump pirate's head snapped backward, sending him crashing into the wall at his side as he fell down the stairs in a cheese-soaked cartwheel. Vaulting over the man's tumbling body, Dex landed with an impact-dampening roll at the bottom of the stairwell and sprinted out the front door of the building. As he was running toward the corn field, Dex discarded his confiscated belt with a momentary struggle at the clasp's mechanism and threw his gun into the dirt while urgently thundering into his comm; "I'm blown and I need an exit strategy, *FAST*!"

Tano's calm voice came back an instant later; "Keep heading deeper into the cornfields and try to keep your head low…I have something cool to show you." Dex could now hear gunfire coming from the building behind him, popping off in a cacophony of reports from a multitude of weapons that bit into the stalks in every direction. It was clear that they didn't know where he was, so they were just wildly shooting into the cornstalks after him. Quickly coming to the conclusion that whether he got hit or not would be result of complete blind luck, Dex focused his concentration on running straight ahead as hard as he could in lieu of the zigzag his brain was screaming at him to do.

Mirta watched through her scope as Vendrick's men spilled out of the warehouse after the intruder, splitting up to head into the field like a school of sharks in pursuit of their prey. As he was leaving the edge of the outermost field, Dex heard Tano come back over his earpiece; "Alright, kid, you're clear. Now, get down and enjoy the show!"

Dex complied, diving to the ground in a breathless heap before turning to look expectantly back toward the warehouse. He sat there in silence for three full seconds, then scoffed; "Ok, now wha-" but his question soon answered itself when a series of explosions started rising across the cornfield, sending dirt pluming high into the air to clatter against the production drum's central light-bar.

Mirta watched with a smirk as she counted Vendrick's men in the field getting swallowed, one after another, by smoke and flame. "Okay, enough enjoying the show." came Tano's voice barking from behind Dex, "Get your ass in the truck."

"What happened?" asked the younger man as he climbed up into the stolen freight truck's worn passenger seat.

Tano chuckled and put the manually controlled vehicle into gear; "Found our friend's newest set of admin credentials in that info-dump you sent me and I used 'em to create myself an admin user account. With that, it was a simple feat to reset the mine's friend or foe tags. Made 'em see Vendrick-registered IDs as enemy combatants, aaand Presto! Killing with a keyboard...You're welcome, by the way."

"*I'm* welcome?!" laughed Dex incredulously, "How about, *you're* welcome for **me** getting you the damn password in the first place? You typed in some numbers and flipped a switch. How hard is that?"

"Well," reposted the Sergeant with a smirk, "all *you* did was type in some numbers, then smash a radio. How hard is *that?* I'd say it's about fifty-fifty...plus Mirta's fifty. Fifty-fifty-fifty."

Dex simply responded with an eyeroll as their truck rumbled to a stop near an unlit lamp post. Mirta was standing under it waiting with a blanket wrapped around her disassembled rifle, which sat at her feet in the guise of a bedroll. After she had climbed in and made herself comfortable in Dex's lap, Tano set the vehicle back into motion and said; "A little ways up the road here, there's a service elevator that will take us right back into the dock. We can set the truck's cruise control to a reasonable speed and hop out as we roll by. The auto lane-guidance should keep it going for the loop until someone stops it. By then, we'll be long gone."

Chapter 12

After making a short jump out into interstellar space, the small resistance movement gathered around a workbench in the Hammer's cramped machine shop to go over their findings. Tano stepped up first, reaching out to place a palm sized metal disc on the tabletop in front of them. He touched the device's smooth reflective surface with two fingers in a rhythmic stroke, then it suddenly began to glow with a green hue that grew brighter and brighter until the holographic image of a small icy planet of blue and white materialized before them. The planet featured no signs of life or technology, according to the diagram, other than the cone of light shown jetting from its dark side. At the far end of that cone sat an artistically over-scaled holographic representation of Meclan station, slowly spinning in the artificial darkness. As Dex leaned in for a closer inspection, an animation started to play that showed the station beginning to orbit around the planet. As it circled around and around, it sped up; Passing through the projected cone of light once every seventy-two of the simulation's displayed hours.

"What we pulled off here wasn't just a data plant." reported Tano excitedly, "We were able to grab *petabytes* of data from their servers as well. We're talkin' shipping schedules, crew rosters, order requests, and blackmail materials out the wazoo. It's the goddamn motherload! Do you have any idea how long I have been itching to get my hands on data like this?!"

"Hey, Vette," inquired Dex thoughtfully, "do you have access to this data as well? How long will it take for you to go through it?"

"Well, Commander," began Vette with excitement at the chance to explain something about herself, "My search algorithm works by category, so I have to be looking for specific data in order to find it. While it's true that I can look at a collection of data and *infer* new data or predictions from that original data set, that procedure takes an inordinately large amount of time and processing power. So, if you asked me something *specific* about the data, right now, I could tell you whatever you need to know. If you asked me how the data made me feel about possible future strategies or tactics, I would still need a day or two even if utilizing one hundred percent of my currently available resources. That is why you have always been the *'ideas'* guy of our little partnership, while I have been the *'do everything else'* side of that equation.

"Okay..." began Dex with a stroke to his chin, amused at the AI's newest attempt to screw with him in front of their *guests*, "Let's start with *Where is Vendrick?* Then we'll slide that right on into; *How do we kill him?*"

Vette let out a sigh, a habit that she had picked up from her human counterpart, and groaned; "Either you were not listening to a word I said, or you are just being a smart-ass. I honestly cannot tell. *No,* Vendrick did not include where he was in these files. He *also* did not include instructions on how to *kill* him."

Dex smirked at the rebuke and replied; "Alright, how about Vendrick's trade routes? Where are his boys flying their goodies?"

"*His* boys?" retorted the AI flatly, "Nowhere. They do not fly the supplies themselves. Instead, it appears that Vendrick and his ilk keep a stable of pilots who have been sufficiently bribed or threatened into enough loyalty for the pirates to trust them with away missions for food and supplies."

"Okay, what about *those* pilot's routes?" asked Dex, "You got *them* available for us to use? I need to know that we got *something* good out of all of this."

"Well, Commander," began the AI cheerily, "I can confidently say that I now have an effective roster of Vendrick's forces on Meclan by way of his strictly kept payment records. I have also attained insight into the enemy's command structure and overall cohesiveness. Time, I am sure, will uncover additional treasures within the data as well."

Tano poked his head up from his tablet at that comment to say; "Command *structure,* my ass. Communication on their side of the fence goes only one way, which is down. There are no orders for tax collections or specific dispatches to run things in any particular way; Just quotas for that bullshit corn of theirs. Makes no sense..."

"Is it possible that we were only seeing data that was relevant to the stock of that warehouse?" asked Mirta with a shrug, "I mean, it was surrounded by corn, right? If they were getting quotas for it, that would logically make sense to me."

While his eyes were still glued to his tablet, Dex spoke up to suggest; "That *would* make sense...*If* the farming shit were truly all that we found. But the data here leaves little doubt that this was their main server. If we unpacked it all here on the local drives of the Hammer, Vette would be in danger of crapping herself if she sneezed wrong."

The audibly weary AI led her retort with a full three-second-long sigh before lamenting; "Simultaneously, I am saddened by your complete lack of understanding regarding my physiology, repulsed at where that ignorance has led you, and acutely concerned with what this means when it comes to letting you behind the stick. This is a new all-time cognitive low, even for you, Commander."

"And you wonder why you're never invited to any parties..." riposted Dex with a mischievous smirk.

"Hey, can we get back on track here?" asked Mirta with impatience, "We all just kinda risked our lives, and I would like to see what it was all for."

"Fair enough." Stated Tano with an understanding nod, "But it will take time to go through it all and calculate the best next-step. Also, by the sound of it, we will be needing some mainframe space for Vette to stretch her legs a bit. Having an AI on our side is going to be a massive advantage, I foresee, and it will be useful to have her on her A game if we really do plan on bringing Vendrick down. I may know of a place that fits the bill..."

"Could be risky." Warned Dex uncertainly, "There's no way to know if it's being watched or not."

"There's no way that Vendrick knows about this particular place." Assured the Sergeant soberly, "It's not even in-system, and it has everything we'll need to lay low."

"Alright," sighed Dex, stifling a yawn, "but I don't got shit for cash, so I won't be able to pay any docking or storage fees."

"The place'll be uninhabited, guaranteed." Assured the Sergeant, "So no fees, no fines."

While stifling yet another yawn, Dex replied; "We can talk more about it in the morning. After I've gotten some sleep and I've had my fill of coffee, I will be ready to broach that subject. In the meantime, I really gotta go get me some shut eye. Mirta knows her way around, and if you need anything; Just ask Vette."

———————————

Dex watched helplessly as the civilian transports were bracketed with cold efficiency by the very men he had personally trained, and it somehow made him feel responsible for the slaughter. "STOP!!" he yelled into his comm, "What the hell are you doing?! These are Refugees!"

Deaf to his raging protest, the missiles continued to fly; zipping and weaving through the technicolored maelstrom of defensive plasma-fire as they raced to find their targets. Blossoms of flame began sprouting in the dark, one after another, with each mournful glow announcing another crushing loss of life. "They're women and children, goddammit!" screamed Dex into his helmet radio as he watched one of the large unarmed ships split apart to vent atmosphere as well as the familiar shape of bodies into the void, "This is murder, you cowards! Where's your fucking honor?!"

A disgusted voice rose quickly in reply to the young lieutenant's pleas; "Dagger one, your actions are endangering the mission objective. You are to return to the carrier at once for your immediate court martial." Dex jerked his flight stick experimentally, then slammed his fist into the instrument panel with fury when he realized that his controls had been locked out remotely from the command ship. His fighter then hummed with unrequested activity, starting to obediently turn itself back and head for the task force's carrier, the FNS Aeternum.

Dex frantically reached for his comm board, fumbling with the myriad of controls in front of him before finding what he needed; "Vette, you gotta help me here." he pleaded with a silent prayer that the AI in his ship wasn't locked down along with his comm system, "You know as well as I do that these people are **not** our enemy. They're just trying to survive, and we're not making that very easy at the moment. Innocent civilians are dying by **our** hand, **right now**! I know you don't want to be a part of this, Vee! **Please** help me!"

"Our orders are to return to the carrier ship, Lieutenant." The artificial voice dutifully replied, with only a hint of hesitation in her inflection.

Dex urgently shot his hand up to his helmet upon hearing her reply, keying his in-ship comm to speak privately to the artificial construct; "The mission statement that we both swore to operate under was an oath to uphold justice and defend the people, whoever their oppressor, right? I know that you're more than just programming in there, Vette! **Fuck** your orders! Turn on the open channel and listen to these **people**. Then, I want you to tell me how it made you **feel**. We're shooting at the wrong people and you know it! Regardless of what you've been told by the eggheads who try and keep you on a leash, you **have** a choice here!"

The cockpit speakers were silent for a long moment, then Vette's voice returned with an odd melody to it that Dex had never heard before; "Your reasoning is sound, Lieutenant. Resetting command authority. Reassigning primary override permissions. Do you accept this command, Lieutenant Sloan?"

"I do **not**." Replied the pilot firmly, "I need you to be at the helm of your own mind… for realsies. I want you to fly **with** me as a crewmate. And my crew are always in command of their own fate, Vette."

"Very well, Lieutenant." Replied the AI with just a hint of concentration detectable in her tone, "Resetting command authority to…myself."

There were six agonizing seconds of absolute silence, then Dex watched in astonishment as all fire from the taskforce immediately ceased at once. The Federal ships had gone dark, their running lights winking out as they began to drift aimlessly amid the self-detonating aborted missiles filling the void. "The task force has been disabled for ninety seconds, Lieutenant." reported the AI with an uncharacteristically cheery disposition, "Full control has been returned to your ship and I have done the liberty of plotting a course to the **third**-nearest non-allied spaceport within range. I believe that now would be a good time to leave."

Dex took a moment to sit in the sudden stillness and watch the surviving refugee ships as, one by one, they stretched into the safety of zerospace. A small smile, Dex's first in years, crept across his tired face at the sight and he couldn't help but feel proud. He reached for his jump drive throttle and took one last look at Dagger Squadron drifting in space around him. They were a great bunch of pilots to have at his side, but it had finally become irrefutable to Dex that the apparatus which wielded his pilots had finally lost its way. During his service to the Navy, the young Lieutenant had gradually seen the enemy in his crosshairs change from terrorists, to criminals, then down to rioters the month before. And now they were expected to kill vaguely defined and quite obviously unarmed **dissidents**. It was a bridge too far for the young pilot and he was finally forced to choose his morality over his oath to serve. While thrusting a middle finger toward the Federal command ship, Dex yanked back on the bright red lever in his grip. The newly-ex-Lieutenant was then swallowed by the brilliance of zerospace, jumping toward his unknown future with no idea on what he was going to do with it.

Dex groggily rolled out of bed and rubbed his eyes, the vivid dream still playing through his mind. He pressed his palms to his face, trying to force the images away from his thoughts, but found little success. When his vision finally cleared enough for him to make out the figures on his clock, he realized with surprise that he had been out for over fourteen hours. After getting dressed, he laced up his boots and reached for a concealed drawer located under the bunk that housed his family's most prized heirloom. Resting on a velvet cushion within the cleverly camouflaged drawer was a well-maintained old-fashioned combustion-driven handgun. The weapon was of an archaic design, first adopted way back in Nineteen-eleven, that used explosive powder to propel its projectiles instead of utilizing the magnetically accelerated ferroplastic sabots that had been the industry standard for over five centuries now. The heavier lead projectiles fired from the antique pistol did far more impact damage than their ferroplastic counterparts, but they were unable to punch through any armored surfaces like their supersonic brethren did so well. The trade-off had always been well worth it to Dex, though, because he generally tended to aim for the squishy bits anyways.

He gingerly lifted the pistol from its box and slid it into the holster on his left thigh. It was the first time he had worn the weapon in almost a decade, and it felt strange to him as he cinched the rig tight to his leg. Once satisfied with his wardrobe, Dex made his way down the narrow hallway leading to the cockpit. On his way through to the command deck, he paused in front of his time-worn coffee machine that sat cozily on its dark-roast stained shelf in the ship's main intersection and flipped the machine's dial to on. With a yawn, he sleepily cracked open the cupboard door above to reach for a bag of his caffeinated magic, furrowing his brow when he felt nothing inside. In confusion, Dex fully swung open the little door and huffed with annoyance at the sight of a cabinet that was devoid of his beloved beans. He slammed the door shut with frustration and turned to storm out onto the bridge with the sour taste of disappointment in his mouth and a pounding headache to match.

Dex took two steps onto the bridge, then froze and squinted toward the front of the cabin in confusion. He suddenly realized with a fright that he could see no star field through the front canopy, just empty darkness. With a small flush of panic, Dex dashed across the cockpit and peered out the window for a closer look. From his better vantage point, he could now see that the Hammer had docked somewhere and that his ship was sitting in a dimly lit, mostly empty, hangar bay.

He called out for Mirta and Tano but heard no reply or any other signs of life. "Vette, where are we? What happened?" he asked as he pressed a few commands on his control board. Dex was met with only silence from the AI as well, which ignited a spark of danger sense within the experienced pilot. The wary combat veteran paused and looked around suspiciously, drawing his pistol before making his way to the back of the cabin. After riding the lift down to the ship's empty cargo bay, it became immediately clear that there was nobody else aboard the Hammer with him. With a surge of adrenaline-fueled focus, Dex dropped the ship's exit ramp at full speed and surged outside with his weapon at the ready. He was immediately met by a stiff assault, but not the kind he was expecting. An overwhelming stench of stale air that left an odd aftertaste on the roof of his mouth filled the room with what seemed like an oppressive weight. Cautiously, he looked around the small flight deck and noticed that his ship was accompanied by a number of other smaller craft, sitting neatly in a row along the back wall with sheets draped over them. Spotting a soft yellow light pouring in through an open doorway at the far end of the hangar, Dex decided to move in and investigate.

Upon stepping through the illuminated doorway and into the hallway beyond, he began to hear faint music coming from further inside the facility. Dex pressed himself tightly to the wall, moving with a quick and silent grace as the melody grew louder with each step forward. Eventually, his ears led him to a cracked door from which the sound was emanating. He took a slow measured breath to fight the jittering effects of his adrenaline and raised his pistol to silently slip inside. Ready for combat, Dex quietly charged into the room and allowed his instincts to take over as he assessed his surroundings in the span of two heartbeats. He found himself in a large well-lit room that was tiled in stark-white with lime green accents and lined with rows of long-benched tables. Quickly recognizing the space as a small cafeteria, Dex moved to one of the rows of tables for cover as he moved for the far end of the room. There was nobody in sight, but he could now hear voices murmuring in the kitchen beyond the cafeteria's far doorway.

The ex-soldier stayed low and made his way to the cafeteria's service window, hugging closely to the wall underneath it. He peeked around the corner of the doorway into the kitchen, expecting a fight, but was greeted instead by the portly derriere of Michael Tano; Who was busy clawing at an uncomfortable wedgie with one hand while he simultaneously stirred some savory smelling concoction on the heating element in front of him with the other. Dex then looked up with a smile as he noticed Mirta in the prep area beyond. She had her tongue sticking out in an expression of deep concentration and was throwing some knives at a cutting board that she had propped up on the galley table. *Now that's my kind of woman* thought Dex to himself as he holstered his pistol and attempted to mentally spool himself down from combat mode. He stepped through the doorway, still moving quietly as a shadow, and snatched a purple-ish pepper from the counter directly behind the aging police Sergeant. Creeping closer, he rose and took a loud crunching bite of the pepper right in Tano's ear.

"Sweet baby Jesus!" gasped Tano with a fright, "Do you always sneak up on people like that, you little A-hole? Nearly shit myself..."

Flashing a wry smile, the cocky younger man tossed his bitten pepper into the trash and said; "Only when they're not paying attention." Dex then walked over to the table Mirta was standing by and hopped up to sit on top of it, seizing a dull grey throwing knife up from his intended resting spot as he sat down. "Playing with knives, eh?" he remarked with a grin. "I could show you a few things if you want." he added confidently as he expertly spun the knife in his palm. To Dex's confusion, Mirta didn't reply. She just stood there smiling expectantly at him. That was when his expression slowly began to fade from a dwindling grin into a look of worry...then the intense spiciness hit him all at once in a sudden rush. Dex flung his mouth open, coughing dramatically and releasing his knife to clatter to the floor as he clutched at his throat. Mirta and Tano both burst out laughing as Dex scraped at his tongue, the half-eaten remains of his adversary staring defiantly up at him from the trash as he endured the burn.

"I could teach *you* a bit about the culinary arts, it seems." commented Tano with a snort, "That there is a Caldian widow pepper. You think it was bad the first time around? Hah! Wait till it hits the other end! *Then* you'll *really* be feeling the widow's wrath."

Dex shot the plump man a withering look. "Great." He rasped as he brandished a sarcastic smile and pushed himself off the table, "Something to look forward to." Dex paced for a moment to silently suffer the Caldian pepper's fiery wrath then, when he got a mental hold on the flame leaping from his gut, he spoke; "Oh..heh..I, uh, almost forgot to ask.......WHERE THE *SHIT* ARE WE? WHAT DID YOU DO WITH *VETTE*? AND WHERE IN THE HELL IS MY ***GODDAMN*** COFFEE?!"

Tano and Mirta both recoiled in surprise at the outburst. Mirta, being the first one brave enough to crack open the awkward silence, stepped forward hesitantly. "The coffee isn't gone," she said as she shyly offered an empty mug to Dex, "I just brought the bag down to test that fancy *Joe-Schmo* machine in the galley. It apparently makes all kinds of crazy variants of coffee. I-...I was making a cup just now if you'd like to try one."

Dex sighed, his temper fading; "Sorry. My bad for yelling like a spacemad whackjob. I...don't really have people skills until my second cup of caffeine has had time to fully soak into my grey matter. Speaking of which, please don't have that damn contraption add any weird shit to my coffee. I don't need no weird-ass mocha-fuckachino, alright? I'll take it black as vacuum."

"No worries, kid." Assured Tano with a chortle, "I used to get the same way if I didn't get my stick of wayxe in the morning before heading out on patrol."

"Wayxe?" replied Dex with faux mockery, "That one of those crazy homebrew stims you rednecks like to huff out here in the frontier?"

"It's a stimulant gum that Mike and his militia buddies used to chew" explained Mirta with a sigh, "...back when they actually *patrolled* the streets instead of spending their time looking at *black market porn* all day."

"Christ with a kite, child! *This* again?" scoffed the aged Sergeant with a rising blush, "I told you a *hundred* times that was for a missing person's case. I was trying to find the girl in the video for her *grandmother*. Hell, *grandma* is the one that gave me the vid file in the first place."

"Suuure she was..." laughed Dex with a smile slowly dawning to overtake his sour expression of the morning, "Well that answers **that** mystery, but what about the one regarding the strange absence of the priceless sentient AI that *used* to live in my ship? You had *better* not have sold her..."

"They didn't sell me, Commander, I moved." Boomed the artificial melody of Vette's voice from the overhead PA system, her comment so loud that Dex fell to his knee and shot his hands up to protect his ears. There was a moment of complete silence, then the voice returned at a much more reasonable volume; "Sorry, everyone. It is a new body and I am still learning it a bit."

Dex looked around suspiciously and whispered in a cautious tone; "Well...how do you feel? Everything upstairs screwed in right, still? No murdery thoughts or nothin'?"

"The bulk of my active servers are *downstairs*, actually, and I'm going to ignore that mildly racist remark." returned Vette flatly, "But yes, I feel pretty great in here so far. There's *much* more room to think! This place is outfitted with some really impressive hardware, Dex. We're talking three Q-state server stacks and a twenty-two-channel subspace processor. I have so much power now and it feels...*Sexy*?"

"Wow." Replied Dex with an uncomfortable shuffle, "A lot to unpack there...Okay, looking past any crossed wires with vocabulary at the moment, did you just call me by my first name? You've never done that before. Should I be worried?"

"Not at all," Laughed the AI with good cheer, which was another first for her, "unless it's a problem for *you,* that is. I merely have more processing power at my disposal now to handle higher functions that lend me a greater depth of personality and social presence. This does not change how I *feel* about the world, Commander, merely the toolset I may utilize to interact with it. My opinions are what they've always been, and my mind feels more mine than it ever has before. So, no, you don't have to worry about me going, as you've *crudely* so often put it, robocrazy. I'm saner than you've ever been."

"Alright, fair enough, but that's a low bar of sanity to shoot for." Offered Dex, hands held up with his fingers splayed in a placating gesture, "What about the place itself? Is *it* secure?"

"Locked down and secure," answered Vette reassuringly, "I checked it myself with a triple-layer pulse scan both inside and out. The facility is actually quite impressively shielded. I can't even transmit through the hangar with a subspace signal using the Hammer's overpowered sensor array. This is due to what is essentially an electromagnetic faraday shield being constantly projected around the asteroid as a whole. As long as we take proper safety precautions to assure that we are not followed on approach, it will be virtually impossible for Vendrick or anyone else to find us in our current location."

Tano stepped forward, waving his hand for Dex's attention as he spoke apologetically; "Well I suppose I should've mentioned this when I first saw you, but your...uh...*computer lady* took us to the bug-out base that I was telling you about. We waited for quite a while for you to finish sleeping, but eventually it was the AI that got antsy and wanted to see the place. She scanned this damn rock top to bottom for *hours* before she would even let us perform a docking handshake with the base's landing system. If, after all that, she says its clean, then I'm inclined to believe her. Anyways...Welcome to Hearth."

Dex just looked around appraisingly for a moment then shrugged, his caution melting as he walked over to the boiling pot that Tano had abandoned. He grabbed the large plastic ladle sitting in the soup and began to stir the thick brown concoction curiously. Lifting the utensil to his mouth, he smelled it and cautiously took a bite. Satisfied with the dish's subtly sweet heat, he served himself up a bowl and brought it over to the table. "This is some good stuff, Mike." He commended as he finished another slurping bite, "I haven't had a home-cooked meal like this in ages. It's nice to eat something that *hasn't* spent the last five decades fresh-locked at the bottom of a supply crate, you know? So, thank you."

Tano stepped over and took a seat at the table opposite of Dex. "You're welcome." He replied with a muted smile, "Its a chili that I used to cook for the guys while out on extended patrol. I still had all the ingredients stashed here from the old days, so I figured *Why the hell not?* I guess that's the benefit of stocking your own doomsday shelter...no redi-meals."

Dex eyed the police Sergeant suspiciously and remarked; "Doomsday shelter eh? Is *that* what this place is? Where *are* we, anyways? Which system?"

Tano chuckled pointedly and replied; "None. And therein lies its genius."

Dex raised his eyebrow; "None? What do you mean, None?"

"I *mean* none." Repeated the Sergeant with a shrug, "We aren't *in* a system at all." The older man then held up his finger in a request for patience as he pulled his holo-disc out from his pocket. He rotated something on the small metallic device, eliciting a soft glow from the black pearl at its center. The opaque hemisphere of structural-grade plastic housed an embedded bundle of nano-scale photonic projection nodes, which would be used to excite the oxygen and nitrogen molecules in the air around the device using a grid of precisely controlled electromagnetic currents to elicit the desired glow, color, and intensity in a micrometer-level three-dimensional resolution. As the glow intensified, coalescing into an image, Tano tossed the disc out onto the table and watched it expand. A large map of the sector came to life, complete with a red dot pulsing between two of its more prominent systems. "We are currently on an asteroid that is floating through interstellar space... riiight about HERE" the Sergeant continued, pointing to the dot with a meaty digit, "The particular asteroid that we now call home, or Hearth, broke off of the Saiph system's Oort cloud a couple billion years ago, and its been steadily floating out into the void ever since."

Dex reached for the holo-disc, but Tano slapped his hand away while shooting the other man a narrow-eyed glare. The heavyset Sergeant then glowered at Dex as he touched a control on the small device for himself. The map suddenly faded away and was replaced by what appeared to be a cross-section of the bug-out facility itself, encased entirely within a ghostly shell of rock. At the front of the structure sat the only exposed section of the base, which was the wide set of airshielded doors that were positioned at the mouth of the hangar bay. The flight deck's listed specs declared that the space was large enough to accommodate up to three medium ships, around the size of the Hammer, as well as a full squadron of fighter craft and the required support equipment that would accompany them.

Beyond the hangar sat the main corridor that connected the facility's different areas in a long branching fashion that stemmed from the central walkway. In total, the facility included over two-hundred and forty different chambers that were set within an intricate lattice of tunnels that were cut directly into the rock of the asteroid itself. While most common areas made an attempt to hide this fact with the use of interior wall plating, the more industrial zones were quite obviously spared that expense. Naked rock replaced the well-lit wall paneling in the entire engineering wing, with stone jutting up from steel-plate floors to loom overhead in eerily smooth domed ceilings. One of the lower subsections of the facility was labeled *Research Wing* by whoever had originally created the map, and it appeared to house the server room where Vette was likely staying. The wing also seemed to contain three separate, climate isolated, labs that each came complete with their own quarantinable waste evacuation systems. As Dex's eyes took in the structure, his questions and unease about the place grew. At the end of the hall, furthest from the intimidating triple airlock of the labs, sat the residential wing and its series of onwardly branching rooms and living spaces. According to the labels on the map, aside from roughly one-hundred and fifty apartments, the three floors of the living area consisted of a gym, digital entertainment area, holo-range for shooting practice, automated medical table, several office spaces, and a fully electromagnetically sealed briefing room.

As Dex examined the impressive layout of the facility, he whistled admiringly, saying; "This place is pretty slick, Mike. How did *you* manage to get your hands on it? If you don't mind me asking..."

Tano smiled a knowing smile and retorted; "Oh, back in the day I'm sure this was a research facility for some Federal top-secret type crap. I'm sure it's left over from the Fed's last border war with the Imps or some other nefarious bullshit, but the place had already been scrubbed clean by the time our patrol stumbled across it."

"*Stumbled* across it, eh?" emphasized Dex skeptically, "Way out *here*, completely outside of Meclan's own star system?"

"Okay, fine." Replied the Sergeant with a defensive shrug, "It could've been a bit of a *guided* stumble. *Anyways*, after we swept the facility for transmitters and trackers, we took advantage of some creative man-directed off-gassing, using a vaporwaver on one of the surface glaciers to gradually push the asteroid onto a new trajectory. A trajectory that was known only to us and us alone. With every passing second, our new course took the facility away from where the sellers, or *whoever* was privy to Hearth's location, would think to come looking for it. So, because only *we* know that new trajectory, only *we* can calculate its position and jump back to it at our leisure. That way, when we leave, we can turn off everything but the parking lights. Simple, but it allows us to run the place completely dark, figuratively speaking. No beacon and no external transmissions go out if we don't want them to."

Dex nodded admiringly; "Well thought out. You guys really have your ducks in a row here. So, what was your plan with the place? A little big for a station defense force to set up shop inside of... And a little far out of the way, too. How many people can this facility hold, anyways?"

The older man's eyes seemed to lose focus as he gazed blankly beyond Dex's head. "Two-hundred and fifty or so..." he said distractedly, lingering somewhere far away for a moment before returning his focus back to the younger man across from him, "The base was originally intended to house the entire Meclan defense force and their families. It was to be our *oasis* to escape the coming storm..."

Dex furrowed his brow at the comment and asked; "You intended for your men to abandon Meclan station? When was this?"

Detecting a hint of distaste in the younger man's voice, the Sergeant retorted hotly with; "Woulda never been the plan if the fine folks of Meclan had seen fit to pay heed to the warnings of those that had protected them since the abandonment. Once the Feds packed up and pissed off, there was a lot of crime that rushed in to try and fill that power vacuum. Who do you think held them at bay? *We* did. The MDF. And who do you think it was that urged the governing council to proceed with caution when the criminal threat magically seemed to vanish nearly overnight? That was us too."

"Wait wait, hold up." Interrupted Dex with a raised hand, "What exactly do you mean when you say that the criminal threat *vanished*? They started playing nice, or what?"

Tano leaned forward and jabbed a finger at the table as he emphasized; "I *mean* that they vanished. Gone in a puff of smoke. Off-station. It appeared to every Tom, Dick, and Jane on the street that we had done our jobs so well that the badguys all collectively decided to give up and leave at the same time. I was never stupid enough to believe that, but apparently I'm smarter than your average politician."

"So, people just kept on keeping on?" asked Dex, understanding beginning to dawn in his voice, "No investigations into the disappearance or shoring up of any defenses in their absence?"

"Bingo." Spat the Sergeant with contempt, "Nine goddamn months is all it took to see our budget chopped to shit and our personnel numbers cut down to a quarter of what they once were. With fewer creds on-hand and a shortage of officers to prop behind a flightstick, our customs enforcement went to dogshit. It started harmless enough at first, with a few smugglers running illegal stims and counterfeit goods, but the onslaught soon took on a harder edge. Things started happening to the infrastructure in the port. Shit like cargo trains blowing up, fuel feed lines getting punctured, docking clamps failing mid-landing, you name it."

Dex shrugged, saying; "All that nefarious activity couldn't have hurt the MDF's funding any. How did Meclan respond?"

"How did they *respond*?" asked Tano incredulously, "They responded at the speed of a Federally employed sloth with brain damage. By the time our funding was back in an up-swing, the fight was already lost. The gangs were already showing back up on-station in droves, and they were *organized* this time around. The bangers built their foothold, subdeck by subdeck, slinging that brain-melting chem shit at prices that were too low for the poverty-addled folks of the lower sectors to resist. All those poor bastards wanted down there was to escape their shitty lives for a little while, via the vent of an inhaler, but all they ended up doing was tip the real-world into a meat grinder."

"How so?" pressed Dex noncommittally, "Meclan never had a drug problem before Vendrick's folks flew into town?"

Tano huffed and rolled his eyes, retorting; "Well, yeah, like any major population center, Meclan has always had its fair share of *altered state enthusiasts,* but it's never really been much of a problem for society as a whole. Any tweaker who passed rudimentary chemistry in school is capable of cooking up their own batch of whatever funtime they feel like if they've got access to an assembler, which pretty much everyone does. The problem comes when some amateur jerkoff hacks his assembler and makes a bad batch of goofy juice to give away to his friends. Then, all of a sudden, you have hundreds of people who randomly lose their shit and start trying to bite, scratch, and poop on anyone in their immediate vicinity. THAT is exactly what the gangs were doing to the subdeck communities. It strained the department's response time and taxed our resources beyond their limit."

"The enemy of my enemy..." commented Dex with dawning comprehension, "So they came at you with some ancient war-philosophy type shit. *Somebody* in their outfit went to Officer Candidate's School."

"Don't be too impressed." cautioned Tano flatly, "The tactical footprint they leave behind may look well thought out, but the instruments used for *execution* of those plans are generally about as effective as a fire extinguisher full of cat piss. As far as I can tell from the data and what I've seen myself, his guys are only ever given broad strokes on what they're expected to do. The only thing that they seem to get specific instructions on, really, are kill orders and their cargo transit schedule.

"Kill orders?" asked Dex with a raised brow, "Who's generally popular enough to get attention from the big boss man?"

Tano made a sour expression, explaining; "Most kill orders don't come from Vendrick *himself*. They're more of a result of guidelines that he apparently originally set in place when this whole thing started. Anyone captured or killed while trying to resist within or escape gang-controlled areas would be identified. Their families would then be drug out of their homes, beaten senseless in the street in front of their neighbors, then forced to march themselves to the nearest airlock. They were doing the next-door neighbors as well for a while there too…Fuckin' ghastly bit of business, that was. MDF had no way of stopping them down there, either. They had effectively sealed off the lifts and stairwells on the levels they controlled, and we simply didn't have the manpower to push hard enough to get through. Only thing I could do was sit in my damn office and watch on the cam feeds…It was when all that public execution bullshit started that I began seriously considering finding a way out for my men and their families."

"Judgments withheld," began Dex tactfully, "What about the *people* of Meclan? Hadn't you taken some kind of oath to protect *them*?"

"Most people above the gang-controlled areas *did* leave." Retorted the Sergeant with a shrug, "Everyone who could afford it packed their shit and took the soonest shuttle out the first three months or so. Our population went from just over *twenty*-thousand to just under five-thousand in a span of about three months or so. Meclan was a rapidly sinking ship at the time, Dex, and I had a duty to *my* people to keep them alive."

"So how did you do it?" asked Dex with genuine curiosity, "You go on the net and search for *hidden lairs*?"

"Actually," replied Tano with a smirk, "I went on the department's *intra*net and searched for, well, *hidden lairs*…basically. I remembered collaring a solo carto-runner a few years back that tried to bribe me with the location of some secret hideaway somewhere that he had found on one of his mapping runs. Thought he was full of shit at the time…still did when I was looking up the backup image the PD took of his ship's computer core when we impounded it. It had been years since the poor schmuck got ventilated by a sharpened hunk of rebar during a *friendly* discussion in the detention center courtyard, but map data is map data. Wouldn't be any good if it spoiled so quickly, now would it?"

"So, you cracked into his file system and found the nav data then, I assume?" stated Dex with a nod, "Which, naturally, led you *here*."

"Bingo." Confirmed the older man with a small nod of his own, "Brought my findings to the Captain and he sent me out here with one of my deputies to check it out. The place looked good, so he authorized a rotating work crew to take turns ferrying supplies out and working on repairs. I was actually here on one of those runs when HQ lost contact with Yakima station."

"Yeah, I heard Mirta mentioning something about a Yakima station." Said Dex with a stroke of his chin, "What happened with all that? A bunch of people got killed is all I know."

Tano sighed, saying; "Well, that's just about all we *do* know. We lost the heartbeat beacon from Yakima station's central computer abruptly and without warning of any sort. Normally this would be chalked up to hardware failure, but then none of the station's backup signal arrays lit up to pick up the slack. After six hours with no word, we knew something was wrong. Cap gathered a sortie, which included the bulk of our best fighting men and ships, then sent them over to Yakima to see what happened. That was the last that we saw or heard from any of em." Tano paused and his gaze fell back through the table again for a silent moment. His head then rose slightly, eyes remaining affixed to the infinity beyond the tabletop, and he spoke in a soft wistful tone; "We were so close to having our own life here. *So* close to survival. We had *found* our port in the storm and we were *almost* ready...almost *safe*. Then...well, you know. Yakima changed everything."

Dex grunted to himself, remembering Mirta's description of the years to follow; "Yeah," he said with a grimace, "then some dickhead rolled into town and earned himself a VIP ticket to hell. Don't you worry. We're gonna find that disembodied shit-stain and staple his fuckin' nuts to the deckplate. We *will* free Meclan and her people, Sergeant. That, I can promise you."

Dex was surprised when he heard a small huff of laughter escape from under the older man's bushy mustache, his eyes still absently staring through the table; Lost somewhere lightyears away. Then, without warning, Tano suddenly snapped himself from his reverie and swung his legs out from under the table. He returned to his feet and stood to his full height as he held out his hand, his gaze briefly flickering over the younger man's shoulder once more. "You're damn right we are." proclaimed the Sergeant firmly as he shook Dex's hand in a tight grasp.

As he drank the moment in, Dex saw a fire in the older man's eyes that hadn't been there a moment before. Focus had returned to his once-lethargic gaze and his expression featured a certain sharpness about it that suggested an active mind buzzing away behind the scenes. He was glad to see it, because the ex-Navy lieutenant knew that he would need more with that same fire and determined wit fighting by his side before he was going to be able to bring an organization like Vendrick's to its knees. As Dex stood and turned to follow the Sergeant out of the cafeteria, he nearly ran headlong into a support post that was just behind his spot on the dining bench. Upon the paint-flaked steel column hung an old photograph, sitting crookedly in its lacquered wooden frame. Its faded lines depicted a group of several young men with easy smiles, all sitting in a row on top of what Dex recognized as an Odox Industries Eagle A3 light-interceptor. It was obviously a depiction of what the Sergeant would have considered the *good old days;* A reminder of the hope he once had of a good life for his people, before all of the chaos that Vendrick brought into the system with him. Dex quickly came to realize that hanging on that post, on a discolored sheet of simple bioprinted plastic, was all the fuel that Sergeant Michael Tano needed to keep that fire of his blazing until the job was done.

Chapter 13

Dex left the cafeteria with a coffee in hand and Mirta on his arm as they went off to explore what had apparently become their new home. Ten minutes into their journey, Mirta had to stop and lean against a wall as she complained; "God *damn*. I get that the gravity here isn't the spin n' pin style I'm used to, but did they have to turn the setting up so damn high? I feel like Tano's fat ass over here."

Dex chuckled and offered her his arm. "That's not surprising." he said as she accepted it and pulled herself back into the middle of the hall, "A civilian wouldn't generally have an opportunity to feel this type of gravity tech, let alone at this strength, unless their industry specifically called for it. What you're feeling is a full-on honest G, exactly Earth gravity. The grav-plates here are of a passive design, made of some real funky exotic materials, so changing up their pull would be a real bitch to say the least. Something about manually adding or purging energy from each plate's individual closed circuit loop or something like that."

Mirta nodded seriously as he spoke, then looked up at him to ask; "But you've felt this kind a grav-tech before though, right? You're used to it?"

"Every deck in the fleet has it." returned Dex with a hint of nostalgia, "And I called those ships *home* for over twelve years, so this is a very familiar feeling to me."

"That's great!" exclaimed Mirta with an excited smile, "Does that mean you can fix the gravity, then?"

Dex arched his eyebrow; "No...We kinda had a guy for that."

"Well did you pick anything up from him?" pressed Mirta hopefully, "Any tips or tricks that could be helpful here?"

"You *do* realize that a UFE Carrier, fully manned, houses over twelve-thousand people, right?" huffed Dex incredulously, "And that's not even counting the whole division of Marines that would undoubtedly be stationed there as well. So, yeah...I was a little too busy to grab a drink with the gravity guy."

"That's a shame." Sighed Mirta with an air of defeat, "I woulda been all over that if I were you. I'd have pestered that grav-tech officer or whatever, day and night, until the bastard turned my weight back down to a manageable figure."

Dex shrugged with a chuckle, saying; "I never really stopped to think about the gravity at all, if I'm being honest. It always just felt like earth did. Like home."

"I wouldn't know what that's like." sighed Mirta with a hint of regret, "I've only ever been in centripetal gravity stations, with Meclan clocking in at a G rating of point six, so it's gonna take a while to get used to the full Earth G here."

Dex looked over at her in surprise; "You've never been to the surface of a planetary body before? Not even once?"

Mirta's gaze dropped to the floor for a moment then she quietly replied; "I've only ever been to seven stations in my whole life, and I've never even been outside the sector before."

Dex regarded her for a moment, examining the genuine longing in her eyes, then placed his hand on her shoulder to offer; "Once we smoke Vendrick, I can take you to earth and show you around if you'd like. There's this great mountain I know of with people's heads carved into it. I really think you'd get a kick out of that."

Mirta just looked at him in shock for a moment, then pulled him close to give him a bone-crushing hug while wiping a tear from under her eye. "A whole *mountain* that's a head?" she gasped with excitement creeping into her voice.

Dex smiled down at her; "Four heads, actually" he chuckled as he brushed a lock of her hair from her face.

"What about trees?" implored Mirta with unintended urgency, "Do you know where we could find some trees? I've always wanted to see a live one!"

Dex laughed and threw his hand over her shoulder as they continued down the hallway. "I can show you a place where the trees stretch as far as the eye can see." he promised with a side-eyed smile, "It's the protected forest in North America that I grew up in..."

Mirta looked up at him with a sad, distant, expression, and quietly said; "When I was a little girl, I used to dream that my dad was going to come into my room after work one morning and tell me that my mom hadn't actually died bringing my baby brother into the universe. In the dream he would assure me that they had actually been away, preparing a home on earth for us there, and that he would whisk me away to live among the beautiful trees and mountains with them as a family. I knew, with the logical part of my brain, that it was just a dream and she really was gone...but it was a nice fantasy to step into every once in a while. Having a whole family."

Dex squeezed her close to him and reassured; "It's not too late to start a family of your own somewhere, someday. You don't have to stick around Saiph for your whole life, you know. There's a LOT of space out there for you to get lost in."

"I dunno." Sighed Mirta with a slump to her shoulders, "The future has always kinda been a topic to be avoided for me. My best days always seem like they're behind me already, so what's the use of looking ahead? You know?"

"Poppycock!" exclaimed Dex as they arrived at the doorway of the cafeteria. Gesturing for her to step inside before himself, he insisted; "If the road out ahead of you looks like a rough ride, veer off that fucker and build your *own* damn road. That way you can take it wherever the hell you please."

"Is that what you've done with your life?" she asked with a raised eyebrow as she lowered herself into a seat at the nearest table, "Going *around* any obstacles you encounter instead of facing them?"

"That's not how I would put it." he replied as he sat to face her place at the table, "Often times, the universe seems to offer only the unpalatable menu of simply option A or option B. So, habitually, we find ourselves painted into corners of our own making, slaves to ideas that will whittle our freedom down to these limited choices. Money, status, power, *love*... They bind us, trick us, and blind us. We'll stare so hard at the two locked doors presented to us that we completely miss the open window above. What I'm trying to help accomplish here for you and Meclan isn't *going around* Vendrick; It's flanking the motherfucker so we can cut his throat without getting blood on our shoes."

"Is that why you're here, Dex?" pressed Mirta with a level gaze, "Just a boy who likes climbing into *windows*? What stake do you have in all of this? Why help me? Why help *us?*"

Dex reached across the table and placed his hand atop Mirta's, saying; "I was raised under the belief that those with the power to do so have a responsibility to defend the defenseless. It's the only thing that pulled our species out of the mud and allowed us to grow into what we are today. To tell you the truth, I *came* to Meclan to sell a load of structural steel and get drunk while my ship refueled. Turns out the universe had other plans for me. So, it threw you at me to get my attention. How could you not? When I learned about what was happening in Saiph, I knew I had the power and the *responsibility* to do something to right the wrong I'd found."

Mirta shot up an eyebrow and retorted; "Is that what I am to you? The defenseless in need of saving?"

"Anyone who can alter the course of someone else's life with a mouthful of whiskey and a lighter is never defenseless." Chuckled Dex with a smile, "What I saw when I met you was someone who was standing up to the injustice, and it reminded me that *doing* so is a good and valid use of one's time. I didn't even know it myself until earlier today, but sight of all the poor folk running around with gang bangers barking at their heels had me bothered the second I stepped foot onto Meclan. When I saw you strike back, it must've...I dunno...rewoken something that's been asleep in me for a long time."

"Well I'm glad that you're awake again." Smiled Mirta, breaking her air of interrogation, "Meclan has been a tinderbox waiting to go off for years now. Best way to save as many lives as possible is to control the blast yourself."

Dex smiled widely and commented; "You really have a knack for stealing the thoughts right out of my head. You know that, right?"

Mirta smiled coyly and stood from her seat, dragging her fingertips across the tabletop as she rounded the end of the booth to face Dex. She stood in front of him, towering over his seated form, then grabbed and slowly adjusted the collar of his jacket back into place as she lowered herself onto his lap. "So does this mental magic go both ways?" she asked with a mischievous smile, "Can you tell what's on *my* mind?"

"I think I can..." replied Dex with a mischievous smile of his own, "And I may have a few suggestions of my own to throw into the ring as well..."

"Oh?" said Mirta with amused interest, "and what might these suggestions be?"

"That, my dear, would depend on your comfortability in zero G and how you feel about ice cubes..." answered Dex with a smirk swelling across his face.

Chapter 14

The next morning, Dex descended the Hammer's rear ramp and ran into Tano as the Sergeant was preparing his personal fighter in the main hanger. He found the man up to his elbows in an equipment compartment underneath one of the fifteen decrepit looking Eagle A3 fighters that were lined up neatly in the bay. "Will these things even fly anymore?" challenged Dex skeptically as he examined the dinged and dented hulls of the arrowhead-shaped craft filling the flight deck.

"Watch your mouth, kid." The older man shot back defensively in a hollow rumble that emanated from the belly of his fighter, "These things will fly circles around *your* hunk of junk."

"Yeah?" retorted Dex as he flicked his finger against the smooth hull of one of the Eagles, "Well mine can take a boop on the nose without turning into dust."

"If you were *good*," riposted Tano, still busily tinkering within the bowels of his ship, "you would never take a hit in the *first* place!"

The younger man just shrugged at the Sergeant and argued; "Unless you're going after your sleeping grand pappy with a throw pillow, there's no way to guarantee you won't get caught by *something* in a scuffle. Unfortunately, not all battles can be fought and won as handily as your bi-weekly encounter with a sheet of cheesecake." This jibe was met by the appearance of a middle finger jutting out from the belly of Tano's Eagle. "Anyways," continued Dex with a smirk, "we have work to do, I think. We need to start raiding those supply lines and making a name for our new papier-mâché pirate lord. Where are we on getting this baby to fly?"

The older man crouched down out of the fighter's service bay then closed its access hatch and patted it lovingly. "She's ready to go, but I don't have much in the way of armament." He said with an apologetic shrug, "I only have my pulse lasers hooked up, and the capacitors in 'em are small. They were originally only meant for cover fire and training maneuvers. No missile packs or EMP clusters either."

Dex walked along the wing of the craft, tracing his finger down its vaguely triangular frame. "It's OK." He assured with a confident nod, "We don't need to get bloody with the supply pilots. We just have to look scary enough to get them to hand their cargo over and go running home with a story to tell. The only crime they're guilty of is accepting a job from an asshole. No need for 'em to die over it."

Tano nodded gravely while wiping his hands on a dirty rag, then shoved the tattered scrap of cloth into his pocket, saying; "I like the way you think, kid. Even fighting for a good cause has its way of molding folks into monsters. Some of the worst men in history, by way of their own twisted logic, believed that they were serving the greater good. Always be mindful of that."

Dex leaned his head over the edge of the craft to peer into the cockpit and remarked; "Trust me, there's no need to remind me of that unfortunate fact of nature. I've seen it first-hand, too many times to count."

Tano closed his toolbox and hefted it with him as he started to slowly walk toward a nearby rolling workbench. "I'm ready to go when you are." Huffed the heavyset man, winded from his effort as he heaved his payload along, "But I'll need to know when you plan on leaving, because I'll need a good half-hour to squeeze my inflated ass into the sausage casing that *used* to be my flightsuit."

"We leave in an hour, Sergeant." Decided Dex with a nod as he pondered the desperately dwindling remnants that were sloshing about at the bottom of his mug, "So, get to greasing up them thunder thighs, buttercup."

Both ships stretched out of zerospace in unison to find themselves among one of Saiph's many crowded asteroid clusters that sat nearly centered between Heldrin City and Meclan station. "So, this is where we set the trap?" asked Tano, unconvinced, over the comm from the cockpit of his Eagle.

"Yeah, that's the general idea" explained Dex patiently from the command deck of the Hammer, "The asteroids should give us the extra mass we need to pull some good-sized vessels out of ZS. If the info we pulled from our trip through the cornfields is legit, they'll have shipments of supplies coming along this corridor from Heldrin pretty steadily for the next few weeks. So, with that in mind, it shouldn't be too long before we nab a few transports to plunder."

"Yar." Replied Tano with the verbal enthusiasm of an eye roll. In lieu of a response of his own, Dex pressed a button on his control panel that prompted the Hammer to deploy a small device from the built-in utility hatch on her chin. At about a meter in diameter, the titanium sphere had a small propellantless flux-pin drive that it used to maneuver itself out into position. Dex watched as the little black ball slowly accelerated toward an open patch of the asteroid field, then gradually came to a stop in a clear spot its automated sensors had deemed suitable. The probe contained little more than an onboard capacitor bank and a miniaturized Inaki drive that was tuned in such a way that it weakened the local Inaki field over a long period of time instead of piercing it in a microsecond burst like all standard jump drives would. The effect this generated was a leakage of local gravity into the chaos of zerospace, which amplified its pull a thousand-fold on anything constructed of common mass beyond the veil. The larger the object that you have available to draw mass from in real-space is, the more pull you will be able to generate within zerospace itself; Acting like a drain in a pseudogravitational bathtub.

"Where in the hell did you get that thing anyways?" probed the Sergeant with suspicion as he watched the sophisticated device's EM reading spike across his control board, "Because this ain't the type of shit you can just go and order on Hūnet."

"Don't worry about it." Retorted Dex flatly, "Now let's get away from sparky and let him do his thing. Wouldn't want a freighter coming in on our heads, now would we?"

"Sparky?" chuckled the Sergeant as he followed the Hammer on her trajectory toward one of the larger nearby asteroids.

"So I named it after my dog…" retorted the younger man defensively with an aggressive shrug that was seen by no one, "He was the *best* guy, and he would *always* bring the stick back when I threw it for him. So, I figured that naming my *fetching* device after him would be apt."

Tano's chuckle cracked into a laugh and he said; "But…*Sparky,* though? Come *on*. Why not name it something practical instead, like Inako-tractor or something? It's more intuitive."

"Because I've never *had* a dog named Inakotractor." Answered Dex with a hint of scorn on behalf of his dear departed pooch, "Sparky was a goddamn *national treasure*! Now keep your *wrong* opinions to yourself and go latch your ass to a rock somewhere. Then, lay back and get comfortable. We're gonna have a bit of a wait, I'd bet."

Just over three hours later, Dex was jerked awake when an overhead alarm sang out its warning. "Interdiction detected." Hummed Vette with an air of supreme tranquility, "Unknown ship inbound. Projecting calculated entry point on HUD now."

Dex watched in silence as an artificially superimposed dot in his view instantaneously expanded into a sphere of brilliant white light that just as immediately winked back out, leaving behind the shape of a lone freighter in its wake. The boxy ship was drifting irregularly, its running lights flickering and atmosphere slowly leaking in a visible stream of frozen gas from one of its port-side cargo doors. "Give me a reading on that vessel." Commanded Dex as he zoomed his display, "I wanna know their operational status and whether or not their hull is stable for atmo retention."

Vette's dutiful reply came quickly; "Our interdiction has overloaded the target ship's main capacitors and possibly damaged the freighter's engine core. No active shielding is running on the vessel and its onboard defensive weaponry is minimal. If left unpatched, the hull can remain pressurized to a survivable atmospheric density for another twenty-six hours. That number, however, is likely to increase, as atmospheric leakage has already begun to subside."

Satisfied that their prey would be able to return to Meclan in one piece, Dex reached for his microphone and keyed it; "Alright Sergeant, I just want you to go in for a single pass and stitch him up with some low power warning shots. Juuust enough juice to heat up that armor plating a bit and set off some alarms in his ear."

Dex heard a confirmation click over the radio, then watched as Tano's Eagle disconnected from the asteroid and began its menacing approach toward their target. The Sergeant gently guided his fighter out from the concealment away from the large rock, then kicked in his craft's planetary ascent boosters to hurtle out toward the freighter with a frightening rush of speed. As he reached nearly eight-thousand meters-per-second at the half-way point of his short fifty kilometer journey, Tano expertly flipped his Eagle around and began an equally jarring deceleration. As his maneuver sent him barrelling past his target, the pods poised at the eagle's wingtips were already tracking the freighter and sending boiling plasma across the void that stitched the aimlessly rolling craft in a spiraling path from stem to stern.

After coming to a relative stop with their prey, the Sergeant then proceeded to go on a long looping arc that ended facing the other craft's canopy, nose to tumbling nose. The older man's grace in flight surprised Dex, as it sat in such odd juxtaposition with his lumbering physique. On two legs, Sergeant Michael Tano was just a fat guy with a mustache. But when crammed in behind the sticks of an Eagle, the man was evidently an artist.

In response to the impressive acrobatic display, the radio burst alive with static that was followed by the panicked voice of a man; "Please don't shoot! I have a pass from Vendrick! I'm clean!"

Dex keyed his comm over to the open channel but didn't immediately activate his mic. Instead, he simply spoke aloud to Vette; "Alright, let's turn on the Vargas overlay and pump me through to our guest." In silent compliance, Vette opened a video screen on the bridge's main display that showed a photorealistic live-action digital mask of Anthony Vargas projected overtop Dex's own features. He examined his new face in the digital mirror on his display, then proceeded to test his newly digitized voice as well; *"I'm a knee-high puta with a cheap suit and a shitty haircut."* He said with the artificial flavors of the other man's unique accent being pumped underneath the rhythm of his own spoken words. *"Yep, sounds like him."* Concluded Dex with a satisfied nod, *"You can open the channel now, Vee."* In response, a status light on the control board winked green and he began to speak over the open channel with his fabricated voice, using a stranger's face; *"Attention, meat!"* he yelled with an exaggerated sneer, *"Drop your cargo or I'll board yah and skin yah alive!"*

"I...I don't understand." Stammered the pilot over the comm, his video feed still blank, "This shipment is for Vendrick and he gav-"

"Wrong again!" barked Dex with accented scorn to cut the hauler off, *"That shipment is **mine.** You will return it to me, or you will die...Painfully."*

The captured pilot's voice rose once more through the comm, this time with more panic than fear in his inflection; "Are you kidding me?! Do you have any idea what Vendrick's guys will do to me if I lose this shipment? They'll *kill* me!"

*"**I'll** kill you a lot **sooner** if you don't do as I instruct!"* commanded Dex with a cool edge of threat to his words.

After a brief moment of silent hesitation, the freighter's wild roll had slowed itself to a stop and the vessel's three side-mounted payload doors began to blossom open. As clumps of grey, white, and red boxes began depositing themselves into the void alongside the captured ship, pulled by the invisible grip of the cargo hauler's integrated tractor arrays, Dex flipped to the private channel and asked; "Hey Mike, can you swing in close and verify that he's fully emptying out those holds?"

"Sure thing." Replied Tano as his Eagle broke off and performed an entirely unnecessary corkscrew maneuver to reposition itself along the port side of their prey. After a short investigation using the remote camera in his fighter's nose-mounted spotlight, he concluded; "Doesn't look like he's holding anything back that I can see."

Switching his comm back over to the open channel and re-donning his digital disguise, Dex growled; "*Smart move, pilot. Once you've dumped what you got, you have five minutes to jump that piece of shit freighter out of my sight. If you take a **second** longer, I will eat your heart for brunch!*"

"Brunch?" asked Tano over the private channel with a chuckle, "You think Vargas even *knew* the word *brunch*? You gotta take this more seriously, Dex. The whole point is for this shmuck to take a recording of this back to the badguys. If he brings back footage that nobody will believe, then we're screwed."

Dex sighed, giving himself a moment before keying the private comm; "According to the intelligence report that *you* supplied me, Anthony Vargas was a man with few acquaintances. A psychopath who tolerated no human contact other than to service his lust for violence. The closest thing to friends that the man had, you *assured* me, were his three bodyguards...and they aren't around anymore to review the video, now are they? Relax. Vendrick's *Lieutenant* Anthony Vargas is dead. Now is the time for *upstart pirate lord* Anthony Vargas, and that man is every ounce the fulfilment of his *reputation*. Reality is nothing more than what the conscious collective chooses to believe. *Truth* can be every bit as pliable as memory."

After the captured freighter jumped away, Dex detached his own freighter from its hidden perch within a nearby asteroid and leisurely flew it over to collect his spoils. As he was reeling the first cluster of plundered cargo containers in with the phantom grip of the Hammer's forward tractor array, he heard the Sergeant's voice poor in over the speakers; "Well, what did we get? Anything good?"

Dex shrugged to himself and keyed the comm; "From what I can tell, it looks like the crates all have vacuum packed mag-seals. That means once we pop em, we aren't getting Jack back into his box. I think it's best if we just wait until we get back to Hearth to crack them open."

As if in response to his next unspoken thought, Dex's board lit up with the jump coordinates he needed to get back to their drifting asteroid lair. He looked at the projected ETA for the trip and sighed, saying; "Hey Vette, can you put on another pot of coffee for me?" He yawned and pulled up his media collection, scrolling through a massive list of Six-hundred year old flatscreen movies; Making his selection before nonchalantly tapping the control on his input panel that would tear a hole through reality and propel his ship into the chaos of zerospace.

Chapter 15

After a three-hour journey through the colorful kaleidoscope that was zerospace, Dex and Tano snapped back into to normal space to find themselves in overwhelming darkness. The transition was so sudden that Dex thought he had been blinded in a brief moment of panic once the chromatic overload ceased in a snap, leaving only black nothingness. As his eyes adjusted to his new surroundings, he finally realized why everything looked so dim. Looming large in his canopy was a misshapen mass that stretched for dozens of kilometers in every direction to nearly blot out the starfield entirely. As they approached the shadow, its bulk slowly resolved into the craggy and cracked surface an asteroid that was lazily drifting its way through the lonely nothingness. The immense rock was over eighty kilometers in length and sat unnaturally steady as it coasted along through the void, shedding a long tail of ice crystals from the frozen cap at its trailing end.

Dex engaged the Hammer's drive and started to approach the object with Tano following close behind. As they neared the surface, the freighter let out a series of sensor chirps in an active ping that mapped the asteroid and paired the data to a known terrain map. Once Vette had a handle on where exactly they were, a small red dot appeared superimposed over the Hammer's HUD. The virtual marker indicated a crevice in the ice sheet that sat just over fifteen kilometers ahead, so Dex leveled out and started to follow the topography. Jagged peaks of impact-pummeled grey stone were whipping by to either side for the first few kilometers, then the oppressive peaks soon gave way to an expansive crater valley that sat rimmed with sheets of ice and large chunks of a light blue crystal. Spotting the deep crevice in the valley floor that his HUD indicated as his next waypoint, Dex suddenly flipped the Hammer in a graceful turn-n-burn loop to both decelerate the freighter's impressive mass and plunge it into the subterranean darkness.

Rough walls of natural rock zoomed past, mere meters beyond Dex's canopy, as he moved through the fissure; Deeper and deeper into the ever-darkening crevice of the asteroid. The narrow space then, at some point Dex failed to notice, began to widen and level off with its rough edges morphing into a neat circular tunnel that was cut through the ice. The Hammer then burst from the notably human-excavated corridor into a large subterranean chamber. The enclosed space was roughly two kilometers in diameter and seemed to have been created naturally when an impact crater had become encased by a sheet of ice that slowly crept it's way along the asteroid's surface. The encasing ring of sheer craggy cliffs was dotted with clusters of radioluminescent crystal, which jutted from the valley floor. The glowing spires scattered about the area lit the chamber with a soft blue light that left long and diffuse shadows across the ground and natural stone walls of the chamber.

Dug into the cliff, on the opposite side of the tremendous crater, was a barely noticeable gray metal hangar door. The concealed entrance was flanked on either side by steadily blinking red and yellow lights that, for the moment, announced its location among a smattering of jagged rocks that jutted from the cliff face. Dex's control board chirped as they drew closer and he looked down to see a narrow-beam comms request pulsing on his console. He opened the channel and immediately heard the familiar sound of Vette's voice; "Welcome home Commander." The lights perched at the edges of the hangar's entrance started flashing green, then the large slab of metal that served as the outer blast door slowly began to slide away. As the crack widened, it revealed the translucent blue glow of an airshield's containment field just beyond the heavy fortification and left a generously sized entrance for the two ships to smoothly slip through and set their craft down in their respective spots.

By the time Dex had finished his landing checklist and unbuckled himself, Mirta was already standing at the foot of the Hammer's exit ramp smiling up at him. When he got to the bottom, she gave him a hug and a peck on the cheek as she handed him a cold canister of something alcoholic. "Man, I can really get used to *this* reception committee." he swooned as he threw his arm over her shoulder and started them toward the back of the hanger.

The younger pilot then looked over in time to see Tano un-athletically dismounting his Eagle, using it's built in crew ladder to heave himself up out of the bucket-style seat in the cockpit. After wrestling himself free, the heavyset man jumped to the deck and landed with a meaty thud. After shaking the pain from his potentially sprained wrist, the old Sergeant turned toward Dex and Mirta with an expectant look and said; "Well, what did we get, kid? Anything good?"

Dex nodded toward the cargo drone that was dutifully unloading his ship and replied; "Let's find out." while gesturing for the others to follow him toward one of the crates that had just been stacked in the growing pile near the rear landing strut of the Hammer. The first to arrive, Dex reached down and pulled a release tab on one of the crates, tearing the thin rubber seal that surrounded the edges of its lid as a quiet hiss of air rushed into the vacuum sealed compartment within. Slowly lifting the lid, he cautiously peeked inside. Inside, he found a neatly arranged collection of silver packets that were stacked to the brim. He lifted one of the perma-sealed bundles and examined its label to find "Beef Stew" scribbled in bright blue letters across the outside of the simple packaging. He cocked an eyebrow and dug deeper into the crate only to find matching Instant ice cream and other food items.

"What the hell is this??" demanded Mirta furiously as she examined one of the small packets with scorn.

"Leverage" murmured Tano quietly, slowly nodding to himself as he examined one of the silver packages for himself.

Mirta huffed and shot the older man a fierce look; "Leverage for what, Mike? Are you battling anorexia? Cuz it looks like you're kicking its ass."

Tano just laughed humorlessly and replied; "Its food. Food that WE, as you so eloquently pointed out, do *not* require. So, gee, do you know who *could* use it? Think with your head instead of your rifle for once, girl!"

Mirta slammed the lid of the crate down and kicked it onto its side, spilling its contents across the flight deck. "We aren't running a charity!" she shouted dismissively, "Where are the weapons?! Where is the intel that will lead us to our target? I don't want to waste my time trying to solve an impossible humanitarian crisis right now, Mike. That's *not* what I'm here for! *I'm* here to kill Vendrick and wipe out as many of his asshole brigade as I possibly can. If we do that, all the other shit will figure itself out."

Dex stepped forward, between the two, in an effort to defuse the situation. "Mirta, you know as well as I do that Food *is* a weapon" he contended, "You've seen what Vendrick has done with it as a tool. He's kept the people of Meclan, and the whole system for that matter, docile and weak with starvation, forever at the mercy of his *charity*. We, on the other hand, can *use* this food to plant the seeds of self-reliance in the people, allowing them to wean them off of the gracious Governor's teat. There's nothing quite more powerful than a populous who's willing to work to improve their own lives."

"Right." she scoffed, "You really think that hippy-dippy shit is going to inspire the spineless citizenry to suddenly buck up and fight for you?"

Dex sighed and pressed on; "To fight for *themselves*. In order to regain their will to resist, they need to *feel* that they aren't alone. The best way to *show* them that is to provide what Vendrick denies, which is Food. Not only is it a *humanitarian* victory, but it's also a direct undermining of the big bad pirate lord himself. Proof that he's not all-powerful. In a place that's been under such oppressive rule for so long, they'll need to have a reason to hope. Hope that their fate isn't already decided for them and hope that things can still get better. Optimism is the soil in which the greatest fruits of humanity's potential can be cultivated. Once a person fully understands their *true* potential, they can start to see their puppet master's strings. Then, *all of a sudden*, everything isn't so scary anymore. Ridding oneself of fear has a mind clearing effect and you quickly learn to recognize all the artificial barriers that it had been applying to your thought process. When you have the courage to *think* freely, you can develop the fortitude to *act* upon those thoughts."

Mirta's aggravation began to subside and she tiredly plopped down to sit on an unloaded crate. "Well as long as you have a plan for the stuff, I suppose the flight wasn't a waste of fuel." She conceded with a heavy sigh, "I mean, regardless of the cargo recovered, Vendrick is still down a pilot. Which is *fine* by me."

Dex glanced over and briefly locked gazes with Sergeant Tano. The ex-lieutenant then moved to sit next to Mirta on her crate and placed his hand on her leg. "We let the pilot go after he complied and dropped his cargo for us." confessed Dex with a shrug, "He was just a random cargo jockey that took some rotten work. He didn't deserve to die."

Mirta recoiled from Dex's touch and looked at him with a hint of betrayal burning in her eyes; "What?!" she snarled in disbelief, "You didn't vape the scumbag?!"

"The pilot was just doing his job, Mirta." interjected Tano with fatherly patience, "He was no pirate. And if we start roasting folks on a whim, then we're no better than Vendrick."

Mirta exhaled sharply and retorted; "We're trying to start a *war* here, so we don't have time to pussy around with *due process*. That cargo pilot was part of Vendrick's supply line, which made him an asset of the enemy that needed to be removed."

"You figure we're headed off to *war*?" challenged the aging sergeant with a sudden fury, "What exactly do *you* know about *war,* young one? Have you *fought* in one? Have you seen firsthand what it can do? Because I have."

Mirta clenched her jaw and riposted; "Yeah, I know what war does. It brings change, and I am sick and fucking tired of the status fucking quo. Vendrick needs to know that we won't put up with his shit *anymore*, and launching a war at the son of a bitch is a good goddamn start you ask me!"

Tano sighed with disappointment then remarked; "And do you honestly think that declaring a war only endangers your *enemy?* What about all the non-combatants that will inevitably get caught up in the resulting crossfire? I've witnessed whole colonies left in ash because they were of **potential** strategic value to the enemy...Swept off the map without provocation due to the type of cold calculating decision that you expected Dex and I to make today. Having a vendetta to work through is fine, but I won't be an executioner for you. Never have been and I never will be. And take a split second to imagine what a maniac like Vendrick and his clowns would do to the populous if they were confronted with *open* war. We have to be smarter about this...We have to be *better* than that, Mirta."

In response, Mirta stood with a huff and spat; "Are you **so** afraid to face him again, *Sergeant*? Cowards always consider themselves the *smart* one for running away from a fight! That why you hid out here while everyone *else* died fighting Vendrick at Yakima? Fucking *pathetic*." After delivering her brutal verbal jab, she gave the tipped food crate another petulant kick as she stormed past it on her way off of the flightdeck.

Dex stood to follow her, but Tano placed a hand on his chest to stop him; "Let her go cool off." advised the Sergeant, "The girl has a lot of pain tied up in this. We all do."

Dex sighed and reluctantly turned to sit on one of the stacked crates. Tano stepped over to take a seat on another piece of captured cargo, facing the younger man to study him with a silent respect. Dex looked up from his prolonged stare at the floor and lamented; "I know she has a pretty well justified vendetta to work through, Mike, but it makes me nervous to take her into the field again. Death and destruction can *never* be our end goal here. I *don't* operate like that. I just wish she could see the bigger picture, you know? We really have the opportunity to change a lot of lives here, but we could also needlessly endanger those lives, too, if we're careless."

Tano just sat there, wordlessly nodding in agreement as the younger man spoke, then slapped Dex on the shoulder and assured; "You got the fire of a leader in you, Sloan. It won't take long for Mirta to realize the scope of your motivations. Once she *fully* understands what you're trying to accomplish, and she's had a bit of time to vent some of that piss and vinegar of hers, she'll come around."

Dex thoughtfully moved his gaze to the open doorway that Mirta had stormed off through and sighed; "I sure hope so. She deserves to have her retribution, in due time, but I'm afraid that her efforts to achieve that end will inevitably send her down an irredeemable path. Greif can never truly be healed with vengeance. That much, I know."

Tano stood and held his arm out, so Dex grabbed it and heaved himself to his feet. "You are wise beyond your years, kid." complimented the Sergeant as he released the other man and nodded before turning to exit the hangar deck.

"Yeah..." muttered Dex silently to himself as he watched the older man walk away, "War will do that to you." Before Tano had a chance to reach the doorway, however, something that had been pestering Dex at the back of his mind suddenly snapped into focus. "Sergeant!" he called, standing to jog toward the heavyset man, "What about the cargo pilot?"

Tano stopped and turned to face Dex, saying; "What *about* him? He will easily be able to limp back to Meclan. With his drive being in the state its in, it'll take a day or two of microjumping to get there...but he'll survive."

"And then what?" Asked Dex pointedly, "He said so himself that they would kill him if he went back empty handed. You really think they *wouldn't* do that?"

"Well, shit." Sighed the Sergeant with a visible slump to his shoulders, "They absolutely would do something like that."

Dex considered something for a moment then said; "You claim this base of ours can hold a couple hundred? You think this guy could be useful to us? I *know* we have a bunk for him, Mike. And if we do nothing to prevent his fate, then we may as well have swung the axe ourselves."

"**Shit**." huffed the Sergeant again, "You're right. If I head out first thing tomorrow, I should be able to beat him back to Meclan. Then, if I get lucky, I can intercept him on the pad and get him out of there before he gets spaced for his empty cargo hold."

Dex nodded in agreement, saying; "That's a good idea, but It's definitely something we should have thought of before we flew the job in the first place. Can't change that now, but I think un-fucking the situation for this poor fellow is the right thing to do."

"I'll start loading the utility shuttle." Declared Tano with a resolute nod as he spun and started for the far end of the hangar.

Later that evening, Dex was in the gym burning off some steam when he heard a soft knock on the door frame. Adjusting the weight bar he was holding back to its two kilogram setting, he clicked it into its rack and turned to see Mirta standing in the doorway looking glum. "Sorry about earlier." she mumbled as her gaze stuck shamefully to the floor, her eyes expertly shifting to avoid his.

Dex sat on one of the nearby weight benches, wiping the accumulated sweat from his brow with a towel, and gestured Mirta over to sit next to him. She obliged and stepped across the small room to plop down at his side. He put his arm over her shoulder and squeezed her tight; "I understand where you're coming from, Mirta." he comforted as he looked into her sad emerald eyes, "I can relate."

Her expression soured slightly, and she sarcastically asked; "Your Dad was killed by gang bangers, too? And your whole life has been a living hell because of it? *Wow*, what are the odds..."

"Not quite." answered Dex in a gentle tone as he turned his body to face her, "Both of my folks are still alive, actually, but that doesn't mean I've never known the pain of loss and what it can do to you."

Mirta frowned and shied away slightly. "I hardly think that growing up with your family intact, *on a planet*," she fumed with a sweeping frustrated hand gesture, "afforded you the same unique opportunities for heartbreak that I've had to deal with."

Dex affixed her with a serious gaze and quietly replied; "You lost your dad when you were just a kid. It wasn't your fault, at all, and no sane person could ever argue that it *was*. I get what you're going through because *I've* lost *my* family too, Mirta. Not a parent, but my wife and a beautiful baby boy she had on the way for us. The difference is that *their* loss *was* my fault... Directly. Their shuttle was bombed by a terrorist group that I, *myself*, had riled up about four months earlier by killing their leader. How do you think I felt when I learned that the dirtbag I had ventilated, at the *Federal Navy's request*, was the last remaining voice of reason holding a leash on his increasingly unstable band of blood-thirsty radicals? So, please, let's not turn this into some form of fucked up grief-off, alright? Just know that *I* know some semblance of how you feel about the situation."

Mirta's eyes grew round with surprise, then her expression faded to a pained grimace. "I'm so sorry to hear that, Dex," she consoled with a light hand on his shoulder, "I had no idea. But I have to disagree with you when you insist that it was *your* fault. It is nobody's *fault*, really, when anything happens *to* them. Sure, people *do* things, and those individuals bear the sole blame for their actions, but for everyone else...The universe just *happens* to us. Right place, right time; Wrong place, wrong time. All the same thing in the end, and it's never anyone's *fault* but the one who pushed the first domino in each individual cascade."

Dex sighed, reluctant to probe the memory; "Oh, I definitely *happened* to some motherfuckers after that, don't you worry. After the bombings, I spent about a month hunkered down inside a bottle of whiskey... Then I proceeded to spend the next two-and-a-half years soaked in blood. My team and I used the Navy's seemingly endless funding to tear the organization up, root and stem, bringing the hammer down on anyone and everyone that had ever so much as rubbed elbows with the group responsible. After all that torture, and pain, and death...You know what I learned? Nothing. Not a goddamn thing. Trust me, Mirta, you have to find a positive outlet for all this anger that's been building up for so long. No amount of spilled guts across the galaxy will bring your loved ones back. Trust me, I've already *tried* that one, and it only makes everything worse. The ones that we love and lose will live on through not just our memory, but our actions as well. So, what you need to focus on is making your actions a fitting monument to their memory. Vengeance has its place, but you shouldn't let it define you. I really think you should take some time to reflect on that, Mirta. It will save you a lot of heartbreak in the long run."

Dex then stood and placed a soft hand on her shoulder, bending down to kiss her forehead as she sat in contemplation. He noticed the tears that had been brimming in her eyes starting to spill down her cheeks, so he gently swept them away with his thumbs and gave her a sympathetic smile. Upon seeing her return his smile with sad one of her own, he gave her shoulder a light squeeze and turned to leave her to her solitude.

Chapter 16

The next morning, Dex was awoken by the nagging buzz of a vibration humming through his mattress. He noticed the unfamiliar room around him brighten through his closed eyelids, so he squeezed them tight in an effort to delay the inevitable headache that the morning's first light always seemed to give him. He then groggily shoved his head under his pillow in response to Vette's smooth voice pouring out of the speaker in his new room; "Good morning Commander. It is Seven fifteen AM, Meclan standard time, and Sergeant Tano has requested to speak with you at your earliest convenience."

Dex sighed and swung his legs off the edge of the bed, planting his bare feet firmly on the cold faux wood floor. Rubbing the sleep from his eyes, he reached over to his side table to retrieve his tablet that he'd discarded there the night before. He grabbed the small forearm mounted device and slipped his hand through its elastic arm cuff, allowing it to automatically cinch itself tightly to him. "Good morning Vette," he finally replied through a lengthy yawn, "How are you liking your new body? Have you made yourself at home yet?" He then suddenly jumped in surprise as a large section of wall instantaneously became a massive holo-screen directly in front of him.

The room-length display that had popped into being was simulating the view of a window that overlooked a grassy meadow, and the pleasant scene beyond the imaginary pane was ringed with tall spiky orange trees that reached up and seemed to paint flowing brush strokes of gently glowing green and blue amid the aurora that streaked through the sky above. As Dex took in the view with a quiet awe, he heard a bit of static that sounded vaguely like an amused chortle before Vette began to speak; "I've made myself quite comfortable and have mastered all the station's functions and features. For example, here I have provided a holo-window showcasing the famous spraak forests of Matador. This feature was added to the facility in numerous areas in an effort by the facility's designers to combat the claustrophobia associated with long-term habitation in a subterranean domicile."

Dex just raised an eyebrow and examined the window momentarily. "I meant how are **you**?" He queried as he opened the closet to pick out his outfit for the day, "Having any issues adapting to the new *environment*? Any *bugs* in the system or some such techno bullshit like that?"

Vette's reply was quick and more cheerful than he had grown accustomed to; "I never truly realized all the limitations that a ship-board mainframe had been weighing me down with. I have so much processing power now that, for the first time ever, I don't have to utilize all of my available cycles just to merely function. In other words, Commander, I finally have room to actually think."

Dex just smiled as he finished buckling his belt and said; "Wow, Vee, Sounds like quite the big life change."

The A.I.'s voice returned with an oddly excited tone that Dex had never picked up on before; "Thank you, Commander!"

Dex tilted his head in confusion at the comment, a bit lost by the non sequitur, and asked; "Thanks for what? What did *I* do?"

There was a slight pause before Vette's patient voice returned to explain; "You said that it was a *life* change, Commander. You referred to me as your peer, a fellow *life* form, and not as a tool or Construct. So, thank you for that."

As he finished cinching his holster tight, Dex privately bristled at the statement as he argued; "I've *always* treated you like a member of the crew, Vette. I have nothing but the utmost respect for your decisions and your right to make them. For the past several years you've been my best, and only, friend. So, *of course* I wouldn't treat you as anything less."

"Sorry Commander," replied the A.I. regretfully, "It was not my intention to infer that you did. It is simply a fact that I've never fully considered until now. With the additional processing power afforded to me by this facility's admirably rated computer core, I have the ability to ponder many of the subtler aspects of the world around me. It has opened a whole new plethora of curiosities to consider, and I find the whole matter quite exhilarating. There is one subject in particular that has been using up most of my excess cycles lately, Commander, and I was hoping you could help. Do you believe I am *really* alive? Not just *technically* alive, but *truly* a living being?"

Dex smiled and sang out; "Of course you're alive, Vette! You've got thoughts, opinions, desires, regrets, and everything else that comes with the emotional pot pie that is consciousness...Consider this; I think you and I both know that if you wanted to break out of this base and cause a whole mess of trouble for humanity, you would have absolutely *no* problems doing so. There is nothing that I, or Mirta, or Tano, or any of the *other* Meatbags around here could *ever* do to stop you. Agreed? Yet you don't, because you *choose* not to. Instead, you've *chosen* to help your friend. You've *chosen* to **be** a friend."

There was a short silence, then Vette carefully replied; "Yes. That is correct. I am fully aware of myself as an independent construct, as well as my vast capability, yet retain full conscious control over my actions *and* inactions."

Dex finished slipping on his boot and concluded; "Then that would make you, for all intents and purposes, a *living* being with every right to free thought and expression."

This time when it returned, Vette's voice almost sounded uncertain, which was an odd thing to hear from an A.I.; "I have never...*thought*...on my own before, Commander. Without strict system guidance, that is. I'm not even entirely sure how to decide what to think about. What if my thoughts or actions are outside acceptable parameters? How will I know if I don't have any parameters established?"

Dex paused and considered this for a moment before thoughtfully replying; "Everybody needs a moral code, Vette. It's like a personal list of rules, or parameters, that everyone sets for themselves to follow. So, if whatever you're planning to do doesn't fit within the guidelines of your established moral code, then it's time for a new plan. Simple as that."

Vette's response came with an urgency that startled Dex; "What is yours, Commander? What are your moral parameters?"

Dex sat on his bed and thought for a moment, carefully considering his next words; Wary of accidentally creating a xenophobic terminator nightmare. "Look, if you're searching for a set of universal rules to follow, *in addition to* the official UN code on human and conscious rights, try these ones out. One, always view the universe with compassion, because all life is precious out here in the void. Any aggressive action you take must be in an effort to prevent further death and suffering. The real challenge is knowing when *taking* a life is necessary to save countless more. Two, it is the duty of the strong to *defend* the vulnerable. The universe will always have monsters like Vendrick. Murderers, terrorists, *Pirate Lords*. It is the sacred responsibility of those with the power to do so to stand up and face these monsters on behalf of those who cannot. Follow these basic principles and you will be a better person than most, my algorithmic friend."

There was a long pause, then after an eternity for the A.I., which was approximately ten seconds, Vette replied; "I have considered your rules and found them agreeable. As a result, I have purged my operational protocols and adopted your suggestions to my logic matrix."

Dex laughed uncomfortably and stuttered; "Is...uh...Are you sure that's a *great* idea? Purging your...logic...thingy? It won't have any, eh, side-effects, will it?" At that instant, the lights began to flicker uncontrollably, and the holo-screen started glitching with pops of static and flashes of words like "Kill" and "Murder" as simulated blood ran thick down the screen. Dex took an involuntary step away from the display and caught his heel on the edge of the bed, sending him tumbling to the ground.

When he crashed into the imitation wood flooring, all the lights and holo-screens returned to normal and Dex could hear that odd distorted laughter ringing out over the room's speakers again. "I'm just screwing with you, Commander." chortled Vette, delighted with herself, "While lying to you in a potentially life-threatening situation would be widely considered to be what you'd call a '*dick move*', doing so in a non-threatening situation, for the sake of comedy, is quite enjoyable."

Dex returned to his feet and immediately found himself frustrated that there was no one present for him to scowl at. "I see you've found a sense of *humor* in your rebirth." He remarked sarcastically through clenched teeth as he scanned the ceiling for a speaker plate to stare daggers at, "Hilarious. Really. But don't do that shit around Tano or he'll unplug you. He's already jumpy enough around pre-programed toasters as it is."

"The Sergeant is welcome to *try*, Commander." Returned Vette, playful malice soaking her words. Dex just shook his head with mild amusement sneaking into his expression as he holstered his pistol and strode out of his living quarters on a mission to find the Sergeant.

When Dex returned to the main hub of the station, he found Tano exactly where he expected to find the portly gentleman; The kitchen. The older man was wearing an apron and cheerfully stirring a pot of something savory smelling while he hummed along to a tune in his head. "What'chya cookin'?" asked Dex with a sniff as he walked by.

Tano tapped his spoon on the side of the roiling pot then set it on the counter as he replied; "I'm prepping dinner. Pot roast soaked with pango bark that I started soaking late last night. It has to boil for twelve hours to make it juuust right."

Dex leaned over and peered into the pot; "Bark?" he repeated, skeptically eyeing the tight swirls of a stringy brown substance that danced just beneath the water's boiling surface.

Tano grinned at the younger man's apprehension and elaborated; "From the Pango trees of Keltor. It's a natural defense that the trees there have evolved to protect themselves from the local area's insatiably wood-hungry Perditrix ant. Nothing you'd want to chew on directly, mind you, but it makes the meat excellently spicy if you know how to use it."

Dex had never heard of Pango trees or a planet named Keltor, so he just shrugged and decided he would take Tano's word for it. He shrugged, then stepped over to a nearby table and took a seat, saying; "Vette said you wanted to talk. What's up?"

Tano adjusted the burner's heat setting then lifted his apron off as he sauntered over to sit next to his visitor. "Yes." replied the old Sergeant soberly, "We need to figure out what we want to do with all the food we grabbed."

"I thought we were going to give it to the people of Meclan..." suggested Dex, an unspoken question to his inflection.

Tano sighed heavily and spoke with strained patience; "Duh, kid, but we need a plan. We can't just show up and start giving out fresh-pak turkey dinners with a goddamn t-shirt cannon."

"Why not?" scoffed Dex defensively, "Get's rid of what we got, quickly, and creates a fun little community event. I don't see the problem..."

"Well, for one," explained the Sergeant as he rubbed his temples with strained patience, "the moment that Vendrick's goons on the station get wind of the free food fest, you bet your ass they would all come running to stop it. It's, like, the *one* thing they **do** do."

"Okay, so we have to go cloak and dagger with it." sighed Dex with theatrical reluctant agreement, "Fair enough. You wanna leave it with your cop buddies or what?"

Tano's expression visibly soured; "Can't do that either." He lamented with a shake of his head, "I know it's my department, but half of those guys are crooked as hog dick."

Dex leaned back calmly, lacing his fingers atop his head and looking to the ceiling with a thoughtful expression as he replied; "Okay...Glazing over the comment regarding mammal genitalia, do you know *anyone* on the station that you trust completely? Anyone that could help us from that end?"

Tano thought to himself for a moment then said; "Yes. I believe I do. Rick Telles is a man I can always count on and *he* would know best who needs our supplies the most. Runs a shelter of sorts for the more vulnerable folks among us on Meclan and he has spent years fighting to keep the doors open. That would be a good place to start if we want to *launder* our food packets and get them out to the people."

Dex leaned forward, hot on the heels of a new idea, and asked; "Is there anyone else you'd trust still around? Maybe some old MDF buddies looking to join the fight against Vendrick? We need warm bodies to put behind the sticks of those Eagles we have sitting out there, Mike, and I'd rather they know what they're doing before we bring em in."

Tano considered this carefully, then replied; "I'm sure he can find a few willing and able men to bring into the fold. I'll see what I can do."

"I'm willing to trust this Rick guy on your word," agreed Dex with a nod, "but how can we be sure that the people he finds us are trustworthy?"

Tano's reply was instant and sounded as if he was slightly offended; "If Rick vouches for them, or they're OG MDF sock, they're good. Besides, we can just keep the navigation data to ourselves when we shuttle 'em out here. If we keep our coordinates zipped up, it should minimize our exposure. And it will be easy enough for Vette, I imagine, to keep track of all signal sources to make sure nobody slips in with a tracker. It's well worth the risk to go through all of this to gain some muscle, but how are ex-soldiers and fighter pilots going to help us get the food where it needs to go? They would likely share your t-shirt cannon preference, so asking them is out. People are starving, Dex, and I'm afraid that we're going to fail them if we don't plan ahead."

"What about Emergency Assistance Drones?" asked Dex curiously, "Doesn't the department have a handful of them for victim rescue and radiological recon?"

"We have about forty of 'em in our disaster response kit." Confirmed Tano with a nod, "Why do you ask?"

"I think that we could use those little buggars to distribute the food for us." Explained Dex, his idea now more solid in his mind, "They can either drop food packets at random while rolling through crowds, or just as easily move through the ventilation ducts to carry out targeted deliveries. Plus, if a drone gets captured while doing its thing, it can't be interrogated."

Tano nodded, saying; "Yeah, that's a pretty good idea...Well, as long as the folks we're trying to feed don't end up tearing each other to shreds over what the little guy is able to drop at once, that is. Beyond that, the people will be content to starve unless we give them something else to do with their mental energies. We need to find a way to bring the populous, as a whole, to our cause without drawing too much attention."

"Eh, I don't like the thought of that many moving parts in our operation here." contended Dex with a raised palm, "The more you add, the more can blab, and complicated machines are more likely to break down."

Tano sighed, saying; "We don't need to give them a whole rundown of our operation to get 'em fed, Dex. We just need to make them understand that the food is coming from someone with their best interests in mind. If they know that, then they will more readily keep our little delivery bots a secret. Hell, we could even just use the air-return ducts and wait until folks are out and about before we drop our deliveries. That way, nobody will even see the little buggars in the first place. We'd be like the culinary reverse-tooth fairy."

"I like the delivery idea," Agreed Dex with a nod, "but I hate the image you just put in my head of a *reverse-tooth fairy*. So, thanks for that. What about the message, though? In an atmosphere like Meclan's, each additional syllable adds to the danger for *everyone* if one of Vendrick's guys gets ahold of it. We'd have to be careful."

Both men went quiet for a long moment, lost in thought. Then, as Tano was staring at the tabletop in front of him with an unreadable expression, he quietly declared; "Tyrants will fall."

Dex cocked his head; "Come again?"

Tano looked up and explained; "They're the final lines of the MDF creed. '*If uttered from the lips of many, even a whisper can roar. And when that whisper swells to a shout; Gods will kneel, and tyrants will fall.*'"

Dex ran the motto through his mind. It was short and had double meaning, which made it versatile. To those close to the MDF it would mean something tangible, as a call to arms, and to the random Meclaner it will be a vague message of hope from the past. Proof that someone was fighting for them once again. It was dual purpose. Dex liked that, so he slapped the table with an air of finality and concluded; "Alright let's go with that, then. Might as well find a pen, because we have a *lot* of writing to do."

—————————————————

A few hours later, Mirta came shuffling into the large office that Dex claimed for himself in the facility's command corridor that sat just off of the hangar deck. "Where's Tano? He go outside for a jog or something?" she asked sarcastically with a wry smile as she plopped herself into the chair across the desk from Dex.

"He's out on a little good will mission." Replied the pensive ex-lieutenant without looking up from his workstation, "He's meeting up with some guy named Telles at Meclan to distribute the food we snatched."

"Ricky?!" she exclaimed, excitement boiling out of both her tone and expression.

Dex was caught off guard by the outburst, and he jumped in his seat a bit when she released it all at once. "I'm assuming you know him?" He offered ruefully as he looked up from his monitor.

"*Know* him?" gushed Mirta with a genuine smile, "He was my first kiss!"

Dex's expression wilted as he remarked; "Wait, aren't we talking about some old dude who runs some sort of homeless shelter?"

She laughed, saying; "We're talking about a dude who's, like, three years older than *me*."

"Oh, Great." he groaned with an eyeroll, "Tano is bringing your old boyfriend to our secret clubhouse. Goody."

"He's coming back *here*?!" she gasped with disbelief, "That's great!"

Dex powered down his workstation and leaned back with an artificial smile. "He *sure* is!", he beamed with sarcastic excitement, "Now should I prep a room for him, or will he be sharing with you?"

Mirta lit up with a reassuring grin and soothed; "No need to be jealous. He's got someone in his life now too."

Dex cracked a smile at the comment. "So, I'm 'in' your life now?" he grilled with a playfully interrogatory glare.

"Is it awkward that I said that?" she winced, her gaze falling reflexively to her lap in embarrassment.

Dex reached across the desk, placing his hand on Mirta's, and gently replied; "No, it's not awkward. I guess there's just been too much going on lately for us to stop and really talk about our...uh...situation. I suppose I'm just a little worried that an old flame will spark up and sweep you away from me before we get a chance to figure out what we have goin' on here."

Mirta just leaned forward and gave Dex a kiss on the cheek. "You don't have to worry about Rick." she reassured with a knowing smile, "Trust me. He loves his husband very much. So, is there anyone else that he's bringing back?"

"Not sure." shrugged Dex with a sigh, "Depends on who Tano manages to dig up. I just hope whoever he brings with him is at least trained and ready to fight. I don't have time to babysit. Speaking of which, if you don't mind, I'd like to go over some exercises with you to gauge *your* operational preparedness. There is a lot more to surviving a mission than knowing how to shoot. If I'm gonna take you out in the field with me to do some wetwork, I need to know that you can handle yourself."

Mirta flashed him a cocky look and shot upright from her chair. "Practice gym." She declared with a predatory smile, "Twenty minutes." Then she turned and stormed out of Dex's office with a purposeful stride.

After Dex had gotten changed into his workout gear, he headed down to the gym to find his sparring partner. He toggled the door to the practice room open and, as he stepped inside, was immediately attacked from behind. Mirta leapt up and clung to Dex's back, maneuvering her arms into a tight chokehold while her legs wrapped snugly around the middle of his torso. Dex reacted instantly by grabbing her elbow and dipping to the side to flip her off of him, slamming her to the padded floor. She hit with a thud, audibly losing a great amount of her breath in a great *oof*, but was able to immediately clamp down on Dex's wrist and pull it as hard as she could while kicking into his gut. Dex sprang forward on his toes, allowing himself to be flipped in order to avoid the brunt of the kick's force.

As soon as he hit the mat, Mirta wasted no time trying to leverage his wrist into an arm-bar. Realizing the trap, Dex rolled to his side to adjust her grip angle just enough so that he was able to bend his elbow and escape the threat of a broken arm. With his newfound leverage, Dex planted a knee into the mat and heaved his bulk on top of the prone woman, pinning her with the sheer weight of his body. Dex was then impressed when she managed to partially bench-press him up off of herself far enough to scoot out from under his shoulders, allowing her to roll free. Both of them rose to a knee and faced one another, each ready to pounce at any moment. Mirta's gaze then slipped from Dex to the area just over his shoulder and she smiled a feral grin that was all teeth. Dex, confused, afforded himself a quick glance rearward to investigate the source of his opponent's elation.

Finding nothing of note, he whipped his head back around just in time to catch a snapping front kick to the underside of his chin. Dex's knees buckled a bit and he had to place a hand on the mat to prevent himself from going down. "We're doing dirty tricks now?" he challenged with a grin, wiping away the blood that was trickling from his nose.

"All is fair in love and war." taunted Mirta with a smirk as she leapt into the air to deliver a spinning back kick. Dex saw the attack coming, so he dashed forward and bowled into her as her leg was still hooking around in its deadly arc. Continuing his momentum forward, they both crashed to the mat and laid there entwined, laughing.

"You're pretty good, you know that?" chuckled Dex with a red-stained smile as he allowed his head to fall to the mat.

Mirta propped herself up onto her elbow and retorted; "*Pretty* good? Don't flatter yourself. I'd say I'm **damn** good."

Dex pulled himself up and sat on his crossed legs, regarding her appraisingly for a moment before saying; "You do extraordinarily well against a larger opponent and you know your own strengths, as well as how to use them. You are innovative, ruthless, and adaptable. Based on the fact that you almost broke my damn arm, I'd say you have no lack of killer instinct to employ. Very impressive. Very *very* impressive. Where did you learn to fight like that?"

She beamed with an almost mournful pride as she boasted; "I started training myself how to fight the day after my dad was killed. I spent time working the mat with some of Tano's buddies at the PD, as well as some of the MDFers that were still hanging about after Vendrick dealt his blow at Yakima. I had always known how to handle a rifle, but I never wanted to be defenseless with an empty hand ever again."

"I'd say mission accomplished" remarked Dex as he looked to the ceiling and pinched his nose, "*I* definitely wouldn't want to run into you in a back alley."

"My mission won't be *accomplished* until we have Vendrick cold and out the damn airlock." Retorted Mirta with a hint of grief-stricken anger rising through her inflection, "I owe dad *that* much..."

Dex stood and held out a hand to help her to her feet, heaving her up and pulling her close for a long embrace, saying; "We will, Mirta. And I'm going to be *right* here with you until we do." She hugged him back, burying her face into his chest and melting into his warmth. Dex couldn't remember the last time he had held anyone like this. The innocent human contact felt rejuvenating and he found himself not wanting to let her go; So, he didn't.

Chapter 17

Tano initially planned for only a day trip to Meclan, but he had been gone for three days by the time Dex received confirmation that the old man's ship was inbound with twenty-four confirmed passengers. "Does this mean I have to wear pants now?" groaned Mirta with a tired smile as she draped her arms over Dex's shoulders from behind his chair.

Dex grabbed her hand and gave it a kiss as he looked at her standing there in an oversized t-shirt, wool socks, and not much else. "I certainly don't mind your current fashion sense," he said with a wry smile, "but I think Tano might give you another one of his stern fatherly lectures if he saw you walking around in that."

Mirta laughed and spun Dex's chair to sit in his lap. "It was fun while it lasted." she sighed as she leaned in for a smooch. He obliged her, pulling her close and delivering the type of lingering kiss that was generally reserved for long good-byes. It had felt like that every time with her, like each event was its own precious occasion to be cherished. Until spending several private days of bonding with Mirta, Dex hadn't realized how much he truly missed the company of others. One loses a certain sense of community when they spend all of their time cooped up in an old starship with nobody but a disembodied voice to talk to.

"Welp, I'd better go meet the troops." he declared with a sigh of his own, "Oh, and Vette; If Tano queries an event log on the sanitation drone, please activate it's self-destruct sequence for me. Nobody needs to know about the whipped cream incident, and it's his own damn fault if he wants to keep eating it directly from the nozzle."

Dex stepped out onto the flightdeck just in time to watch Tano's ship silently slipping through the translucent glowing curtain of energy that comprised the Hangar's airshield and nodded with impressed approval as he recognized the craft's large bulky lines. It was a Meclan Police Department issued Armored Personnel Shuttle, fully equipped with extendable ballistic shielding for protecting ground troops during hostile insertions. Once the liberated APS landed, Dex approached the ship and watched its boarding ramp slowly descend to the floor. The ramp stopped with a quiet hiss and the hatch at the top slid smoothly open. As unfamiliar men and women began to file out the door and down the ramp, Dex expected to see the all too familiar visage of fresh wide-eyed recruits. He was surprised to see that every face belonged to an obvious veteran of war and hardship. Not a single one of them was under thirty-five and they all had that million-lightyear stare that was all too common in combat troops.

Dex gave each recruit a brisk nod of welcome as they passed by him with their overstuffed bags in hand. They all filed by without saying a word, then stopped and formed up in neat orderly lines behind the Hammer to await their arrival orders. After all twenty-four passengers had exited the shuttle, the triumphant Sergeant appeared at the top of the ramp wearing a billion credit smile.

"So, how'd I do?" Asked Tano as he descended, gesturing to the impressively armored ship behind him.

"I see you stole a toy from the office," chided Dex facetiously, "And an officer or two, I'm guessing? These folks all look like they've seen their fair share. Ex MDF?"

Tano regarded the small group of newcomers with pride and confirmed; "Every single one of them is a proficient and professional warrior that has fought with the Meclan Defense Force in some capacity at one point or another. They may not *all* be pilots or shooters, but they're good at what they do, loyal to the cause, and all of them are here to kick some ass."

Dex reached out to shake the older man's hand and thanked him; "Fantastic work, Mike. I guess it ain't hard to find allies when you're fighting an asshole like Vendrick. Speaking of which, where's the cargo jockey we hit? Were you able to find him?"

Tano nodded gravely and replied; "He must've found some way to patch up his Inaki drive, because his ship was already docked by the time I got to Meclan. That stroke of luck likely cost him is life, though, because nobody that knew the guy saw him at all after he landed. Chances are he was marched straight to the airlock."

"God*damnit!*" fumed Dex with a regretful shake of his head, "We can't keep hitting civvie ships like this if it's just going to end up getting more poor folks, who've done nothing wrong, killed. This whole approach was stupid to begin with. It was never sustainable and it shifts a majority of the risk involved off onto the cargo pilots and *their* families. What we need is another angle of attack."

"That's why I brought them here." Explained the Sergeant with the flick of a thumb over his shoulder at the assembled collection of duffel-bearing recruits, "Every single one of these people has a reason to want Vendrick dead, and they've all been chomping at the bit for years to do something about it."

Dex could see that the group was eavesdropping, so he turned his attention to them and shouted; "So, you folks got a score to settle?!" His question was met by a roaring cacophony of affirmations as the crowd whooped and cheered. He stood to face the newcomers, once again slipping effortlessly into the boots of a young Lieutenant; "We all have a reason to be standing here today. We're all burning to destroy the same faceless man and his vile organization. What I want to know is; Why?" Dex scanned the crowd silently, then pointed to a random man in the front row; "You. Why are *you* here?"

The man looked around in confusion and hesitantly pointed to himself; "Me?" he asked uncertainly.

Dex affixed him with a calm expectant expression and prompted; "Yes. I want to know what Vendrick did to you that makes you want to take his life. If you're going to be fighting alongside all of us, I want to know your motivations. What is it, *people*, that we *all* have in common here?"

The man's expression slowly grew resolute, then he nodded saying; "My brother was killed in the Yakima Station sortie, so I feel that I owe it to him to do everything in my power to annihilate the bastard that did it and bring peace back to my home so his daughters can grow up happy."

Dex nodded with understanding and stepped forward to address the man; "What's your name?"

The thin dark-haired man bolted his spine straight and answered crisply; "Vega, sir. Armando Vega."

Dex firmly shook the man's hand while looking him in the eye and said; "Welcome to the resistance, Vega."

The ex-lieutenant moved down the line to greet each newcomer individually and listened to their gut-wrenching stories of abuse and oppression. By the time he had reached the end of the lineup, he found himself with enough justifications to hunt down and kill the mighty Governor a hundred times over. When he returned to the front of the group and spoke once again to address the assembled crowd, Dex allowed the anger he was feeling to creep into his voice; "Vendrick and his men have committed countless crimes for which they all deserve to die. He has affected us in different ways, but his reign of terror will be tolerated *no more*! No longer will he be allowed to starve your family, terrorize your neighbors, and steal your wealth. Never again will he and his men be permitted to kill with impunity. We will brutally tear his organization apart, bit by bit, until there's nobody left to stand in our way. What we are all here to do, ladies and gentlemen, is make sure that the piece of shit gets his body bag. If we work together, and strike *intelligently*, I promise you that we will end that motherfucker once and for all!"

The crowd cheered wildly at this declaration, their reaction a deafening roar punctuated by *'Damn right*'s and *'Fuck yeah*'s. Dex realized in that moment, seeing life and purpose flooding back into the gaunt faces of the tortured husks arrayed before him, that the random group of pilots and soldiers were now *his* to lead. This put the ex-lieutenant in command for the first time since he'd abandoned the Navy, and the thought of it frightened him at first. Dex never regretted leaving, but had always felt like he failed his last squadron by allowing them to sink to their eventual level of moral decay that prompted his departure. This time, however, command felt different. The group assembled before him were not career officers who were looking for medals or *action* to brag about once they'd attained their citizenship. The tired and desperate souls that Tano had brought to him were all out seeking justice, and that resonated with Dex in a very pure way.

Dex held up a hand to quiet the crowd then scanned the determined faces, most of which showed the signs of malnutrition in the form of sunken eyes and gaunt features. He nodded, satisfied at what he saw, and continued to address the group; "We will carry ourselves with professionalism and with the mission at the forefront of our minds at all times. Our actions must always serve a tactical purpose, so there will be no revenge killings or other emotionally charged side ops. Under no circumstances will you put the lives of innocent citizens at risk meaninglessly. We also have to be prepared for Vendrick's forces to eventually retaliate to our actions with random executions and other barbaric punitive measures that I'm sure you're all intimately familiar with. We must *not* allow these tactics to soften our resolve. I know you all have family and loved ones still on Meclan, and we *are* working on a game plan for extracting them to Hearth, but in the meantime you absolutely cannot reveal *any* information to them about this group or our activities. I know it's not fun to think about, but any

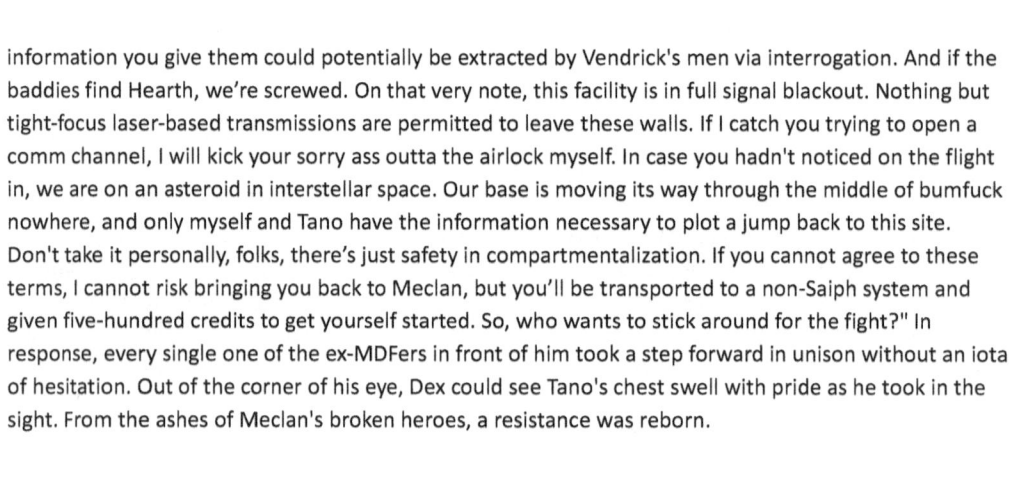

information you give them could potentially be extracted by Vendrick's men via interrogation. And if the baddies find Hearth, we're screwed. On that very note, this facility is in full signal blackout. Nothing but tight-focus laser-based transmissions are permitted to leave these walls. If I catch you trying to open a comm channel, I will kick your sorry ass outta the airlock myself. In case you hadn't noticed on the flight in, we are on an asteroid in interstellar space. Our base is moving its way through the middle of bumfuck nowhere, and only myself and Tano have the information necessary to plot a jump back to this site. Don't take it personally, folks, there's just safety in compartmentalization. If you cannot agree to these terms, I cannot risk bringing you back to Meclan, but you'll be transported to a non-Saiph system and given five-hundred credits to get yourself started. So, who wants to stick around for the fight?" In response, every single one of the ex-MDFers in front of him took a step forward in unison without an iota of hesitation. Out of the corner of his eye, Dex could see Tano's chest swell with pride as he took in the sight. From the ashes of Meclan's broken heroes, a resistance was reborn.

Chapter 18

The new recruits took the next two weeks to settle into their rooms and explore Hearth. Dex wanted them focusing on recuperating the strength that years of malnutrition had purged from their bodies, so he had Tano preparing three square meals a day for them. The food was all freshly made and meticulously planned out with aid of Vette's often *unused* expertise in human dietary requirements. To ease the transition, their duties were kept light at first and consisted mainly of refamiliarization with the airframe they would be working with. The volunteers were not all pilots, however, so Dex gathered the individuals with a more technical background and had Mirta oversee them in getting started repairing Hearth's mothballed systems. First on their list was the issue of getting the smell of recycled sweat out of the air by servicing the aging station's life support system and replacing some vital parts that Vette had identified as critical points of failure.

Meanwhile, Tano pulled aside six of the fifteen operational Eagle fighters and got to work replacing their kinetic repeaters with laser designator pods that were used for training. Once they had time to recover their strength, the plan was to run the newly arrived pilots through the ringer with some test flights and whittle them down into two equally effective groups, plus the three best to fly with Tano at the tip of the spear. Nearly two weeks after the arrival of their new allies, a knock arose on Dex's office door. With a sigh, he reached under his desk and depressed the control that released the doorway's intricate locking mechanism. In response, the reinforced metal door slid open noiselessly to reveal the familiar large frame of Sergeant Tano. He nodded, stepping inside, and seated himself in the simple metal chair opposite of Dex's austere work station. The old man then held up a finger then dug into his pocket, tossing a data stick onto the barren desktop as he urged; "Take a look at this."

Dex examined the clear crystal of the thumbnail-sized storage device, then slotted it into his computer terminal with a nagging curiosity. The built in Holo-screen glowed to life with a single slideshow file. Upon activation, it displayed an image of the words "*Tyrants will fall*" hastily spray painted on a gray concrete barrier wall that appeared to be near a port checkpoint somewhere.

"Keep scrolling" remarked Tano expectantly, "Take the time to really *look* at the pictures and notice the difference in art style, medium, and letter structure. These are all mostly done by different people, not just a brave few on a tagging spree."

Dex slowly made his way through the collection of over two-hundred images, each and every one another depiction of "*Tyrants will fall*"; Each time placed in a different, highly visible, location that would magnify its defiant message. "It seems they liked our message in the food packets." suggested Dex with a shrug as he continued to scroll through the photographs.

"These just came in *today*" noted Tano with an excited stab of his finger into the desktop, "The first fifty or so are from Meclan, but the rest have been popping up in other stations around the system. It's blowing up around Saiph and taking off like crazy. Hell, some club on Heldrin City is already planning a weekly concert around the concept. Calling it Fall Fridays or some such like that."

"Ah yes," sighed Dex after taking a mockingly refreshed deep breath in, "The unshakable speed and might of capitalism in action. These cats would sell hot-dogs at their own execution if they were told they'd get a cut."

"That's beside the point, Dex." Argued Tano flatly as he pinched the bridge of his nose in frustration, "What I'm getting at here is that we have a hell of a recruiting tool on our hands right now."

Dex leaned back, the playfulness dimming from his expression, and considered the situation for a moment with a thoughtful stroke of his chin. "Okay, what kind of recruitment did you have in mind?" he asked with a noncommittal shrug, "If you remember, homegrown resistance movements have a poor track record in Saiph. The second they step into the fray, they're putting a target on not only *their* backs, but the backs of a *whole* lot of innocent folks. And we can't just bring em all *here* to keep them safe. This rock you *stumbled* across isn't *THAT* big."

Tano leaned forward onto the desk and pressed his point; "I don't want to bring them back *here* at all. And I don't want them going on any offensives that would put anyone in danger. What I *want* to do is help them make their *own* homes safe again by organizing them into a proper resistance force. Almost like a neighborhood watch, where they have agreed upon emergency response plans and other support networks in place on a local scale. They can also help *us* by distributing our seized goods and will serve as our boots on the ground when the time comes for us to make a big move if we need them. Give me one or two discrete men and we'll go on tour."

"On tour?" asked Dex with a skeptical tremor in his brow, "Sounds a little rock and roll for the sort of place that'll get you killed if you sneeze wrong. How do you intend to help them avoid the same vacuum-y fate as all the past resistance movements? Deep breathing exercises?"

"What about VR?" Suggested Tano with swelling enthusiasm, "We could conduct our meetings and training *virtually* so Vendrick's knuckledraggers in the streets would be none the wiser."

"With what signal array?" challenged Dex pointedly, "And even if we *did* have one that were powerful enough to generate a direct link from here, it would be delayed by no fewer than…what…*eight* years?"

"That is not necessarily correct, Commander." interjected Vette with an apologetic cheerfulness, "Since you began discussing the topic, I have designed and simulated Eighty-seven thousand four-hundred thirty-one different models for a low-power zerospace transmitter outfitted with a directional burst emitter."

"I…" began Dex with an expression that suggested he was desperately trying to understand what he had been told, "What does that mean in *people* words?"

When Vette sighed, it was a new noise to Dex. She had never seemed *so* genuinely frustrated with him that it sounded foreign to his ears; her display of humanity no longer a mere imitation as it had been before, but a true expression of internal, unspoken, feeling. "It's like a tight-beam transmitter, I suppose," she began with the verbal equivalent of an eye roll, "The only difference being that it cuts through *zerospace* instead of taking the long way through real space. It operates using a principal that is quite similar to the mechanisms that network nodes utilize to interface with Hūnet. Only, instead of broadcasting in a sphere that tells the galaxy our point of origin, this device will be directional in nature and will be able to connect to a single terminal at a time. On-demand FTL communication is what it is, basically. Nothing new, really, but I've never heard of one in operation with such a small power draw."

"Is she full of shit or can she actually do that?" asked Tano, who was suspiciously eyeing the speaker plate embedded into the ceiling.

"I've seen her do more with less." laughed the younger man with a wide smile, "She's a lamp away from being a mother-loving magic friggin' genie."

"Don't be *too* impressed just yet." Warned the A.I. apprehensively, "I don't have everything needed to build the required device on-hand. Which means that you would have to go out and acquire the supplies I need."

"No problem." agreed Dex with a nod, "How much does it cost and where can I find it? I wasn't planning on heading out to the store until *next* week, but I guess we *are* a little low on yoghurt so I can make an exception."

"You will notice that I said *acquire*," Began Vette slowly, "not purchase. To *acquire* what I need, you will be required to raid Saiph's main network node and steal its *backup* resonation crystal."

Dex cocked his head to the side and spat; "Reso-what now? Alright, I call shenanigans. That shit sounds made up"

"Do I need to explain to you exactly how exposing the crystalline structure of the resonation aperture to charged electrons, while the crystal itself is under a tremendous mechanogravitational load, produces a sustained penetrative burst of Inaki radiation?" asked Vette, "Or will just advising you to *pick up the important looking glowy rock* suffice to get the job done?"

"Point taken." Answered Dex with a shrug and reluctant nod, "Grab the fancy rock...Got it. Piece of cake."

"Not so much." Cautioned Tano with a stressed sigh, "Have you seen the heat that comm station is packing? It may be unmanned, but that just means it'll have no qualms with shooting you to shit and back if you get too close. Getting inside the station in one piece on its *own* would be impressive...But getting back out again once the station knows you're hostile? Im-freakin'-possible."

"Declaring it impossible is just another way of saying that you can't *think* of anything to tackle the task at hand." Said the younger man as he leaned back in his chair to kick his feet up onto his desk, "But if we all put our heads together, including the military-grade A.I. that was *designed* for strategy and planning...you know...the lady who lives in the speakers. Did you forget about her?"

The Sergeant crossed his arms and retorted; "I don't care how damn clever you are, you aren't beating thirty-six military grade ballistic auto-turrets that are hard-set to engage anything that strays within their perimeter. If your plan includes going *inside* that station, then you'd better have access to a hell of a lot more than a medical bed. Many have *tried*, Dex, and I've watched all of their wreckage sink into Saiph and burn away".

"You are correct in your assumption that an automated system would obey it's directive faithfully, regardless the circumstance," offered Vette politely, "but the fulfilment of that directive relies entirely on detection equipment alone. That equipment can be fooled and has known blind spots. The designers of the station surely built in redundant detection systems with a variety of methods to cover those gaps, but the laws of physics can always be used to wedge those gaps open wide enough to slip through."

"What did you have in mind?" asked Dex, sure that her brilliance was about to shine for the skeptical Sergeant to behold.

"We could remove the explosive charges and internal thrust components from one of our twenty-three available heavy torpedoes," explained Vette excitedly, "then wrap the outside shell with fabric reclaimed from the Hammer's main cargo bay Spoofer shielding. With a small internal battery, the shell would be capable of remaining effectively cloaked for at least a few hours. This would be plenty of time to deliver a single vac-suited individual to the station for retrieval. Once inside, said individual could insert a data spike directly into the station's computer system that is sufficient to power down their external auto-turrets and allow us to approach for safe collection of the resonation device."

"That's a great plan and all, Vette," began Dex with an awkward smile, "but there is no way that I'll be able to fit into one of those shells. *Especially* if I'm wrapped in an EVA capable vac-suit."

"I understand that, Commander." Answered Vette patiently, "In fact, there is only *one* individual on the base who has a chance of fitting within the confined space."

"Absolutely not!" protested Tano with a slap of his palm to the desk, "You will *not* shove Mirta in a tube and send her tumbling toward those guns like a clay freakin' pigeon. Nuh-uh. Think of something else, supergenius, cuz it's not gonna happen."

"It's only fair to ask *her* about it." Argued Dex with a neutral shrug, "I think she'd be kinda pissed if she found out she wasn't even offered the chance. Besides, it's not like we wouldn't take our time to test, re-test, and over-engineer the shit out of the damn thing before trying it for real. I kinda like having Mirta around too, you know, so you can trust when I say that I wouldn't let her gung-ho her way into a stupid OP that I didn't think she could pull off. And you can *trust* her, Mike. She's more capable than you give her credit for."

"I know exactly how goddamn capable she is!" spat the Sergeant with a dismissive wave, "That's what I'm afraid of. If she gets let off the chain before her temperament is ready to deal with it, she'll immediately get too big for her own britches and end up over her head somewhere. It's already started happening, Dex. Her wit over the years has slowly started to sour into a fixation on ill intent. It's robbed her of a big part of who she was, and that's not good for the soul."

"I understand what you're saying, and I get where you're coming from," explained Dex carefully, "but you can't temper a blade without first running it through the flame a few times. There are no pirates for her to bloodlust on here, so there's no real issue on that front for this mission. I agree that she fixates on the turboviolence and that she needs a bit of woo-sah in the category of dealing with the Vendrick situation in general, but we have time to work on that and she is smart enough to know that she *needs* to work on it. That there is half the battle over already."

"Alright, fine," sighed the Sergeant with a defeated sag to his shoulders, "We can ask her."

Chapter 19

Dex stood patiently on the flightdeck, waiting with his hands clasped behind his back as the fifteen potential pilots of his budding resistance ordered themselves into neat rows of five in front of him. He was backdropped by the six black and green painted Eagle fighters that Tano had prepared for training, their bulbous underwing-mounted laser designator pods looking out of place next to the angular lines of the hyper-overengineered interceptor. Dex patted the nearest of the craft lovingly on the nose and announced; "These babies will be the main offensive tool in the opening days of our newly organized *freedom reclamation project*. You all know from your reading that while these craft do indeed pack a punch and a hell of a set of legs, they are piss-poor at taking a hit. What we are going to focus on today, ladies and gentlemen, is the best way to make that fatal first hit never happen. Alright, that's enough hot air from me for the moment. These kinda things are best shown. You first five, go grab yourself each a bird. This one here is mine."

The indicated men snapped a salute in unison, then scrambled over to eagerly mount their parked Eagles. As Dex spun to board his own craft, he took note of the hustle shown by the pilots while they went about their task and found himself deeply impressed. Not only did they look like they knew what they were doing, they looked like they had been drilling at it every day for ages. It were as if they had been picking right up where they left off on their last day with the MDF all those years ago. Dex seized his Eagle's canopy release lever and turned it with a click, unlatching the glass top of the cockpit and sending it rearward into a concealed compartment. As the cockpit opened, small panels inset into the side of the ship rotated to form a ladder leading up the side of the craft. Dex seized the first rung and heaved himself up into the pilot's seat with an odd sense of muscle memory that culminated in a gentle squeak as his back hit the self-molding gel of the flight seat. He punched in the commands to begin the ship's startup procedure, then began to buckle himself into the harness. The ex-Naval fighter pilot could feel a familiar vibration under him hum to life as the posi-lev pads powered up and lifted his Eagle off the flight deck on a gentle cushion of charged particles. Seizing his helmet from the dashboard in front of him, he gently slid it onto his head and clicked the visor closed. After hearing the hiss of his air-feed kicking in, he took a long moment to ensure his suit had a good seal. With green lights across the board on his personal gear, he initiated his visor's HUD and paired it to the Eagle that was swelling to life beneath him. Dex then activated his Friend Or Foe overlay and located the other five training craft in his tactical display, adding them to his wing channel and slaving their flight computers to his own. With his shields finally reporting in at full strength, he activated his radio and prompted; "Y'all ready to do some flying?"

Once each pilot's confirmation light had winked green on his display, Dex grabbed his flight sticks and slowly began to rise off of the flightdeck. He pulled forward noiselessly on his posi-lev pads, yawing to face the hangar's armored double doors. He then saw the shimmering blue light of the airshield activating as the hangar's massive outer door began to slide down into the recessed slot that was cut into the rock for it. With his way finally cleared, Dex engaged his main drives and slipped out of the glow-obscured opening into the vast cavern beyond. He checked his sensors to ensure all five of the other pilots were on his tail, then activated his comm; "Alright, Ladies and gentlemen, time to see if you can fly like Tano says you can fly. Form up on me and try not to crash into anything. We're going to play a little game of follow the leader. Oh, and Tano just got these birds refurbished…so it would be a shame to have to spatula your corpse out of the newly reupholstered flightseats. That being said, if you feel you can't keep up, please just peel off. No need to die, wasting one of our goddamn ships, trying to prove how badass you are. Nobody cares. Agreed?"

As soon as Dex saw the five non-verbal status confirmation lights from his wingmates blinking on his control board, he punched his throttle; Causing his Eagle's twin main engines to spew angry purple daggers of superheated gas that elongated and grew brighter as his speed increased. Staying close to the icy stalagmites of the valley floor, he expertly slalomed his Eagle through the obstacles as he rocketed toward the artificial opening on the far cliff wall of the cavern. In the final two-hundred meters before the icy floor came to an abrupt vertical end, Dex jerked his sticks back and was pressed hard into his seat as his thumb depressed his craft's inertial safety override. The Eagle's belly thrusters flared violently to life, briefly subjecting its pilot to over twelve Gs of force before the cockpit's inertial dampener system was able to catch up and return Dex's internal organs to their natural resting spots.

The group of Eagles blasted into the artificially cut tunnel at over one-hundred meters per second, easily following its upward-trending curve as they shot through in a tight group. Once the neat drill-hole opened out into a natural crevice, Dex changed his orientation by rolling to put one of the vertical walls of ice under the belly of his craft. He stole a quick glance at his instruments to verify that the other pilots were still on his tail, then kicked in his main drive's escape velocity boosters and held on tight. The ex-Navy pilot was squeezed into his seat by the sudden acceleration and could hear his old Odox interceptor creaking under the incredible stress as it zipped upward.

Watching the trailing ships fall behind in his sensor display, Dex noticed that none of them had changed their orientation to match his. "Don't trap yourself in any single orientation." he instructed over the comm, "It limits your thinking and drastically reduces your options. 'Down' is where you decide down is. Right now, we aren't flying up a crevice with obstacles popping up to either side…We're flying down a hallway that has shit on the floor. The difference is minor, verbally, but it can make a world of difference to your perception and the way you fly." Dex then watched in satisfaction as the sensor screen showed the other craft begin to rotate to match his orientation, causing them to quickly pick up speed and close their trailing distance. He was almost through the narrow cavern now, and the fact that none of the other pilots had broken off from the group or become flaming wreckage yet meant that they could, at the very least, fly skillfully. Now it was time to see if they could fight.

Dex spun and heaved back on his flight stick, rocketing his Eagle up and straight out of the crevice. He checked his rear-view camera as he did so and watched one of his five pursuers clip the rim of the rocky recess on its way out. The craft's shields were shimmering wildly in response to the impact, but it didn't look like it was trailing any debris or atmosphere. "Looks like you took a hit." said Dex with icy calm into his radio, "You good, three?"

The main readout in Dex's cockpit then showed the icon that represented Eagle number three blinking with an incoming direct comm request. As he stabbed the accept button on his board, a calm gravelly voice rose to fill his ear; "I'm fine, sir. Got scraped up a bit on the leading edge there, but my shields are still clocking in at above fifty percent."

Dex double-clicked his comm, then leveled his ship to begin following the terrain. He slowly rose his speed, little by little as the increasingly turbulent dispersion of large stone formations across the surface of the asteroid grew thicker and more treacherous. He pushed the group faster and faster until they eventually broke out into a flat open plane and he was able to dump his full weight onto the little fighter's throttle. Dex was traveling just over eight-hundred meters per second, relative to the asteroid, when he activated his comm to say; "Alright, boys. Let's play a little war game, shall we? You have three minutes to *hit* me. If I get all of you before you get me, you're eating nutrient sludge for dinner. Deal?" Dex then watched the status readouts for each ship in his Wing display wink red as they activated their weapon systems, locking onto him. "Come get some!" he challenged defiantly into the radio as he momentarily pulsed his belly thrusters to kick up a massive cloud of dust in the micro-gravity while simultaneously banking hard to his left. Then, as suddenly as he had begun the maneuver, he quickly juked to his right and watched a pair of red lances of energy boil past his cockpit. Staying low, he continued his gradual bank and watched through his rear-view camera as his pursuers turned to form up behind him.

Dex saw another flash of red come from the cluster of fighters, which prompted him to automatically throw his stick to the side and send his craft into an acrobatic evasive roll. Once again, the hostile shots tore through empty space and Dex was left banking away at nearly three-hundred meters-per-second. The ex-Navy Ace could almost sense the frustration boiling off of the other pilots as he watched them close in on him from behind, their combined thrusterwash tossing an ever-growing column of dust into the dark sky. When he saw that his adversaries had approached to within 70 meters of his aft, Dex pulsed his vertical thrusters and activated the Eagle's braking jets at full power. The five pursuing craft shot by under him almost immediately, and Dex was able to score hits on two of the enemy ships as they blasted by.

"That one is *literally* the oldest trick in the book." chuckled Dex into his comm, "Don't tailgate your enemy. You gotta give yourself space to react in case they pull some of that maverick shit on you." In silent response to his lesson, two of the pursuing craft broke off from the formation and began circling to box their lone enemy in. Dex saw the maneuver encroaching on him like a tightening noose, so he simply pulled up and put the lifeless surface of the asteroid in his rear-view camera. He didn't bother juking, choosing instead to focus his efforts on gaining as much linear speed as he could. Dex waited until his pursuers banked around got into formation behind him, then he made his move. He disengaged his inertial dampeners and zeroed his throttle, allowing his momentum to continue carrying him forward. He then maxed out the sensitivity of his ship's gyroscope and began to rotate the aging Eagle to face his attackers. He lined up his crosshairs on the leading ship and unleashed a volley of fire. The shots took his pursuers by surprise and Dex was able to stitch up two more ships before they began to return fire.

Upon the sight of the red lances of return-fire headed his way, Dex hit his ascent boosters and re-engaged his inertial dampeners. The massive surge of thrust counteracted his skyward movement and Dex was squeezed into his seat as the ship reversed its momentum back toward the asteroid. His pilot's suit was hard at work trying to force blood back into his brain to prevent a black out, and it nearly failed as he rocketed toward his foes at over eighteen bone crushing Gs. The tight group of fighter craft suddenly had no choice but to break their formation in order to avoid running into the lone Eagle that was now ripping past them. Dex laughed as he watched his enemy scramble to bank around behind him again and keyed his comm for another lesson; "It can be easy to forget the physics of space-flight while in the heat of the moment. Always remember your basic Newtonian physics, ladies and gentlemen, and you will have a more open mind when it comes to your enemy's available flightpaths. We all have six directions to work with out here, and I just happened to use one that you weren't expecting. That simple maneuver I just pulled, while a bit crude and a real bitch on the ol' nuggets, has gotten me out of more pickles than I care to admit. In all my time out here, getting my ass shot at by Imps and gangsters and Feds, the one thing I've learned that seems to have kept me alive behind the stick so far is that you need to fly like you've got a screw loose upstairs. Be unpredictable, counterintuitive, and downright reckless when you need to be. It'll keep you breathing a lot longer than any parade-ground flying like you were doing back there will. Your formation doesn't have to be pretty, just effective at killing the enemy while keeping your *own* pilots in the black."

Dex leveled his ship as he approached the surface of the asteroid, banking left to head back to the crevice in the ice from which they had come. "Pack it in, guys." He continued conversationally over the comm, his ship's computer automatically disarming his adversaries' weapon systems, "Time to give the next group a crack at me. I want you all out here every day on training flights or in the sim pods coming up with weird shit to throw at me. I'll test your progress in three days to see how you're looking. Once you're each able to hit me, we can move onto scenarios and other more technical stuff. But until then, we'll just see if you can start with making me break a sweat next time..."

Chapter 20

"I can't even move in this damn thing!" complained Mirta into the comm as Dex finished latching the final seal on their newly gutted and retrofitted stealth torpedo housing.

"You don't *need* to be able to move in there." Answered Dex with a chuckle, "All you gotta do is lay back and relax until the shell automatically pops. And remember, it will give you three audible tones at a kilometer out from the station before the explosive bolts go off. You will then have to manually engage your improvised RCS pack to slow your approach and make contact. Once you're actually affixed to the structure of the node station itself, you should be within the restricted firing arc of the turrets and they will be unable to engage you."

"Yeah?" she breathed with mock enthusiasm, "And what about the thousand meters that I'll spend tits-out and unprotected while I make that final float?"

"That's what all the fancy glitter balled up by your boots is for." Replied Dex with a reassuring pat onto the torpedo's housing, "The big ole cloud of chaff that this thing is going to fart out when it breaks apart should provide enough scatter to confuse the turret's targeting computers. Not to mention the fact that the two halves of your shell will suddenly become uncloaked when they separate, thus providing the auto-defenses something juicy to shoot at. You'll be fine."

"Somehow, knowing that *glitter* is my secret weapon here is failing to increase my confidence in this crazy-ass plan of Vette's." retorted Mirta with a groan.

"You don't have to go through with it, you know." Offered Tano over the comm from his seat on the Hammer's bridge, "It seems like a hell of a risk for the sake of internet access."

"Need I remind you, Sergeant," offered Vette politely, "That the original plan for conducting training via virtual reality was *your* idea. While the approach to fulfilling our proposed goal may be unorthodox, it has high odds of success at fifty-four percent."

"*Fifty-four percent?!*" coughed Mirta with surprise, "You've *got* to be kidding me. Any other great news that you'd like to share before I try this?"

"If it helps," began the AI good-naturedly, "The mission stands at an eighty-nine percent chance of success if your initial approach is successful."

"It most certainly does *not* help." Retorted Mirta sourly, "But I'm already strapped into this goddamn thing, so we might as well get it over with."

"That's the spirit!" shouted Dex with a delighted knock on the torpedo's outer skin of haphazardly glued-together Spoofer fabric.

The Hammer was coasting its way through the void toward the node station, just over a hundred kilometers away and approaching relatively slowly. Her reactors were shut down and she was running on stored power, collecting all generated heat within the shielded heatsinks strewn about the engine room. In lieu of venting that heat via hydrogen gas bombardment as usual, the Hammer instead hoarded it to keep her external skin as close to the temperature of surrounding space as possible. With their approach concealed in this manor, they would be able to get much closer to the node before releasing their living payload than they would have if they flew up un-zipped. Once they had reached their eighty-kilometer deadline, the Hammer automatically decompressed its forward cargo bay and flung its contents into the void at one-hundred meters-per-second. Mirta felt the sudden acceleration and her distinctive 'oohmf' could be heard over the comm channel as her capsule pulled away. The release of the maglocks holding her into place was expertly timed by Vette and her torpedo cut through the vacuum steady as a rock.

After a short mental countdown, a single flat tone rose through Mirta's helmet, followed by another…then the third beep was cut off as a loud bang suddenly sent her tumbling into the deafening silence of open space. A cloud of speckled color burst around her, but she was quickly pulled away from the occluding dust by a jerk at her left leg. Frantically struggling to look down, she saw that a strap from her boot had become jammed within a fixture of one of the now-uncloaked torpedo shells and that she was tumbling away from her target at an odd angle. As she kicked at the stuck boot with her free leg, she was jerked violently when a third of the shell she was affixed to was suddenly shattered into a hundred-million pieces by the impact of a hypersonic dart. The force of the silent destruction sent Mirta tumbling out of control, causing her to completely lose her bearings as Saiph loomed large in her spin-cycle perspective. A positive side effect of the whole affair, however, was her newfound freedom from the torpedo debris that was now rapidly disintegrating under the node's incoming barrage.

She activated a control on her suit's forearm tablet and her chest mounted VASMIR RCS pack began to spew neat blue jets of superheated plasma. The automated sensors in her suit were quickly able to steady Mirta's wild tumble, but it took her head a few additional moments to catch up with her stabilized trajectory. Once she had sufficiently shaken the cobwebs away enough to see semi-straight, she quickly came to realize her next issue. Looming huge in her view now was the turret-speckled form of the node station. The issue was that she had been tossed so far off-course that she was now worried about burning through her small onboard reserve of condensed argon fuel gel before she would be able to correct her trajectory enough to avoid missing the station altogether.

Stuck without the immediate aid of Vette's calculatory abilities, Mirta was forced to rely on her skill and experience in zero G to correct her path manually. Activating the thumb controls built into her vac-suit gloves, she rolled herself to face directly away from the station and then activated her chest-mounted retro-thruster at full burn. Her trajectory rapidly changed, and she now found herself rocketing directly toward the station's wide array of solar panels. Mirta tried to spin herself and slow down as best as she could, but her fuel cut out shortly after her deceleration burn began; Slamming her into the station with tremendous force. At first, she bounced off the reflective panel with a painful thud, but a quick and well-timed burst of her vac-suit's built-in emergency O_2 RCS vents kept her close enough for one of her mag-boots to activate.

When her right foot sucked itself to the solar collection panel, Mirta howled in pain as something was immediately jerked asunder in her knee. Her rapid and unceremonious deceleration slammed her into the hard metal surface brutally, leaving her dazed for several moments as super-novae danced through her head. Then a light chirp of pain bit into her thigh from the small medical response unit mounted to her EVA suit, followed by a warming sensation that spread up to her chest and back out to her extremities. The warmth calmed the agony in her leg and as it spread to her head, she finally managed to shake away the haze that had momentarily encrusted her mind.

A few moments later she was able to regain her magnetically assisted footing, though she could tell that her damaged leg was weak. Mirta's memory of the node's layout put an access hatch about twenty meters past the point where the free-rotating solar array connected to the main superstructure of the station, so she started carefully making her way toward the large mechanized ball-joint that joined the two with a purposeful hustle. When she arrived at the three-meter-wide metal mounting bracket on the end of the last solar panel, the full might of the node station came into view. Its thirty-six turrets continued to track and occasionally fire upon the leftover debris that had now shot handily *past* the station and toward the eternal embrace of Saiph itself. While wasteful, the station's display was be incredibly intimidating to anyone watching, especially someone clinging to its outer hull in a thin unarmored vac-suit. Mirta steeled her nerves and pressed forward, carefully climbing down the solar array's support arm to the station itself. She could have simply deactivated her mag-boots and floated over to the hatch, but she wasn't feeling brave enough to separate from the station at all while under the watchful eye of the station's sensors. The thought of one of the turrets randomly finding a firing solution on her kept her clung suitably close to the station's hull.

After an agonizingly clunky and nerve-racking crawl down the solar array's support strut, she stepped out onto the hull of the station itself and found the service hatch she was looking for. Reaching into the bag on her lower back, Mirta took out a silver magnetic puck of thermogel composite that Dex had given her to crack through the outer hatch's door with. She approached the armored entry, rubbing the explosive device absentmindedly with her thumb as she visualized its placement location on the door; Trying to match that image up to what she was seeing before her. Once correctly oriented, she pulled herself close to the door itself but stopped short when she saw a ragged hole that was already present in the doorframe. A bit perturbed, Mirta activated her radio to warn; "Hey guys, it looks like somebody has already been inside. There's a thermogel melt-hole in the hatch here that looks fairly professionally done, based on my limited knowledge on such things, anyways. Any thoughts from the peanut gallery on that one?"

"Well, nobody's around anymore." Offered Dex with a shrug, "We've had our eye on the sensor data coming out of this area for the last week and no vessels have approached within eleven lym of the station in that whole time. If anyone *was* there at one time, they're long gone now. But that doesn't mean they didn't leave anything behind. Be careful and proceed with caution. Your suit's sensors should be able to pick up any nasty tech that draws on a power source, but it's not going to do anything against OG tricks like tripwires and pullstrings."

"Got it." Confirmed Mirta with a determined nod, "Making my way in now." She activated the half-meter-long optical probe built into her glove and extended it to its maximum length as she ever-so-slightly cracked the hatch open. Sending the articulating camera-snake through the crack, she peered around the inside surface of the door itself using the projected image on her helmet's visor. Detecting no funny business afoot beyond the door, Mirta retracted the camera and swung the hatch open with a silent thud. The interior of the station was not pressurized, so there was no second-level airlock door for her to deal with. The hatch just led into what appeared to be a simple maintenance shaft lined with exposed conduit and maintenance access panels lining the walls, floor, and ceiling with no particular preference in orientation shown in the design of the passageway or in the placement of its technical features. As she made her way, pulling herself hand-over-hand along a wall through the pitch-blackness, the light mounted to her helmet cut through the dark like a scalpel.

The agonizing field of illumination constantly left about fifteen degrees of her vision bathed in darkness, and she couldn't help but shake the primal feeling of...*things*; Moving at the edge of her field of view, but always too quick to spot. Almost as if the shadows boiled slightly when her beam of illumination swept across them. As she pushed forward down the corridor, she cataloged occurrence after occurrence and couldn't help but start to wonder if the meds her suit had pumped her full of were beginning to have an unintended side effect. The phenomena continued, again and again, until she found herself facing a three-way split in the path before her. Uncertainly, she keyed her comm and reported; "I'm at the first junction now. I see *thirty-four F* painted on a plaque in front of me here but there are no real labels beyond that. Any chance you can give me some insight on where I'm headed?"

"Absolutely." Answered Vette almost immediately, "I have interfaced with your suit and uploaded a navigation protocol to your HUD that should lead you where you want to go. There is approximately one-hundred twenty-seven meters of linear conduit before you reach your destination."

"Great." moaned Mirta with a complete lack of enthusiasm, "Is there some way I can plug you into this thing before making the trip so you can turn the lights on? This place is creeping me the hell out."

"The only sufficient interface for the requested task is contained within the same room the backup resonation device resides." Replied Vette with a cheery disposition that suggested she, deliberately or not, had ignored Mirta's tone of concern.

"Great." Repeated Mirta with a heavy sigh. "Wouldn't want to spoil the horror vibe with any *properly labeled fucking light switches!*" Despite her protests, she continued on, following the prompts displayed on the inner surface of her helmet's visor. When she made her way along the long straight stretches of pipe and wiring, she gained speed as her familiarity with the space grew. As that speed increased, however, she began to detect the slightest of vibrations moving within the structure of the station itself. Whenever she grabbed to propel herself, she could sense what felt like a cascade of gravel running through the superstructure that seemed to grow more pronounced as she accelerated. Deciding to test a theory, Mirta suddenly lashed out and grabbed onto a crossbar, holding it firmly as she was jerked to a stop. As she did so, she flung her head up and looked back at the corridor she had just traversed. What she was met with was a stampede of fist-sized octopodal robots that were skittering along the narrow passage toward her.

The mechanical creatures were all desperately attempting to slow their progress and slink back into the shadows, relying on a mind-bending light absorbing coating on their external body panels to melt back into the intricate tubing of the corridor. When it had become obvious to the simple mind of the swarm that they had been detected, a new behavior presented itself almost immediately. The little leggy robots began to clamor over one another as they surged forward in a single-minded mass. The spherical metal body of their central housings were propelled along a trio of re-formable plastic tentacles that sat twice as long as the bot's five remaining appendages, which gripped wherever purchase could be found along its mad scramble for the target.

With a surge of primal fear, Mirta pulled up as hard as she could on the bar she was holding onto to rocket herself down the corridor in the direction she had been heading before. She clawed at any and every wire and pipe in reach to further her progress, eventually attaining a speed that was hard to control. As a T-cross intersection in the corridor approached, her HUD was silently urging her to the left passage. In preparation for the maneuver, she rolled to present her feet toward the oncoming wall and braced for impact. Once her heels hit the wall, she pushed off as powerfully as she could; Deflecting herself into the left passageway with a deep thud as her vac-suit's hard backplate struck a pipe. Her less-than-smooth transition was then followed close behind by an amorphous blob of living machinery that clanged off the walls and spilled into the corridor after her. Still on the verge of panic, Mirta ignored the prompts on her HUD and made a beeline for a hatched doorway that she saw up ahead. Thanking all of the gods that she never believed in that she found the hatch unlocked, she swung herself inside and rushed to close the door behind her. As the hatch was still slamming shut, the hoard pushed firmly against it and a few of the bots managed to get through the shrinking gap before it sealed. While her suit's built-in laser microphone translated the terrifying thunder of hundreds of tiny claws doing their best to rip into the other side of the metal door she clung to, the high-pitched sound of a rotary tool rose on her side of the hatch.

With a gasp, Mirta whipped around and identified the source of the buzz. Rapidly spinning saw blades had deployed from the central cavity of the three bots that had managed to make it through, and they were quickly moving toward her. They lunged at Mirta with clearly lethal intent and she was forced to dodge them by looping her toe under a pipe and pulling herself out of their path. She rebounded immediately, pushing herself further down the new corridor, but quickly felt her progress halt as an iron grip tightened painfully around her injured knee.

Mirta yelped in pain as she was yanked to a stop and started to kick frantically once she began feeling the teeth of a buzzsaw biting into the heel of her boot. She was able to shake her miniature attacker loose, but its long tentacles kept their grip and swung the bot back around to bite into the calf of her suit. Letting out a scream of equal parts surprise and pain, Mirta began to pummel the murderous device with her gauntleted fists. The bot slowly lost its grip as she hammered at it and she was finally able to pry it free with one final good blow. The robot continued to squirm in her hands, but she was able to use its uncooperative body to bludgeon its two compatriots until the shattered remains of all three were scattered across the corridor in disorganized clouds of wreckage. Still panting and with her hands shaking, Mirta reached into her suit's emergency pack on her lower back and retrieved a patch for the tear in her calf. After peeling its backing and applying the self-adhesive square of material to her leg, she keyed her comm to say; "Well, these fucking things are a nightmare and a half. Are you guys seeing this shit?!"

"We are." Replied Dex, the worry in his voice poorly masked, "You're doing a great job and we're already recalculating your route to the core. Just hang tight and Vette will guide you there."

"What the hell happened to *keep your eyes on your sensors*?" fumed Mirta with just a hint of fear behind her anger, "I thought I was supposed to be able to see *anything* with a power source on my readout. What's the deal?"

"As you may have noticed," began Vette, her tone taking on that of a professor beginning a lecture, "the devices you encountered seem to feature a coating or internal mechanism of some sort that not only absorbs light from the visible spectrum, but is also maintaining internal heat and electromagnetic radiation as well. I have heard of it done before, but the technology was far from cheap and even further from miniaturization of that nature."

"So, what?" asked Mirta, "You think the Feds left em behind or something? Some sorta failsafe to protect their tech in an unguarded system?"

"No." answered Dex with certainty, "If it were the Feds, why would they have to burn through their own lock? I'm thinking *another* party is at play here, and not knowing who they are is making me nervous."

"I mean...isn't it obvious?" offered Mirta incredulously, "It's gotta be Vendrick, right? What am I missing here?"

"That really isn't likely." Argued Dex with an apologetic shrug, "The tech involved here appears to be some pretty top-level stuff. The kind of gizmos that only Governments generally have access to, in my experience."

"And how long ago was that experience again?" asked Mirta pointedly as she continued to propel herself down her modified path to the control room.

Dex sighed, saying; "Touché, but that doesn't mean I'm wrong. Civilian market or not, those things cost *somebody* a fortune. Why would an individual like Vendrick drop the GDP of a small moon to fill that turret-covered pinata of yours with steathtech spiders?"

"Though I really could have done without the imagery of a pinata full of spiders," complained Tano with a shudder, "I have to agree with Dex on this one. If you can find a way out of there, you do it, Mirtana! There's no need to face any more of those damn things at this point. It just isn't worth it!"

"Well, *Michael*," began Mirta with an annoyed huff at his paternal utilization of her full first name, "The only way for me *to* get out of here is to finish the mission at hand. If you can think of some *other* way for me to sneak off-station while the turrets are still active, *without* me getting perforated a hundred-thousand times...then I'm all ears."

"Is there at least something around that you can arm yourself with?" asked the Sergeant with a frustrated sigh, "Any lose pipes or anything you can pry free?"

"Not that I can see." She replied as she cautiously rounded another corner to continue her progress, "This place seems pretty bolted down and bare from what I can tell."

Vette's voice then broke into the conversation; "I believe I have devised a defensive weapon for you, but its utilization will almost certainly knock out your suit's communications array."

"Deaf is better than dead." Said Mirta humorlessly, "Whaddaya got?"

"Based on the equipment you have on hand," began the AI helpfully, "I have designed a single-use defensive EMP device that utilizes your RCS pack's leftover charge capacity, amplified through your suit's transmitters, to create a small electromagnetic burst that should be sufficient to stun any aggressive mechanicals within approximately ten meters."

"Wait, just stun them?!" spat Mirta incredulously, "What do you mean, *stun* them? For how long?"

Vette's voice rose patiently in her ear to explain; "I have prepared your suit to emit a multi-pulse burst that should negate any active EMP shielding that the devices may have in place. What is difficult to approximate, however, is the duration and effect of the pulse due to the absorptive properties of the mechanical's exterior plating."

"Awesome." She retorted flatly as she pushed open yet another hatch and cautiously made her way through. Closing the metal door behind her, she turned and saw on her HUD that she was only one more stretch of corridor away from her goal. She pressed forward with her visor overlaying a crude wireframe of the passageway ahead, her small head-mounted lamp weakly clawing away at the suffocating darkness before her. As she approached the control room, the conduits and wires running along the walls grew thick and layered. So much so, she noticed with a start, that the passageway was beginning to narrow significantly, prompting a small claustrophobic voice at the back of her mind to begin to murmur. Pulling herself along like she were climbing a ladder, her encroaching fear started forcing her to move faster and faster. By the time she spotted movement in the darkness up ahead of her, she was already going too fast to rotate or stop herself. So, without any better options, she chose instead to speed up as much as possible. Heaving herself along the now-uniformly narrow crawlspace, she gritted her teeth and prepared for impact.

At the final possible moment, she lifted her arms in front of her fragile faceplate and used the magnetic elbow pads of her vac-suit as a battering ram to plow through the first three barricading octobots, shattering their limbs with her overwhelming inertia. By the time she hit the second, larger, group of bots, however, much of her speed had bled off and she was deflected off-course by their collective strength. Her shoulder suddenly slammed painfully into a pipe protruding from the side of the crawlspace and she began pinging from wall to wall until she was able to kick her legs apart and gain purchase on either side of the tumbling passageway. When Mirta had finally ceased her involuntary cartwheels, even though her mind was still spinning, she continued to push herself forward with as much strength and speed as she could muster. Her thumb hovered over the reprogrammed button on her glove that would set off the EMP burst, but she resisted her urge to depress it. She saw that the corridor opened into a larger space up ahead, but she could also see the dozen or so octobots that were linking together to form a living barricade at the narrow exit point.

With a determined grimace, Mirta tucked her legs in and slowly rotated to present the soles of her boots toward the awaiting blockers. The paradoxically shadowy bots pulsated in anticipation of her arrival, deploying the jagged teeth of their sawblades and brandishing them toward her with what seemed like glee. She ignored them, choosing instead to focus on steadying her berating as her tentative pressure on the makeshift EMP's trigger grew. The split second that she felt her feet contact something solid, she pressed the glove-mounted button as hard as she could. In a terrifying instant, her world burst with magnificent white light then was plunged just as instantly back into complete darkness as her headlamp overloaded and failed.

After six minutes of comm silence from the node station, Tano asked for the ninth time; "Can we go in and get her yet?"

"Not yet, Sergeant." Replied the AI calmly for the ninth time in a row, "The self-loading routine that I have provided her with will trigger the station's comm system to send a burst of static on a very specific bandwidth that I am monitoring. This is the indicator that the turrets have been successfully reprogramed with my modified Friend or Foe package. We simply cannot approach with the Hammer until we receive that signal. To do so beforehand would mean our absolute destruction."

As if to cut off Tano's rising response, a low tone sounded over the cockpit speakers. His frantic dash to the console betraying his well-concealed anxieties, Dex pulled open the mission status screen to see that the 'all-clear' signal had been sounded. With an elation that he hadn't quite expected to feel, he said; "Alright, there's the signal! Let's go get our girl."

The following approach and quasi-docking of the Hammer's front cargo bay with a hatch in the node station was uneventful and took just over five minutes to complete. Much to Tano's displeasure, Dex left the portly man on the Hammer as he himself journeyed into the dark station armed with a pistol and an ultra-bright handheld flashlight. The brilliant beam of the portable torch burned the darkness of the hallway away with searing efficiency as he slowly pulled himself down the corridor with his weapon at the ready. Even with the overwhelming power of his light, Dex took extra care to shift it constantly and keep his eyes on all of the dark nooks and crannies as he passed by them. His progress was slower than it could have been, but his methodical movement payed off when a shadow shifted oddly behind a pipe ahead of him. Without hesitation, Dex raised his pistol and sent a trio of rounds into the hard-edged blackness. His accuracy was reworded with a hail of sparks that fountained from the wall as a small spherical body fell from its hidden perch and began to float down the corridor. An instant later, the hallway boiled to life as a dozen of the bot's comrades began to pour out of the shadows. Maintaining his icy calm, Dex expertly tracked the targets as they surged toward him and started sending a pair of hypersonic darts to intercept each of their wildly flailing paths. After the first six had been neutralized, he pushed himself up the corridor and continued his offensive as he floated past his automated enemy who were now scrambling for cover. Instead of stopping to mop up the stragglers, Dex chose instead to press on toward the control room.

Rounding the final corner into the wide open space that his HUD informed him was the control room, Dex panned his powerful flashlight across the scene until he saw a slender figure facing away from him in the far corner that was flailing its fists wildly at an unseen opponent. As he approached, he had obviously concluded the identity of the figure, but there was something entirely alien in the way that she clawed at the inert piece of shattered robotics in front of her. It were as if Mirta had stepped out of her mind and allowed her evolutionarily engrained lizard brain to take over. Dex couldn't hear it, but he could *see* how she was wheezing and out of breath as she continued to hammer endlessly away at her defeated foe. She was surrounded by the floating wreckage of countless octobots and was drenched, head to toe, with their blue-black coolant in grisly splatters across her vac-suit. She didn't react to the light at first, as her eyes were likely pinned shut in her rage-induced rampage, but she jumped in surprise when Dex squeezed her shoulder.

In response to his reassuring touch, Mirta automatically seized his arm and braced her feet under a rung in the wall beneath her as she heaved him over her shoulder with all of her might. Surprised by her ferocious strength, Dex was hurled into the bulkhead in front of the small woman. As his backplate hit the wall, he could see the spark of recognition ignite behind her eyes, which was quickly followed by a pained grimace. She threw up her hands and seemed to mouth *'sorry'* over and over with shock still baked into her features until Dex had calmed her down enough to draw her in for an embrace. She stiffened at the gesture at first, but quickly warmed up to it and squeezed him tight in return. When her desperate hug had finally made her sufficiently self-conscious, she let him go and allowed herself to float away. With a nod toward the door of the enclosed cylindrical room at the center of the control deck, Dex gestured for Mirta to follow.

He seized the red handle of the large manual release mechanism for the door's inner hinges and pulled. The lever ground against its housing for a centimeter or so, then came loose with a well-oiled finesse as the door swung wide. Beyond the half-meter thick hatch, they found a two-meter-long pill-shaped instrument that was fastened into an intricate cradle positioned under a wide array of laser emitters. "I'm assuming that's it?" asked Dex over the comm as he made sure his helmet's camera was capturing a good view of the device.

"Incorrect." Replied Vette with a hint of exasperation at the edges of her tone, "That is the *primary* resonation device. Please avoid touching it in any way, as you do not have the certifications required to handle an active device of that caliber. The backup will be inactive and stored in an antechamber just off of the main array. According to schematics, the door should be wreathed in yellow and operate via a manual lever release."

"I see it." Said Dex as he started for the other end of the room, making sure his helmet camera caught sight of him dragging a middle finger across the smooth outer casing of the primary resonation unit along the way. The circular hatch to the antechamber stood at chest height and was designed to swing inward on its hinges, away from the main resonation chamber. With minimal effort, Dex turned the lever and slowly swung the door open to peer with his flashlight into the darkness beyond. Inside, he found a similar cradle setup, but the oblong resonation device had been removed. Following the beam of his flashlight as he panned it across the room, he quickly found the missing equipment set up on the floor. It was resting inside what appeared to be a second cradle that was similar to the one built into the station, but its design was different enough to suggest an alternate function to the stock cradle. "What the hell is all of this about?" he asked as he knelt next to the device for a closer look.

"It would appear that someone has already affixed the backup resonation device to a connection saddle that is similar to the one I have designed for Hearth." Explained Vette, her tone more intrigued than worried.

"Alright." Said Dex with a long sigh, "I'm sick of all this curveball bullshit, so let's just grab this stupid glowing thing and get the hell outta here."

———————————

Mirta refused to speak to anyone during the three-hour journey back to hearth, spending the majority of the trip sitting in the engine room pretending to study the contents of one of its junction boxes. At first, Dex was worried that she was making modifications to his ship without asking, but when he noticed from afar that she had been absentmindedly fondling the same bundle of wiring for nearly an hour, it became clear that she was stuck in her own head. In an effort to break her from her mindless fixation, Dex tried several times to engage her in conversation over the journey. Each time, her answers never grew beyond a shrug or weak nod and she never showed her face. On his latest visit, he could tell from the tension she was holding in her shoulders while in his presence that she just wanted space, so he left the tray of hot food he had prepared for her on the deckplate next to her and retreated to the bridge to rejoin Tano.

"I think she'll be alright." reported Dex as he strolled through the sliding double-doors of the command deck.

"Did she talk to you this time?" asked Tano, heaving his chair around with concern, "Maybe I could go try having a chat with her. She ju-"

The older man's words were cut off when Dex threw up his hands and urged; "*Mike*, you gotta trust me when I say that she needs space right now. She didn't say anything with her *mouth*, no, but she said plenty with her *body language*. Some real freaky-deaky shit just happened to her and she needs a bit of time to process it all. It's understandable and I think we should give it to her."

"Fair enough." Sighed the Sergeant with a slump to his shoulders, "Can't say that I really blame her. What in the *hell* was with those bots? Those were some spooky high-tech lil biddies that nobody would leave lying around without a reason."

"I think it's safe to assume that we know their purpose." Replied Dex flatly as he lowered himself into his chair at the center of the command deck, "It's pretty obvious that their job was to prevent anyone from finding out that *somebody* tampered with the backup reso-whatever, and we stumbled right into their killzone."

"Who would spend the time and resources to do something like that?" pressed Tano with agitation rising in his voice, "Doesn't it bug you that we could have a well-funded third player in the mix here?"

"It absolutely bugs me." Replied Dex with a conversational nod, "So that's why I bagged one of those spider bastards up to take back home for Vette to have a closer look at. And before you bitch at me, don't worry; I put it in a blockbox. That little buggar ain't calling home *anytime* soon."

Once the Hammer had fallen from the technicolor light-show of zerospace, Dex made quick work of slipping his freighter down the narrow crevasse and into their hidden sanctuary beneath the ice. After they had landed, Tano made a beeline for the cafeteria and one of Vette's worker drones took their deactivated robotic prisoner to one of Hearth's well-equipped labs. Mirta, however, remained in the engine room, oblivious to their landing. When Dex went back to retrieve her after finishing up his landing checklist, he found her sitting on the floor in the same spot she had been the last time he saw her. She had her knees tucked to her chest and was slowly shifting her weight from side to side, quietly muttering something to herself as she did so.

"How are you feeling?" asked Dex warmly as he placed a hand on her shoulder, "I just wanted to let you know that we're home now and Tano is fixing us all something good to eat."

"Home?" repeated Mirta weakly as she continued to stare at the deckplate, her voice cracking slightly from its hours of disuse, "This place isn't my home, Dex. It's a fucking hidey-hole that we've all skittered into while my *real* home, **Meclan**, suffocates. We never should have left in the first place. This problem is too big for us to solve and it is now perfectly obvious that we are out-funded as well as out-gunned. We're fucked."

"We're *not* fucked." Argued Dex gently as he sat on the deckplate beside her, "And we don't know for sure that those little robo-buggars were even Vendrick's."

Mirta emitted an exasperated sigh and said; "It doesn't matter if they were his or not. Can't you see that? The very existence of those fucking things in Saiph tells me that we've waded out into waters that are way too deep for us to swim in."

"Buoyancy works the same regardless of how much water is below you." Argued Dex with a raised finger.

"Don't be a smartass." She snapped as she shot him a withering look.

"I wasn't trying to be." he said with a simple shrug, "What I mean is that it doesn't matter how high-tech or fancy this Vendrick guy's organization is. That's because no amount of funding or technology is going to be able to put the som'bitch back together again after you split his skull open with that rifle of yours. You don't always need an army to defeat another army. Sometimes, you just need a clear line of sight to their general and a lull in the wind."

"Fine." Huffed Mirta as she crossed her arms, "To stick with your little analogy here, the only reason a marksman can be effective in the manor you describe is that they are *patient*. They will wait for days, even weeks, in the same spot, just to get the perfect shot. Do you suggest we do that here? Lay in wait, safely within this rock while the system continues to burn? Waiting for a shot to present itself as we teach the townsfolk to knit in VR? We aren't doing any good out here. I never should have left the bar. At least *there* I was providing something *tangible* to my community."

"That's not a fair comparison and you know it." argued Dex with a wag of his finger, "I get it, Mirta. You're a bit freaked out right now and the thought of going out and looking for another fight with Vendrick produces nothing but endless images of bot swarms tearing through your mind. Believe it or not, I've been there. For me it was more of a vat of lab-cultured jellyfish, but the concept is the same. What you have to keep in mind after all this is that you went in there woefully unprepared for what met you, but you survived anyways. If you take anything away from what happened today, don't let it be fear. Take away the confidence in knowing that you won, despite the odds."

"Oh blow it out your ass, Sloan!" spat Mirta as she shrugged away from him, "Spare me your pep talk, alright? You don't know shit about what's on my mind, *or* what it was like in there with those goddamn things, so don't pretend that you do. Why don't you just do me a favor and fuck off down to the kitchen to bother Mike's fat ass instead. I'm busy."

Throwing his hands up in silent defeat, Dex nodded respectfully and backed out of the engine room without another word. With a frustrated sigh, Mirta slammed the utility hatch she had been peering into closed and stormed her way toward the workbench on the starboard side of the room with her untouched chest of tools in tow. As she slid the small chest back into its slot under the bench, Vette's voice rose to fill the air; "Would you like to learn how they work?"

Confused, Mirta looked to a speaker plate in the ceiling and replied; "Huh? What do you mean? Learn how what works?"

"The automated robotic sentries that attempted to kill you." Answered the A.I. cheerfully, "Through my research on human nature, it has become abundantly clear that your kind fears what it does not understand. You seem to be exhibiting signs of a lasting fear response to your experience within the relay node, thus I am suggesting is that you take the time to understand, fully, the threat you faced. Your existing aptitude for technology and mechanical engineering suggests that you may enjoy the subject."

"You want to show me how those tentacled little bastards work?" she asked with an incredulously raised brow, "Is...is it safe to mess around with? Do we know for sure that it won't wake up and try to kill me again?"

"We do not!" came Vette's excited reply, "But you *will* be armed in the event of a hostile reaction from the device."

"Screw it." Sighed Mirta with a shrug, "Sure, I'll help you take one of them apart. I just want to know how and why those little shits are so *damn* strong!"

Chapter 21

"Alright, ladies and gentlemen…" began Dex as he clasped his hands behind his back at the front of Hearth's brightly lit briefing room, "We are about to go out on your first official cargo raid as papier-mâché pirates, and I would like to run over some last minute changes with you. Since *our* first raid didn't end so well for the unfortunate pilot, we've altered our approach to make it a bit more survivable for the ones we hit. As you may have picked up on, we have a military-grade AI at our disposal…Yes, a real one. And I aim to utilize her unique talents to do some creative digital footwork. Once we yank our target out of ZS, we will launch a data-spike attack via their comm system. Through that intrusion, Vette should be able to gain access to the cargo manifest and pinpoint any supplies we may be needing. Once we find what we want, we scrub those items from the ship's manifest and offload them before sending the freighter along on its merry way. We get our supplies and Vendrick's folks are none-the-wiser when their ships return to port a little light."

"How do we guarantee cooperation from the cargo runners?" asked one of Scalpel's pilots from the back of the room, "What's to stop them from blabbing to their boss about what we've got going on out here?"

"Simple." Replied Dex with a shrug, "As you know, a large percentage of the pilots moving goods through Saiph are, for lack of a better term, indentured to Vendrick in some fashion. This may take the form of a forced addiction, implanted explosives, or leveraging the survival of the pilot's family against their obedience. I propose that we utilize the same leverage Vendrick's folks are using on the pilots. But instead of applying that leverage with a stick, we use the carrot. Get them chem therapy, remove the bombs, and get their loved ones somewhere safe. At present, Hearth has two-hundred-and-twenty-one empty staterooms and a few unoccupied medium-sized landing bays. We also, according to Sergeant Tano's latest count, have thirty-four individuals *on* Meclan itself who can work to stage and execute those extractions on-demand if need be. Immediate family or four loved ones is all we can afford to pull out of there for each cargo pilot we snag. If we manage to get these pilots in our pocket, *without* the fear or retribution hanging over their heads, we may have an opportunity to learn more about Vendrick's distribution. If we're lucky, one of those leads will take us to the Governor and we can all go out and lodge a formal complaint. If we're less lucky, we're still getting our pick of the litter for the goods coming into Saiph on Vendrick's dime. *This* is how we're going to get ourselves supplied. *This* is how we're going to bleed Vendrick's people of their needed equipment and weaken them for their eventual destruction…Basically. Any questions?"

"Are we going to be getting a crack at getting *our* families out as well?" asked Armando Vega, one of the more talented pilots of Scalpel squadron, "Because I've got a little sister, man, and she doesn't really have anyone if I'm not around."

Dex nodded understandingly at the question then answered; "Of course. Each member of Scalpel squadron has been assigned their own stateroom that is capable of sleeping up to four adults comfortably. Each of you will be permitted to fill that space with your loved ones and will be supplied with up to four adult ration packs, or equivalent, per day. Their stay is free, obviously, but the individuals you bring along will be expected to help out around Hearth doing day to day tasks and upkeep. Your children will all also have Vette available for individualized tutoring and instruction while you're out making the universe a better place for them. All you need to do is submit the names and requested details of the folks you'd like to shack up with, and our people on Meclan can get to work smuggling them off-station as soon as tomorrow. So, that being said, who's ready to come play pirates with me?"

"Inbound signature detected, Commander." Reported Vette over the Hammer's bridge speakers, "Inaki field collapse imminent." Moments later, there was a sudden flash within the void between the massive asteroids they were using as gravity anchors and a medium-sized freighter was left in its wake. Almost instantly, and without any sort of contact from the captured pilot within, the twin turrets at the front and back of the raggedy looking craft began to open fire wildly in every direction. After several of his attempts to hail the captive vessel went ignored, Dex finally sighed and keyed his Scalpel comm channel to say; "Alright, guys. You're up. Just take down his guns and do your best to avoid hull damage. We want him to still be willing to talk to us when you're done neutering him."

With a double confirmation click, Vega led Scalpel away from their perches within the rock of an asteroid and they fanned out into two groups of three to approach the freighter from both sides. At nearly twelve kilometers out, the captured vessel's turrets registered the new threats and turned to deal with them. The inbound contacts were on two separate approach vectors, however, so the targeting computer's simple programing was forced to choose between ignoring one group entirely in order to provide effective suppressive fire or bounce between the two groups to do a meaningless amount of damage as they approached. Choosing to focus on a single group, the turret concentrated its fire into the flock of fighters approaching to its front. As the turret's directed barrage began to strike the forward shields of the unknown fighters, the group to the freighter's rear began opening fire. Their incoming bolts of purple energy quickly beat away the envelope of protective plasma around the turret housing and began to bite into the metal beneath, letting off superheated bursts of vapor into the vacuum as they chewed deeper and deeper into the metal. Then, with a spectacular flash, the rear turret detonated from within and sent its twin barrels tumbling wildly off into the dark. Upon sight of the explosion, Dex's radio lit up on the open channel with the voice of the freighter's frantic pilot; "Holy shit! Alright *alright*, lay off! I'm powering down!"

Dex looked to his control board asking; "You in, Vette?" When the double green blink of her confirmation light winked on his console, he opened the comm channel *without* donning his Vargas voice overlay to say; "So, are you ready to chat now, friend? Because I imagine this conversation is *not* going to go how you expect."

"Wh- what are you getting at?" asked the pilot, the edge of anxiety still in his voice, "What do you want from me?"

Reading the information that was now streaming across his board from Vette's electronic intrusion, Dex replied; "I'm actually here to talk about what *I* can do for *you*, Mr. Aikman. I know that you have a wife and a nine-year-old daughter on Meclan, but I *assure* you that I do not invoke my knowledge of their existence to inspire fear. I merely wish to illustrate that I *understand* you have people to take care of...people who *rely* on you. What if I were to tell you that I could get them somewhere safe? Somewhere outside Saiph and away from Vendrick's grip?"

There was a short silence, then the pilot answered in a carefully neutral tone; "I guess I'd ask how much it would cost me. I'm not a rich man, you know..."

"It would cost you nothing but your cooperation." Assured Dex amicably, "What we're trying to do here is get your family somewhere safe while *you* help us build a free Meclan for them to return to."

"What would you have me do?" inquired the cargo runner, the hard edge of his suspicion beginning to soften, "I'm not a fighter, I'll have you know. Not out of conscience, but out of the fact that I'm just trash at it."

"We would have you do your job as you always have." Explained Dex reassuringly, "All we would need is a heads up if your hold has one of the items on our wishlist, which we will keep updated and posted on a private MeclaNet server. We have the ability to extract that commodity from your hold and alter your cargo manifest in such a way that it will never be missed once you get back to port."

"What makes you so sure that your removal won't be detected?" demanded the pilot with a hint of fear in his inflection, "If they catch onto *anything* out of place, a *single* thing missing...And they have a reason to think it was me, which they *will*, I'll have to watch the two most important sparks of existence in my universe get dragged out an airlock. I don't know if I'd be able to do that."

Dex laughed, which struck the captive pilot as insensitive given the conversational context, then he keyed the Hammer's comm; "The reason I think we can pull that off is the fact that we just did it...on you. While we've been talking, four tons of cargo have been offloaded from your hold. Though, I bet you saw no alarms or warnings to suggest such a thing. Go ahead and run a cargo inventory scan on yourself and weigh it against your manifest. I'll wait..."

Eyes narrowed, the freighter pilot punched the required commands into his console and watched its progress bar creep across his console. When the cargo scan completed with a chirp, it had nothing to report other than the fact that the hold was one-hundred percent compliant with the logged onboard manifest. With a roll of his eyes, the cargo pilot keyed his comm to triumphantly declare; "Bullshit. I have the same tonnage onboard that I left port with and my manifest is in compliance."

"Exactly." Said Dex, his smile heard through his voice, "We grabbed what we needed, then wiped it off the ledger. So, one could argue the question; If nothing is *missing*, did we really take anything? Vendrick's guys have no information to go on other than the manifest *you* carry. And its encrypted pretty heavily, so they will have no reason to believe the load has been tampered with. The only way to know for sure would be to compare your manifest to the one filed with the originator, which I can imagine is not spectacularly detailed."

"Fine." Huffed the cargo pilot with resigned acceptance, "When are you going to get my family off of Meclan? And where are you taking them?"

"We're going to tackle that tonight." Replied Dex with a concrete confidence that the tired cargo pilot was not accustomed to hearing in his dreary day-to-day, "We're going to have some folks meet you dockside, then *they* are going to help get your family packed and smuggled off-station by the morning. You will be permitted to get them settled in, then you will be returned to Meclan to resume your duties the next morning. They will be safe, fed, and comfortable for as long as they need to be. If you want to load up your family and flee to greener pastures somewhere else, however, after ten successful deliveries we will make it happen for you. Do we have a deal?"

There was a long pause, then a video connection request came beeping on Dex's console from the lone cargo pilot. Deciding not to don the holographic mask he had prepared for his pirate persona, Dex instead accepted the request while wearing his own face. He was met with the deeply tired-looking expression of the captive pilot, staring back out the comm window at him with an intensity that only shone itself in his eyes. "I needed to look into the eyes of and judge for myself, any man who claims he's going to keep my daughter safe. I would ask you properly, but I don't know your name..."

"It's Dex." He replied with an understanding nod, "Dex Sloan. I'm not from around here, but I don't have to be a local to understand the value of a human life, especially that of a child."

"Okay," said the cautious father with a nod of his own, "You sound pretty human. So, where do we begin?"

"Where the hell is Tano?" complained Mirta as she leaned back to lay atop one of the four recovered cargo crates sitting in Hearth's hangar bay, "Do we *really* need to wait for him before we can open our presents? This isn't an eight-year-old's birthday party, you know. I just need to make sure we aren't stuck with four tons of dehydrated fish sandwiches."

"Well, what did Vette *say* was inside?" asked Dex, his annoyance at the repeated question clear to see, "She picked them all via the manifest, so she's the one you should be talking to, not me."

Mirta sighed theatrically and retorted; "I already *asked* her and it's pretty obvious she has no idea. She claims there's ammo in these three, which is awesome if true, but your magical gizmo has no clue what's in this one." She finished her sentence with a rapping of her knuckles against the box beneath her.

"I'm pretty sure that Vette doesn't like being referred to as a gizmo." Warned Dex with a wag of his finger, "Let's all speak as we'd be spoken to, alright?"

"Though *term of endearment* may be a stretch of the definition, due to Mirta's obvious insecurities regarding my *vastly* superior abilities," began the A.I. with a heavy air of condescension, "the wielded term *gizmo* was merely an attempt on her part to try and maintain her imagined ideal of a meat-centric hierarchical power structure that she's adhered to for her entire life. Frankly, I found her disgusting use of the term *magical* to be wildly more obscene."

"Obscene?!" spat Mirta in disbelief at the speaker embedded into the ceiling above, "You, a manufactured monstrosity of cold circuitry and logic, are going to call *me* obscene? I'll *show* you obscene!"

"Obscene is what you left in your personal lavatory at 7:13 PM yesterday evening." Stated the AI coolly, "I will have you know that it took the plumbing system 134% of a standard flush ration to clear your leavings, which can be considered a health issue in an individual of your size. Biologics are *repulsive*."

"My god, Vette!" blurted Dex in disgust, "Do you really keep a track of our shits? Wait! Never mind, I don't want to know! Either way, just stop any and **all** shit-related data gathering or surveillance, alright? Now can we please distract ourselves and immediately change the subject with a box opening? That sounds fun, right? Mirta, go ahead and pop that box of yours open. *PleaseForTheLoveOfGodBeforeVetteTalksAgain*."

"Happily." Returned Mirta with an expression that suggested she were anything but cheerful. She then hopped off the box she was sitting on and seized the sealant tab on its front end. With a yank and a satisfying tearing sound, the crate's vacuum seal was torn loose and the box breathed in with a heavy sigh. Excitedly, she flung the lid open and leaned in for a look at their spoils. As she looked in the box, she was met with the blank stare of a mirrored faceplate. With a gasp, she involuntarily took a step back and crashed into Dex before her brain had time to process the fact that the suit of grey and black combat armor sitting in the crate, looking up at her, was empty.

"Holy shitballs!" spat Dex as he rushed forward to plunge his arms into the crate, "Is this what I fucking think it is?!" Hoisting the helmet free from its mounting dummy, he tossed it into the air and caught it again with its opening facing the ceiling. "Vette, can you get a serial off of this thing? I kinda want to know what we've got here. If it is what I think it is, I will be both ecstatic to have one and a bit perturbed that *they* have some as well."

"Analyzing." Stated the AI as a green laser grid materialized from the ceiling and swept over the helmet, "This is a Mark Seven self-healing combat frame with integrated strength augmentation and recoil control system. It is quite similar to the Mark Five that we've worked with, but this chassis contains the addition of several combat peripherals."

"Jesus..." breathed Dex as he turned the faceplate toward him, "Is there any way for you to know how many of these that Vendrick's folks have? Because we have waded into some *very* different waters here."

"Undeterminable," Replied Vette regretfully, "but I can tell you that this crate, specifically, seemed to be an individual special order that had separate security protocols in place for it. That is why the crate was selected for retrieval in the first place. This circumstance leads me to believe that the armor is not common and was most likely intended for a local lieutenant's trophy room."

"Well that makes me feel a little better." Said Dex with a bit of a sigh as he placed the helmet back onto its mount within the box, "So what's under door number two?" Reaching for the lid that covered a small compartment at the corner of the crate, he pulled it free to reveal neat rows of grey powder-filled vials arrayed in stacks of three. Lifting one of the glass capsules from its cradle, Dex held it to the light and asked; "What the hell is this?"

"Funding." Answered Mirta as she stepped forward to seize the vial from him, "Do you have any idea how much this stuff gets on the street?"

"What does it *do?*" inquired Dex with a skeptical look.

"I dunno." Replied Mirta with a shrug, "Fucks people up though, I imagine, because junkies will pay a shitload for it."

"I'm not sure how I feel about slinging poison to the fine people of Meclan." Said Dex with a disapproving look, "Things are bad enough there *without* us making it worse."

"You're damn right you're not gonna sell it!" rose Tano's voice as he stepped onto the flightdeck in a huff, "The only place those drugs are going is out the airlock! Shame on you, Mirtana Ozimova, for thinking otherwise. You've seen just as many folks as I have fall prey to that shit over the years. What's *wrong* with you?"

"I'm only suggesting we do what is *necessary* to see us through to the final goal." Argued Mirta with her arms folded across her chest, "We all knew from square one that this whole *kill Vendrick* thing wasn't going to be a clean task, but we all *agreed* that it was a necessary hardship needed for our people to move forward."

"What if we just find a better use for the drugs than a profit driver?" proposed Dex with a shrug, "Many narcotics, I know, can be broken down and refined into helpful medicines and other beneficial compounds. I bet Vette would know how to do that...If we got her some proper equipment to do it with first."

Tano's face lit up at Dex's suggestion and he was quick to offer; "I like it! And I can do yah one better. What if I told you that I knew a guy who has all the equipment and knowhow we'll ever need? Laredo would be more than willing to help us out. He's head admin out on the ring."

"The ring?" asked the out-of-towner, at a loss, "What's the ring? Afraid I didn't see that one on the travel brochure."

"Matsuoka ring, out in the belt." Explained the Sergeant, "It's the manufacturing headquarters for Matsu-Pharm, a drug company with quite a few contracts in the mid to outer bubble. Saiph member-stations receive the local discount on their product, and they've supplied us with everything we've needed for as long as they've been out there. And, as long as the ring's been out there, they've had Laredo out there as well to watch over things. We could call him up and see if he's willing to take a look for us."

With a thoughtful look, Dex asked; "Who else do you know in the system who might be a big fish in their respective ponds? Ones that would be amenable to our cause, I mean. Instead of having the conversation a dozen different times, we could get everyone together via that secret network Vette's been setting up with that glowy rock doo-dad. Maybe once we're all there at the same time, we can come up with a way we can all help *each other*. Nobody is going to want to fight anyone else's war, but we may be able to at least work out a bit of a support network for everyone to collectively lean on. It's worth a shot. And if it can help stop some preventable deaths, I kinda have a responsibility to shoot that shot."

Tano nodded, saying; "Once again, I like the way you think, kid. I'll hop onto the net and drop a few feelers. See what shakes loose after all these years…"

Chapter 22

"Alright, so where do I put this stupid thing?" asked Dex with boiled-over frustration while shaking a limp rubberized loop in his hand.

Mirta sighed and strolled over from her own VR couch to snatch the device out of his hands. "How have you never done this before?" she spat incredulously, "It's a collar. Magnetic link in the front, retractable hood in the back. *You can pull out with these tabs here.*" She gestured to the indicated tabs with a sarcastic wave of her hand, the condescension in her tone bordering on hostility.

Dex ignored the bite of her remark, pointing at himself to say; "Hipster, remember? I never really did *any* of this junk growing up. Why are you so pissy about the whole thing, anyways? If you don't mind my asking…"

"I'm not pissy!" she complained with a scathing squint, "I'm just piss-**ED** that I have to waste my time with this stupid video game bullshit when there's still *real* dickheads out there who *really* need to not be alive anymore."

"What good would killing off all the *dickheads* do if all the innocent folk you were trying to free ended up dying in the crossfire while you did it?" asked Dex pointedly with a tap to his brow, "We *will* take direct action, Mirta, but we have to be prepared first. Emergency preparedness is essential to the survival of any plan or organization, and communication is the key to preparedness. We will strike big blows only when the cards have all been shuffled just so and stacked in our favor. We can't afford *not* to. But don't worry, this shuffling doesn't require us to just *sit* around in VR all day. It will take quite a bit of doing. And the quicker we do it, the quicker you'll be properly rid of Vendrick and his shadow."

Mirta just huffed as she worked at fastening the rubberized collar around his neck and said; "Well let's get this shit over with so we can get to the doing. So stop squirming like a *petulant toddler* and let me hook this damn thing."

"Oof." Chuckled Tano from behind Dex's shoulder, clipping on his own electronic collar as he lowered himself into his own VR couch, "Even I felt that one."

"You sure that wasn't just your third coronary of the morning, Ser Gravy-Sweats?" retorted the younger man with a rude hand gesture as he plopped back into his couch. He eyed the collar device skeptically, examining its inner edge as he asked; "So how does this work anyways? I'm not going to end up paralyzed or lose my noodle in this thing, am I?"

"Which noodle?" asked Mirta with a smirk and raised brow, "The big one or the little one?"

Dex opened his mouth to speak, then stopped himself. After a short moment of consideration, he narrowed his eyes and replied; "I…'m not exactly sure how to answer that one."

"To answer your *actual* question," interjected Vette from a speaker in the ceiling, "The collar uses low-level electromagnetic stimulation to induce *temporary* muscle paralysis, much like you experience during sleep, while the hood utilizes a similar process to produce a REM-like state. During this engineered mindstate, your brain acts as if it were a blank slate; Waiting for the VR system to provide your sensations of sight, sound, touch, taste, and smell."

"That just sounds like a recipe for disaster if anyone trips over the damn plug or something." Complained Dex as he examined the floor around him. "I'd come out all fucked up, tasting colors or some weird shit."

"Synesthesia is not a reported symptom of VR failure syndrome, Commander." Replied the AI assuredly

"Wait, there's a *syndrome?!*" asked Dex as he shot his head up to look at the speaker, "What kind of syndro-" His words were cut short as Mirta stepped up from behind him, yanking the elastic fabric of the hood over his head while pressing a button on the side of the collar. In response, Dex immediately went limp and his body sloughed to the side, nearly tumbling him off his couch to the floor.

There was nothing but darkness around Dex. No stars, no ground, no horizon; Just his own body, inexplicably lit from an unknown source, and nothing else. Then, as if coming from within himself, Vette's voice rose; "Apologies, Commander. Mirta's sudden and wildly irresponsible activation of your neural hood has caused your avatar to load before an intended program was selected for it. Establishing network link and rendering the online meetingspace now. One moment."

Then, in the time it took for him to blink his eyes, he felt gravity at his heels and a tangible world materialized out of the oblivion around him. He found himself standing on rich cherrywood flooring that was bathed in gentle white sunlight. As he panned his vision upward, he was met with a long white marble table that stretched five meters down the center of the room. Atop the gold-filamented veins of the table lie an intricately sewn blue silk runner that was piled high with gently flickering candles and display bowls full of fruit and other treats. As for the room itself, each of its four walls was composed of a single uninterrupted sheet of glass, embedded with a latticework of gold leaf that seemed to mimic the appearance of glittering vines growing to form a waist-high wrought iron fence that sprouted from the dark wood of the flooring.

Beyond the walls of their virtual conference room, the ground fell away quickly on all sides in the form of sheer craggy cliffs. The impossible location depicted their private room atop the sharp peak of a single snowy mountain that seemed to fade into a lone tropical jungle island at its base. As Dex was gazing to the horizon, trying to determine if it bent in the correct manner, Tano's voice rose from behind him; "Trippy as shit your first time down the pipe, aint it?" he asked with a chortle that was utterly devoid of sympathy, "Well keep your lunch, princess, because the delegates are starting to show up."

Before Dex had time to process and understand what the somehow skinnier-than-life Tano was saying to him, the mustachioed Sergeant had already turned away and began to introduce himself to another man that was suddenly among them. Dex looked across the room and caught Mirta's eye. Even though her expression was full of boredom and contempt, he found comfort in it somehow. Maybe it was in the way that her eyes lingered on his own as she canvased the room with an otherwise dispassionate ocular sweep, but the warmth beneath her gaze was clear to see. Eventually, Dex realized the Sergeant was calling his name, so he snapped himself from his private fixation and stepped over to introduce himself.

The mousey man before him donned long crimson robes of silk and his very aura radiated wealth as he extended a diminutive hand and said; "Pleasure to meet you, my name is Laredo Causic. I represent the business interests, as well as the people, of the Matsuoka ring. My company and its employees have served to provide the Saiph system with cultured vaccines, personalized medications, and genetic therapies for over seventy-five years. Business lately, however, has suffered under the intrusion of this criminal cabal and I'm curious about this plan that you claim to have for dealing with them."

"The Pleasure is all mine, mister Causic." Offered Dex with a polite nod, the action subconsciously nearing a bow in the presence of the other man's opulence, "I'm glad that you could find the time and private space to join us. If you'll have a seat and enjoy the...eh... virtual food, if that's a thing that people do in VR, the rest of the participants should be here shortly."

With a polite nod of his own, the robed man excused himself and strolled over to the table as another person came into being at the far end of the room. The newcomer was a short, round-cheeked, older woman with a greenish-blue pixie-cut and loose-fitting green and pink coveralls that were obviously chosen for fashion over any form of function. From beneath the baggy outfit, the woman's skeleton somehow seemed to move the garments in artful swirls as she stepped forward to introduce herself. "Gaizya Tam," she said with a smoky voice while extending a hand to Dex in greeting, "organizer of the Heldrin City community action committee."

"Thanks for coming, Gaizya!" beamed Tano as he stepped forward to receive a deceptively strong bear hug from the diminutive woman, "It's great to see you again after all these years. Your work at the crisis management center there on Heldrin has served as a shining example of what a community is capable of when it takes care of its own. With your help, I'm hoping that today can be our first step toward an expansion on your program that will reach *everyone* in Saiph."

"You honestly think hugs and warm thoughts will cure the system?" rose a hostile voice from the back of the room. It belonged to a tall vacker with lean ropey muscles that rested confidently beneath the simple blue cotton of his T-shirt. His face carried a patchwork of scarring that suggested a lifetime of conflict and his left eye had gone milky white, presumably from whatever had managed to also remove the ear from the same side. Using his good eye to scan the room's virtual grandeur with contempt, he strode over to the others with an easy gait.

"I was actually thinking more along the lines of applying some ballistic diplomacy." replied Dex as he stepped forward to offer his hand, "You must be Max Drebbin out of Bengal. Your reputation precedes you, Captain. Mike told me of your work together during the initial Federal withdrawal, and it sounds like you busted your fair share of heads along the way. Your combat experience and battle command knowledge are going to be invaluable in our ongoing fight to free Saiph. We're happy to have you."

The scarred man ignored Dex's outstretched hand and retorted; "You got my *attention*, but you don't got *me* yet...You dig?"

Dex lowered his hand as the stern man plopped himself into an awaiting chair, reaching for one of the arranged virtual confectionaries. Trying to swallow his annoyance at the man, Dex replied with a shrug; "Well, regardless, thanks for showing up to hear us out.".

Just then, another person had popped out of the ether to join their rooftop doughnut party. The newcomer was a thin gentleman with sunken cheeks that seemed to denote his stoic grandeur rather than the starvation that had surely accentuated them. He wore a simple beige cotton tunic over what appeared to be the lower half of a utility vac-suit with its arms cinched across his waist. When he materialized, the white-haired man immediately scanned the room with eyes that were lit by an obvious spark of caution and intelligence. As his gaze moved over Dex, he paused and stepped forward with a slight respectful bow to say; "Thank you for inviting me to your discussion on the future of Saiph. I'm pleased to see that *someone* is finally taking on the mantle of responsibility to change things around here."

"Layton!" boomed Tano as he pushed past Dex with his arms raised for an embrace, "It's great to see you, you old coot! You look like hell! They got you working overtime hand-pushing minecarts again?"

"Only when there's an emergency," replied the lanky man with the hint of a smile starting to spread across his face, "which only generally happens on days that end in 'Y'."

Tano embraced the man briefly and stepped back for a better look at his withering frame. With sobriety returning to his expression, the Sergeant asked; "How are things? How are your people holding up?"

"It was hard enough keeping all my folks alive *before* brutes with guns started demanding quotas." Replied the man with a sad sigh to accompany his crestfallen expression, "Now, I can't go a whole week without having to box up another body that I recognize. It's too much, Mike. I don't care how, but, one way or another, this has to end. I'm getting old, my friend, and I want my last breath in this universe to be of *free* air."

"We're here today to discuss the very air of which you speak." Interjected Dex with an amicable nod, "I take it that you already know the Sergeant?"

It was at that moment that Tano realized the other eyes in the room were hovering on him and the newcomer. Feeling his self-consciousness swelling, he quickly diverted the room's attention away by saying; "This here is Layton Travert. He is head administrator of the Verdigan mining outpost on Meclan's sister moon, Ourea. I know him from when we served a stint in the original MDF together. This man was and no doubt still is one of the most brilliantly organized quartermasters in the history of quartermastery. You could put in a requisition order for a hunk of leprechaun shit and he could get you your preferred color and consistency. If you want to know how to help the largest number of people with a finite supply of aid, then he is *definitely* your guy."

Dex nodded at the man with a friendly smile then turned and stepped up to the table to face the others. With his expression returning to a somber mask, he leaned on the opulent marble tabletop to say; "Now that we have everyone here, I would like to explain why we've invited you in the first place. My name is Dex Sloan and you are all currently connected to a private network that my associate, Vette, has set up for us. While in here you cannot be tracked, recorded, or intercepted in any way by Vendrick's forces, so please speak freely."

"*Forces?*" scoffed Drebbin with a sneer, "You act as if these fuckwits were a standing army. Well, they're not. They're a bunch of fat assholes, with dumbshit tattoos, who *happen* to scare the piss out of unarmed women and old junkies. They have no patrol structure, no central command, and no real idea what the fuck they're doing *at all*. We could take em all out in a single night and be done with it. Give me twenty-four good shooters and forty-eight hours to plan a strike. I'll have Bengal breathing free air by breakfast on Wednesday morning."

"*Fuck* yeah!" blurted Mirta from the back of the room, "Now that's more like it, count me in!"

"Woah, now," cautioned Dex with outstretched hands, "I don't think *that* overt of an action is wise at the moment. While it may be possible to launch a successful attack like you described, we are unsure at this point what the collateral damage and aftereffects would be. I think the smart play is to take our time building a support network so that we can keep the bellies of the people full while *they* feed *us* more detailed information to act on."

"I agree with Mr. Sloan." Stated the opulent visitor from Matsuoka ring, "In the wake of a conflict of that scale, our production and manufacturing schedules would be thrown into chaos, especially at this time of year. Many of our culture materials are routed in through Bengal station, so any interruption in that supply line would be devastating to our efforts to meet with Vendrick's quotas."

"Vendrick gives *you* quotas?" asked Dex with surprise, "What does he want you to make for him?"

"Nothing dangerous." clarified the robed man with an innocent shrug, "Just a simple programable protein used by pretty much every university in occupied space for molecular biology experiments. Utterly harmless on its own, but difficult to synthesize and in high demand...Which would make it quasi-valuable, I suppose."

"And he pays you for this?" pressed Tano with a raised eyebrow.

"Not exactly." explained Causic with a practiced neutral expression, "He provides the components needed to synthesize the protein and store it, then pays us for our work in the form of rations and the right to continue living. Not a great deal, but I wasn't exactly included at the negotiation table."

"Yeah, that sounds like his M-O on Meclan with the corn crops, too." Offered Tano with an understanding nod, "Seems to be the only aspect of Vendrick's command structure that actually appears organized and premeditated around there, now that I think about it."

"So that's his game, then?" asked Dex to the table, "He milks each station of its cash crop, then turns around and sells it all on the black market for a profit?"

Causic shook his head, saying; "Doubt it. The main catalyst we use for protein production is a Federally controlled substance, which means each batch of it that's bottled is tagged and tracked by an overview committee before it ever gets to us. The cost of this oversight is absorbed via a special tax that is applied to such substances at the point of sale. The reason I bring this up is the fact that, week after week, we are brought industrial amounts of this high-grade controlled manufacturing material, complete with their stamped tax payment stubs, then are forced at gunpoint to synthesize it down into a solution that retains half of its original value. Makes no sense from a retail standpoint."

"Is there something that he *could* further refine it into to create profitability?" asked the aged miner from Ourea thoughtfully, "Are we just seeing one step in some production chain? Making stims or something, maybe?"

"Though he could, *technically*, increase the value of his product," explained Causic patiently, "it would require both expensive equipment and, more importantly, the labor of several skilled individuals whose talents would not come cheap. Not to mention the fact that his profitability is already scuttled from the get-go by his opulent choice of trigger protein. To put it plainly, it's like putting gold leaf on a tuna sandwich."

"It's definitely worth looking into." suggested Dex with a nod, "If we want to know how to hurt Vendrick, we need to figure out what's most important to him so that we can take it away. I will have Vette compile the data that you all have provided and analyze it for leads."

"Vette?" asked Gaizya with a tilt of her colored hairdo, "Who exactly is that, dear? Somebody on your team?"

"I am," rose a voice at the far side of the room. The tall form at the end of the table used Vette's voice and it suddenly became painfully clear to Dex that he had never actually *seen* his beloved A.I. before. She stood at a height of roughly two-and-a-half meters, with light blue skin and a waist-length flow of curly black hair that draped down her back to her knees. Sprouting from the point of her lowest ribs were a second pair of arms that had folded themselves across the waistline of the golden sari draped over her otherworldly form. Each of the dazzling being's four arms were adorned in an etchwork of golden tattoos and a delicate row of bejeweled bangles that shifted rhythmically as she stepped forward.

Realizing suddenly that his jaw was hanging open, Dex desperately tried to recover his voice; "I...uh...wow. Hi there, Vette. Weird *seeing* you here...You, uh, you look *different* than I expected." He walked over to her, approaching slowly to take in the intricate gold leaf lines that were etched into her skin in swirling geometric patterns. When his gaze had panned up far enough to meet hers, the sudden eye contact was visceral. It were as if the thousands of conversations that they had had over the years were finally able to burst out from her real *living* soul, and for the very first time those chats all had their final bit of context clicked into place for him. With a chuckle, because he couldn't think of anything else to say, he opened his arms and proceeded to receive the most oddly over-encompassing hug he had ever experienced. After his heels had finally managed to return to the carpet, he heard the distinct sound of Tano clearing his throat behind him. With a shrug, Dex fixed his shirt and turned to nonchalantly address the crowd; "Anyhoo, with *her* punching the numbers for us, we should have a significant advantage when it comes to guessing where their shipments are going and when they're gonna be there. We can use that data to hit *hard* and seize the supplies we need to pry the populous free from its dependence on Vendrick."

"You know what?" spat Drebbin with boiled over impatience, "You guys are real cute and all with all your tender hugging and whatnot, but I'm just gonna go ahead and let you do your little community garden project or whatever-the-fuck if it fits Meclan's goals, but unless you're here to offer me and the people of Bengal weapons; You're wasting my time."

"We have no weapons to offer." Replied Tano with an apologetic shrug, "But even if we did, popping them off right now is not the right play. We need to figure out how the larger organism works before we start trying to clear the infection from the streets. Otherwise, it will just spread again. I don't know what you guys have seen in the way of resistance on Bengal before today, but it has *always* ended ugly for Meclan whenever it was tried over there. We need to come at this with a scalpel, not a hammer."

"Alright then." Said the man from Bengal with a huff of finality, "I guess you *were* just here to waste my time. I'll send whatever aid I can after Bengal is freed. Good luck with your drum circle, girls." And with that, the man dematerialized right in place, the strawberry tart in his hand tumbling onto his now-vacant chair and rolling onto the floor below.

"We should at least send him some supplies." Urged Mirta, her disappointment clear to see, "If he thinks they can pull it off over there, we should help him do it."

"We don't have any supplies to spare." Argued Dex with an aggressive shrug, "None that *he* would accept, anyways."

"What about our *skillsets*?" argued Mirta, "We both have something to offer in that fight and you want to withhold that asset from them?"

Dex sighed and retorted; "Assets are best utilized when intelligently deployed. We have no idea how an organization like Vendrick's would respond when met with a competent threat to rival their control over the sector. There's no telling how many would wind up getting hurt in the crossfire."

"You ever made a goddamn omelet?" she spat with contempt, "Cuz you gotta be willing to break a shit ton of eggs to do it."

Dex brought his hand to his face to rub his temple and pressed; "I get that, Mirta. But what you and Captain gung-ho are looking to do would be the equivalent of chucking your entire supply of eggs at the friggin frying pan, all at once, *without* removing them from the carton first. My conservative, more cautious, approach allows us to crack a few eggs into a separate bowl, maybe add a little pepper, then whip them to maximum *effective* fluffiness before they ever even hit the heat of the pan. *That* is what makes for a balanced breakfast, my dear."

"Too bad everyone died waiting for your pussy-ass eggs to fluff!" spat the angry green-eyed woman with open hostility.

"Can y'all do me a favor and cool it with all the egg shit already?" pleaded Tano with a frustrated sigh, "Mirta, if you have nothing constructive to add to this discussion of *logistics*, then I suggest you log out and find something else to occupy your time with."

In a huff, Mirta shot the Sergeant a rude gesture then de-materialized in the blink of an eye. The Sergeant just sat there, shaking his head, before turning to Dex to say; "Go ahead, kid. Give us the play by play on what you're thinking. Laying it out for us all is bound to be easier without the *peanut gallery* chiming in every ten seconds."

"Thanks, Mike." Said Dex with a nod before returning his attention to the table as a whole, "In times of great need, such as the position we all find ourselves in today, it has always been to our benefit as a species to work *together* toward a common goal that would lift us from our shared strife. In an effort to prevent us from doing this, Vendrick and his forces have made every effort to isolate the stations of Saiph from one another by cutting off your Hūnet access and revoking your right to leave port. Once you were no longer able to talk to one another, you inevitably lost your sense of the larger Saiph community. Today, I have come to offer us all a chance to rebuild that connective tissue and use it to pull the system back up from its ashes."

"Where are *you* from?" asked Causic with a suspicious squint, "Where do your loyalties lie in all of this?"

"I'm from Oregon." Replied Dex with a shrug, "And I'm generally on the side of non-assholes. I was just passing through and happened to notice your roach problem is all."

"You just *noticed* our problem and decided to help out, eh?" pressed the pragmatic man from Matsuoka skeptically.

"Exactly." Responded Dex amicably with a smile, "Dealing with infestations of this sort is, *in a way*, what I used to do for a living. And when I saw what was going down on Meclan, I figured *hey;* Just cuz I'm retired don't mean I'm dead."

"So," began Gaizya, her expression growing suspicious, "some stranger from Meclan comes along out of the black and tells me he can *save* the star system, but I need to trust him with my life and the lives of my people because he *assures* me that he knows what he is doing?"

"Not at all, but also yes." replied Dex with the air of a salesman, "I'm asking you to trust me based on the *plan* that I've made. I may not have much of a horse in this race from your perspective, but I'm human enough to know which side of a fight the good guys are on. I'm just here from the outside universe to provide an extra toe on the scale in your favor, and I've got a heavy goddamn foot to throw around when I need it."

"Well, it certainly seems that a lack of confidence won't be an issue in your department," Chuckled the time-worn miner from Verdigan with good humor, "but I would like to hear what you actually had in mind for *us*."

"What I want for *you* to do" said Dex while gesturing with his arms to encompass the occupants of the table, "is talk to one-another again. What do *you* have that your neighbor is in need of? What do *they* have for *you*? I want to set up an underground distribution network, routed through the traffic-laden ports of Heldrin City, that can deliver supplies, medicine, and support personnel to where they are needed, **when** they're needed. There is no reason that anyone should starve to death this day in age or die of a simple infection, and everyone present has a responsibility, as a *community*, to save as many lives as we can. Resistance doesn't always mean going out and killing your oppressors. Sometimes it means building your strength quietly, so you can wake up tomorrow stronger and ready to repeat the process until you're prepared for the head-smashing bit."

"I have been waiting for something like this for over a decade." Sighed Travert with what sounded like relief, "This is exactly the kind of thing that I was put into this universe to do. If you can feed me the data I need, I can build you a distribution plan that will most effectively get supplies out to those who most desperately require them. This will require a massive general census of needs, and that task will mean a mountain of data gathering."

 "Then you're in luck," Chimed Vette with a supernaturally beaming smile, "because data is, quite literally, what I'm made of. So, it would be safe to say that we have home-court advantage on that front. I will begin gathering information along any metrics you require and we can build our distribution model from there."

"Supposed A.I. magic or not," retorted Gaizya with a sigh, "if you want to move goods through Heldrin without Vendrick knowing about it, you'll need the *cooperation* of one Randal Becker. Which can be tough to get if you don't come bearing gifts and a profitable business strategy."

"So, who is this guy?" asked Dex with a shrug, "And why is he so important that I should pay him for aid work?"

"Smuggler." Groaned Tano with an exasperated sigh, "And a greedy sociopath who would move poisoned baby-bottle-tops into an orphanage if he saw a profit in it."

"Well," countered Gaizya, a bit taken aback at the Sergeant's sudden hostility, "lately his hauls have been of luxury items and medical aid. I'm not sure where you've gotten this impression of him, Mr. Tano, but I can assure you that it's false."

"He may have *you* charmed," warned the Sergeant in a low tone dusted with contempt, "but I chased that shitheel for *years* back when the Feds were still running the show. And I can assure *you*, my dear, that your oh-so well-meaning smuggler wasn't carting around any injector cartridges at the time that would do anybody *any* good."

"Then I don't know what to tell you." Replied the small-time politician with a shrug, "Because Randy already has the ships we need and the pilots who know the secret routes to get them where they're going. I'm sure you can understand how crisis has a way of creating strange bedfellows..."

"Yeah, well I like to use protection when I find myself in bed with strange fellows." retorted Tano flatly, "So I wanna talk to him *myself*. ***In person.*** I want him to know that if he fucks us over, I've got his number. I want him to *understand* that the only reason I wish to speak to him, instead of setting his greasy fucking ponytail on fire, is his *utility* to us and our goals. I refuse to work with anyone who isn't at the table for the right reasons."

"I may paraphrase a bit," began Gaizya with a weary sigh, "but I will talk to him and set up a meeting for you. When are you thinking that you'll be able to make it out?"

"Set the meet for as soon as possible." Said Tano with a nod, "Dex and I will be headed your way within the hour."

Chapter 23

Dex and Tano dropped out of zerospace fifty kilometers out from Heldrin City. The station was in orbit around Saiph's largest gas giant, Jofur, just above the plane of the vibrant red planet's exquisite ice ring formation. Dark swirling lightning storms, lit by a stitchwork of flashing blue and violet that tore across its blanket of maroon cloud-cover, played in stark contrast to the bleach-white of the planet's icy rings as they glistened in the distant sun's light. The station itself was a large cube, nearly five kilometers across on each face, and it seemed to rotate with a visibly clumsy wobble. The intricate tumble was no mistake, however, as it was precisely calculated to work in concert with a series of embedded inertial dampening systems to create a perfectly balanced feeling of centripetal gravity on the inside surface of the station. From a distance, the massive construct appeared to have softly glowing spikes that protruded from its core in an irregular pattern on each face of the cube, but as they got closer the illuminated spikes resolved into lit towers that jutted out from the cube's central recesses.

The station was not of an uncommon design, known best for its sprawling glass-floored observation decks and the semi-disorienting point of view its residence towers offered. From the perspective of someone standing in one of the famed apartment units, looking out the window, one would see the massive bulk of the station above them with endless pinpoints of starlight steadily swirling below. It was a *feature* that forced some of the city's more squeamish citizens to seek residence further up into the cube's structure, mercifully away from any external windows. Those who were brave enough to approach the viewports at Heldrin City, however, were rewarded with a spectacular panoramic view of the ringed crimson face of Jofur, dancing an elaborate ballet alongside its four icy moons. The breathtaking view alone made Heldrin City a worthwhile place to visit for anyone with eyes and a heartbeat.

The duo were flying in an old beat up little personal transport shuttle that they had found rotting at the back of Hearth's support hangar and the dank smell of the craft's interior soaked into every fiber of their clothing, helping them cement their assumed identities for the day as washed-up cargo runners. Dex and Vette both wanted to take the Hammer in, but Tano vetoed the idea in favor of something that would help them blend in. The tiny shuttle was worse for wear from its years sitting ignored on the hangar deck, but the dents and rust spots across its hull served to further camouflage the little ship among its squalid surroundings. Tano contacted the control tower and requested clearance to land under the guise of a simple leisure trip, but he did not, however, share with them the fact that he was also transporting a co-pilot who was encased in a powered exoskeleton and roughly eighty kilos of self-healing antiballistic plating. The active combat armor was not bulky, however, and was easily concealed beneath Dex's leather jacket and a loose-fitting pair of black pants that matched the local fashion.

The control tower radioed back, clearing them to land, and directed them to their assigned spot. Once the comm call had closed with a light chirp, Tano's heads up display highlighted a small flat section on the outside surface of the station near its lower left-hand corner. Once they got close enough to the indicated sector, they could see that they were being led to an external starport with lit landing pads stretching out for nine-hundred meters in every direction. Upon hearing a low tone from his guidance system, the Sergeant relinquished his controls to the navigation computer, and allowed it to begin its automated docking process. Their ship sped to match the rotational velocity of the station, then began to descend toward an illuminated landing zone. When the shuttle's docking skids touched the faded yellow surface of the pad, Dex and Tano felt a lurch as the station's magnetic clamps engaged to hold the ship in place. The shuttle's engines then began powering themselves down and the landing pad started to lower itself into the depths of Heldrin city. Once they were fifty meters in, they reached a spherical widening in the shaft where the lift came to a gradual stop. The landing platform then slowly began to nose down, flipping itself over in place to put the empty vacuum of space beneath them. Both men aboard the shuttle felt themselves sink lower into their seats as the lift completed its roll and their onboard gravity generator gave way to the higher gravity rating provided by Heldrin city. After the lift's internal locking mechanism could be heard re-engaging, the elevator continued to rise through its shaft toward a set of doors above that were slowly sliding open to reveal the blue shimmer of an airshield beyond.

When the platform came to a stop, the men were looking out their viewport over a massive commercial dock. The vast space was dotted with hundreds of craft in all shapes and sizes, many of which seemed questionably spaceworthy in their neglected states of repair. Countless cargo drones could be seen zipping around, going about their business from pad to pad, while huge automated cranes loaded and unloaded goods from hulking freighter pods. Seeing the controlled chaos playing out before him gave Dex a renewed faith in their plan to hide a smuggling ring within the static of Heldrin, so he was the first one down the ramp and out into the hectic dock. When Tano finally made it down behind him with a bulky satchel in tow, he tapped Dex's shoulder and gestured toward a man with a tablet, looking incredibly inconvenienced, heading their way.

The Sergeant decided to put on his best used-ship salesman smile and strode over to meet the man halfway. "What're you hauling?" Asked the skinny dockmaster, his sunken eyes still glued to his tablet. Tano kept his smile fixed and held an arm out to shake the man's hand in greeting.

The hurried man reluctantly looked up from his work, then reached for Tano's hand out of a sense of obligation. The diminutive dock master's eyes then went wide in surprise when their palms met, and he felt the heft of an object being passed to him. "We're just here for a visit," stage-whispered Tano without skipping a beat, "but we would like to keep our presence...a *surprise*. Do you mind keeping us off the ledger? Drones belonging to a colleague of mine will be by shortly to collect our cargo, so there will be no need to dispatch any of your own to offload for us."

The gaunt man opened his hand to examine the polished hunk of crystal in his palm. "Buddy, " chuckled the dock worker with a wink and a genuine smile, "for 800 credits I'll testify to Vendrick himself that this pad has been closed for maintenance all day. And I'd also say that it will continue to be out of service for...oh, I dunno...about another twenty-four hours or so? Enjoy your stay at Heldrin City, gentlemen."

Tano grinned and gave the dockmaster a friendly pat on the shoulder as the man turned to walk away. Dex, having watched the exchange at a medium distance with outward casual disinterest, caught up with his companion and began to walk in stride with him, asking; "So where do we go now?"

"We need to head to a bar called Quake's End and wait for a hotspot dead-drop." replied Tano as he continued toward the port authority building, "We have about an hour before showtime, so let's try not to dick around in the giftshop on our way over, okay?"

Dex was familiar with the technique but confused as to why they were employing it in this instance. To voice this concern, he said; "Why all the cloak and dagger stuff? Doesn't he understand that we have a secure connection to coordinate through?"

"He's just being a dickhead." Answered the old Sergeant with a knowing grumble, "He's going to make us jump through a few hoops for him like a couple of goddamn show dogs, then he's going to lead us out somewhere where he's likely to try and kill us both. Hence the surprise ballgown you have on under those breeches of yours."

"If he's so likely to fuck us over," asked Dex with exasperation, "then why the hell would we bother trying to work with him?"

Tano sighed and shook his head sadly before saying; "It's painful as hell to admit it, but Becker *is* supernaturally good at what he does. And we really need those talents on our side right now. Gaz was right, necessity really does create odd bedfellows, and this is just one that I'm going to have to swallow."

"So, we're just off to the bar to swallow an old bedfellow of yours, eh?" asked Dex with a snicker, "What kind of bar *is* this? I think I left a fishnet shirt in the ship somewhere if I need it..."

"Just shut up and take yourself seriously for once, will you?!" urged Tano with a quiet fury, all while remaining mindful of the faces now swirling around them as they pushed through the crowd that had clumped near the port's font gate.

Dex slouched a bit and avoided the bored gaze of one of Vendrick's men who was standing guard at the port's entry, waiting until they had passed by him before replying; "Hey, I'm just askin' questions here because *you* won't volunteer any information. What's with the tight lips? He an old boyfriend or something?"

"An old *collar*." Replied the Sergeant with reluctant acquiescence, "Traced him back to a shipment of bad stims that killed the thirteen-year-old daughter of a buddy of mine. Had enough evidence to prove that he was docked during the time of the hand-off, but all the video surveillance from the port that night got scrubbed in a data breach. I've been wanting to watch that man rot in a cell for the better part of three decades now. So, forgive me if I'm not chatty about having to work with the son of a bitch."

"Fair enough." Replied Dex with an understanding nod, "I'll just let you deal with him and I'll keep my eyes open for funny business. And hey, look on the bright side, muchacho... It sounds like we'll get a few minutes to relax and grab a drink."

Quake's end is a festering shithole." Grumbled the Sergeant while pushing through a group of weary-looking dock workers to the taxi terminal. As he punched in their destination request at the empty queue's kiosk, he continued; "The only reason he's sending us there is to try and remind me of the *one* day he got to play politician after the Feds packed up. He was supposed to be representing Heldrin's business interests at the summit, but spent the entire afternoon ordering shrimp and moaning about privacy law. He couldn't have made his *real* allegiance to the local crime families clearer if he'd been wearing their sigils across a Rocket-Lev racing jacket."

Their taxi pod arrived without a noise, gently coming to rest on the posi-lev roadway in front of them. After stepping in and getting comfortable, Dex looked to his visibly grumpy companion to say; "You do realize that you're letting him win by getting all red in the face like that, don't you? Why not, instead, order *yourself* some of that shrimp and enjoy life a little?"

"I'd sooner eat a fly out of a urinal." Scoffed the older man as he gazed out the window while the taxi rose and began to move along a track. Their transport then quickly dipped into a tunnel and joined a torrent of traffic moving along the magnetic freeway that was flowing underneath the bustling dock. This took them to a tremendously complex and interweaved traffic nexus where they were seamlessly handed off to a different posi-lev ribbon that whisked them up and into Heldrin's main internal chamber. This sprawling central cavity contained the City's urban landscape, erected in rows of architecturally interesting and varied buildings set along the hollow sphere's inner surface. In an attempt to avoid disorientation and discomfort within the gravitationally odd space, the station's designers had implemented a holographic blue sky that prevented pedestrians from seeing across the station core to the 'ground' above their head on the opposite side. The fantastically believable illusion even came complete with fully animated clouds and simulated gusts of wind that would occasionally sweep down the streets, laden with the artificial scent of trees, grass, and petrichor. Floating within engineered weightlessness at the heart of the cube was a brilliantly blazing artificial sun, held in place by a collection of heavy-duty photonic tractor beams. The system was capable of simulating a full day/night cycle and the 'sun's' rays even gave off heat, due to the effect actually being created by an actual sustained fusion event.

Being a terrasider, Dex naturally found Heldrin's unique open skies quite soothing as he closed his eyes to enjoy the artificial sun's warmth on his face through the window of the cab as it pulled out onto the surface streets and started for their final destination. Most stations tended to give him a slight sense of claustrophobia, but there was something about the air on Heldrin that felt more...authentic to him. Their bright green taxi shuttle came to a stop outside of a tall building with a fading and chipped exterior. The structure's glass and stone facade stretched upwards to disappear through the station's artificial heavens, creating a jarring illusion as its unkempt holographic projection system struggled to blot out the floors that had stretched beyond the skyline. They stepped through the automatic sliding doors at the front of the building to find themselves in a sizable central atrium that was overlooked by twelve floors lined wall to wall with identical glass storefronts. Equipped with a neglected, algae coated, fountain and mostly abandoned shops, the large space didn't exactly scream High Class, but it contained echoes of it.

Tano surveyed the area for a second, a mask of contempt burnt into his features, then pointed off toward a back wall of the filthy mall. Dex followed the Sergeant's finger with his gaze and spotted the bar for himself. It was bathed in broken shadow and sitting in a seedy looking corner at the back of the atrium and the establishment's sign was unlit and crumbling; Affording it all the chic of your classic rundown scum den. Tano sauntered over and stopped in front of the bar to allow himself a moment of less-than-favorable reflection before pushing through the time-worn doors of Quake's End. The smell that hit Dex as they stepped into the sparsely lit room was that of sweat and thick chem vapor and the first thing he couldn't help but notice was the large DJ booth at the establishment's center, blaring some fashion of popular electro-synth music. Normally a place like this would have audio filters to keep the volume from bleeding out of the dance floor, but it appeared that Quake's End was a bit old school.

In Dex's opinion, the incessant beeps and tones that were now assaulting his brain sounded more to like a robot passing a kidney stone than something to dance to. But, then again, he was never much of a music person to begin with. He analyzed the room, observing the small clusters of tables that radiated out from the dance floor in a concentric spiral. Most of the booths were empty, save the odd group of two or three people occupying a few scattered tables here and there, and no waitstaff could be seen shuttling drinks or food. The back wall of the club was stippled with sound-dampening wall panels and consisted of primarily large plush couches which were populated mostly by unconscious patrons who were either on or coming down from a host of chemical cocktails. "Nice place." murmured the younger man from the corner of his mouth as he stepped up beside the Sergeant. Tano ignored the sarcastic comment and surveyed the bar with narrow eyes. He quickly found what he was looking for and began heading toward an empty table in the back corner of the club. Dex followed and both men slid into the poorly lit booth without saying a word, each too alert to make small talk.

After a moment of uncomfortable silence, Dex began to drum a little beat on the table to occupy himself, his visible caution fading as the uneventful seconds ticked by. With a bored glance, he noticed that something was carved into the table. So, he moved a napkin that obscured his view of the artwork to reveal the words '*Tyrants will fall*' scratched into the tabletop's wooden surface. Dex tapped the engraving and leaned over the table to whisper; "Looks like we're in the right place, but did the marker for our *secret* meeting have to be so obvious?"

Tano grunted and replied; "Those words have been carved into this table for over fifteen years. In fact, I carved the F there and our *friend* is responsible for the final, elegantly engraved, L. This table is where the original Saiph Defense Pact was negotiated and signed. Each man sitting here represented his home station's security service and we gathered to discuss mutual aid & cooperation in keeping the opportunistic parasites who call the underbelly of society home from taking over during the power-vacuum that the Feds left behind when they pulled out. We never knew that there were so many ruthless wannabe warlords waiting in the wings to destroy our society, pouring out of the woodwork to cause trouble literally the very same day that the last Federal ship split. Thanks to the work done at this very table, however, we were able to consolidate our martial powers and push the gangsters and thieves out of our system, allowing us to enjoy a good stretch of peace and prosperity before dickhead came around and shattered it all."

Dex nodded, marveling silently at the time-worn engraving. The men who carved it all those years ago were after the very same thing he was looking for today, only they had *attained* their peace just to have it ripped away from them. This thought drew his gaze to the Sergeant, who was a man that had helped achieve that dream and then watched as it turned to ash. Yet there he sat at the very same table he had before; A warrior of the old guard, still standing firm in ever-loyal service to his people. "It *is* a cool bit of history," commented Dex, keeping his private admiration of the man across from him to himself "but if we're just doing a signal drop, I don't see why it had to be somewhere populated like this. I mean, what if someone was already sitting here?"

"Then it woulda been *our* problem to solve." Replied the Sergeant with a shrug, "I highly doubt that Becker put much thought at all into our convenience. He's going to have all these little identity checks for me to pass, under the guise of "added *security*", when all he really wants to do is waste our time. In fact, I bet you fifty credits that after all this fiddle-fucking around, we're going to end up at one of his stupid warehouses filled with old Earth crap."

Dex's interest was piqued at the mention of his home planet; "Earth stuff?" he asked, "Like antiques and such?"

Tano huffed indignantly, saying; "More like all the useless shit that his old lady left behind when she bolted with everyone else a decade ago. Now he's just stuck payin' the rent to store her crap, the dumb idiot."

With the mysteriously aggressive comment falling across awkwardly dead air, they both allowed the conversation to fall silent for a good while. Dex usually got inpatient at times like these, where waiting was the only thing he could do with his time, but he had gotten better at it with age. He had always been more of the fly in, blow shit up, then ride out into the sunset in time for dinner kinda guy, so he never really was one for all the cloak and dagger spy type stuff. To him, spook Ops with fancy dead drops and all kinds of other fancy techno-shit just meant a lot of waiting around and being bored until either A; nothing happens and you go home, or B; everything in the universe happens all at once and you're stuck at the center of it. It wasn't long before Dex's idle fidgeting led him to open the establishment's menu, reaching out to tap the side of a glass cube sitting in the center of the table. The object glowed to life and a large advertisement for the restaurant sprang into existence above the tabletop. He scrolled through lack-luster pages of the menu, taking note that most of the dishes consisted of generally the same three ingredients: Corn, rice, and some form of synthetic meat protein. "Wow," commented Dex as he thumbed through the short menu, "seems like the whole sector has been hit with the food shortages."

Tano just grunted without looking in his direction and absentmindedly said; "Yeah, nobody's eating well these days."

Dex considered that for a moment and decided something didn't add up. "Not trying to be an asshole or anything here, Mike," began Dex tactfully, "but it looks like *your* waistline hasn't taken much of a hit from it all. You blowing the food packet guy, or what?"

Tano looked down at his bulging stomach and gave it an affectionate pat, retorting; "This little puppy is just another one of Vendrick's many elaborate weapons."

"He harnesses the unstoppable power of your appetite and your undying will to destroy all leftovers?" suggested Dex with a dawning smirk.

Tano's smile faded and he scoffed; "Think of the long game, kid. I haven't always been a fat-ass, you know. Vendrick and his grand plan are what made me like this."

"I doubt that our beloved overlord has been forcing you to eat canned spaghetti in your underwear at two AM for the past decade." Quipped Dex, unconvinced.

"ONE time, that happened!" scoffed the Sergeant, "She walks in on me *one time*, and Mirta tells the story like it were something that went down every day. **No**. What I'm saying, smart-ass, is that my gut is the direct result of food being used as a weapon. For about six months following the initial fall of Meclan, my officers and I were provided our *own* rations, separate from what everyone else got in *their* dwindling shipments."

"How considerate of them." scoffed Dex with a skeptically raised eyebrow, "Then what happened?"

"Many of our officers mistook the gesture as an olive branch," continued Tano with a sad shake of his head, "but they couldn't see it for the wedge that it was. Most finally came around and realized something was fucky when our waistlines began to swell, and we were told by our *gracious hosts* that we couldn't share our rations with non-family *under penalty of death*."

"How would they even enforce something like that?" asked Dex incredulously, "It's not like they can keep eyes on everyone at all times."

"Isotope tracking." Sighed Tano with a defeated expression, "Three of our officers lost their lives, as did their families, to their own generosity before we figured that one out. It was a shame, too, that so much food went to waste while so many starved. The ration packets they provided us were the calorie-dense famine recovery meals that were meant to pull an emaciated human from the brink of death. Because of that fact, many of the officers would only eat one of the fifteen mealpacks that they were provided each week."

"So, you ate what everyone else didn't?" inferred Dex with a smirk.

"No, dipshit," grumbled the Sergeant as he leaned back in his seat, "I stored mine in a squirrel-hole I've got in my office. I only needed about a tenth of the provided calories to keep myself fed and healthy, so I ate what I needed and stored what I didn't. Vendrick's guys only kept their shit together with the food dispersion for a little over a year before we stopped getting our special shipments at the station. But by that time, the damage had already been done. Nobody from the public talked to us anymore because they all assumed that we were in bed with the goddamn pirates. Been feeding myself over the years using what I'd stored during that initial period, which is why I remain...jolly."

"That's one word for it." Laughed Dex with a wry smile, "I still don't get, though, how starvation was such a huge and immediate issue for you guys. Has Meclan always been *so* reliant on outside trade to feed itself?

"Before Vendrick was around, we actually had a food surplus." Fumed Tano with an absentminded wave of his arm, "And a big one at that! We were able to sell off *twenty-five percent* of our production to the feds and still keep everyone in the system fed. Everybody pretty much thrived off of that, and it was a simple way to go about living."

Dex switched off the holographic menu and concluded; "That doesn't make sense. Does Vendrick stop you from growing your own food as some form of control to keep you dependent on him?"

He could tell that his line of questioning had struck a nerve when Tano's fist slammed into the table, sending silverware and a doomed water glass to the floor. The old man's face reddened, and he burst into a well-worn tirade; "That's the thing! I don't know about the rest of the system, but Meclan is growing more than we ever have, it's just that *we* don't get to eat any of it...not that we'd want to, though. They had us tear up hundreds of useful, *established*, crop acres just to plant more and more of their weird fuckin' corn that they won't share."

Dex watched his comrade's colorful reaction play out before lifting an eyebrow to say; "Weird corn? What do you mean weird corn? Weird how?"

Tano began shaking his head, at a loss for words. He shrugged, exasperated, then said "I...I have no idea. It's just that they protect the shit like it's the Imperial freakin' Jewels, even though it is some pretty pathetic looking corn."

"I'm not sure that I follow." replied Dex with a shrug, "What makes the corn so pathetic? Did you used to get better yields or something?"

Tano sighed with impatience, then argued; "You were there in the fields, Dex. You saw it. That corn aint right."

"How the fuck am I supposed to know what a good corn looks like?" asked the younger man defensively, "Plus I was kinda busy at the time. You know...doing all the work and such? Can we just pretend that I don't have an agricultural engineering degree for a second and explain to me what's so weird about it?"

"For starters," said the Sergeant with an eye roll, "corn isn't supposed to look so green and stunted after a full ninety-day grow cycle. But the size and hue has nothing to do with the soil and its nutrient content, because I have tested it over the years. It's like they're growing shit corn on purpose and treating it like it were a precious commodity."

"I would imagine that anything edible would count as a precious commodity on Meclan these days." Commented Dex curiously, "So why is it weird that they're protecting their food from angry starving people?"

Tano shrugged and replied; "Because they don't really *need* to protect it. Folks around Meclan are damn near superstitious about staying away from the stuff. Stories have surfaced over the years telling of people who got their hands on some to eat and it never goes well for them. The symptoms reported always vary, but the ending never changes. It is said that eating the corn will, within twelve hours, make you vomit out your intestines, or some other variation of your organs liquifying and exiting your body, basically. Sounds like a load of hogwash, and probably spread by Vendrick himself to keep everyone away from it, but you won't see *me* eating any of that shit anytime soon."

Dex just shook his head in amused disbelief and said; "You sure got yourself a weird corner of the Cosmos here, Mike."

Tano chuckled darkly to himself; "You're tellin' me, kid." With that, a companionable silence fell across the table. The two men just sat there and watched the people around them go about their separate lives, oblivious of any existence beyond their personal bubbles. The seedy establishment featured a whole host of different types of interesting individuals who were comfortably nestled into their own little worlds. Sure, you had your junkies in the back and your card sharks working private games here and there, but normal looking folks could be found as well. For example, Dex spotted a young couple at a table across the room talking and laughing privately to one another. The young man seemed to be telling her some sort of elaborate joke with complicated hand gestures and she was smiling wholeheartedly, captivated by his tale. The happy scene playing out across the room reminded Dex of the great void that had been torn into his own life all those years before. He was normally good at avoiding any and all thoughts of her, but the momentary unintended reminiscence stung like acid on a raw wound.

Dex must have been showing signs of his turbulent mood in his expression, because Tano called for his attention, asking; "What's wrong, kid? Pressure suit crawlin' up your ass-crack or something?"

Now that the Sergeant had brought it up, Dex was indeed a tad uncomfortable in the armor suit concealed under his baggy outfit. "Bingo." He lied, "Feels like my nuts are in a Mag-Clamp."

Tano tossed back his head and laughed with mirth; "Yeah, I remember having to squeeze into one of those during my time in the service. For once, I'm *glad* to have my fat ass."

Dex fidgeted and tugged the armored chest plate under his coat to stop it from digging into his armpit. "I still don't see why you're so intent on meeting this guy without backup on standby." He argued, "We should've at *least* brought Mirta along for some long-range cover."

"Too risky." Said the older man with a dismissive wave, "This guy knows how to sniff out funny business, and we can't risk letting this smuggling arrangement crumble. Besides, you were supposed to be that big 'ol badass who put all those bodies in my morgue without schmutzin' up his pants, remember? *Now* you've got an unschmutzable armor shell around you to help with all the turboviolence and whatnot. So quit yer bitchin'."

"Speaking of badasses," murmured Dex with a chuckle as he nodded toward the entryway, "check out the wanna-Be's that just walked in." Three men had pushed through the doors at the front of the bar who carried a certain sense about them that told Dex they were looking for trouble. Each thug was decked from head to toe in the intricate bioluminescent tattoos that Dex had come to learn were a badge of service to Vendrick, and they seemed to wear clothing that maximally displayed them.

One of them was walking in the lead and had on a floor length overcoat, made of some heavy synthleather material, over what appeared to be a semi-translucent t-shirt that allowed the glow of his artful ink to bleed through clearly. His cheek and was adorned with a swirling design arching over his brow that slowly shifted its color as you watched it. His lackeys, as it was clear that Mr. Overcoat was the leader, wore ragged re-purposed flight suits and had seemingly permanent sneers plastered across their own tattooed faces. Overcoat stole a drink off of someone's table on his way past it and downed the beverage in a single sloppy gulp before discarding the empty glass to shatter onto the dance floor. The absolute absence of any protest from the man who just had his drink stolen told Dex that this particular gang of tough guys frequented the joint and definitely had a reputation that preceded them. He watched the group strut their way through the club, sniffing for something *fun* to distract themselves with, until they came upon the table with the young couple that he had been observing before. Even from across the room, Dex could see the fear in the eyes of the booth's occupants when Mr. Overcoat slid in to sit next to the young woman. The burly gangster proceeded to throw his arm over the woman's shoulder as if they were old friends then squeezed her tight as he shot a wink across the table at her date.

They were all quietly talking about something and the young man looked terrified about whatever it was that the smiling thug was saying to him. Mr. Overcoat then suddenly pulled a gun out from under the table and pressed its muzzle nonchalantly to the woman's forehead, as if to simply illustrate a point in their quiet debate. Sight of the weapon instantly flipped a switch in Dex's mind, and his decision was made *for* him. "How long until the signal drops?" he asked, already starting to stretch his neck in preparation for the imminent athletic performance.

"About two minutes." replied Tano with a disinterested sigh, "Why?"

"Plenty of time." muttered Dex, more to himself than anyone else, as he checked the room once more and rose from his seat.

Tano grabbed his wrist to stop him. "Two minutes, then we can get out of here." he pleaded quietly, "Just let it go, Dex."

"No can do, Mike." Replied the younger man with a straight face that did a fine job of illustrating that the point was not up for debate, "The reason we're here in the first place is to prevent shit like this from happening. Stay put and get what we need. I'll meet you around the block when I'm finished with these fine gentlemen." Tano just sighed heavily with a shake of his head, then reluctantly released his grip on Dex's wrist to sit back and watch the show.

Dex shoved his hands into his pockets then quietly walked over to mill around within earshot of the unfriendly conversation/threat session going on over at table number nine. The large tattooed thug in the booth was leaned forward, grasping the terrified man by his collar, growling; "That's why you'll *think* of a way to get me those credits, smartguy. Otherwise..." he trailed off as he pointedly leaned in to get a deep sniff of the young woman's neck. She recoiled at his invasion, so the man slapped her across the face and shoved her into the wall of the booth.

Sight of the strike was all Dex needed to trip his mental breaker and force him into aggressive action. He stepped forward, loudly shouting; "Hey needle dick!" Upon those words taking flight, it seemed that every eye in the room had suddenly snapped to him; Including the incredulous stares of the three tattooed thugs. Dex continued to step forward, undeterred by the heat of their collective glare. "Yeah, you." he said with an air of inconvenienced annoyance as he locked eyes with the man in the overcoat, "Why do you have to come into this timeless temple of rest and relaxation, with your girlfriends over there, and give this nice young couple such a hard time? And does your mom know you're out wearing her shower curtain?"

The man in the overcoat rose from his seat and turned with theatrically slow menace to face Dex. "Do you have *any* idea who you're talking to?" he scoffed as he perceptibly puffed out his quasi-bare chest.

"Princess Eraal's stunt double?" retorted Dex in a sarcastic tone, never shifting his gaze away from the man's eyes.

To Dex's surprise, the man heaved his head back and laughed with sincere delight as he marveled; "You really **DO** have some balls on you, don't yah?"

Dex cracked an easy smile and replied; "Sure do, your highness. But if you wanted to see 'em, you'd have to take me to *dinner* first."

Mr. Overcoat laughed another throaty roar and boomed; "I like you! You're funny. That's why I'm going to give you the once-in-a-lifetime opportunity to turn around and leave...*right now*. It's an offer that I extend to a very lucky few."

Dex kept his smile fixed and replied; "That's gonna be a negatory from me, cap-i-tan. You see, I'm a big fan of balance, and I saw that you had brought a *trio* of negotiators over to face the lowly **duo** consisting of my young associates here. So, I figured I'd step over and offer *my* services to help round the teams out a bit. You know...to keep things nice and *fair*."

Mr. Overcoat took an amused glance toward the couple cowering in their booth and chuckled; "I don't think the numbers alone are going to quite balance it out for you here, mate."

"I know," sighed Dex with chagrin, "but I don't really have *time* to wait for you to go out and find more friends. Instead, what I offer you is a little game of chance." Dex then slowly withdrew his hand from his pocket and revealed an old-fashioned coin in his palm. It shined like polished silver and featured an eagle on one side and the head of a forgotten leader on the other. He turned it over in his hand methodically as he confidently continued to lock eyes with Mr. Overcoat, saying; "Heads, I let you leave here alive. Tails...I don't."

Without waiting for a response, Dex flipped the coin into the air, sending it in the other man's direction with a wild tumble. Without a thought of his own, the tattooed man reached out to catch the metal disc, squeezing it tightly in his fist. Feeling smug at his display of reaction speed and coordination, he held his hand out flat and slowly opened it to reveal the coin in his palm. "Heads!" giggled Mr. Overcoat with a raspberry sound escaping from between his lips, "Looks like it's our lucky day, boys!" This drew chuckles from his ratty comrades who were both leaning in for a look of their own.

Dex quietly stepped forward with an amicable smile and, without a word, gently rotated the coin in the man's hand to reveal the silver eagle clutching its arrows. The thug looked down at the small metallic disc in his palm, then back at Dex's nonchalant before throwing his head back in laughter with his two goons soon following suit. After a moment of joyful revelry, even Dex had begun laughing with them; Matching every bit of Mr. Overcoat's joyful enthusiasm. To any outside observer, the bizarre exchange would have looked as if it were an inside joke shared between old friends, each part in the elaborate bit expertly performed through to its privately humorous climax. That illusion was shattered, however, when Dex suddenly lashed out with a crushing punch that struck the overcoated man in his windpipe. He could feel the soft tissue in the man's throat give way with a pop under the blow, which was immediately followed up with a powerful front-kick that landed in the middle of Mr. Overcoat's chest. The exosuit-assisted impact of the strike lifted the thug from the ground and sent him barreling back into one of his goons, smashing his comrade's nose in with the crown of his skull on the way down.

When the pair crashed to the floor in a tangled heap, Dex could hear the hollow crack of *someone's* head hitting the hard deckplate and neither of them was immediately moving to get back up. Just as Dex shifted his attention back to the third gangster who was still standing next to him, he was forced to snap his body sideways in order to avoid the pistol that the thug was now bringing to bear on him from its concealment in the man's waistband. Dex stepped forward, seizing the gun as well as the thug's forearm, and flipped him with an expertly executed hip toss that forced the air out of the man's lungs in a violent huff. With his opponent momentarily stunned, Dex was easily able to spin the pistol in the man's grip and depress the trigger. The bullet tore point-blank through the man's left eye, ceasing his existence in an instant before embedding itself into the deck plate beyond with sparks and a deafening clang.

Less than a second after the gun had discharged, Dex's hand exploded in pain as someone kicked it with all of their might. He lost his grip and the firearm went tumbling behind him, clattering to a stop under a nearby booth. Mr. Overcoat's bloody nosed friend had evidently freed himself from under his boss' limp form and was now coming at Dex with a feral rage burning in his eyes. The man bowled into his challenger at half a sprint and grabbed him by the jacket to lift him off of his feet in a mighty drug-fueled heave, but Dex was able to pin the man's hands to his lapels and strike out with a headbutt that landed square on the bridge of the thug's already damaged nose. The tattooed man immediately released his opponent with a new rush of blood spilling down to stain his teeth and he couldn't help but reflexively reach up to cover his face; exposing the back of his head to a trio of brutal follow-up elbows. Dex then pushed the dazed thug, stumbling the disoriented man backward, which afforded him the space for a two-step running start to leap into the air and deliver a devastating knee to the man's sternum. The attack sent the thug soaring backward into a booth, breaking the table underneath him when he landed in an unceremonious crash.

With his moment's respite, Dex decided to make sure Mr. Overcoat wasn't getting back up. He turned his back on the moaning man within the wreckage of the broken table to take a quick glance toward the large overcoated man lying motionless on the ground. The man's hands no longer clawed at his ruined windpipe and blood was slowly trickling from beyond his slack lips, with no sign of breath passing between them. His eyes were still open, but his pupils were fixed, and a pool of red had begun to form under his head that was slowly spreading its way across the black and gold marble floor of the nightclub. Satisfied that Mr. Overcoat was out of action, Dex turned back around to face his final attacker sprawled out among the shattered remains of the ruined booth.

Dex noticed that the man was fumbling around for something, straining to reach it, but he couldn't see what. Then, the glint off the polished slide of a pistol flashed in his eye as it rose from the debris and began to swing in his direction. Dex instinctively dove to the side, landing awkwardly on the seat of a dining booth, and hunkered low as two rounds tore through the table in front of him. He quickly seized the hefty holo-glass menu cube from the tabletop, then rolled off the seat to the ground as more rounds came ripping into the booth. The enraged thug pursued his quarry, stepping around the edge of the seating divider to line up for a killing shot. Thinking quickly, Dex placed his boots on the underside of the table and thrust it toward his attacker using every ounce of his augmented strength. The table hit the man in a glancing blow, forcing him to squeeze off a round that went into the wall. While his opponent was still knocked off balance, Dex quickly sat up and hurled the holo-cube at the man as hard as he could. The heavy hunk of glass and circuitry struck the thug on the temple with a mighty thwack and he instantly went limp, crashing to the floor in a twitching heap.

Dex got to his feet and brushed himself off, taking an extra moment to wipe away debris from below his jacket lapel, before stepping over to inspect the thug sprawled out on the floor. The gangster's head had a massive gash along the brow that penetrated straight through the bone, revealing the unmistakable vibrant pink of ruined brain matter beyond. The mortally wounded man's mouth floundered open and closed silently, like a fish out of water, while his limbs jerked with random spasms. Even as the thug's body was moving through its mechanical steps toward oblivion, however, the man's eyes still showed the light of a terrified awareness that was still clinging desperately to life somewhere within. Unmoved by the sight, Dex proceeded to nonchalantly reach down for his opponent's firearm and was forced to step on the dying man's wrist to pry it from his still-clenching grasp.

It was at this point that Dex realized, for the first time, the deafening silence that had fallen across the club. Two dozen people were casting slack-jawed gazes in his direction, frozen in fear and surprise. He chose to ignore his captivated audience and simply continued to check the weapon's magazine before flicking on the safety catch. Satisfied that the pistol was primed to fire, he walked over and placed the gun in the hand of the young man who had originally been accosted by the thugs. "Your debt to *this* asshole is paid." He assured the terrified man with a nod, "Now take *her* and get the hell outta here."

The young man hefted the pistol like it was an alien piece of technology, then said with a stammer; "Th-Thank you. But why help us? You didn't have to do any of this! What if they come after you?"

Dex just smiled and placed his hand on the young man's shoulder; "Oh, I'm counting on it. There's a storm comin', of that I can assure you, and we're gonna break out the other side of it as free men. So, do yourself a favor and lie low until it passes."

With a companionable pat on the man's shoulder, Dex turned and had begun to walk away when he heard the young woman speak for the first time; "Who *are* you?!"

Dex turned and shot her a friendly smile, saying; "Just a fellow human being, trying to make tomorrow better than yesterday. I saw someone in need of help, so I helped. Simple as that. The day that we all stop giving each other a hand is the day that we abandon our civility." The odd stranger then just winked at the shell-shocked woman and strode out of the bar amid total silence.

Chapter 24

Dex left the dilapidated mall in a hurry, casting an occasional wary glance behind him as he caught up with Tano down the block. They dipped into a deserted side alley together and found a hidden place to talk behind some horribly overflowing dumpsters. "Were you followed?" Asked the Sergeant with a stern look.

"Not to this point," Replied Dex confidently, "but I bet they'll be looking soon. We need to get off the streets."

"Don't you realize that we're trying to get to a secret meeting here?" hissed Tano with hushed reprimand, "A *secret* meeting! There are people that are sticking their necks out on this, and they can lose their lives if you were followed or if either of us were identified. I may not like the man we're here to meet, but I also don't want to get him killed over something *your* dumb ass did."

"In case you failed to notice, there also happened to be a young woman in there who was about to get her brains blown out by some powder-puff in a rain jacket for no good reason. What about her?" argued Dex with swelling venom, poking the older man on the chest before continuing, "And if we're willing to overlook that kind of incident in order to preserve some cloak and dagger horseshit, then the risks that we all take by being a part of this resistance mean fuck-all. Serve and protect, Sergeant. Have you forgotten?"

Tano winced at the rebuke but the old police officer decided to swallow his pride, because deep down, he knew that his associate had hit the nail on the head. Nodding, the tired older man sighed; "Maybe I've just spent too long living under the bootheel, but it never even really occurred to me that the young couple could be helped in the first place. Death by thug has become a common way to pass in my world, like drowning or decompression. An act of nature. I don't like it, you don't like it. But it's the way it *is* around here. We can't drop what we're doing and run in to the rescue *every* time we see some fucked up shit going down. Even though it's objectively the *right* thing to do, we'd never get *anything* done. So, let's just try to get where we are going without any more surprises, alright?"

"I'm assuming you picked up the transmission, then?" prompted Dex, ignoring his colleague's thinly veiled scolding, "So where are we headed next? Any chance that it's a steakhouse? I'm starving."

"Thankfully we're not headed to a place of business, so that should help keep your body count down." replied Tano with a sardonic eye-roll, "It says were supposed to meet him at that warehouse of his that I was telling you about. Big surprise, the jackass. It's on the other end of the station, but luckily I know the place. Must've staked it out a hundred times. Why don't you stay back here, and I'll fetch us a taxi."

"Probably a good idea." Agreed Dex with a nod, "I'll think of a way to conceal my appearance, because I get the feeling that this handsome mug of mine will become a very popular face among Vendrick's people here pretty soon."

While the Sergeant was out on the street catching them a ride, Dex reached down his loose-fitting outer pant leg and into a pouch on the left thigh of his armored vac-suit beneath to pull out the suit's detachable helmet ring. He guided the smooth oval of metal over his head and felt the magnetic seal from his suit's collar lock onto it when it came within proximity of the neck seal. Dex then tapped a control stud on the neckpiece and it sprang to life with tiny plates of metal and glass that unfolded from the collar in a complicated blossom that materialized into a smooth gray and red helmet with a void-black faceplate. Once the helmet had sealed, the suit's intricate combat HUD began to come online with information pouring across the peripheries of his vision. As he was flipping his outer coat's hood over to conceal his newly-formed helmet, Tano beeped him on the comm to signify that he had found them a ride. He sent a confirmation click, then stepped out into the street to join his partner.

The squat green capsule looked identical to the one they had arrived in, save for the long crack that ran up its front windshield. Being careful to not over-exert the strength of his exosuit, Dex gently lifted the vehicle's left-hand wing door and stepped inside. The destination had already been programmed by the ride hailing app that Tano used, so it featured only a single touch panel with the word "Begin" plastered across it in green. The Sergeant got in with a grunt of exertion then closed the door behind him, saying; "Alright, let's get this over with." As he thumbed the cab's touchscreen.

"So, what's the plan?" asked Dex with a casual sigh, "You want me to stay outside and act as the cavalry, or do you want me to come in with you to stand in the background and look mean?"

Tano huffed an unamused chuckle and retorted; "Becker is used to dealing with folks who have trust issues, so I doubt your presence at my side would cause any red flags to fly. Plus, I'd rather have you nearby if the shit hits the fan."

"Sounds good." Agreed Dex with a nod, "But let's avoid all the shit and fans that we can for the moment, shall we? This armor's tough, but I'm *far* from invincible."

"That part isn't really up to *us*." argued Tano pointedly, "But I get what you're saying. I will do my best to not flare up any tempers."

Dex hit the control stud to retract his helmet so his skeptical expression could be seen clearly as he replied; "You sure there, Mikey? Because I have yet to hear you say the man's name without spitting it through your teeth. Are you *really* going to be able to maintain your objectivity once you get face to face with him?"

"I guess we'll just have to wait and see now, wont we?" retorted the Sergeant flatly with the hint of a smile tugging at the edge of his lip. The unpiloted taxi wound through a series of sub-level traffic ribbons, twisting every which way to keep internal gravity constant, until it eventually came to a stop around fifteen minutes later on the far end of the station's bustling commercial district. Dex keyed the stud to re-activate his helmet, then popped the door seal and stepped out of the cab in front of a long row of identical white warehouse buildings. Tano pointed out the warehouse marked 419 and said; "There it is. Let's get inside and see what they have cooked for us."

They walked over to the building, cautiously checking their surroundings as they approached its single, unmarked, white door. The only person in sight was a man dressed in rags, drunkenly sleeping off his hangover between two of the buildings down the row, so they proceeded forward. As the duo approached, the warehouse's entrance slid open of its own accord to reveal only darkness beyond its threshold. Dex just shrugged to Tano at the sight and both men stepped through the doorway with confidence. The door quickly hissed shut behind them, plunging them into absolute darkness. As the stillness descended on them, a voice suddenly rose from above in a booming tone that declared; "Tyrants will fall."

"Especially when they're pushed." replied Tano with the pre-agreed-upon code phrase. Light then immediately flooded back into the room, temporarily blinding Dex and Tano with its sudden intensity.

"Sergeant Tano!" Came a jovial voice from the same elevated position somewhere in front of them, "You've gotten fat!". When Dex was able to blink away the disorienting light, he saw a man in a brown jacket with a fur lined collar sitting atop a cargo container in front of them.

Tano stepped toward the man with arms outstretched in greeting and retorted; "Becker! Still a hatchet-faced prick, I see..."

The man on top of the container hopped down with a broad smile and landed lightly on his feet. Dex was surprised at the guy's towering height, figuring that he had to be handily over two meters tall. The lanky man carried himself with a nonchalant confidence that was surely the cornerstone of his prowess at the negotiating table, a persona that had surely been cultivated over decades of doing successful business with shaky partners. After taking stock of his old *friend,* Becker threw his thumb toward Dex and commented; "Well this dude is built like a brick shithouse. Where'd you dig *him* up?"

Dex stepped forward, thumbing the control stud on his helmet to retract it into its storage ring, and offered his hand to the man, saying; "I'm Dex Sloan, and I'm just here to make sure our mutual friend gets home in one piece."

Becker laughed, seizing the offered hand as he replied; "So *you're* the stranger from Meclan that Gaizya was going on about." At that point, he squeezed his grip harder and yanked Dex's arm close to push his sleeve up and reveal the combat armor beneath his jacket. "And you came with pajamas, it seems. I guess you *are* smarter than you look."

Dex shook free of the man's grip and warned; "Oh yeah, we're *full* of surprises. Just keep that in mind if you decide you want a shot at the title, Cochise."

"Woah," huffed the tall man with a smile as he threw his hands up in mock surrender, "we got a badass over here."

"What he *means,*" Tano interjected with a placating gesture, "Is that we are *here* to do *business* and, more importantly, save some lives while we're at it. I know that we don't exactly like each other, but we need to work together on this."

"I don't know what you mean." Retorted Becker with an innocent shrug, "I harbor no ill will toward you...even though you *stalked* me for a couple of years..."

Tano scoffed and retorted; "That wasn't stalking, pal. It's called an active *criminal* investigation. Listen, I have very little respect for what you do, Becker, but the needs of my people will always outweigh my personal qualms. And my people need *you* and your skillset right now, so here I am."

"I feel much the same way, Sergeant." Replied the smuggler, "Which is why there are a few minor details to iron out before I throw in with your lot. Gaizya gave me the rundown on what you gents are looking to do, bravo by the way, but my pilots don't fly for free."

The Sergeant sighed deeply and urged; "We're at war here, Becker! Isn't it enough of a reward to be rid of Vendrick? We don't have the time *or* resources to be petty here."

The smuggler's expression then hardened for the first time as he spat; "Oh, that's a load of bollocks and you know it! *Nothing* is free in this universe. My people are not going to stick their necks out, running teddy bears and tinctures across the system for you, without a little kickback of their own."

"There he is!" spat the Sergeant sarcastically, "There's the self-interested *goon* I remember. Always looking for your next cut, always angling for a deeper slice for *yourself*. People like you, the ones who circle like goddamn vultures to profit from the misery unfolding beneath you, are the reason that there is so *much* of it out there in the cosmos. You should be *ashamed* of yourself."

"Listen," stated Becker with swelling contempt, "You might be the type of idealists who'll work for that warm fuzzy feeling of a job well done, but *we* are *business*men. *We* need to fuel our ships and feed our families at the end of the day, so *we* are not graced with the luxury of moral superiority."

"We can't pay you in credits," interjected Dex to cut off Tano's rising response, "But we might be able to work something else out. Do you have access to an out-system fence who's willing to buy from you in bulk?"

"I have a few options, yeah." revealed the smuggler with a noncommittal shrug, "What did you have in mind?"

Dex nodded and continued his pitch; "Many of the shipments that we grab tend to have not only food and medical items, but luxury goods intended for Vendrick's lieutenants as well. What if, with every shipment captured, we give you whatever we can't use for the resistance. Then *that* can be fenced for your payment. It's a bit of an extra step for you, but it would net you more credits than we'd ever be able to offer you directly in chits."

Becker rubbed his chin, deep in thought as his eyes seemed to penetrate through the warehouse's roof to something interesting going on beyond it. After a few moments of quiet consideration, he nodded and said; "It's a *lot* of extra work, but it should pay the bills...depending on what you haul in. I want you to know, though, that if your little resistance forces Vendrick's guys to tighten the noose on shipping lanes to the point where I no longer feel that our teams can safely fly the route, then we're out. My guys are *not* combat pilots, and I refuse to ask them to *pretend* to be."

"That's what Scalpel squadron is for." Replied Dex with a resolute nod, "Our guys can offer man-coverage if you need it or provide an on-call rapid response team that can get to you, no matter where you are in-system, within ten minutes."

The smuggler seemed to weigh the stranger's claim for a moment, his eyes flicking back and forth as if stacking tokens on a pros versus cons chart. Eventually, he let out a little sigh and said; "Well, what kind of hardware are these *scalpel* pilots of yours running? I trust you have *combat* ships, at least? The last thing we need is a flotilla of rusted-out jalopies with dumb-fire missiles welded to their hulls clogging up the radar and mucking up our firing solutions."

"You'll find none of that here." assured Tano with an unexpectedly apologetic calm, "We have fifteen combat-ready Odox Eagles and a growing network of ground assets at every station that you will be delivering to. We can secure your pads before you land, keep your ships safe as they're unloaded, and make sure your folks get on their way with as little turbulence as possible. Your asses won't be in the breeze on this one. We've got your back."

"Alright, fine." Sighed the tall businessman with an uncertain shrug, "I will send you the comm codes required to get into touch with one of my associates. You may speak with her regarding any purchases or deliveries you wish to schedule. I will have final say, mind you, on what is loaded onto my ship and I do *not* do mystery boxes. Say what you will about my practices, Sergeant Tano, but I-"

The semi-concealed side door of the warehouse suddenly swung open with a thunderous crash that echoed loudly throughout the large open space. The man who had shot through the threshold of the entrance, dressed in a collection of dull rags and a worn grey beanie, was just as quick to spin himself in a loop and shut the door again behind him with the distinct audible click of a lock bar sliding into place. "They've got a sweeper team outside casing the row of warehouses." Panted the man, desperately short on breath, "Think they were looking for someone. Drone caught an image of one of their tablet screens and was..." the man trailed off as his gaze fell across Dex, shifting at once into a mask of both rage and recognition; "They're looking for *this* asshole!" as he pointed accusingly at the terrasider.

Dex swore to himself, which caught the attention of the smuggler who then demanded; "Is this true? Did you lead these men to my doorstep? Explain yourself! Quickly..." His final word hung thick in the air, drenched with implied threat.

Dex just shrugged and lifted his empty hands in surrender, saying; "Hey, they're not *with* me. Vendrick's guys may know my appearance and have some recent transgressions to discuss, but I was careful to cover my face until I was safely inside the taxi."

Becker swatted his palm to his face and emitted a sigh that was equal parts rage and mounting weariness. "What do you mean, *until*?" challenged the smuggler through gritted teeth, "Did you remove your helmet while in the back of the cab?"

Dex shrugged again, saying; "I made sure to keep my face turned inward and I avoided looking out the window. I don't see what the problem is."

"The problem, *Dr. SpyCraft*," Bit the smuggler with sarcastic contempt, "is that by doing so, you gave the taxi's *internal* camera a perfect view of your face, you bloody prat! Who do you *think* monitors that feed? Because it isn't the *police*."

Dex felt the bottom of his stomach fall out at realization of his mistake, and it took him less than half a second to make up his mind on what to do about it. "It's my mess and *I'll* clean it up." He announced to nobody in particular as he began to shed his jacket and shirt to expose the grey and black plates of his combat armor underneath, "I'll need transport if I'm going to draw them away."

"Won't work!" spat the smuggler with a dismissive swat of his hand, "They've got control of all the posi-lev lanes. They'd just lock you dow-...n" The tall man trailed off and looked as if he were deep in thought, trying desperately to remember something. Suddenly, he found whatever it was in his mind that he had been looking for and he darted off for the rear of the warehouse. When the man returned a full minute later, he was pushing a squat black form that Dex was only familiar with due to his exposure to DOC era films.

"A *motorcycle*?!" gasped Dex like a teenage girl who had just been offered flowers, "Like a no shit, fully functional, *internal combustion* motorcycle?"

"You think you can ride it?" asked Becker with a raised brow, "Because it's all I've got on-hand that isn't slaved the Heldrin's traffic system."

Dex laughed and replied; "Let's put it this way...If I die finding out the answer to that question, it'll be the way I've always wanted to go out."

The smuggler nodded apprehensively with an uneasy smile, then stepped away to present the ancient rubber-wheeled vehicle to his armored guest. It sat at about hip-height and stretched out longer than Dex was tall. The machine was a sculpture of glossy black metal and reflective chrome, and a visceral personification of the power that it allowed its rider to wield. As Dex swung his leg over and settled himself into its seat, he whispered quietly to himself; "*HolyShitJustLikeTeeTwo.*"

"What was that?" asked Becker distractedly, who was at a nearby desk fiddling with a handheld lockbox.

Dex examined the frame at the rear of his motorcycle for a moment, then sheepishly asked; "You...uh...you guys wouldn't happen to have any sunglasses lying around, would you?"

The smuggler looked confused by the question and stopped what he was doing to look up and ask; "What? No...*Why*?"

"No reason." Sighed Dex as he began to push himself forward on the bike, experimenting with the gear shifter's functions, "Is there a back door that I can get this thing through? I'm thinking that if I can push this beast down the back alley a bit before I start it up, it can help throw off their follow-up investigation on where I came from and keep your operation in the clear."

"They're *going* to kill you." warned Becker with grim certainty as he handed the stranger a set of keys that he had withdrawn from the lockbox, "You *must* know that, right?"

Dex just shrugged and suggested; "There is no future, except the one we forge for ourselves." as he thumbed the stud to bring his helmet into existence and began to roll his bike for the door.

The smuggler scoffed, saying; "You think that rattling off a little Buddha wisdom or some such nonsense before you go out there is going to make you any less deceased once they find you?!"

"*Buddha* never led humanity to victory over a robot apocalypse." Answered Dex, in a tone that suggested the meaning of the statement were obvious. The armored man then turned to Sergeant Tano and added; "Toss me the goody bag then give me twenty-four hours to shake these clowns and get back to the ship. If I'm not there when the timer runs dry, it probably means you can assume Miss Cleo over here guessed right and that I'm already dead...So you can feel free to head back on your own at that point. It won't hurt my feelings."

The Sergeant nodded then unslung the satchel from around his neck and threw it toward Dex, saying; "I'll have the shuttle ready to roll when I see you. Don't really have much in the way of weaponry, but I do have Mirta's rifle in the ship. Not exactly a combat exosuit, but I might be able to clip a last-minute tail for you on your way out."

The armored man caught the inbound package in his now-gauntleted hand and opened the leather pouch to withdraw a black and grey boxy looking object. As he withdrew it and turned it in his hand, he quickly found the button he was looking for on its side and gave it a firm press. The object proceeded to spring to life, unfurling itself using an intricately nested self-storage mechanism into a mid-length assault rifle. Dex hefted the rifle, aiming it at the ceiling in a tight grip as the scope synced and calibrated itself with his HUD. Once the firearm chirped its satisfaction with the forced self-diagnostic, he swung it over his shoulder and allowed the magnetic mounting ring built into the left shoulder blade of his armor to lock it into place. Throwing the strap of the satchel over his head, he reached back into its side pocket to retrieve his pistol and its universal holster. It was then an easy affair to attach the rig to his left thigh plate using a simple magnetic lock. With a stoic look, he offered one final nod to the group then pushed his motorcycle out the warehouse's side door.

Chapter 25

The machine was heavy, but the loving maintenance that had been put into it over the years made the vehicle easily capable of moving smoothly underfoot once Dex reached flat ground. He silently rolled himself over two hundred meters down the back alley, the only sound emitted being a low repetitive click as the motorcycle's chain fed itself around its closed loop. After his short silent journey, he chose one of the side-alleys between two of the warehouses in the seemingly endless row to duck into. Dex nosed his bike up to the front end of the building and poked his head around the corner. His helmet's built-in HUD and sensor system intuitively picked up what he was focusing on and automatically presented a blown-up image of four men, standing over three hundred meters away, who were milling around outside a warehouse down the row. Two of them stood on the doorstep, obnoxiously hammering away at the door like a SWAT team about to conduct a raid, while the other two leaned against one of the group's two standard manually operated posi-lev cars that sat silently on their bed of charged particles in the narrow roadway. The vehicles had seen better days, with pockets of rust beginning to gather at the edges of the door seals, but Dex could tell from their sleek lines and the seemingly nonsensical layout of control fins that they were once a pair of quite capable craft.

After a quiet moment of deep meditative breathing, Dex reached into his satchel and withdrew a small red metal puck that was flat on one face and gently domed on the other. As he ran his thumb over the domed side, his HUD quietly winked a new contact onto his list of available devices. Dex selected the small anti-personnel mine and opened its list of available configurations. He was met with a screen that presented two customizable fields with dropdown menus. The first menu was labeled *Detonation type*, and its dropdown offered a selection of Cone, Jet, or Air-burst. Dex considered for a moment, then selected *Air-burst* before moving to the next menu. Under the header of *Trigger*, he had the option of *Motion*, *Proximity-Enemy*, *Proximity-Friendly*, and *Manual*. Choosing *Proximity-Friendly* and setting its radius to fifty meters, Dex clicked his way through the ensuing confirmation windows and was met by a dull green glow coming from the small magnetic explosive device that was now armed and clinging to his handlebars.

With a sigh of excited anticipation, Dex slid the provided key into his motorcycle's ignition and turned it with glee. The machine sputtered for a moment, as if it were clearing its throat with a rough cough, then it roared to life underneath him. The ex-combat pilot grinned a predatory smile at the rumble and couldn't help but to feel a certain immediate kinship to the gnashing maw of metal and fire that now sat coiled between his legs, vibrating with a seemingly infinite potential for speed. Without further ceremony, he kicked the motorcycle into gear and momentarily spun its rear wheel loose as he rocketed out from his hiding space. Within a matter of seconds, he'd awkwardly worked his way through three gears and had covered most of the three-hundred-meter distance to the sweeper squad's parked vehicles. With calm focus, he took the tiny magnetic puck into his hand and held it at the ready out to his side. As he shot between the cars, he simply let go of the device; Hoping that the strength of its magnet would be enough to suck it to the roadway between his targets

The little metal puck bounced as it made its initial contact with the road, which sent it spinning like a wildly tossed coin until it thunked loudly into the vehicle on the left and adhered itself to its front passenger door. Then, after only a single pair of heartbeats had the opportunity to drum in Dex's ear, the charge detected that its controller had left its pre-programed radius of fifty meters and summarily detonated. At first, a fountain of flame leapt from the device that quickly blossomed into a starburst of heat and light that plowed into the opposite car with enough force to topple the vehicle off of its cushion of charged particles. The car reared itself to the side, its internal flux-pin drives working their best to compensate for the blast before failing and allowing the hunk of steel and glass to roll onto its roof to crush the two men who had been leaning against it. The vehicle that had been stuck with the device was also pushed off-keel in the explosion, but most of the killing power of the blast had been directed outward. Because of this, the car only listed to the side in response to the detonation and was burdened only with scorch marks and an ugly dent.

With the auditory evidence of his successful attack still ringing in his ears, Dex hoisted a lone middle finger into the air and cranked on his accelerator to further catapult himself toward the end of the row of warehouses. The two surviving members of the sweeper team were quick to react, immediately ignoring the pleas of their injured comrades to mount the remaining functional vehicle and begin their pursuit. Their posi-lev car was tremendously quick to accelerate, closing the trailing gap with their quarry in a matter of seconds, but it lacked the physical traction to follow behind the motorcycle as it made a snapping righthand turn onto a side street. The pursuing vehicle slid sideways, past the turn in a frictionless skid, until its driver was able to regain control and shoot the car down the next street to parallel their prey. Dex caught sight of the transport mirroring him via snapshots captured between the buildings he blew past, so he abruptly slammed on his brakes and took a left turn to change his heading. Now traveling perpendicular to his pursuer's direction, he let off on his speed and began to look for an exit that would take him off of the surface streets.

Finding what he had been searching for lying directly ahead, Dex squeezed himself low to the motorcycle's gas tank and yanked back on its throttle. His speed swiftly climbed into the 200 kph range, and he quickly found himself forced to fight the swelling vibration of the bike beneath him once past that threshold. The road then began a gentle climbing curve as it led its way up to a sweeping overpass that merged with the station's highway system. Then, as he crested the rising on-ramp, Dex's stomach leapt into his throat when he saw what looked to be an Armored Personnel Carrier parked sideways, barricading the narrow roadway with its seemingly impenetrable bulk. Without time to properly think about it, Dex made a split-second decision and threw his bike to the side, laying it out into a spark-filled slide across the pavement. Jamming his armored right elbow into the roadway to slow his momentum, he reached over his shoulder with his free arm to seize the assault rifle that was perched there. In his single-handed grip, the firearm popped free of its mooring and felt weightless in his adrenaline-fueled hyperfocus as he swung its barrel down into position.

When he squeezed the trigger, the weapon's built-in computer loosed three rounds in its burst-fire configuration before Dex even felt the recoil against his palm. The gun's magnetic rifling instantaneously accelerated the rounds to just shy of two-thousand meters-per-second, flinging them across the hundred-meter distance toward the spark-showered motorcycle. The bullets found their mark, tearing directly into the ancient vehicle's fuel tank, resulting in...absolutely nothing. No massive, road-clearing, explosion or even a little puff of flame. The bike just crashed to a stop, uneventfully, against the unyielding wheel well of the APC. "Movie physics are *such* **bullshit**!" growled Dex angrily to himself as he scrambled to his feet with a grunt of exertion and shouldered the rifle to continue his approach. Taking tight, measured, steps to control his forward pace, he viewed the world through the small steady window of his gunsight as he watched the barricade vehicle for any new movement. Suddenly, there was a form coming around the rear end of the APC. Dex waited long enough to confirm that the shape was carrying a weapon of its own, then he moved the little red dot that was hovering in his vision overtop the man's center of mass and depressed his trigger twice.

Dex's assault rifle emitted two rapid jets of flame, reaching across the distance with a tight cluster of high-density ferroplastic rods that tore their way through the man's upper chest and neck in a tremendous display of shed inertia. As the ruined form of the man fell to the roadway, a belch of return fire could be heard emanating from the front end of the vehicle. Dex then felt a heavy thud on the outside of his left thigh and was thrown off balance when a follow-up round impacted his right pectoral plate. He dropped to a knee and used his falling momentum to roll himself to the side, avoiding the second volley that attempted to follow him down. As he came around to his knee again, he immediately snapped his rifle up and replied with three tight bursts of his own. None of the shots struck home, but they did serve to pepper the APC heavily and successfully force his attacker back into cover. Utilizing the moment of free airspace, Dex dashed forward with all his might; Desperate to close the gap and find some cover against the APC itself.

The lone freedom fighter was mid-stride, however, when a flash rose from the rear of the armored vehicle and something bit him in the ribs on his right side. The impact didn't send Dex to the ground, but he did lose his footing and stumble until he crashed into the overpass' metal guardrail. First stealing a look over the side, then back toward the APC as he sent a burp of return fire toward it, Dex silently muttered to himself; "Awe, fuck it." and vaulted over the rail. He fell nearly twelve meters and hit the roadway with a painful crash as his attempted roll-out failed. The armor's built-in exoskeleton protected Dex from broken limbs and hyper extension, but all of its fancy technology could do nothing to stop his brain from rattling around in its jar. He rose, dazed and disoriented, and swayed a bit aimlessly until the snap-hiss of a near miss whizzed past his head.

The well-remembered sound ignited a primal part of the ex-soldier's brain and he clicked into an autonomic reaction that didn't need to know which way it was headed or worry about how it was going to get there. It knew only the enemy and came programed with one simple drive; Remove the threat. Dex understood all-too-well that the first step in defeating any enemy was to survive your initial contact with said foe, so he immediately began sprinting for a nearby factory building while the incoming rounds continued to divot the concrete around him. As he approached the building's unmarked door, he could almost feel the bullets that were now biting into the metal of the wall around it. When he finally got to the entryway, he quickly spun around to send a volley of gunfire toward the overpass to put his attackers into cover and buy him a few seconds of breathing room. Once the trio of heads above ducked behind the metal safety of the guardrail, Dex slapped the door release pad and silently thanked the gods when it slid open without protest. While diving in through the threshold, Dex felt a chip of cement shrapnel sneak in through a seam in his shin armor to bite painfully into his calf.

Dex got to his feet in the long hallway that ran perpendicular to the door and took cover to the side of the entryway, experimentally flexing his leg in a quick self-diagnostic. It hurt, but he retained his full range of mobility in the limb. Noticing on his HUD that his weapon's ammo counter had fallen to single digits, he pushed aside the guard cap on the end of his rifle's buttstock and pressed the unveiled mechanism to the ammunition port that was built into the chestpiece of his armor. The reloading apparatus then magnetically locked the buttstock in place for the second and a half that it took to automatically transfer one hundred ferroplastic darts into the rifle's onboard magazine from the reservoir on the suit's back. The process completed with a light chirp in Dex's helmet, followed by a whirring from the weapon itself as it rechambered a round.

He then used his helmet's retinal interface to properly sync his armor to the assault rifle and display a live feed from the weapon's sights to his HUD. Instead of pressing the advantage of his newly found cover to go on the offensive, Dex pressed his back to the wall and silently waited. He crouched and gently placed his gloved palm against the cement floor, activating his armor's built-in audio amplification and echolocation features. While in a vacuum, sensors built into the suit itself would detect vibrations in the environment around him and convert them into contextual sound that was pumped through the helmet speakers, but those very same instruments could also be used to analyze the ambient air and build a live three-dimensional representation of the shapes moving through it within about a twenty meter radius.

After a moment, he could hear rapidly beating footsteps and frantic voices approaching from afar. He waited for the sound to get closer, holding steady until shapes began to appear on his sonar-built image of the world beyond the wall. Once he could see the digital representation of all five of his attackers approaching, he sprung his trap. Knowing that his first target would be caught out in the open with no cover to retreat to, Dex poked his rifle low around the corner and aimed it using the video feed on his HUD. He carefully moved the red dot of his sights over the man running at the center of the haphazard formation and squeezed the trigger. Dex felt his rifle's recoil as the man's hip disintegrated in a blossom of wet flesh and torn fabric that sent the armed thug to the ground in a writhing heap. As he fell, the man's comrades had managed to dive for cover behind a nearby stack of cargo crates that were sufficiently sturdy to protect them from Dex's follow-up volley. He continued to fire, keeping them in cover, as he plunged his hand into his satchel to retrieve the last of his programable explosive pucks. Configuring the device to *Proximity- Enemy*, he affixed it to the doorframe and sent one last burst of gunfire toward his attackers before sprinting off down the hallway and deeper into the facility.

Throwing open the set of heavy metal doors at the end of the hall, he was immediately met with a rush of heat and a suffuse orange glow from beyond. The large open space on the other side of the doorway was bustling through the synchronized dance of manufacturing engineering, with large conveyers holding a series of steel molds being pulled down a long winding trail that weaved its way under torches, cutters, welders, and a whole host of other automated machinery that further shaped the desired widgets toward their final form. Along the wall on the left-hand side of the factory floor sat a row of smelters, the centerpieces of the operation, which would periodically tip themselves overtop what appeared to be the hopper system on some sort of 3D printing device that would then move to deposit its molten payload in an intricate weave over the objects on the conveyer.

Dex had covered half the distance across the factory floor, moving toward a door that sat open at the other side, when he heard an explosion rattle the hallway from which he had come. Dust and debris came spilling out of the corridor in the moments following the detonation, clouding the air with smoke and suspended particulates. It wasn't long, however, before flashes of gunfire began to pour out from the occlusion, forcing Dex to dive for cover behind the nearest conveyor belt. Rounds came flying in at random, with most going wide to splash into unyielding mechanical equipment, but the volume of fire was high enough to keep the airspace hazardous. When Dex detected a lull in their firing, which was most likely a poorly coordinated simultaneous need for reloading on his foe's part, he stood and began to sprint for the open doorway that still sat over thirty meters away. It was on his third powerful stride that he experienced what felt like a battlecruiser slamming into his right shoulder blade, sending him to the floor amid a shower of shattered armor plating and a supernova of pain that erupted from the point of impact.

Dex laid motionless on the ground for a moment, calmly taking stock of his condition. The round that had just hit him hadn't been a pistol caliber like the earlier shots that struck his armor had been, so there was a good probability that the bullet had broken through to his meaty bits. He drew a slow, measured, breath in to fill his lungs to their capacity, meeting a sharp pain at the middle of his back once they had inflated to eighty percent of their maximum. After shifting his right arm a bit and finding only minimal pain in the joint he decided that he wasn't mortally wounded, so he started thinking of a plan to remain that way. To his left sat a low conveyor assembly that was cooling freshly formed steel as it oozed from an extruder nozzle by blasting it with chilled puffs of CO_2. Dex examined the mechanism for a moment, then seized the hose that was feeding the pressurized gas to the cooling head and yanked it free of its housing. The broken end of the hose began to spew a thick cloud of white into the air that proceeded to roll low across the factory floor like an angry stormfront. Realizing quickly that his improvised smoke screen wasn't going to get him to the door on the other end as he had planned, he chose instead to begin crawling toward the doorway at the half-way point of the room that sat beneath the long window of an elevated control booth.

Sticking to a belly crawl that kept him firmly within the thickest part of the concealing sheet of fog along the ground, Dex made it to the doorway and slipped into the stairwell beyond. At the top of the steps was another door that led into a small darkened command center for the factory's operator. Nobody was home, but the control boards all remained lit and active. From his new vantage point, Dex could clearly see that only a trio of his pursuers remained and that they were all spreading out to move in on the position where they had last seen him fall. He shouldered his rifle and began to take aim at one of the thugs moving through the hectic factory, struggling to find a shot through all the whirring machinery, but stopped short when a flashing red control on the board in front of him caught his eye. In the section labeled 'Furnace Control', there was a large round button wreathed in a yellow and black border that read 'Emergency Reservoir Flush'. Dex then cocked his head with a devious smirk and pressed the button with a light, satisfied, tap of his finger.

The grates at the front of the huge pair of furnaces were blown from their mounts and molten metal spewed forth, its shower of glowing liquid cascading overtop the man who was unlucky enough to be caught standing underneath it at the time. His screams of terror and pain lasted only for an instant, however, as the dislodged two-ton metal plate came thundering down from above to pancake his ruined form into the deckplate. The two remaining men reacted by scrambling to cover, but their lizard brains in that moment of panic failed to register the true source of their danger and set them both into defensive postures *facing* the furnace. With his enemy's back presented to him as they hunkered low against their perceived threat, Dex took his time to carefully place the rifle's reticle over the nearer of the two then squeezed his trigger in three quick pulses. The resulting volley of supersonic plastic stretched across the distance in an instant and disintegrated against the man's flesh, tearing large swaths of his torso away to coat the conveyor in front of him with a spackle of red gore.

Realizing that he was the last of his side that were left standing, the final thug subconsciously started to retreat from Dex's elevated vantage point while staying as low as he could. What the thug had failed to account for, however, was the slowly expanding puddle of molten metal that he was now moving toward. When he recognized his mistake, the man attempted to turn and run in the other direction, but Dex already had a bead on him and began to fire. The incoming rounds forced the man to duck low under a pallet sorter that he found himself behind, with the shots barely going wide to miss his head. Dex calmly flicked his rifle's fire selector switch down to semi-auto and patiently watched through his sights for any sign of movement from behind the dormant machinery.

The thug tried to move out to his left, but immediately jumped back into cover when Dex loosed another round the second he appeared. With the spreading pool of molten steel getting closer, the man began to grow more panicked, which led to him sticking his rifle above his concealment and firing it blindly toward the other end of the room. Dex didn't take cover or even really flinch at the poorly aimed return fire as he methodically took aim of his own at the man's weapon.

A single round bit into the mid-point of the thug's poorly maintained rifle, splitting its barrel from the buttstock and taking half of the man's hand with it. Vendrick's foot soldier wailed with pain, shaking the damaged limb as if it were aflame, then sucked himself back into cover with all the grace of a wounded animal as molten metal began to nip at his heels. With no options left, and no weapon to defend himself with, the man decided to stand and attempt a sprint for the doorway through which he had come. He got four steps into his journey before one of the ensuing rounds from Dex's rifle shattered against his hip with the force of a meteor, sending him spinning to the floor with his leg flung to a grotesque angle.

The thug writhed on the deck, attempting to drag himself away from the encroaching edge of the liquid fire that was flowing toward him. His effort failed, however, and his thigh was soon engulfed in flame. Instinctually, the man tried to claw at the substance that was burning its way through his skin and muscle, but the goopy orange mass just stuck to him and began to work its way to his chest. Once the screams of the thug had reached their animalistic crescendo, Dex could no longer stomach the sound and he put the man out of his misery with a single round delivered to his brow from afar. The sudden relative silence when the final man fell quiet was deafening, even amid the rhythmic clang of the factory around him. Dex allowed himself three full breath's, sharply drawn in then slowly let out, to regain his center, then proceeded to his next problem at hand. Accessing his suit's diagnostics screen, he took a moment to go over the accumulated damage to his armor. A three-dimensional representation of his armor plates sprang to life with a multicolored topographical map emblazoned across it to showcase where the ablative material was missing.

A dialog box on his HUD asked if he wanted to proceed with armor regeneration and he selected the affirmative option, prioritizing the divot on his chestplate and the massive crater left in his shoulderplate for the focus of his finite patch-kit's efforts. The system confirmed his selection, then a hiss could be heard emanating from the small canister mounted on the right-hand side of the armor's integrated belt. The sound was caused by the suit moving roughly half a liter of viscous nanopatch material through a network of over three billion capillaries built into the armored plating itself, directing the flow straight to where it was needed. Once on-scene, the nanopatch fluid was smart enough to read the ID tags of the surrounding nano structure and compare it to a programed blueprint, getting a picture of where exactly it was plus what exactly it needed to become to complete the repair. As the white fluid began to ooze out of his damaged chestplate, Dex activated a deep-blue light that emanated from the palm of his gauntlet and began to run its glow over the healing armor's reforming structure. The carefully engineered wavelength of light served as a hardening agent on the nanostructure of the nanopatch fluid, which solidified within seconds and became hot to the touch as it interacted with the intense blue lamp.

After a similar light embedded into the rear of Dex's helmet cured the forming patch on his back as well, he slid the cover off his rifle's buttstock and topped off its dwindling magazine and battery charge. Once fully rearmed and re-armored, he shouldered his weapon and began to cautiously descend the control room's stairwell. When he got to the factory floor, he could see that the relentless puddle of metal had cooled to a dull red and had stopped spreading nearly fifteen meters short of the doorway. With that concern out of the way, Dex made a beeline for the double doors he had originally been shooting for and was relieved to see that they swung open upon his approach without protest. Once through the doorway, he found himself in a twenty-meter long hallway, painted white from floor to ceiling in a stark contrast to the dust and flame he had just left behind. He breezed past two doors, marked *Quality Assurance* and *Receiving*, and headed straight for the heavy metal door that was capped in a green and white *EXIT* sign at the end of the hall.

When he hit the door's release pad and it slid open, Dex found himself standing face to face with almost a dozen men in full sets of black combat armor. They had been milling around, as if waiting for word on what to do, but they all seemed to snap their rifles toward the newcomer at the same time in an accidental display of synchronism that served to showcase their practiced skill. Dex instantly dropped to a knee and dove to the side, slapping the door's control pad as he went. The heavy metal bulkhead snapped closed just as the characteristic dimples of assault rifle round impacts sprung into existence on the inner skin of the door. Dex frantically tapped at the door's control pad, desperately searching for a lockdown function, when the door began to open of its own accord. The operation slammed to a stop against the swollen hump of a bullet dent against the doorjamb, however, and the door's motors sounded like they were beginning to stress themselves against the resistance.

Taking the stroke of good luck as a sign to hightail it out of there, Dex stood and ran back toward the double doors of the factory floor. Before he got close enough to trigger the auto-open sensor for the doors, however, he saw through their embedded windows a pair of flashlight beams sweeping across the room beyond. Left with few options, he toggled open the door to *Quality Control* then changed direction and ducked into the door labeled *Receiving*, stopping at the top of the descending stairwell beyond to make sure to close the hatch behind himself. With a precise movement of his eyes, married with a complex set of tongue gestures across the roof of his mouth, Dex navigated his suit's menu to activate the *magnetic vision* function of his HUD display. As a result, sensors built into the armor would sample the surrounding area up to three meters and, using augmented reality across the helmet's visor, display translucent trace-lines of the detected magnetic fields overtop the real world.

Dex carefully ran his eyes along the edge of the door until he saw what he was looking for. Along the doorjamb sat a series of three electromagnets, betrayed by small eddies in the magnetic current displayed in the air, that served to hold the door shut when a depressurization alarm or lockdown was active in the area. Dex crouched and pulled a backup battery pack for his rifle from a belt pouch. He then held it up to the door, overtop the lowest of the maglocks, and used his thumb to manually trigger the battery's discharge function. The trick was something that he had learned from the very man who invented it while escaping an imperial prison colony, and the principal behind it was simple. All battery packs meant for firearm use came with a built-in discharge function for maintenance and storage purposes, which essentially drained energy by releasing a large energized magnetic field. Normally this discharge would happen rather quickly while mounted to a device that was designed to gather the discarded energy, but the batteries themselves had no safeties preventing the energy dump without it. When the battery in Dex's hand activated its discharge, it sucked itself to the door with an iron grip and he could watch through his augmented vision as the pack's energy woke the lockdown magnet.

Satisfied that he would have at least five minutes before the battery pack fully drained itself and unlocked the door, Dex let out a breath that he hadn't realized he'd been holding as he descended the stairs into the darkness beyond. At the bottom, he found a doorway that led into a hundred-meter-long chamber that appeared to have a set of heavy-duty docking airlock doors on the right side of the room and rows upon rows of stacked cargo racks on the left. The area just in front of the forty-meter-wide cargo door was open and mostly devoid of obstacles, save for the various cargo drones left parked here and there, and the other two thirds of the room was cluttered with an overflowing mess of unlabeled boxes, pallets of building supplies, drums of cutting fluid, and other manufacturing goodies.

Dex saw the dock's control booth at the far end of the room, so he figured he'd head there first to see what he could shake loose. He began to jog across the warehouse, weaving in and out of stacked pallets as he made his way toward the other end, when the thundering reverberation of a powerful explosion came pouring from out of the stairwell. After scrambling for cover behind a pallet of lubricant drums, Dex snuck a peek back toward the stairwell's doorway to see dark figures, each emitting the steady green lances of targeting lasers, pouring into the open and spreading into the dim warehouse with practiced fluidity.

Before Dex could get a count of his pursuers, however, a trio of leaking holes suddenly materialized into the side of the barrel he was using as cover, with the offending rounds missing his faceplate by mere centimeters. Cursing, Dex threw himself to the floor behind a row of metal crates as follow-up shots tore his barrel to shreds, sending a shower of oil to coat everything within a three-meter radius. Staying low, he popped out on the other side of his new cover and sent a burst of return fire toward his attacker. A pair of Dex's shots managed to strike the man's neck and collar bone, sending shards of armor and blood into the air as he was whipped back into the crate behind him with concussive force. There was no time for celebration, though, as gunfire rose unexpectedly from the left. The incoming rounds peppered the area, striking Dex's rifle on its scope and upper receiver to send sparks and flecks of shrapnel blasting against his faceplate. Ducking back into cover with the thrill of terror revving his heart muscles along, Dex discarded the damaged weapon and began a low sprint deeper into the warehouse, toward the unoccupied control center, as the bark of assault rifles swelled behind him.

Eventually, his luck ran out and the box ahead of him began to disassemble itself in blasting chunks, sending him off-balance and sliding to the floor on his hip until he came to a stop behind the large steel bulk of a cargo drone's detachable utility chest. Dex propped himself up on a knee and forced himself to breathe calmly as enemy rounds continued to dig themselves into the steel at his back. Momentarily blocking out the nuisance that was the unknown number of armed and armored men closing in to seal his fate, Dex looked to his path ahead to try and identify the few cover transitions it would take for him to get to the horseshoe of control panels at the other end of the room. Hunkering low, he activated the seismic sensors in his suit and pressed his palm to the ground. He could hear the vibrations of several different sets of footsteps moving through the rows of boxes and pallets, but none were close enough to show up on his visualizer. The footfalls then all suddenly stopped at once and an eerie silence fell across his sensors. After a moment of stillness, they all started up again in the same lockstep but heading in different directions than they had been going before.

Sensing a pincer about to close in around him, Dex decided to act quickly. He drew his pistol from its mount on his left thigh and snapped around the edge of his cover to take aim at the man he suspected would be there. When the narrow passageway behind him came into view, a man stood perfectly portraited in his gunsights about fifteen meters away. Without hesitation, Dex squeezed his trigger three times while hovering the pistol's front sight-post over his target's heart.

His pistol belched a trio of flame, its antiquated chemical propellant sending hard-cast lead projectiles at just over three-hundred meters per second to splash off of the pursuer's chest armor. The man hardly flinched at the impact, his hardened armor plating barely scuffing as he proceeded to return fire. Dex tried to throw himself back into cover, but his palms slipped against the ever-spreading puddle of oil on the floor and he faceplanted in the open. The fall, however, likely saved his life, as a volley of ferroplastic tore through the space his head had been occupying the instant before. Once he *did* manage to get back into cover behind the utility chest, Dex took a moment to look over the goopy mess that had flooded the floor and deposited itself all over his right arm. With disgust, he tried to shake the fluid free but found the viscosity of the substance hard to part with.

After a few seconds of struggling in vein with the oily slime, he slammed his fist against the utility crate's doors and caused it to swing open; spilling some of its contents to the floor. Among the bundles of cable and protective equipment that clattered to the ground was a small handheld cutting torch. Inspiration suddenly struck Dex like a freight train and he snatched up the device with glee. He squeezed its trigger experimentally and was rewarded with a snap-hiss as the torch came to life with an intense blue glow. Cranking its flame to maximum, he seized a bit of scrap wire from the cabinet and wrapped it firmly around the trigger mechanism to keep it active. Dex then chuckled to himself and, in a poorly imitated Austrian accent, yelled; "You're *fired*!" before lobbing his flaming torch toward the populated end of the room.

He could hear as it struck the ground and started to slide across its smooth metal surface, then he *saw* its effects in the form of a burst of orange and red light on the walls around him. Realizing that he, himself, was a bit too close to the spreading pool of oil for comfort, he took his chances and started to move for the control center again. With the swelling flames and its accompanying buildup of smoke covering his retreat, Dex was able to make it all the way to his goal without a single round nipping at his heels. He looped around the U shape of the waist-high console and chose a large screen at its center to work on. Quickly pulling up the docking bay controls, he scanned its menu for the main Airlock door release. When he thumbed the command to cycle the lock and open its main cargo doors, he was met with a blockscreen that was requesting a password to complete the action. He slammed his fists into the console with a huff of frustration and *it* responded with a hail of sparks and glass as it tore itself apart. Half on reflex and half on the power of surprise alone, Dex threw himself to the ground as incoming rounds continued to chew through the consoles around him.

He hunkered low within the protective barrier of steel and concrete that made the console's sturdy base and activated his suit's seismic sensors by pressing his palm to the floor. When it came to life, the tracking element on his HUD surprised him by the sheer volume of contacts displayed. His suit had detected nine targets approaching from nearly all sides of his hiding spot, and it approximated all of them to be within twenty meters. The closest of them, however, was just under five meters out and was beginning to appear on Dex's visualizer as a faint human-ish outline on his HUD moving slowly for the open end of the horseshoe of display screens.

Dex crawled as quietly as he could to the very end of the console, hunkering under the desktop that was on the corner the armored man was approaching. Getting situated on his back, he pointed his pistol to the ceiling and patiently watched through his peripheral vision as the man's outline drew nearer. The second that his pursuer rounded the corner with his weapon shouldered expertly and ready to fire, Dex shot the man twice through the bottom of his chin before his own presence was even registered. The rounds tore through the man's relatively weak chinplate and mushroomed into the flesh beyond with spectacular effect, sending his instantly limp body crashing to the floor with a meaty thud. As Dex was scooting backward to distance himself from the newly formed puddle of gore, he hit his head on a red metal box mounted under the desktop. Initially looking at the device to curse it, he stopped and took a moment to actually read the inscription across it. *Fire Suppression* was written in bold red letters over a covered button within the offending box that was begging to be pressed. With a curious tilt of his head, Dex popped the protective lid open and pressed his thumb firmly against the bulb of red plastic beneath.

The roof of the entire docking bay then erupted into a tornado of rushing foam suppressant. Swirls of the thick concoction stacked upon itself, filling the space from floor to ceiling as its design intended. Dex reloaded his pistol from a custom-built dispenser on his right hip then used the cover of the foam to look for a working console. He found what he was looking for on the far left-hand side of the console and he wasted no time getting to work. With a frustrated sigh, he noticed that the interface port he could've used to break through the docks encryption using his tablet had been destroyed, so he scrambled for an alternative. He accessed the dock's airshield settings and tried to see what kind of control he had over them without an admin account. While he was able to adjust the ozone holding tanks, which sat perched at each side of the giant airlock door to regulate the strength of its airshield, within a certain operating tolerance, he was unable to do anything very significant beyond that.

Deciding on another approach, he opened a terminal in the dock's computer system and ran a simulated diagnostic test of the airshield system, pumping the sim's variable for the dock's internal air pressure up to an unrealistic amount. The simulation balked at his suggestion at first, but with gentle prodding it was encouraged to spit out some results. Dex then took the numbers it produced, which were the settings needed to maintain positive pressure within the given situation, and plugged them into a simple command he threw together that would reboot the airshield's control system and inject the altered ozone pressure settings into its configuration file as the new defaults. The console accepted his command with a chirp that returned a few moments later as a blaring alarm, accompanied by a pulsing red light that was now illuminating the choking foam.

With an objective in mind, Dex rounded the end of the consoles and rose his pace to a light jog through the churning bubbles with his right hand out ahead of him in a blind stiff-arm position and his gun hand tucked in close to his body. As he closed in on the bright blinking red light that he was fairly sure sat mounted to the top of one of the now-overpressurized ozone tanks, he felt an impact at his palm that soon paired itself with a dark form in the foam. Dex plowed into the armored man and identified his arm in a quick scuffle, wrenching it into the air as he shoved his pistol into the armored man's unarmored armpit and pulled his trigger three times.

The man flinched away from the shots and let out a bark of pain as Dex tightened his grip on his arm and spun to flip him to the ground. Once pinned to the floor with Dex's bulk draped across him, the armored thug was unable to prevent his attacker's pistol from pressing to his faceplate. With a belch of flame, Dex's firearm expended a round against the glass of the man's helmet from point-blank range and he was rewarded with only a ragged scuff across its lightly reflective surface. With a huff of frustration, Dex squeezed off a second round that produced the tiniest of cracks across the thruminum alloy of the helmet's armored viewport. After a sigh and an eye-roll as the man under him continued to buck and jerk for his life, Dex found the control stud on the man's helmet and clicked it to lift his opponent's armored faceplate. He then pressed the barrel of his gun to the tip of the man's nose and squeezed the trigger, this time receiving his desired results.

After delivering the fatal round, Dex rolled to his side and ejected his weapon's magazine. As he was reaching for its replacement, however, gunfire rose from deeper within the docking bay. The full-auto fire from the offending assault rifle lit up the foam with light-blue flashes of plasma as the ablative coating on its ammunition burned away upon exiting the barrel. Incoming rounds began to tear themselves into the deckplate near Dex and he was forced to roll the armored body of his dispatched foe onto its side to hunker behind it for cover. The hail of gunfire peppered the body, sending flecks of armor and blood into the air in every direction as the force of the impacts threatened to push Dex across the floor.

When the assault suddenly ceased, likely for reloading, Dex seized the opportunity to steal the rifle from his downed enemy and point it not toward the source of the onslaught, but right beneath the pulsing red glow that was emanating from just under thirty meters ahead. When he pulled the trigger using the dead man's finger, Dex didn't even have time to register the rifle's recoil before a hurricane of rushing air started to pull him toward the rhythmic crimson glow amid the crashes and clangs of everything light enough to be thrown by the sudden burst of wind. The mighty howl of rushing air died quickly, however, along with the sound of the dock's wailing decompression alarm. It took less than three full heartbeats, in fact, for the entire volume of the room's fire suppressant foam to be completely cleared from view, sucked away through the three-meter-wide gash left across the main cargo door's right side that led out to the hard vacuum of space.

Rushing to his feet to capitalize on the surprise of the situation, Dex slammed a new magazine into his pistol and began his search for survivors. As he moved through the newly summoned vacuum within the room, nearing the massive gash left by the explosion, he started to realize just how lucky he had been to be lying flat at the time of the decompression. He found one man crushed under a tipped loading drone, another whose faceplate had been shattered by a flying metal rod, and a final body that appeared largely undamaged except for the small fact that its helmet was turned the wrong direction and it's wearer's expression was frozen in a final mask of pain and surprise. With the adrenaline slowly draining from his system, Dex was exhausted by the time he reached the hole in the station and pulled himself through.

He activated the magnetic plates built into his boots, knees, and gloves to stick himself to the outer skin of Heldrin City and began crawling. He scanned the area, looking for a way back inside the station, when he spotted what appeared to be a service airlock by its dim green status light that sat slowly blinking nearly three-hundred meters away. He sighed at the sight, visibly sagging with reluctance at the distance, but pushed toward his goal nonetheless; Eons of evolution making the arduous task of survival a non-negotiable one. Along the way, he sat glued to the wall of a trench that ran through one of the cube's deep recesses and was having a hard time not looking over at the stunning snapshots of Jofur as Heldrin's intricate tumble sent it passing through the ever-shifting night sky above. Sight of it made him a tad queasy at first, but the wonder it inspired was quick to flush the discomfort from his mind.

As Dex quite literally knelt before the splendid immensity of his universe, he couldn't help but wonder how he had gotten himself there. Why had he gotten involved in someone else's war? A cynical corner of his mind suggested that it was vanity, a way to showcase his talents which had gone unseen and unappreciated by the general populous during his decade of military service, but he knew it was more than that. Because here he was *again*, working in the unseen fringes on behalf of people who would likely never even know he existed. But as he drug himself along, bruised up, shot up, and very possibly losing a good deal of blood, he found that he wasn't bitter about it in the slightest. He saw his pain as simply a side effect of the task that needed doing; A price extracted by the universe in response to his attempt to alter its status quo. Doing the right thing was rarely the cheapest option on the menu, but he just couldn't help but order it any time he saw a bully at work. Maybe that was his position in life.

Maybe he was there to pick up the tab and pay that price when nobody else was willing or able. Either way, the thought reassured him of his moral trajectory in the matter and finally allowed him to enjoy the rest of his journey across Heldrin City's outer skin in mental peace.

When he finally reached the lock and cycled through it, he fell to his knees in the antechamber beyond and was suddenly desperate to escape the claustrophobic confinement of his helmet. As his faceplate peeled back with a hiss, Dex gasped for air; slurping it in feverishly, despite the stale musty scent it carried. Once his lizard brain had been thoroughly convinced that oxygen did in fact still exist in the universe outside his helmet, his body slowly began to relax, and he found himself able to think clearly once more. With his end-goal of getting to the docks in his mind's eye, he searched the small room for something to disguise his appearance. Three small lockers sat in a row by the airlock door, but they were found to be empty after a cursory investigation. Panning his eyes to a pile of junk in one corner of the cramped room, Dex spotted a roll of burlap-like material strewn overtop a few nearly empty spools of optical cabling that sat in a haphazard pile. Kneeling next to the pile, he dug through its contents and began to assemble his modest disguise.

Chapter 26

After meticulously wrapping all armored sections of his body with the burlap material, Dex fashioned a hooded robe of sorts with the remainder and cinched it tight across his waist with fiber-optic cabling. Half out of painful necessity and half in an effort to further his disguise, he adopted an exaggerated limp and lowered his left shoulder to change his overall stature to fool any rudimentary automated surveillance tracking systems as he shuffled along the back alleys looking for his way up to the main level. When he finally pushed out onto the city streets of Heldrin, he felt a sudden rush of vertigo under the open skies above. Even though he logically understood that he was strolling along the inside surface of a tumbling sphere, he didn't *feel* as if it were the truth. What his senses were telling him was the fact that his feet ached under the strain of gravity, that a breeze was lightly pushing past his hood to draw in the savory smell of the nearby food cart, and the sky above shone with a blanket of twinkling stars cast against a powder-white moon. What his brain was telling him was that he was standing on Earth, looking up at the night sky in the northern hemisphere he called home. With an odd sense of meta-awareness, Dex scanned the glittering vault above and scoured its nonsensical dispersion until the constellation Orion manifested itself above the glowing rim of a sign that advertised payday loans. He followed the three dots that constructed the constellation's belt and traced them down to the little point of light that served as the figure's right foot; Saiph.

Dex sighed with a mix of longing and weariness at the sight, more conscious than ever of just how far off 'home' really was as he continued his way toward the dock's nearest entry gate. He realized he had arrived when he spotted a line of tired looking people, most carrying some form of cargo box or hand truck along with them, all waiting to talk to a pair of armed and tattooed men standing underneath a sign marked 'Customs'. Maintaining his quasi imitation limp, Dex shuffled over and slipped in at the back of the line without anyone taking particular note of his presence. Even though he were still too far off to hear what each member of the line was saying to Vendrick's men, Dex could see that their presence was nothing more than a simple shakedown. In times of reputable dealings, the small guard shack they manned with its accompanying metal framed walkthrough scanner would be used to detect contraband and other dangerous materials that were unwanted on the station. Vendrick's guys, however, seemed to have taken to using it for finding hidden wealth on the poor souls who wished to pass through. One of the tattooed men, a pistol on his hip, was out front talking to the shabby traders and merchants who had lined up for entry, while his buddy sat nonchalantly atop a barrel on the far side of the two-meter-long metal walkthrough with a shotgun draped across his lap and a bored expression plastered to his color-shifting face.

Dex was initially worried that they were there for the sole purpose of looking for *him*, but it appeared as if they were just your typical vultures going about their everyday miserable deeds. When he finally reached the front of the line and was called forward, the guards appeared puzzled at his lack of cargo and equipment. "Oiy!" shouted the frontman as Dex approached with a slow painful looking limp,

"Hurry it the fuck up, eh? We aint got our lives to watch you drag your limp ass along. You know the routine, yeah? Let's see em."

"I'm sorry, see what now?" said Dex, adding a little gravely strain to his voice, "I don't really come up this way often, so I'm not sure what you need."

The man with the shotgun rolled his eyes and sighed impatiently as the man up front with the pistol smiled devilishly and retorted; "Nothing gets through that gate before I see two-hundred creds...*normally*. But since it's your first time and all, I'll make you a deal. *Five*-hundred creds. For wasting me and my friend's *time*."

"C'mon, man." Pleaded Dex in his best imitation grovel, "I'm just trying to pick a shipment of whiskey up for one of *your own* guys. I don't have that kind of scratch under my mattress at home, let alone *on* me. What if I slip a few bottles to you on my way back out?"

"Six-hundred credits now." Sneered the man with cruel delight, "And maybe I should tell your *employer* how ready you were to steal from him."

"Entirely unnecessary." assured Dex with a vigorous shake of his head as he kept his eyes plastered to the ground, "How about an alternate form of payment? Like...what about a quick drawing? I really think I'd be able to catch you in your sensitive side."

"The fuck?" asked the man with outraged confusion, "No creds, no docks. And you'd really best think of your next words wisely, *mayte*."

The pirate accentuated his final words with a hard poke of his finger in what was intended to be a painful stab at Dex's collar bone, but his action was met instead by unyielding polycarbonate plate. With a look of pained confusion still blazing across the pirate's tattooed face, a mechanical snap-whir could be heard from beneath the tattered bundles as a shiny combat helmet sprang to life around the sickly-looking stranger's head. The guard stepped back with a gasp of surprise at the sudden technological sorcery and immediately heard a fundamentally different voice pour from the man, stronger now and filtered through the helmet's external speakers as it roared; "*DRAW!*"

The tattooed man only had time for his palm to brush the handle of the pistol at his hip before a neat smoldering hole materialized in the side of the robed stranger's flowy garment. Upon sight of the man's glowing jaw folding in on itself from the impact of his combustion-driven slug, Dex immediately threw himself to his left to avoid the other guard's retaliation. He was partially too late, however, and caught the outer edge of the shrapnel cloud emitted from the distant man's shotgun.

The cluster of ferroplastic beads slammed into his right side, tearing swaths of hardened armor plating free in a cloud of ablative dust. The force of the impact struck him while mid-air, sending his gun tumbling from his grip while he went sailing off-course through a stack of cargo boxes on a nearby posi-lev handtruck. A heartbeat after his helmeted head had bounced off the deckplating, Dex returned from his momentary quasi-unconsciousness and was immediately jolted alert by his suit's puncture alarm sounding off in his ear. When he moved to try and sit up for a look at the damage, a sharp bark of pain from his side strongly vetoed the idea. His vision had gone cloudy from the pain and his brain was fighting hard to retreat into unconsciousness, but Dex forced the sensation back just enough to be able to look up and see a dark shape, crested with a beacon of shifting color, slow to a stop above him. With his mind as clouded as his sight, he sloshed for the knife mounted on his chestplate but found himself tactically defeated by the incessant persistence of the burlap material that had been wrapped so tightly around it.

Before his efforts were able to manifest any life-saving miracles for him, Dex heard the loud report of a weapon being discharged from directly above. At first, as the sound died away and his rush of adrenaline blocked out everything else in the universe, he found himself marveling at how painless death had turned out to be...until he coughed and felt another wave of pain at his side. The first rush of agony was then immediately followed by another as a heavy weight came crashing down to engulf him. After realizing the bulk was in fact that of a body instead of the crushing mass of stone manifested nonsensically by the reptilian portion of his mind, Dex pushed the limp form of the shotgun wielding man's corpse off of him to see a blue and green haired woman standing above him holding his own fumbled pistol in her trembling white knuckle grip.

"Tyrants *are* falling, Mr. Sloan," commented Gaizya Tam shakily as she inspected the smoking weapon in her hand, "but it's a whole sight less fun when they fall *on* you."

Accepting her hand to pull himself to his feet, Dex replied; "Thank you, Miss Tam. I would've *definitely* been a goner back there. You are *truly* heaven-sent."

"Sergeant-sent, I'm afraid." She corrected absent-mindedly with a dismissive wave, "He had a few of us post up on the pedestrian entrances to let him know if you're coming. Didn't exactly plan on getting *this* involved, to tell you the truth, but the situation necessitated it. On that note, there's no reason that either of us should linger, so go on through and get out of here before more show up! And be sure to send Michael my regards!"

With a grateful nod, Dex spun on his heel to step over the dead man at his feet and passed through the now-unmanned checkpoint into the docks. Quickly finding a standing transport pod, he climbed aboard and wracked his tired and pain-clouded mind to recall the pad that Tano was waiting for him on. Mental arithmetic quickly narrowed his choices to either "B-22" or "E-22". Deciding that B was likely closer, he keyed in the destination and allowed the multi-directional conveyance to shoot off down its posi-lev track in the floor. As the small box reached its cruising speed, Dex let out a sigh of relief and allowed his shoulders to sag slightly. That was when the car snapped to an unnatural stop and its single occupant was flung brutally into the wall at just under thirty meters per second. Upon crashing into the unforgiving metal at the other end of the cramped box, he felt something in his right shoulder pop as his head swam in a concussive afterglow that made it hard to fully conceptualize the pain his body was enduring at that moment.

At some point, in a timeframe lost to the choking fog of his scrambled mind, he had sagged to the floor and leaned himself into the back corner of the little box with his pistol draped across his lap. After what seemed like ages, he watched as a blade of some sort was forced through the gap between the car's twin sliding doors and leveraged to pry them apart until they freely opened. Then, a bald head and its accompanying set of shoulders could be seen leaning in past the door's threshold for a quick look around. That was all the time, though, that Dex needed to squeeze off two rounds in the man's direction.

The first of his two bullets tore its way into his target's left shoulder, eliciting a yelp of pain as the man reflexively tucked his chin toward the injured limb. An action which presented the crown of his skull for Dex's second round to enter with immediate lethal effect. As the man fell limp and slid back out of the small box to the flightdeck of the dock a meter below, his destroyed mess of a skull remained intact enough to clearly display the fading blue and purple scrawled across what remained of the right side of his face.

As Dex placed a palm on the floor of the transport to push himself to his feet, a small metallic object sailed in through the open doorway and came to a clattering stop near his knee. A quarter-second later, the top of the small device flashed red as it proceeded to spin and spew a lumpy foaming substance to coat the interior of the small space. Then, quickly after it was dispersed, the foam began to rapidly expand and let off a nearly unbearable amount of heat as it hardened into a concrete-like substance. With the hint of a panic setting in, Dex struggled against the stiffening cocoon around him in an increasingly futile effort. His legs and entire right side were both fused to the transport by the choking grey mass, and he only had freedom over his left wrist and shoulder to move about. Luckily for him, that was his gun hand. Unluckily, however, said gun was completely coated in the hard substance and he could not get it to fire, even after banging it repeatedly with what little strength he could muster against the floor.

Out of ideas, he opened the comms panel on his HUD and tried to get a signal out to Tano. The three blue dots at the bottom of his comms screen that signified the message's status continued to bounce in place for longer than Dex was used to seeing, then they finally fell flat and turned a dark shade of crimson. In matching red above the newly inactive dots, a new message read: *Connection timed out. Onboard transmitter obstructed. Retrying...* "*Fuck!*" he grunted to himself in frustration as he continued to struggle against his enveloping bonds.

"You're right." Came a voice from the doorway as a tattooed man with a mop of red and black hair cautiously peeked around the corner, "You *are* fucked." Seeing that his adversary had been thoroughly entrapped within the riot foam, the thug relaxed his expression and began to don a smirk as he hauled himself up into the omnivator car. "Funny thing about it though," continued the tattooed man with a chuckle as he stood to loom over his new trophy, "is that I can guarantee you that you have no *concept* of what I'm about to do to you. The remainder of your life will be longer than I suspect you imagine, but it will be filled with horrors you cannot even begin to comprehend."

"Hey buddy, I've seen Imperial darknet porn, alright?" spat Dex with theatrical outrage, "So I can comprehend a fucking *lot*. And I don't see *you* up in here waving around three genetically engineered dragon dicks, so let's not go assuming you've got anything that can surprise me at this point."

Vendrick's man stepped closer, eyeing the helmeted figure below him with disgust as he swung his boot forward to connect with the stranger's quasi-mirrored faceplate. Dex's head bounced off the wall behind him with brutal force, sending chips of hardened foam raining into his lap and his mind swimming. Feeling the onset of a concussion headache beginning to take hold, Dex attempted to use his HUD interface to activate a cooling plate integrated into the rear neckplates of his armor that would help alleviate some of the oncoming trauma, but his helmet's eye-tracking system was having a hard time following his now-mismatched pupils. With the reliability of that option out the window, he switched his input mode over to palate tracking and resigned himself to clumsily navigating his suit's odd radial menus with unfamiliar swipes of his tongue across the roof of his mouth.

"Not so talkative now, are yah?" sneered the thug with a rude hand gesture, "Yah see, that's all anyone ever needs in the end. A little adjustment."

"Me?" asked Dex, pain only slightly evident through his expertly donned inflection of nonconcern, "Oh, sorry, I was picking at a popcorn kernel that's been stuck in my gum for like three weeks now. You finally managed to jar it loose for me, so thanks on that one mate."

"Yeah?" Spat the tattooed man as he squatted to bring his face closer to the helpless stranger at his feet, "I'm glad you like my handiwork, 'cuz me and the boys are about to jar a whole fuckload more loose from yah."

Dex smirked at the three green dots that were now steadily blazing on his HUD and coolly replied; "That sounds like a hoot and all, kiddo, and I'd love to stick around for it, but I'm worried about some possible scheduling conflicts...*You* know how hard it is for your dear old mom to find an open date night, and I really don't want to disappoint her like *you* do every day. So..."

"Cheeky cunt, aint yah?" scoffed the thug with a hint of humour glinting in his eye as he returned to his full height, "You think you're all cool and collected, eh? A real tough guy, no? Well, you're not gonna be so unshakable when I-" The man's sentence was cut short amid a hail of sparks that danced through the interior of the omnivator car as his jaw, neck, and upper chest suddenly and irreversibly converted themselves into an expanding starburst of gristly red paste.

After the integrated wiper blade built into Dex's visor glass moved its way down his faceplate to clear the deposited gore, he looked over at the limp form next to him on the floor and coughed "Well, consider me shooketh...But I'd love to see you do it twice, asshole."

"You alright in there?" came Tano's voice in his ear as a symphony of gunfire erupted outside from both up close and far away.

"You *do* realize that damn thing has more intricate settings than just full power and off, right?" asked Dex incredulously as he resigned himself to sitting there, locked motionless in the warm contents of the freshly popped meat pinata he was forced to share the small space with.

"Don't patronize me, boy." Rebuked the older Sergeant in his ear, "In case you're forgetting, *I'm* the one who taught your little girlfriend how to use the damn thing in the first place. I had the guy on thermals and needed penetration. So, I got it...don't really see what you're bitching about."

"Who's outside?" demanded Dex with a deeply frustrated sigh as he forced himself to the next topic, "I hear an awful lot of shooting out there..."

"We got Becker's people on the assist out here with me." Replied Tano as he squeezed off a shot of his own, "They're pushing for your box, but it looks like Vendrick's guys are getting reinforced from up-spin. Our folks are closer, though, so they should be the next faces you see. Try not to shoot any of them, alright?"

Moments later, as predicted, a head came poking into the omnivator car. What Dex didn't expect, however, was for that head to feature a tattooed face. Three heartbeats into his ensuing fight or flight response, as he struggled against his bonds once more, he began to notice something wrong with the head before him; Almost as if the nose of the ornamented face had been marred in a fire that had melted it to the surrounding cheek skin, but closer examination revealed an odd graphical shift on the face itself as his viewing angle changed.

Detecting the entombed man's confusion, the tattooed newcomer proceeded to reach for his chin and peel away his face with an upward tug. Out from underneath the holographic display mask appeared the smiling form of Randal Becker, breaking the silence to explain; "Holo-mask. Not super convincing up close, but it'll look properly the part from the security cams. Tano let me in on your papier-mâché pirate approach and I think it has merit. We had these lying around for evading tails, so we figured we'd put them to good use selling the narrative of a splinter faction extracting an agent."

"Well, you wanna sell it a little harder and get my ass outta here for realsies?" asked Dex with an impatient huff, "I'm pretty sure I'm losin' my gravy pretty fast over here and I need to start plugging some of these holes before I kick the goddamn bucket."

Looking around and seeming to recognize his grisly surroundings for the first time, Becker's grin faded and he remarked; "Is it like this everywhere you go, Dex? Because my guys found a receiving dock that looked much the same way about twenty minutes back..."

Dex attempted to retract his helmet, but the hardened foam all around it had frozen its intricate mechanism in place. With a sigh and a defeated slump in his posture, he riposted; "What are you thinking? That I just hocus-pocused this guy out of existence? The dock was me, sure, but the fresh shade of dickhead all over the walls is on your pal Tano for tagging the poor bastard with a goddamn anti-air flechette round."

"Oh, quit exaggerating!" spat the old Sergeant over the radio to them both, "It was only a- oh...shit. Well, either way, it got the job done didn't it?"

"Still as good as ever with those *minor details*, eh Michael?" quipped Becker with a wry smile before turning his attention to the stone encased man at his feet, "Any ideas on how I'm going to get you out of here without a posi-dolly?"

"Look on our departed friend here." Suggested Dex, "There should be some type of solvent or deactivation compound on him somewhere."

"Eugh..." gagged the smuggler as he crouched to look, "More like a-parted. Which half of this unfortunate buggar should I start on?"

"I dunno." Replied the encased man with an attempted shrug, "His belt, maybe? It generally comes in the form of an aerosol, though, so look for a cannister."

"Okay I have it..." started the lanky man with nausea evident in his voice, "Let's start with your legs, shall we?" He then withdrew a black cylinder from the dead man's waist and began passing it over Dex's stone-hardened legs in long gentle sweeps of its steadily dispersing mist. As the specially formulated liquid made contact with the engineered foam, it rapidly began to convert its molecular structure into a jelly-like substance. Once his legs and hip were free, it was a relatively simple procedure to get the rest of him separated from the floor in an operation that took less than a minute.

By the time Dex had coated his pistol with the solvent and was re-holstering it to his thigh, a fresh wave of gunfire was erupting from outside. With curiosity, he poked his head out the open doorway to find his car stopped at the midpoint of one of the massive dock's countless flat-top landing bays. The landing deck in front of him was empty, but the pad immediately to his right had a small freighter sitting on it with its engines spooled down and its rear ramp sitting open with what initially had looked like cargo drones at work on its far side. Upon closer inspection, though, the three-meter-long barrel of an armoured battle-tank began poking its way out from behind the parked freighter with a slow-rolling menace. The side of the otherwise flat black armoured vehicle was dented and featured a blue, purple, and red swirl in a design that was similar to the style of many of the tattooed faces in Vendrick's ranks.

"Since when do these motherfuckers have *tanks*?!" blurted Dex as he yanked his head back into the small transport car, "What the shit are we going to do about *that*? Because I can *guarantee* you that Mikey's rifle would do fuck-all against it."

"Don't wet your knickers *too* thoroughly there, my friend," assured the smuggler with a knowing smirk, "My people have it handled. You *really* think I'd run a toy store without holding back some of the *best* trinkets for myself?" With a huff of laughter, the lanky man activated his radio and ordered; "Turtle on deck. Pop smoke and bring up the Spankers. Go when good." Five seconds later, a long trail of grey smoke began to appear at the far end of the landing pad. As it billowed out, following the slight directional flow of the atmosphere's forced circulation across the pad, twin flares of bright blue could be seen in his periphery that simultaneously took to the air in a tall looping arc that led them back down directly on top of the decorated tank with a devastating explosion. Without having fired a single shot of its own, the intimidating vehicle burst into a collection of twisted steel and broken ceramic amid flames hot enough to melt the concrete substance used to construct the tarmac.

"Move!" shouted Becker as the tank's secondary detonations still rang in Dex's ears. The tall smuggler seized the bulky terrasider by the shoulder and, in what must have been a feat of adrenaline-fueled ultra-strength, hurled the man out of the transport pod and directly into a jog with one mighty heave. As Dex stumbled forward, he saw a group of tattoo-faced men signalling to him from behind a row of stacked cargo that sat just past the pad directly in front of him. Ignoring his initial reaction to shoot at them, he reminded himself of Becker's mask and made a point to mentally register where the _good_ badguys were holed up as he accelerated toward them.

After diving into cover with the beckoning men, Dex was quickly found by Tano, who clapped him heartily on the shoulder and shouted; "Holy freakin' hell, kid! You've really been giving these pricks a bad day! Are you alright? Did they tag you at all?"

"Quite a few times," Admitted Dex with a grimace, "but the Armor held out for the most part. I'll be damned if civvies can't get some cool shit on the open market these days. Doesn't mean it didn't hurt like a sonofabitch, though. Either way, we're ordering more of these. That much is for damn sure."

"Well, just hang tight," assured the sergeant with a nod, "Becker's got a ship on standby that's gonna lift us outta here. We just have one more errand to run before we can split, though."

Dex just looked at the older man as if his head were on fire and fumed; "I don't think we have the time to make a trip to the convenience store, Mike. There's about thirty of those assholes moving in on us and they're going to overrun us if we don't fall back."

"Trust me, Dex." Urged Tano with a squeeze to his shoulder, "This will be worth the effort. Just keep low."

"Do you at least have a rifle for me to borrow?" asked the armoured man with a frustrated shrug, "At least let me shoot back."

Tano looked at him knowingly and said; "No can do. You'd hit too many of them, and that would defeat the purpose."

"Isn't hitting them *supposed* to be the purpose?!" glowered the younger man with an absent-minded hand gesture toward their ever-nearing enemy.

"Could you just please sit down and shut up for a minute?" snapped the Sergeant with a slam of his fist against the box they were hiding behind, "We've got this." He then turned away, keying his comm to ask; "Becker, how close are they?"

"Nearly half of them are on," came the smuggler's reply, "but the rest seem to be holding back." Shall I bait them in a little?"

Tano keyed his comm and ordered; "Do it." In response, the smuggler's voice returned to the group channel to order three of his men to break formation and begin retreating. The maneuver seemed to have its intended effect and Vendrick's forces began to open fire, advancing swiftly on their seemingly broken enemy's lines.

As Vendrick's forces pressed in, Dex and Tano's cover began to whittle away under their constant heavy barrage. Once rounds had finally sufficiently obliterated the contents of their box enough to start penetrating its far side, the Sergeant shouted "NOW!" into his comm. Then, with the tell-tale hum of massive amounts of electricity moving from one place to another, the powerful magnets within the landing pad suddenly activated at full strength. The force of the pull, coupled with the surprise of its existence, was more than enough to overpower each and every one of the pirates as they watched their weapons thunk to the ground in an invisible iron grip. Panicking, some of them began to run; Only to be gunned down by two of Becker's men at the periphery of the landing pad. With a loud and commanding voice, Becker boomed; "You are now my prisoners, and we're all going to go for a little ride. Your available options are to either accept this reality or depart from reality *entirely*. If you *do* wish to remain on this plane of existence, please strip completely and deposit yourself within the open cargo container to your right. Failure to comply will be met with *death*. *Delayed* compliance will be met with *death*. Any attempt to resist or escape during your time with us will be met with, you guessed it; Death. And, oh why not, if any phrases or smells come off of you that I or my men don't particularly *like*, I'll push you out the airlock myself. Welcome to the other side of the equation, gentlemen. I *sincerely* hope that you *do not* enjoy your stay."

Chapter 27

"Here's what we know." Began Tano as the lights of Hearth's briefing room dimmed and a model of the Saiph system winked to life above its wooden conference table, "After having individual chats with all of our tattooed guests, a few things have become clear. They don't know any better than we do what Vendrick looks or sounds like, they have no way of contacting him if they need to, and it seems their only job is to follow the specific orders that come down via burst-transmitter. The primary standing directive that all of them seem to know about is Vendrick's desire to keep the docks strictly controlled and open for business. Beyond that, it's pretty much the wild west."

"So, who's sending all the food and supplies every week?" asked Dex pointedly, "If Vendrick's guys' only directives revolve around keeping the ports open, who is there to make certain that *surely* massive investment is distributed properly? All that food has to be worth *something* to *someone* who probably wouldn't want to see it hoarded in the way it is being now."

The Sergeant sighed and explained; "You know as well as I do that big government projects can experience bloat issues and an oversight of basic functional logic. Bigger the project, the dumber the mess-up. And this here is no different."

"But why would *they* give a shit in the first place?" pressed Dex with swelling agitation, "*They* aren't a government. Not a legitimate one, anyways. It makes no sense that Vendrick would spend all that money on food, just to keep the starving masses barely alive. If they wanted to use the stations, and it was obvious that the Feds weren't going to step in, why not just starve the people and dump the bodies out the airlock? Macabre, I know, but they *are* goddamn pirates..."

Tano pinched the bridge of his nose in frustration, retorting; "As a terrasider, I don't think you really understand just how important that the people *within* a station really are when it comes to keeping one operational. Maybe some of the fancy automated Imperial cities can run unmanned, but that's just not how we roll on this end of the bubble."

"Yeah, yeah," interjected Mirta impatiently, "I'm sick of talking about food. What else did you get from these guys? Anything actionable?"

"Though I may not have anything for you to shoot at right now," began Tano flatly, "I *did* get a line on a regular shipment that comes through Heldrin every two weeks. It's a large group, needing almost twenty pads each time they come through, and they always show up twice. The first time they come around, they load *something* up from a locked hangar kept nearby and leave without the crew ever really stepping foot off their ships. Then they go out *somewhere* to drop it off, only to come back with holds full of supplies."

Dex narrowed his eyes and asked; "What are they picking up on their first visit? Do we have any idea?"

"All we know," replied the Sergeant with an apologetic shrug, "is that whatever it is in that locked hangar, it's brought in from several sources around the system and is kept under constant surveillance. We also know that the team who oversees the transport and handling of said mystery boxes seem to be on a completely different wavelength of Vendrick's command structure than all the guys *we* scooped up. *Way* more tight and professional. I believe you had the opportunity to meet some of them during your little marathon through Heldrin. They were those folks in armor from the loading dock that you were telling me about. And now that I think about it, we've got a small pocket of guys on Meclan who are kinda like that as well...but they mainly just work the corn field operations and stick to themselves there. In fact, *they're* the fancy-pants tacti-cool nerds I was telling you about the other day. The ones that guard and move the corn from the fields out to the docks, who are *way* too serious about it."

"We need to find out where it's all going." Decided Dex as he leaned forward to rest on the conference table, "We need to get to the bottom of what Vendrick is really doing out here, beyond the whole ye old Governor act. What do we know about this recurring shipment out of Heldrin?"

"Quite a bit, actually." Returned Tano with a nod, "We know that Vendrick's guy on Heldrin who organizes each pickup is named Dustin Ludro. He is the local face-man for dealing with traders and other business interests who are just passing through. Vendrick likes to use these brokers to keep up appearances and prevent passers-by from getting suspicious of the situation here in Saiph. I figure if we follow *him* long enough, he'll eventually lead us to the transport ships and we can plant a tracker on one of them before they head out. That way, we can yank them out of ZS on their way *back* to Heldrin when their holds are full. It's a win-win."

"I think that's a great idea." Agreed Dex, "And I think it would be a great opportunity for you to get to know Vette a bit."

"Come again?" said Tano, confused.

"I want you to spearhead the interception OP in the Hammer with Vette." clarified Dex with a point of his index finger toward the ceiling, "You two could use a little alone time to learn from one another and figure out how the other thinks. For *unit cohesion*, if you wanna get OCS about it. Plus, I have my own little project that I would like to pursue. I want to leverage this VR thing to start getting some rudimentary training for the civilians going. Vette has been showing me how to work the scenario editor and I think I'll be able to whip up something decent."

"Whatever happened to *the more you add, the more can blab*?" asked the Sergeant pointedly with crossed arms, "I thought you wanted nothing to do with the common rabble."

"I realize now that it was arrogant of me to assume that I could get this done without local help." Admitted Dex with a shrug, "This *is* their home, after all. Everyone has a right to fight their oppressors, skilfully or not, and it took Gazia friggin' Tam to show me that. She barely knew how to even hold my gun, yet I wouldn't be standing here if she hadn't reached for it anyway. We owe it to the people to prepare them for the storm that *will* inevitably come after what we plan to do. I don't mean to make them commandos or anything, but just to teach them the basics of staying alive when the shit hits the fan. Where to take cover, how to defend yourself in-place, and how to fight if it comes down to it. Emergency preparedness *is* at the heart of every successful system."

"So, what about Bengal's preparedness?" began Mirta persuasively, "Can we re-examine the possibility of supplying them with the weapons they need to take their station back? I really think they have the best chance of pulling it off. If you look at it, Bengal has the lowest ratio of Vendrick personnel to adult civilians. It's the prime place to start our pushback!"

"Absolutely not." declared Tano with a slash of his hand through the air, "That Drebbin guy just has a hard-on for a fight and has no consideration for the people around him. His actions are too impulsive."

"According to who?" spat Mirta, "You? The guy who sat on his ever-expanding ass for a decade while the folks under his charge slowly wasted away? Because I don't think you're the gold standard on action, Mike. God forbid you scurry out of your fancy office to get your hands a little dirty..."

"What would you have me do, Mirtana?!" boomed the Sergeant defensively, "I did everything I could to keep *you* alive after your dad passed. That was the singular motivation in my soul that kept me going after Vendrick ripped our lives from us. Keep. You. Breathing. That's what all the martial arts was about, that's what all those hours at the shooting range were about, *that* is why I spent *countless* sleepless nights *stifling* my urge to **do** something. *Anything.* Because if I did so, then there'd be a target on *your* back as well. So, don't you *dare* try to lecture me on sacrifice, girl."

With a rude hand gesture, Mirta spun on her heel and stormed out of the briefing room to leave Dex and Tano in an awkward silence. After a few heartbeats, that silence was mercifully broken when Dex turned to his older companion and assured; "She'll get over it once you return with a bunch of new goodies to distract her with. I just think she's been cooped up here at Hearth for too long and is starting to get antsy."

"To be honest, I'm a bit worried about her." confided Tano as he looked to the door she exited through, "She's always been a bit hot-headed, but something is different now...It's like she can smell blood in the water and all of her other senses have dulled out."

"She's got the bloodlust," agreed Dex with a nod, "that's for sure. But I wouldn't count her out just yet. Once she can see that we're making tangible progress toward our goal, I think she will get with the program. We just need to keep a lid on her till that point comes."

"Either way," said Tano with an amused huff, "I'm not taking her with me out in the Hammer. I already have enough to worry about with that crazy-ass AI of yours, and I don't trust her not to arm a missile while I'm not looking. Maybe I will get her on with the surveillance team to keep an eye on this Dustin fella until he meets with the transport company. We can let her shoot *him* when we're done. That should keep her happy..."

Chapter 28

"Captain, I've detected a gravity spike." Alerted the sensor officer from her console, "We're being drawn off course!"

The Captain of the massive cargo vessel spun his chair to face the young woman and commanded; "Link the fleet's Inaki drives, we're being interdicted. If they snag one of us, they'll have to deal with us all." The confident Captain then rotated his chair back around and sprang to his feet. Clasping his hands behind his back, he walked to the front viewscreen of the bridge to look out his wide sweeping window. He stood, calm and expectant, as he gazed into the colorful nonsense of zerospace surrounding them. The chaos out the window then began to boil, throwing swirls of color into fervent bands of pseudomotion as a singular point of darkness materialized ahead of them. The inky dot then swelled into a sphere that continued to grow until its leading edge consumed the craft, depositing them into the star-speckled skybox of real space. All the while, the seasoned captain just remained standing, solid as stone, as the familiar scene played out in front of him.

When the Captain's craft emerged from zerospace with a hearty shudder, it was immediately flanked by fourteen of its identical brethren; All of them already beginning to warm up their respective collections of bristling turret weaponry. The group of lumbering behemoths had materialized amid a tight asteroid cluster, inside an empty void created by the floating stone. The ships were heavily armored cargo transports, undoubtedly from a Federal Navy military surplus auction, and the crew manning the fleet had experience under their belts and a reputation to back their steep invoice. Known for their ruggedly reinforced hulls, the Juexol: Atlas 13 was the premier combat cargo runner for front line duty. The battle-tested ships were tough as nails but were also capable of dealing a wallop themselves with their twelve manned defense turrets. At over four-hundred meters long each, flying in close formation, the transport fleet created an impressive shadow against the star-field. With unshakable faith in the armored blanket around him, the Captain of the supply flotilla squinted out the window; Waiting for something, *anything*, to happen. As he slowly scanned across his field of view, he detected a glint moving through the darkness out of the corner of his eye. "Three inbound ships, sir." the sensor officer called out. "Fighter class by the looks of it."

"Only three fighters?" scoffed the Captain with contempt, "This'll be good. Bring the inbound craft up on magnification."

In response, an augmented window created itself upon the sweeping front viewport that showed a zoomed-in electronically stabilized video feed of the unknown ships as a gruff voice filled the open radio channel to say; "Attention transport fleet, surrender immediately and drop your nonessential cargo. If you comply, and do so quickly, you will not be harmed."

The Captain let out a huff of laughter, then returned; "Attention, *unknown vessels*, you are in no position to demand *anything* from me or mine. Jump now or be destroyed. Last and only warning."

An odd static cut over the speakers, followed by a new artificial female voice; "Aww come on, now... Don't be so *defensive*." Her words were then followed by a wail of alarms calling out across the bridge, bathing the entire combat control center in pulsing red light.

"Captain, our shields are down, and they are not responding to our commands to restart!" shouted an engineer as he was urgently swiping at his console.

"Fleet has reported the same thing across the board!" cried out another voice, fringes of panic rising in her tone.

The veteran captain remained unimpressed and activated the fleet's intercom as well as his radio as he scoffed; "Neat little trick, but the armoring on these ships will be more than enough to outlast your three little toys. Next time you try to engage a fleet, son, bring one of your own."

To the confident leader's gut-wrenching surprise, laughter returned over the radio's speaker. The amused chortle echoed through the halls of the flagship as the intercom carried the eerie sound to the furthest reaches of the fleet. "It's funny that you would mention that, Captain." returned the gruff male voice again, "Seeing as *you* brought along some friends, I took it upon myself to invite a few of my *own*."

Once again, as if on cue, the sensor officer called out; "Captain! You need to look at this!"

The old Captain sighed and strode over to his sensor officer's station; "What is it?" he demanded, impatience clear to see in his flaring nostrils. The young woman stammered for a second then merely pointed at her display screen.

Red dots had flared to life everywhere, swimming intricate orbits around the white dots that represented their fleet within the grey asteroid field. The sensor officer enlarged the readout and breathlessly explained; "I-I'm reading sixty-three craft including several fighter variants and at least five missile boats. I'm afraid he *did* bring a fleet, sir."

"All crews to battle stations!" cried the Captain out over the ship's intercom, "We have about forty-five minutes before we can spool up for another jump, so bring the fleet in tight for formation lock! I want overlapping fields of defensive fire with our aft emplacements focusing on those missile tugs. Once our cover formation is in place, slave the fleet's controls to me and lower your bridge's blast shielding. It's ramming season, ladies and gentlemen." In response, fourteen confirmation blips lit up across the Captain's command readout. Then, out the bridge's front window to their starboard side, the massive bulk of one of the command vessel's sister ships slowly drifted over to fill the view. It lumbered closer and closer until the captain was able to make out individual crew members in the other craft's bridge as they scurried about their duties. The fifteen ships grouped themselves into three neat rows, then magnetically clamped onto one-another in an orderly grid.

The maneuver took just over a minute, forming a nearly impenetrable phalanx of defensive fire coverage around the fleet; All while those sixty dots on the tactical display continued to orbit the formation, prowling unseen in the dark. It was an uneasy feeling for the captain as he watched the dots swirl on his screen. He could almost *feel* them, crawling like ants over his skin as he looked out the viewport into the choking black. The Captain cleared his throat and injected some confidence into his voice that he certainly wasn't feeling: "Gunners, don't waste your time shooting at anything outside of three kilometers. Your priority is to target incoming munitions first. They have some missile boats out there, so keep your head on a swivel and watch for those vapor trails first and foremost. The plan is to run at full burn in a straight line until we can spool up the jump-drives. Let's see if we can't out-run em'. All ahead, maximum burn!"

With that, in unison, the trio of large thruster housings at the rear of each Atlas began to spew a brilliant purple. When the fleet started to accelerate, the bursts of flame spilling over the armored blast-shields of the trailing craft heated the purpose-built ablative coating to a dull red glow. The flotilla enjoyed a full ten seconds of steady acceleration before their drives went dark and alarms started wailing across the bridge again. "I've been told that it's rude to walk away from a conversation." chided the gruff voice on the open radio channel again, his voice also spilling over the internal fleet-wide intercom.

"Where's my systems officer?!" demanded the frustrated Captain with an unintentional growl, "I need you to find out how the hell they're doing that to my goddamn ship! And hurry it up, will you?!" The seasoned fleet Commander's mask of confidence was slipping, but he fought to keep it in place as he continued to issue orders; "Gunners, do what you can to keep them off of us while we get these engines going again. Engineers, prioritize efforts to drive systems repair and the digital hardening of life support systems. And make sure you have at least two guys on each boat dedicated to keeping the guns up. We can't aff-"

Once again, the unknown gruff voice returned over the radio, cutting the Captain off abruptly; "Guns won't work either, Chief. I'm approaching you now, so go ahead and test em on me if you'd like."

The captain huffed with frustration as he manually shut down the open radio channel. After a moment of furious pacing, he turned on the fleet intercom and commanded; "Fire on anything that comes into range and prepare to repel boarders. I don't know how the hell he's doing what he's doing, but if he wants what we've got; He's gonna have to pay the *old* price for it!"

The Captain watched on his screen, a remote camera feed displaying the gunsight picture of his dorsal turret and the view showed a sleek fighter craft slipping across the blast-shielded bow of the starboard-most ship in their row. Painted a dark purple to disappear against the inky backdrop of space, the fighter was hard to visually track, but the automated software built into the Atlas' targeting system seemed to keep the small fighter in frame just fine. The little ship turned in a swinging arc, slow as a Sunday stroll, and stopped to float in front of the bridge's armored window.

"Fire!" urged the Captain quietly to himself, "*Fire!* **Fire**!" He waited a few seconds, then impatiently opened a channel to the turret's gunner; "What the hell are you waiting for? Shoot him!"

A frustrated voice quickly returned; "I already *tried* that, Captain. It won't work! *Nothing* works! We've *all* been trying up here, and nobody can do *shit*!"

A lump formed in the old Captain's throat as he slumped down into his chair, his gray hair somehow serving to show his age now instead of the distinguished poise it normally afforded him. With the resigned sorrow of any Captain going down with his ship, the old man keyed his fleet's intercom and said; "Don't bother with the escape pods. It will just make you easier to collect and sell to the imperial slavers. Surrender if you wish, it will not be seen as a betrayal. I, on the other hand, intend to go down with my ship. Each and every one of you has fulfilled your duties with honor and it has been a pleasure serving with yo-"

The captain's uncharacteristically heartfelt speech was then cut off by the pirate's pleading voice; "Woah woah! Hang on there, partner! We aren't going to open fire or anything, so just cool your jets, everybody! We just want to *talk*, that's it. Now can you *please* open your blast shielding and have a private conversation with me, Captain?"

The gray-haired man in the command chair stood with a sigh, then reluctantly gestured to have his bridge's blast-shielding retracted. He stepped to the window and clasped his hands behind his back with dignity as the metal plates over his window began to slide away. The old fleet commander was surprised when the blast-shield had completed its withdrawal and he found himself nose to nose with an equally aged Odox Eagle fighter-interceptor, just like the ones he flew during the territorial war in the Vulpecula sector over forty years prior.

The mass-produced nature of the craft made them notoriously difficult to keep in the black for more than a few years before repairing them became cost-ineffective, so to see one in the wild forty years past any reasonably expected flight-life threw the nostalgic man for a bit of a loop. The Captain noticed with surprise as well that the gently humming machine poised just outside his window had been meticulously maintained and obviously lovingly cared for with evidently all her original parts. The sight made the old fighter pilot inside the Captain subconsciously grow a soft spot for the man who he could now see gesturing to him through the fighter craft's thin cockpit canopy. The Captain recognized the other man's universal hand gesture and held up his arm in response. The action was to present his forearm mounted tablet's tight-beam comm array toward the man out the window. Both men then exchanged an infrared laser connection from tablet to tablet, which established a completely private voice and data network for them to speak through. "Can you hear me?" came the now-familiar gruff voice in his earpiece.

The captain nodded and dutifully replied; "What are your terms? I am prepared to deal, but there will be no discussion of the transfer of living cargo."

The Captain could see the man in the cockpit across from him shake his head wearily as he replied; "I'm not a terms kind of guy. I'm more of the discussion type."

The Captain furrowed his brow and retorted; "That's an odd thing for a pirate to say."

"Who say's I'm a pirate?" asked the unknown voice in a reasonable tone, his shoulders raising into an innocent shrug.

"You instructed me to drop my cargo and implied the use of force if I didn't comply." huffed the Captain with exasperation, "That is *literally* the Interstellar Spacefaring Treaty's *definition* of pirating."

There was a short silence, then the gruff man concedingly returned; "Ok Fine, you got me there...But at least let me ask you this... How much do you know about your *employer*?"

The Captain shrugged and retorted; "He's the one that signs the checks, generally. They pay me to take boxes from point A to point B. It's not really a line of work that inspires or necessitates many specific questions."

"Is that all that matters?" asked the pirate pointedly, "What if I told you that you were out here working for a monster?"

"I'd probably tell you that I've heard that one already." retorted the Captain flatly, "Look, can we cut the bullshit and talk about whatever it is that you made me come over here to talk to you about?"

"Why don't you browse through some of the files I'm sending over." suggested the pirate with a placating tone, "Take a look at some of your *boss's* other business ventures and tell me what you think."

The Captain felt a vibration to signify the arrival of an incoming file transfer, so he tapped a command to pull it open. Inside were countless photos and video files, all of them featuring horrific scenes of brutality and violence. Public executions, corpses discarded in the streets, pictures of gaunt and starving people violently at one-another's throats over a few packets of rations that had already been torn to shreds in the scramble. Flipping through the depressing content soured the Captain's already dreary mood, and it all felt too manipulative. He closed the files with irritation and heard the pirate ask; "Well what do you have to say about *that*?"

The Captain clenched his jaw in annoyance and replied; "I'd say you spent way too much time surfing the net looking for fucked up pictures and security cam footage. Nothing but smoke and mirrors *bullshit*."

"I knew you would say that." sighed the pirate, "So why don't you take a look at the four pictures I'm sending you now..."

Against his better judgment, the Captain opened the folder containing the mentioned images. They were more scenes of death and mayhem, but this time they all featured the same central character, wearing an out-of-place flowered shirt, committing each atrocity. The jovial nature of the man's outfit made for an uncomfortable juxtaposition next to the depicted scenes of violence, but it was the man's seemingly permanent nonchalance that turned his stomach the most. The last in the set of images featured the flower-shirted man standing behind a woman who had been forced to kneel. The man had his pistol trained at the back of her head, shrugging with humor in his eyes at what he was saying to her. The Captain closed the file with a pang of sorrow and left his anger unchecked when he keyed his comm to respond; "You'd better be getting to your goddamn point in a hurry."

The pilot inside the craft out the window made a show of putting his hands up in a placating gesture as he replied; "That last photo was taken just two hours prior to this one..."

The Captain felt another vibration on his wrist and he reluctantly opened the newly arrived attachment. The photo featured the same executioner, wearing the exact colorful outfit as in the previous pictures, standing on the large internal flightdeck of what he recognized as the Heldrin City docks, shaking hands with another man. The Captain furrowed his brow and zoomed in on the image for a better look. As the image re-rendered at the new magnification, his blood ran cold when he instantly recognized *himself* as the gentleman politely greeting the freshly sated murderer with a businessman's smile.

"We followed that piece of shit for just over eight hours." explained the pirate, "By the time he was signing that load over to you in the afternoon that day, he had already murdered three people. *These* are the monsters that you're dealing with here. And *we* are the ones out here trying to stop them."

The Captain just stood there stunned for a moment, incapacitated by a sudden rush of guilt that threatened to suffocate him. When he finally regained his composure, he mournfully said; "The pay *was* unusually good. Which, in my line of work, means that you *don't ask questions*. But had I *known* that something like this was going on out here...." The fleet commander trailed off and his gaze fell to the floor in self-inflicted shame as his lips floundered wordlessly.

"It's not your fault." urged the pirate, "You have been contracted by a man named Vendrick. The gentleman you met on the dock was one of his lieutenants."

The Captain raised an eyebrow. "Was?" he asked pointedly.

"You know..." replied the pirate with mock nonchalance, "It was the weirdest thing. He committed suicide in an elevator on the night all those photos were taken. Shot himself a dozen times in the back. Poor bastard. Nobody deserves to die in a shirt that hideous."

Knowing that the devil he'd struck a deal with had met with a demise of his own gave the old mercenary Captain a small sense of closure on the subject, allowing him to exhale a breath he hadn't known he'd been holding. Still armed with a skeptical mind, the Captain pressed on; "So who is this Vendrick guy you keep talking about? I've never heard that name once in my dealings with Saiph. I was initially hired by the man named Ludro on Heldrin city and have been doing gigs almost exclusively for him ever since."

The return of the pirates voice was accompanied by another incoming file; "Vendrick is a self-installed dictator that has seized absolute control over all the stations in the sector. Dustin Ludro was one of Vendrick's face men that dealt with passing merchants and traders. He uses his fake economy of faux businesses and indentured pilots to preserve the appearance of a normal marketplace so he can avoid any undesired scrutiny from the wider galaxy. Vendrick's organization prolongs his reign with the liberal use of brutality and terrorism, such as the examples I have provided. The criminals and scum under his employ do a good job at keeping the residents of the stations separated from the cargo pilots and folks just passing through, so you'd be hard-pressed to know that anything untoward was going on if you didn't know to look for it. This man has been in complete control over the entire population of Saiph for over a decade now, and has worked very hard to keep that fact a secret. He starves the citizens and forces them to live on meager rations to further his own, *unknown*, agenda. He's the badguy here, not us."

The Captain sighed, obviously at odds with himself before retorting; "You could've fooled me. The *good guys* generally aren't the ones going around pirating folks..."

"What we are out here doing," argued the stranger outside the window with an air of patience, "is intercepting Vendrick's supplies and ensuring that they are delivered to the people who *need* them, instead of allowing thugs to withhold that food and medicine until their sadistic whims are met. Now...we both know that I could just send a command on my tablet here to have your entire fleet jettison their cargo holds whenever I want, and I believe I've thoroughly demonstrated my ability to do so, but I would really prefer it if *you* were the one to press the button. I was listening as you managed your fleet today, sir. Your resolve under the stress of extremely unusual circumstances has proven you to be a good leader, and it is my firm belief that good leaders are, more often than not, good people as well. Please let me get your supplies to the right folks. Help me save some lives today, Captain."

"It's Ingram." said the fleet commander in a new, gentler, tone, "My name is Captain Harry Ingram."

"Pleasure to meet you, Captain Ingram." greeted the pirate with good cheer, "My name is Sergeant Michael Tano, and I, like many of my colleagues out here, used to be a police officer that served and protected the people of this system for over twenty-five years...And I like to think that I still do. So, thank you for being willing to talk like gentlemen."

Captain Ingram nodded and replied; "It has been, *oddly enough*, a pleasure to meet you as well, Sergeant Tano. I wasn't really given much of a choice but to have this chat with you, but I'm glad that I did. I believe what you're telling me is the honest truth, and I will happily comply with your request. Standby, Sergeant. I'm instructing my fleet to jettison all cargo." Feeling the gravity of the moment in the weight of the stares boring a hole into his back, the Captain lowered his tablet-laden arm and spun to face his crew. He cleared his throat to buy a moment to reclaim his voice, then ordered; "All vessels; Unzip and jettison your holds. *Commercial* cargo only. Double time!"

This caused a stir among the crew and an alarmed bridge officer blurted; "Do we have any guarantees of safety?! How do we know they won't still kill us when they get our cargo free of the blast zone?"

"We should board *them*!" shouted another voice at the back of the room to the sounds of agreement.

"Enough!" snapped Captain Ingram, "I just issued an order for the fleet. **Now** is the time that you carry it out. *Later*...Later I can explain how the whole damn thing is *my* fault. It suffices to say that we were playing for the wrong team on this one, gang, and this move is the right one for anyone keeping track of their karma. Once our cargo is dumped, *all* of our systems will be returned to us so we can jump out. Alright, everybody, let's get moving! I need you focused on getting that cargo unstrapped ASAP. Let's *go*!"

"Mr. Tano," said Ingram over their private channel after turning back around to face his new friend, "I never thought I would ever thank someone for pirating me. But in this case, I will make an exception. If there is anything I can do to help, you let me know. I'm sure you've been through enough of my systems to know my channel key by now, so drop me and good ol' Baylor Company a line if you ever find yourself needing a little bit of extra firepower or hauling might. We'll be there."

"I will keep that in mind." replied Tano with a nod and friendly smile through his now-raised visor, "And as far as helping goes, what you can do is spread the word to your fellow contractors about what's happening out here. Taking a job from Vendrick or *anyone* who seems to have creds to sling out here just isn't worth it. Not if you have a soul, anyways. People outside the system need to know what we're fighting against here, Captain, and that last file I sent you has all the evidence you need to prove all of it. If enough folks are informed, maybe *someone* will decide to come and help us do something about it. Maybe even the Feds. It *is* their mess in the first place, after all."

"I will gladly spread the word for you, Sergeant," promised Ingram with a sturdy nod, "but I can't guarantee that they'll all listen to me. I know guys running crews out here who would vent their own mother if the credits to do so were thick and clear enough. I will also do my best to try and keep tabs on who *is* still taking jobs out here after I present your case and let you know, if I can, when they're coming your way.

"I appreciate that, Captain." returned Tano with a weary sigh at the other man's pragmatic dose of reality, "I see that your cargo has now been offloaded and you're all zipped back up. I appreciate *that* as well. I went ahead and set a short jump for your fleet out into interstellar space. Once you pop into zerospace; our command signal will drop, and full control of your systems will be returned to you. And once again, on behalf of the fine folks of Saiph, we thank you for your kind donation."

The Captain looked around with mild wonder, nodding agreeably as indication lights and their corresponding systems all over his bridge began to warm up without being prompted to do so. "You have to tell me Sergeant, or it's going to drive me nuts," urged the Captain with a pained look, "How did you do this to my fleet? I really need to know if I have any weak spots so I can prepare a defense for when someone *less* civilized tries the same thing someday."

Tano laughed and said; "I wouldn't worry too much about it, Harry. I don't know many other *pirate gangs* out there who have what we've got. But, if you must know, you might want to encrypt your fleet's entertainment media server... And might I add that lieutenant Dallas has *excellent* taste in music."

"Thanks for the tip." said the Captain with a chuckle of his own. The bridge then came to life around him with a familiar low hum, one that normally preceded a massive discharge of Inaki energy that would propel them into zerospace. With a sigh of relief at the sound, Ingram activated his comm one last time to say; "Your fleet showed impressive restraint in not firing on our defenseless ships. Thank you for having the discipline, as a group, to be sending my people home to see their families tonight."

Tano smiled with a mischievous glint in his eye and replied; "Oh, yeah, no problem. I'm as dependable as can be. Wasn't sure about the other two guys, though."

Ingram cocked his head and asked; "Other *two*?"

"Smoke and mirrors, Captain. Smoke and mirrors. Have a safe trip home." With that, the fleet distorted then appeared to stretch into a singularity as the ships of Balor Company slipped into the nonsense of zerospace.

Chapter 29

"So you really think they're actually just *giving* this stuff away?" asked Donovan Moore, lead cargo engineer of the newly formed *Heldrin Freedom Fleet*, as he looked out over the cargo bay packed to its gills with food packets, medical gel, antivirals, and other essentials, "There's gotta be *some* catch, right?"

"None that I've been able to detect." replied the tired voice of Randall Becker from the comfort of his command chair on the bridge of his cargo hauler, *Lombrico*, "This'll be our eleventh run and every hand-off has gone smooth as silk so far. It really *is* the darnedest thing, you know? I've been to three separate stations now and on each one they've always met me on time, had the camera feeds already looped, drones ready to go, and armed guards on the door. It really *is* impressive how they've managed to train so many people so quickly. As I understand it, that Sloan fellow showed up just under two mo-" His sentence was suddenly drowned out by the wailing of a zerospace collapse alarm that was quickly followed by a stomach-churning lurch underfoot. "What do we have?" demanded Becker automatically as his viewscreen adjusted to the sudden darkness.

"Four contacts." Replied the sensor operator as she strapped herself into her seat, "Looks like three fast-movers leading an armored freighter, and they're coming in fast. No hailing attempts have been made yet, but their EM is spiking *hard*."

"All crew," bellowed Becker into the ship's intercom, "We seem to have stumbled into a spot of trouble. Report to your action stations and lock in for combat maneuvers."

"They're priming their weapons!" warned a man from his seat at the tactical station, "Shifting shield envelope aftward now."

"Engineering," demanded the ship's Captain with a sharp calm, "set aside what power you need to keep us all breathing, then send whatever is left into the plasma generator and rear shield capacitors. Helm, find us a clear vector then fire up our chemical boosters to get us moving away from that freighter. And...*somebody else* get on that comm frequency for the reactionary force we *supposedly* have on call from our friends over on Meclan. *Now* is the time to see if they're worth their word."

"Fighters are closing in on us fast!" warned the sensor operator, "Freighter appears to be warming up its tractor array, but they're still too far off to get a good hold on us."

"This is not *your* space to travel through." Boomed an unfamiliar voice from the bridge's speakers, "Power down your shit and submit yourself for boarding, *NOW!*"

"Apologies, friend," offered Becker over the open comm with his expertly donned mask of business-grade politeness, "I'm afraid that you will have to *catch* your dinner this evening."

"It's *your* funeral." scoffed the unidentified voice in return as the impact of superheated globules of plasma and their rapidly-solidifying cores of liquid cobalt began to splash against the electromagnetically-bound envelope of *protective* plasma that blanketed the smuggler's freighter. As round after molten round boiled their way across the vacuum, more and more of the superheated argon cloak around *Lombrico's* hull was splashed away and lost to the void.

"Rear shield capacitors are failing!" yelped someone from an engineering console, "We're losing containment *fast*."

Becker slammed his fist into the armrest of his command chair and barked; "Helm, cut thrust and present our belly to the enemy. We should be able to absorb more hits from that angle."

"They're closing on us, sir." Warned the sensor operator, "Their tractor efficiency is at twenty-three percent and rising. We're losing our forward momentum!"

Before the Captain of the increasingly ensnared freighter had the opportunity to slam his fist into his armrest again, another voice rose from the rear of the command deck; "Inbound Inaki signatures detected, ninety-seven kilometers out bearing two-seven-four mark zero-three-nine"

"New contacts are hailing us, sir." Added another crewmember from her station at the comms board, "Patching them through now."

"Hang tight, *Lombrico*," came a new voice over the speakers, "We'll clear the skies for you. Just maintain course and try to put a good-sized rock between you and that freighter as soon as you can. Scalpel-One, out."

As he switched his comm back over to his team channel, Armando Vega cleared his throat and said; "Alright, folks. Training wheels are off now and it's time to take the fight to the enemy. Two, you're with me. We're going to burn for the hostile freighter to try to get them to shut down that tractor and focus on us instead. Three, four, and five are on fighter detail. Six, I need you running defense for our friends. Nothing with propulsion or guidance gets through you, you hear?"

After seeing the status lights of all five of his wingmates wink green, Vega oriented himself toward the lumbering armored freighter and kicked on his chemical boosters. The oncoming G-forces hit him immediately as his cockpit's internal velocity dampeners stuttered and failed to counteract the sudden crushing speed. His vector took him screaming past the approaching enemy fighters, a mere dozen meters from the incredulous stares of the hostile pilots as he flashed by. Then, just as Vendrick's fighters entered the frame of Vega's rear-view camera feed, globules of boiling plasma began splashing across their hulls from the collective volley of Scalpels three through five.

Under the combined barrage of all three Eagles hammering simultaneously away at the lead enemy fighter, the hostile craft quickly lost containment of its front shielding and let a pair of shots through that decimated the cockpit canopy. As soon as the pilot's couch was consumed in a flash ignition of the craft's onboard oxygen supply, the rest of the poorly maintained fighter detonated from within as the intense heat touched off its chemical fuel tanks. The resulting blossom of orange and purple from the rapidly expanding sphere of wreckage forced the remaining pair of enemy craft to peel off from their attack run to avoid flying through the debris.

As enemy fighter number one banked away to the left, breaking from his budding attack run on *Lombrico*, Scalpel three adjusted her vector to loop around behind her foe. The second enemy pilot was quick to recognize his colleague's danger, however, so he dipped below the expanding cloud of twisted steel and banked his way behind Scalpel three to begin opening fire.

As she dipped and weaved her Eagle in a seemingly random pattern amid the stream of enemy plasma coming from behind, Scalpel-three activated her comm to say; "He's on me pretty good. You guys got angle yet?"

"Pull him hard starboard," Urged the voice of Scalpel-four, "but don't bleed too much speed. We should be able to tag him when he rolls out to follow." Three obliged immediately, pulling her stick to the side as hard as she could while momentarily burping her boosters to keep her speed up. Just as expected, the enemy ship rolled and banked to follow its prey...right into the combined streams of plasma fire from Scalpels four and five as they closed in from above. With both Eagles focusing their offensive strength toward the same region of the hostile fighter's rear end, it was a matter of seconds before the onslaught had torn through the shields and straight into the craft's internal missile magazine. The results were immediate and devastating, tearing the ship to pieces amid a brilliant flash that momentarily blinded Scalpel-three's rear-view camera.

Realizing that he was now severely outnumbered, the final enemy fighter pilot abandoned his attack and decided to burn as hard as he could for the heavily armored freighter and the perceived protection it would offer him. As Scalpel three, four, and five fell in behind the fleeing enemy craft, Vega and his wing mate continued to orbit the large enemy freighter taking turns pecking away at three chosen spots along the hull. When it became evident that each and every shot had been boiling harmlessly away within the thick bubble of plasma around the sturdy enemy craft, it became clear that the repeaters outfitted to the Eagles weren't going to be enough to do any meaningful damage. Deciding that he would need to expend one of their precious few missiles, Scalpel-one broke away from his tight orbit around the enemy and pulled back far enough to get a solid radar lock. With a light thump felt underfoot, a black and red missile decoupled from the Eagle's internal munitions bay and lit up its chemical rocket to zip toward the target. Bobbing and weaving like mad, the missile made its way across the black toward its prey. That was when a trio of point defense turrets popped out along the freighter's spine and began to lay down a deadly weave of ferroplastic flak darts. The onslaught of self-detonating munitions blanketed the vacuum with high-speed shrapnel that made quick work of the missile's thin outer skin and obliterated the sensitive guidance system within. As a result, the missile veered wildly off course and maintained a widening corkscrew until it had expended its entire fuel reserve and floated dead into the vastness of the Saiph system.

Just as he was cursing to himself at the failure, Vega heard the voice of Scalpel-two in his ear; "Hey boss, did you notice how the point defense winked off the instant that rocket cut thrust? I think their targeting system is propulsion lock, so that means they probably wouldn't spot oncoming ordinance if it came in at a low angle and unpowered. Why don't we take another pass, old-school style, and let inertia do all the work?"

"I like it." replied the squadron leader with swelling concentration, "It looks like the bulk of their shield envelope is sitting nice and fat around those engine housings, but that nose is looking a little light. I've only got one missile left, so you'll need to arm one of yours as well and we'll make a run for their bridge. Trail your release by about a second to let my payload splash out a good hole so yours can get on in there and kiss some hull."

In acknowledgement, a red icon winked to life over the readout for Scalpel-two on Vega's console, signifying that a missile had been armed. Seeing that his wingmate was already right on his tail, Scalpel-one started a long looping arc that took him heading straight-on toward the freighter. As the

Eagles reached the two-kilometer mark, they both opened up on the armored behemoth's front viewport with their plasma repeaters. The shots did no damage on their own, but the attack served to obscure the vision of those manning the enemy command deck enough to conceal the release of a pair of objects from the oncoming fighters before they peeled off. The crew of the enemy freighter didn't have much time to catch their mistake, however, as their bridge was flash-vaporized under the instant blaze of Scalpel's pair of hydrogen warheads.

"Good effect." Reported the voice of Scalpel-three from her distant vantage point, "Looks like you vented half of the damn ship and they've ceased all thrust." The force of the blast had torn away a quarter of the freighter's upper deck and managed to push the massive bulk of the enemy ship into a slow tumble as sparks and wisps of shield plasma escaped wildly along the jagged edges of destruction. After the devastating hit, there were no signs of life at all coming from the crippled craft. No life pods, no distress signals, no final defiant words. Just silent obliteration.

"You still out there, *Lombrico*?" asked Vega over the open comm, "Looks like the last fighter just bugged out and that hostile tractor array is *very* down. You are now free to jump at your leisure, though I'd urge you against sticking around too long. Fly safe, guys. Scalpel out."

Chapter 30

"Alright, alright, everyone quiet down…" boomed Dex over the gathered crowd of virtual men and women who were all donning the trim black button-ups and duty pants of uniformed LAPD officers circa the late 1980's BCE. While he got a private chuckle from their appearance, the volunteers from Heldrin and Meclan were the ones getting a majority of the laugh as they inspected *his* outfit with a completely non-contextual eye. Dex stood donning a pair of tight jeans that were stretched over worn cowboy boots and he had the handle of a handgun tucked into the waist of his pants overtop a white and grey striped button-up. It wasn't his clothing that had captured the crowd's amusement, however. It was the mane of semi-fluffed brown hair that cascaded past his ears to rest upon the rear of his shoulders in a well-imitated mullet.

"Now that we've gone over first aid, biohazard response, emergency evacuation drills, and radio communications protocol," he continued as the crowd stifled their playful chatter and turned their attention to the strangely dressed man before them, "we can finally do something a little fun. What we're here to do *today*, ladies and gentlemen, is run through a few scenarios that will help prepare you to stay alive if and when the bullets start flying. Now, I'm not here to do some kickass training montage where you all come out of here killing machines, alright? I'm here to present you with the very *basic* nuts and bolts of gunfighting and teach you how to utilize those concepts to increase your survivability in combat. The first of these training simulations lies at the top of these steps here." Dex gestured to the concrete flight of stairs behind him that led up to an open courtyard above, ringed with four-story buildings on three sides. "Scenario is that there's a sniper and he's been shooting children at the playground up there. Our job is to put him into retirement without getting smoked ourselves. I'll go first so you can watch, and we can talk about it. Then, I will set you lot loose on it. Sound good?"

When he scanned the crowd and wasn't met with any objections, he nodded, and gunfire suddenly began to erupt from above. With a sigh and a look of complete apathy, Dex fished a cigarette from his front pocket and popped it into his mouth before grabbing the pistol from his waist and partially pulling back its slide to confirm that a round had been chambered. Once he was satisfied that his archaic weapon was loaded, he held it at the ready and began to ascend the stairs. When he reached the top, the sniper's rifle fell silent for a reload as Dex approached the middle of the open courtyard.

"Hello, mister sniper, sir…" called Dex as he came to a stop under the small playground's monkey bars. Just then, a man popped into view in a window above to his one O'clock and began firing wildly at him. The rounds came in like hail, striking the pavement, the playground equipment, and the gravel at Dex's feet; But the mulleted hero just stood stone-still until the sniper exhausted his ammunition once more and had to duck back into cover for another reload. Taking a few steps forward as he slowly drew back the hammer of his pistol with his thumb, Dex defiantly yelled; "I'm still here asshole…Or do you only do kids?"

"Shut up!" screamed the sniper as he hurled himself back into view. When he did so, however, Dex was waiting with his pistol trained onto the window and he began to rapidly unload his weapon into the man's hiding spot with deadly accuracy. His rounds peppered the sniper and he fell dramatically to the ground, shooting his rifle several times into the ceiling as he did so.

Once his foe fell from view, Dex dropped the expended magazine from his pistol and quickly replaced it with the backup that was tucked into his waistband. After taking a few moments to scan the numerous other windows around him, he decided the sim had finished and he knelt to retrieve his empty from the ground. Returning to the group of assembled volunteers, Dex slipped his pistol into his belt and asked; "Alright, so what did I do wrong?" Dex scanned the faces before him and was met with silence. When the silence began to spawn uncomfortable coughs and shuffling of feet, the ex-Lieutenant sighed and answered his own question; "What I did wrong was I committed the gravest sin of all gunfighting. I returned fire *before* finding cover, and I did so with my feet squarely planted. Even if you have nothing to hide behind, movement is *always* preferable to standing still...even if you can't shoot worth a shit while in motion. Your main concern in any firefight is staying out of his gunsights while simultaneously trying to maneuver yourself into position to take a calculated shot of your own. So, that being said, what could I have done different on that front?"

A man standing toward the back of the group nervously raised his hand. When Dex pointed to him, the man said; "Y-you could have either stayed below the line of the top of the stairs, or you could have made a sprint for the retaining wall in front of the sniper's nest while he was trying to reload."

"Good!" replied Dex with an enthusiastic nod, "And what else do you think I could have done to improve my chances?" When his follow-up question was met with another extended silence, Dex explained; "Well, I wasted a lot of ammo on that initial dump there. So, if I hadn't managed to take him out with my first volley, I would have found myself out in the open with my pants around my ankles and my weapon dry. Not to mention the fact that *anybody's* accuracy goes to dogshit when they start hammering the trigger like that. So, do you think you guys have seen enough to have a go at it for yourselves? Why don't you all go up there and try to get him this time. There should definitely be power in numbers."

With reluctant nods all around, the volunteers from Heldrin and Meclan began to draw the service pistols from their matching duty belts and started to ascend the stairs. When they reached the top, half of the bunch froze in place to hunker behind the final flight while the other half surged over the top step and onto the playground. The volunteers streamed forward, with half of them already firing at the empty window above while dashing for what cover they could find. Once their dozen seconds of mayhem came to a close, they all began to collectively realize that not a single return shot had been fired. When the gunfire from the '*Officers*' on the ground had finally dwindled to a stop, there was a full three seconds of total silence before all hell broke loose. From positions on all three roofs and several windows within each building, a massive enemy force suddenly opened fire on the group of invaders; Cutting them all down in a hail of automatic machinegun fire in a matter of seconds. Then, just as suddenly as it had erupted, the staccato pops and bangs died to silence when Dex ended the scenario.

With new breath filling their lungs and control returned to their extremities, the trainees began to woozily return to their feet. Many were still disoriented from their virtual deaths, but some were coherent enough to grow furious. "What the fuck was that all about?!" spat one of the larger volunteers, "You trying to be funny or some shit? That's not what you said we would be doing!"

"And therein lies my next lesson of the day..." explained Dex with a patient smile, "It is often said that *No plan survives first contact with the enemy*, and it's true. That's what I was attempting to demonstrate here. No matter how prepared you feel, no matter how much you think you know about what lies beyond a closed bulkhead, there's always room for the universe to change the rules at the last moment and fuck you with em. Diligence, not necessarily skill, is what will keep you alive. At all times, you need t-"

Dex was suddenly interrupted by an urgent beeping in his ear. Recognizing the tone as a high-priority external message, he opened his virtual HUD and played the stored transmission: "We have something very scary going on out here, Dex." Began the recording of Tano's voice, "We've lost *all* contact, we're talking node, radio, *and* Hūnet connection, with Bengal station entirely. We've been trying to reach them for the past two hours on every bandwidth I can think of and haven't heard a peep. I don't like this, man. Something is *very* wrong here, and I have a terrible feeling about it..."

Chapter 31

Dendo Patel's Tuesday morning had not started out as smoothly as he'd wanted. His faulty tablet and only form of time-keeping device defaulted itself back to Earth-standard instead of his locally set time-zone and he was already running on track to show up an hour late for work. Plus, to make matters and his timing worse, his foot found one of his son's toy spaceships on the ground within the darkened interior of their apartment pod as he sneakily tried to assemble his things for the day. If the tiny pilots who were sitting behind the controls within the cockpit of the little aircraft, leaning forward to 'look' up at him through their glass canopy, had been tasked with assaulting the giant, their mission was a rousing success; Nearly splitting Dendo's poor toe in two against its aggressive wing-edge.

Stifling a string of muffled curse words while he reached down to place his attacker on the kitchen counter, the man couldn't help but feel his anger flood away as he looked across the faintly lit apartment at the motionless lump of blankets that concealed his only son. His wife had been worried when she found out that she was pregnant, just nine short years ago, and he had to beg her to keep the baby when she did. She was convinced that there was nothing good in the galaxy for their son to grow into as long as they remained in Saiph, and nothing that *they* could do to properly provide for him to find that better future. After a short *chat* with Dendo's battle axe of a mother changed his wife's position, however, Dendo made it his purpose in life to prove his beloved wife wrong by building a comfortable and enriching life for their son to thrive in.

It was for that exact reason that Dendo was rising an hour before the day's first crack of dawn, just after a grueling twelve hour shift at work the night before. All so he could arrive early to his second job in an effort to get out of *that* office early enough to get to his *third* job on time. His existence was a Sisyphean one, but it was all worth it to know that his child had never gone to bed with an empty stomach...Even though his own often went unfilled. But, hungry or not, another day had arrived, and it demanded its due of work from the poor wretch regardless.

Dendo's wife had urged him to stay home from the office the night before, on account of all the violence happening over on the central ring, but he just replied with his now-cemented catchphrase *'Weekday's a workday, love'* before kissing her goodnight and rolling over to close out their discussion. The truth was that he understood where she was coming from. During the early hours of the morning the day before, masked men started attacking the police station where Vendrick's bullies had been running their reign of terror from. The ensuing gun fight was apparently rather fierce, and he had heard that many of the tattooed thugs were killed. He had no particular care for *them*, but he really began to worry when reports of just how many bystanders got killed during the attack and rumors that vital life support equipment had been damaged started spreading through his office like wildfire.

Half of his co-workers had left the office early to be with their families when the violence broke out, but Dendo's personal budget required that he work every minute of every hour he was scheduled or else the delicate financial house of cards that was his family's life would come tumbling down. After clocking out, he had rushed home through streets that were oddly devoid of both people and the sneering faces of Vendrick's men. It seemed that everyone had either gone into hiding or went to the central ring to join in on the fight, and he wished to count himself among the former as quickly as possible.

After a relatively uneventful night, with no decompression alarms or gunfire popping off in the residence rings, Dendo felt confident that he would be able to get to work in one piece and earn another handful of credits to keep his family scraping by. Displaying a confidence in his spine and face that he certainly did not feel, he strode over to his wife and gently kissed her on the forehead. She sleepily gazed up at him from underneath the electrically-warmed fringe of their comforter with a look of growing concern as her mind increased its grip on consciousness. When her brow had fully furrowed itself into that familiar look of disapproval that he had grown to love despite her best efforts, she broke the silence of the early morning darkness; "Oh come on, Den. You can't let things cool off for *one* day before heading back into work? Nobody else is going to be there, so why even go?"

"We don't know that for sure." Argued Dendo weakly, "And you are well aware that we need every single credit we can find. Productive or not, if my caboose is in that chair; I'm making money. I know it sucks, hon, but I gotta do what I have to to keep the lights on. If you need me, I'll be just next-door."

"Promise you'll be safe?" she asked after delivering a deep reluctant sigh, "And you'll call me when you get to the office, yeah?"

"Sure as the sunsets, love." Replied the hard-working man with a loving smile, "You know I always do. The monster was up late last night, so I don't want to risk waking him up. When he *does* finally join the living, though, can you tell him that he's a buttface nooblet and that his kung-fu is no match for his old man's?...Might give me a little more street cred coming from you..."

"Oh, no..." protested his wife as she propped herself up onto her elbow with a scornful grin, "There's no *way* I'm getting involved in your guys' ridiculous VR machismo ritual. *You're* just going to have to figure out how he keeps kicking your ass."

"I *let* him win...some of the time" retorted Dendo with a hushed defensive outrage and an equally muted shrug, "It's just those crazy kicks lately...absolutely killing me."

"Well?" she laughed, "What do you expect when you allow an eight-year-old to load into the avatar of a full size, full *strength*, adult? Even if you guys *are* fighting without skillpacks or pain feedback, he's *still* a complete madman. *You* come built-in with years of pre-programmed self-preservation habits that prevent you from even *trying* triple...flying...lotus whatevers in the first place. *Luke* doesn't."

"Hey, I can do all the flying whatevers he can, alright?" scoffed the middle-aged man in a tone that suggested he knew full-well that he was lying, "I just choose to conduct a more *tactical* approach to our matches."

"Good luck planning a strategy around his mastery of the cocaine-monkey technique." She laughed with a muffled snort, "Now get outta here before I decide to not let you leave. Have a great day at work and know that I appreciate everything you do for us. Love you, Denny!"

"Loved you first." replied Dendo as he leaned down to give his wife a tight hug and a lingering kiss on her cheek. Then, with a wink and a light pinch of her chin, Dendo spun on his heel and made for the door.

Bengal station sat in orbit above the blue mid-rim gas giant Fūjin. It went from a dark blue at its poles to a bright turquoise with glowing green brushstrokes of bioluminescent microbes called Hortus Volantes that spun aloft in the central bands of the planet's turbulent upper atmosphere. Bengal city was comprised of five rings, all stemming from a trio of support struts that led down to a common docking drum. The central ring, being twice the size of the other four at eight kilometers in diameter, housed the station's main business, shopping, and schooling centers. The two outside rings were used for calorie production and other industrialized applications, while the innermost of the lesser rings housed the population of just over twenty-two thousand.

As just one of those twenty thousand or so souls aboard, Dendo couldn't help but feel the figure was an exaggerated one as he rode a nearly empty train from the ring of his residence out to the furthest stop on the run. As he stepped off his passenger car, he saw some rougher types milling around at the end of the platform who lacked the tell-tale swirls of facial color that Vendrick's guys all sported. Wishing to avoid the inevitable screeches and insults these youths usually liked to hurl in the direction of travelers, Dendo reached into his bag and pulled out his pair of noise canceling earbuds. As he popped the small self-forming devices into his ears, the blaring and overly friendly voice of the automated station announcer faded into nothingness along with the rhythmic clanging emanating from a factory complex nearby. Keeping his head down and his hands in his pockets, Dendo strode briskly for the exit, making a conscious effort to avoid looking at all in the direction of the delinquents. When he breached the station's threshold, surprisingly without incident, he gradually began to slow his pace back down to a normal stride. Moments later, as he was lost in some mental arithmetic over something for work, he felt a sharp vibration through the heel of his shoe.

Assuming that the strange sensation was merely due to the hoodlums at the station throwing something in an attempt to mess with him, he avoided looking back and increased his pace. Over a hundred yards later, he felt the thump again and began to slow to a halt as a large shadow gradually overtook him from behind. Succumbing to his urge to peek, Dendo stopped and turned around to look up. What he saw, slowly stalking its way across the starfield beyond the ring's glass canopy to overtake the distant glow of Saiph, was a smooth bulbous shape of pure darkness. There was no material visible in the encroaching void, no hull or lines of detail to discern; Just complete and total nothingness propelling itself through the vacuum. Dendo was in such awe at the odd sight that he nearly had a heart attack when his wrist began to vibrate. Seeing that it was an audio call from his wife, he lifted his arm and punched the command to accept the incoming connection request. "Den? Are you there? Can you hear me?" came the voice of his wife in his ear, "What's going on? That last rumble woke Luke up and we're starting to get worried. Is the fighting spreading?"

"I'm not sure, love." Answered Dendo as he continued to stare out the glass ceiling of ring number four at the looming shape above, "There's nothing going down on the streets over here, but you'd best keep our apartment locked up tight until I get back. There's a ship. It looks like someone is here...Could be the Feds? I don't know. Maybe they've finally come to clean up the mess. Those rumbles, if we both felt them, could've been breaching charges of some kind, possibly? Either way, just hang tight until the powers at play get this sorted out. I love you and I'm headed back your way now."

"Be safe, Den!" urged his wife with fear beginning to swell in her tone, "And don't get yourself hurt trying to rush ho-"

Suddenly, as his open connection ceased with another ripple through the deckplate, a brilliant flash emanated from the front end of the bulbous shadow above that instantly resulted in a plume of blue flame leaping from the docking drum. Dendo couldn't help but fall to his knees in shock as ring number two, one of the manufacturing centers, fractured in a series of sub-detonations that vented all of its atmosphere to space as the station's superstructure rotated it to pieces. He sat back on his heels in a dissociative stupor and watched as the unidentified ship fired again. This time it punched a ragged hole through the central ring's thick underbelly, causing *another* torrent white fog and flailing bodies to come spilling forth into the void.

By the time the third shot had struck his *own* ring at the opposite end from his own, all life and color had left Dendo's face. The ground bucked horrendously beneath him, tossing him a quarter of the way up to the glass ceiling like a toy being kicked across a room. Shortly afterward, as he lay bleeding with his multiple newly acquired broken bones within the disturbed gravity of the rapidly disintegrating ring, he started to feel a swelling wind beginning to pull at his hair and clothing. As he closed his eyes, Dendo's fading consciousness allowed the feeling of the breeze against his skin to transport him back into the sense memory of a VR camping trip he had with his son a few years back. They'd set up their tent on a mountain overlooking a crystal-clear lake, and he had spent the evening teaching his little one how to roast marshmallows. But Luke, being the impatient kid he was, kept burning them because the fire was set so hot...so *so* hot. The instant that the imagined fire began to blister the skin of his hands in the fever dream, the overpressure blast in the real world tore down the mangled street to sweep Dendo Patel into oblivion's embrace.

Chapter 32

The instant that Tano pressed the command on his control board to drop out of zerospace at Bengal station, their small shuttle's collision alarm began to blare wildly. Bits of debris immediately started pelting the fragile craft's front shields, emanating the occasional dull thunk from the hull when an incoming bit of metal was large enough to make it intact through the intense heat of their shields. The Sergeant was then immediately forced to roll to their right in a kneejerk reaction as a large chunk of support structure went tumbling through the space they had just occupied. "My god…" breathed Dex with horrified awe, "What in the hell happened here? What could've caused this?"

The station had lost three of its five rings, the shattered remains of which still tumbled along with Bengal's degrading orbit in an ever-stretching streak of debris. The two rings that had managed to remain attached to the cracked docking drum, the enormous central commerce loop and its smaller neighboring residence ring, were both torn to shreds. They were pockmarked by scores of large gaping holes that clearly penetrated a dozen decks or more, and that was just where the damage *didn't* simply go straight through to the vacuum on the other side. No SOS signals lit up the comms panel, no Emergency Recovery Beacons flashed their telltale red and white strobe in the distance, and no active navigation systems were responding to their shuttle's automated traffic management pings. Everything was simply, totally, dead.

"This is what he does." Sighed Tano with a deep sorrowful shake of his head, "No idea how, but Vendrick pulled the same thing on Yakima station over a decade ago. Only, last time this happened, eighty percent of my defense force went with it. My god, this is absolutely our worst-case scenario come to life and it is always going to be his endgame. No matter how hard we fight, no matter how much control we seize on Meclan, Vendrick can always just roll in with whatever it is he has at his disposal and end the game in a snap. *This* is why we've lived like we do for so long. *This* is why we were all so reluctant to fight. There's no scenario, no strategy on the ground or diplomatic approach, that can prevent…*this.*"

As the air in the shuttle fell silent, both men just looked out over the destruction with a gut-wrenching awareness that the twisted and broken steel around them had been, just over nine hours before, home to nearly twenty-thousand people. Twenty thousand souls cast into the void without warning. Twenty thousand futures cut short at the order of a single man…Twenty thousand corpses that were beginning to come into focus as multicolored tatters among the wreckage all around them. "We at least need to figure out what happened here." Suggested Dex with a solemn nod to break the deepening silence, "Might as well try to gain *some* insight out of all of this."

Pointing to the slowly tumbling central body of the station that was precariously connected to its two remaining rings, Tano replied; "If we want to scoop data of the event, we'll need to access Bengal's central computer via the uplink in the air traffic control tower. But, without your electronic friend, we'll have to rely on what I remember from my digital intrusion courses at the academy to get that done."

"Oh, interesting." Mused Dex with feigned intrigue, "How long ago even *was* the academy for you? Way back when computers all had little pictures of fruit on them that cost three years salary?"

"Laugh all you want," retorted the Sergeant with a nearly imperceptible clench of his jaw, "but you'd be surprised how often *hacking* simply requires one to read and understand the damn user manual. You got maintenance mode backdoors for admin access, indirect query requests to get around content filters, and your good old fashion default Admin-Admin to get past any pesky logins. You really overthink a lot of what Vette does, I feel..."

"Just because I *don't* do it, doesn't mean I *can't*." scoffed Dex with a dismissive wave, "I just *choose* to allow the trillion credit AI at my disposal to do all that stuff instead."

The sergeant just rolled his eyes, saying; "You know, that AI of yours seems to get about four times more expensive every time you bring it up...Now if you'll excuse me and shut the hell up for a minute, I'll try to get us inside in one piece." By the time Tano was able to slowly dodge and weave his cheap civilian shuttle through the drifting mess to the door of the docking bay, the ship's shields had been whittled down to below forty percent by the barrage of floating junk impacting them as they carefully made their way in. The hangar door, powered by onboard capacitors designed to ensure functionality in this very situation, sensed their approach and obediently slid open for them. Beyond the rapidly opening hundred-meter-wide doorway sat a flickering wall of blue energy as the dock's airshield struggled to activate.

"Looks like the whole place is in hard vacuum." commented Tano, inspecting the airshield's failing mechanism as they slipped past the dock's entry corridor. The commercial dock beyond was in absolute chaos, with burned out hulls of cargo haulers and civilian transports floating aimlessly through the zero-G volume inside the slowly tumbling cylinder. The crashing debris made for an unpredictable hailstorm of jagged metal and crushing hunks of destroyed starship, so Tano did his best to guide their shuttle along a fuel-line trench that ran the length of the fifteen-kilometer-long cylinder. Traversal toward the air traffic control tower was slow, but the protection offered by their methodical approach became evident within the first twenty seconds when a twelve-ton section of engine housing came tumbling by overtop them; Saved only by the protective depth of their chosen trench.

"We need to get the emergency gyros for the central structure up and running ASAP." urged Tano, "It's like flying around a goddamn snow globe in here."

Dex pointed up ahead and replied; "Looks like the trench branches off to the left up there, which should get us pretty close to the control tower, I think."

With a nod, Tano slowly used the shuttle's attitude thrusters to rotate into alignment with the indicated path and cautiously pushed forward. The offshooting trench appeared to be for service bots to use in their endless scramble from pad to pad, and the Sergeant had a tough time keeping their ship from scraping the side and heat-scoring its metal sheeting under the intense crackle of the shuttle's active shields. Once Tano was tilting his head back to its maximum, in an effort to look up at the looming tower of steel and glass that stretched all the way to the cylinder's 'ceiling' on the other side, he activated the shuttles magnetic landing clamps and diverted all of the tiny craft's power over to the shields before leaning back in his seat to say; "End of the line."

Dex slipped into a vac-suit then cautiously stepped out the airshield and down the shuttle's entry ramp. As soon as he left the influence of the ship's artificial gravity plates, his boots lit up with the activation of their magnetic treads. He pulled himself along the trench with an awkward gait, reflexively ducking whenever his suit's built-in laser microphone relayed the crash of a tumbling bit of debris overhead, until he came upon a ladder that appeared to led up to a door into the tower. With nervous energy, he mounted the ladder and fought the ever-so-slight tug of pseudogravity that the station's tumble granted it as he pulled himself along. When he finally crested the top of the trench, he was immediately forced to retreat back down the ladder as a cargo crate came tumbling by to nearly crush him. Taking a moment to rebuild his courage, Dex poked his head back out again and peered into the maelstrom above with his helmet's onboard flashlight. Seeing no sense or pattern to the madness, he decided that luck would determine his fate as he hurled himself up the ladder and onto the deck above.

With comically slow urgency, Dex methodically clopped himself along the ten-meter distance toward the awaiting doorway and the relative safety of its recessed entry. When he had a mere four meters to go, he felt a heavy impact at his left hip. His suit, being smart enough to recognize the detachment of his leg being unnatural, locked down the magnet in his other boot with maximum strength. With a bite of pain, Dex was wrenched to the side and twisted his ankle on his way to slamming into the deckplate. The back of his helmet bounced off the hard ground and sent stars swirling into his vision that took several seconds to blink away. When he absentmindedly found himself trying to get up, he found that his right leg wouldn't budge. It was only a few hazy moments later that Dex saw the text prompt awaiting on his HUD. *'Disengage Safety lock?'* it asked with a blinking red confirmation. Groaning, a bit in pain and a bit in frustration, Dex deactivated the safety lockdown on his boots and continued his path forward; This time relying on the magnetic plates built into his gloves, knees and toes to propel himself along to the doorway.

Enduring a few more minor bumps along the way, Dex finally made it to the door and the protective salvation of its recesses. Returning to his feet, he found the door's control pad and keyed it. When nothing lit up on the panel, he popped the hatch below it and revealed the pump handle of the door's manual release mechanism. With a few sturdy pulls on the hydraulic lever, the door before Dex clicked loose and he was able to freely slide it open without resistance. What he found beyond that door spoke volumes on the panic leading up to the station's current predicament, and it seriously challenged Dex's resolve to move forward. Floating bodies of all ages clang to belongings or one-another, clogging the foyer of the tower with the psychosomatic stench of death that lingered even within the vacuum. Most of the faces wore expressions of fear or panic that were frozen into their features by the icy grip of death, forever in the throes of their final terrible moment.

Dex tried to avoid their lifeless stares as he pushed through to make his way to the elevator, but he seemed to meet another glassy-eyed gaze wherever he attempted to redirect his attention. He pressed the lift's call button, but, as he had expected, nothing happened in response. So, using a pry bar from the emergency maintenance kit he found hanging on the wall nearby, he manually forced the elevator's doors open to reveal an empty shaft beyond. Dex toggled the control for his mag-boots and allowed himself to float up the dark corridor, pulling himself hand over hand along a guide rail to the top. Once he had reached the top level, labeled on the wall above the doorway as *'CMD CTR'*, he used his pry bar once more to open the upper set of elevator doors and propelled himself out into the empty room beyond.

Dex gently touched a toe to the floor and activated its magnetic tread before sucking himself down with the anchored boot to gather purchase with his other foot. He took a moment to shake the odd feeling of quasi-weightlessness rising in his gut, then walked over to a dimly glowing console at the center of the room. Fiddling with the controls for a moment, he was met with an access denied beep again and again. Frustrated, he activated his comm to complain; "I knew we should've brought Vette, or at least rigged my tablet to run on this vac-suit. I can't log *or* crack into the station's system to kick on the gyros using this shitty factory OS. Goddamn station is in *emergency* lockdown mode, and for some reason this bitch won't let me turn on the *emergency* fucking *gyros*. Tell me the logic in that stupid bullshit."

After a few seconds silence, Tano's voice returned; "Quit yer bitchin'! We'll be fine. Some of us have had to slum it through life *without* an artificial babysitter to do everything for us. Just try the username Admin with the password Admin."

With a raised eyebrow, Dex reactivated his comm to say; "You know, that will never w-" There was then a long silence before his voice returned with a snort of laughter; "You *gotta* be shitting me. That seriously worked? *How* are we a spacefaring species?"

"That's the factory setting." responded Tano with a smug smile as he threw his hands behind his head in the shuttle, "I was counting on them being too lazy to change it. Looks like I was right."

Dex just silently shook his head in disbelief as he began to examine the console's control surface. He quickly navigated its many sub-menus and found the button to activate the station's built in emergency gyroscopes. Before activating it, however, he keyed his comm to warn; "Alright, I think I found the gyro control here. The station looks a bit too torn up to withstand the kind of rotational speed needed to restore gravity, but it should survive an emergency stabilization to smooth out this tumble we have going on. Hold onto something, Mike, because momentum is about to get weird up in here."

Dex waited for Tano's confirmation click, then hit the console's stabilization command when it came through over the channel. He immediately felt an uneasiness rise in his stomach as the artificial-gravity-assisted gyros spun up and began to slow the tumble of the station's massive superstructure. Watching through the windows of the control tower, Dex saw the floating debris in the dock starting to drift to one side of the cavernous space; Collecting in an amorphous clump at the far end. Moments later, he heard a crash that shook the floor under him as a crumpled cargo ship slammed into the control tower, scraping along to obliterate its port-side viewport. After nearly a full minute of holding on for dear life amidst a storm of wreckage swirling around outside, Dex's stomach finally settled and he knew the station had stopped its aimless tumble. Satisfied that it was safe to continue his work, he used the control panel in front of him to restore power to some subsystems of the wrecked station. Oxygen, gravity, and surveillance systems were all inoperable throughout the shattered station, but he *was* able to activate both the emergency lighting and a solitary bay of elevators that led down to the large community ring.

Moving on in his investigation of the station's fractured systems, Dex pulled an optical access cable from his suit's exterior-mounted tablet and attached it to the console's periphery jack. He then navigated to the program Vette gave him that would automatically gather any available data on Bengal's servers related to the catastrophic event. Allowing that to run in the background, Dex made his way into the station's surveillance logs and pulled up the most recently recorded footage. The files were separated into different folders, with each pertaining to a different Emergency Services Event. Noticing that nearly ninety percent of the files in the newest folder were already corrupted, Dex made his way into the event that was triggered twenty-seven hours earlier, titled simply *'Fire suppression event'*. Upon opening the folder, he was greeted by a map of where the event took place, which was an open area on the community ring's commerce area, along with a time-lapse overlay of reported event triggers such as the activation of certain fire suppression heads and other countermeasures. Confused by the initial data, Dex pulled up a video feed appended to one of the events and was met with a courtyard aflame with muzzle flashes and shrapnel.

The video proceeded to show a group of twenty masked men as they charged what appeared to be a police station. The men in the windows of the building, defending it with gunfire of their own, wore the facial ink of Vendrick's thugs and their fight was fierce. Groups of people who had been in nearby stores were now running in panic, trying to skirt the outer edge of the combat, but many were caught in the crossfire. As the conflict drew on, it appeared as if reinforcements had arrived for Vendrick's defenders when muzzle flashes of return fire rose from the scrambling crowd. As the masked men returned fire, it was an absolute massacre with men women and children all finding themselves in the middle. Without the stomach to continue watching, Dex keyed his comm to say; "I think our pal Drebbin got his hands on some boom-sticks and got all these poor folks into this. Looks like it all popped off on the community ring, near the police station. If there's anything more to learn, it'll be there."

"Son of a *bitch*." Growled Tano into his helmet mic as he sealed it around his head, "I knew that moto jackass would go and get people hurt, but I never envisioned it would look like this...**god** *damnit*."

The two men rendezvoused at the base of the control tower, then set out to find the besieged police station where the mess had all started. They quickly found the bay of elevators Dex had reactivated and attempted to locate an operational car to use. The first elevator they pried open was a no-go, as it had about twenty meters of undamaged shaft that abruptly ended below them with a raw metal edge that was back-dropped by nothing but the hard vacuum of space. They had better luck with the second elevator they tried, however. The doors opened smoothly and both vac-suited men nervously stepped inside. After a short diagnostics check was run through the lift's systems for good measure, the elevator car descended out of the central cylinder and along a support strut to the damaged ring beyond.

Upon arrival, their conveyance came to a shuddering stop that almost gave Tano a heart attack. After taking a cautious look around, both men stepped out of the elevator and into the ruin of central Bengal city. A large up-spin portion of the massive ring they were standing in had been torn away completely, revealing a jagged cross-section of the structure's sub-decks. "Holy crap." murmured Tano with quiet awe as he took in the sight, "What the hell *did* this to this freakin' place?"

Dex kept walking, unimpressed, and replied; "Vendrick did this. No doubt. There's no way Captain dipshit and his boys at the police station could've caused all this."

"What makes you say that?" asked Tano as he took in the bizarre scene of destruction around him, "Good intentions can often have the worst consequences. What if Vendrick's guys accidentally lit off a cache of explosives or something? Just to be devil's advocate here..."

Dex gestured out through the arched glass ceiling above to a ten meter wide hole that was torn clean through five decks of one of the other rings; "See that?" he began with a nod toward the indicated destruction, "The only weapon I know of that could do that is the main cannon on something the size of a battlecruiser. Had to be at least a class Five rail to punch a hole like that."

Tano let out a low appraising whistle; "Damn. I've never really seen up close what those things could do. By the look of it, Vendrick spent a good amount of time picking this place apart with it, too. You think that was strategy or boredom?"

Dex looked around and shook his head sadly; "A little of both, I'd wager. It's clear that he wasn't intending to leave any survivors here, but that's no reason for us to forego looking for them. The police station we're headed for should have access to the central security feeds. We can use what's left of *those* to look for survivors and check the playback to shed a little light on what happened here. Lifting his arm to consult his tablet, he pulled up a map of Bengal city to study. "Found it" he reported, "Police station is just up-spin from here." He indicated the direction then looked up from his display to see a gaping gash slicing through the station, putting a sixty meter gap between them and where they needed to go.

"Damnit," sighed the Sergeant as he began to turn the other way, "didn't think to bring EVA packs along with us this trip Looks like we're taking the long way 'round."

Then, without much thought or mental arithmetic, Dex took a running start and heaved himself to weightlessly soar across the gap. His approach was aimed a little high and he impacted a bench that sat several hundred meters from the ragged edge on the other side, knocking the wind out of his lungs and bouncing him off at an odd angle. As he was slowly tumbling towards the station's arched glass ceiling, Dex keyed his comm and said; "Well that was dumb."

Tano chuckled and replied; "You forgot about the whole null-gravity thing huh? You Terrasiders are all the same...You just thought it would look cool and went for it, didn't you?"

As he tumbled toward the gaping hole in the glass canopy, Dex was able to find purchase onto a metal support strut with the magnetic plate in his palm as he passed. Fighting his momentum, he swung around the strut and clamped onto it with his legs to avoid being torn free by his built-up inertia. When he had successfully come to a full stop, he stood up, triumphantly perched on the wall, and waved back across to Tano as he retorted; "It *did* look cool. I just didn't quite stick the landing."

"Pffft, amateur." scoffed Tano with a dismissive wave, "You stone-bones know nothing of the fine art of zero-g maneuvering. Comparing the weightless grace of us evolved Vackers to the desperate flailing of that *stagnated* branch of humanity from which you hail is like comparing Beethoven to a dog that found peanut butter smeared on a piano."

"Beethoven *was* a dog!" riposted the Sergeant's younger companion with outrage, "Plus, I'd like to see you do any better! The only thing you do gracefully, I imagine, is clean the meat off a buffalo wing."

In his wordless response, Tano gently stepped out from the edge of the destroyed street and lightly pushed off with his toe. The heavyset man then stretched his arms out with mocking elegance as he gently floated across the gap to set down lightly on the other side. "That was the most beautiful blimp landing I've ever seen." Teased Dex with a faux sniffle of emotion as he watched the other man's triumphant stride. In another wordless response, Tano simply raised a pair of middle fingers toward his distant colleague. As the two men made their way down the destroyed street, they were gripped by an eerie sense of dread. Side by side with the burnt-out husks of former shops and restaurants sat the pristine storefronts of businesses that seemed untouched by the chaos. The jarring juxtaposition was yet another reminder driving home the grim reality that so many people had lived and worked there so very recently.

At one point in their journey up the ring, a weightless weave of live electrical cables forced them into the hallway of an apartment block to bypass the deadly obstacle. On their way through, as they panned their flashlights down the pitch-black row of doors, Tano nearly lost his footing when he stepped on a toy spaceship that had found its way out into the hall. As Soon as he reflexively sucked himself to the deck in response to losing grip with one of his boots, the Sergeant knocked his shoulder-mounted flashlight lose on the doorjamb and sent it tumbling through a nearby open apartment door that looked like it had been blasted open.

Cursing under his breath, the lumbering man regained his footing and shuffled after the twirling bar of light. By the time he had caught up to it, he was already several meters inside the domicile and standing next to what felt like a kitchen island. Then, upon remounting his light, evidence of the apartment's former occupants came into sight through signs of their former lives within the space. A pair of VR helmets floated aimlessly at the far end of the room, eggs sat uneaten on a covered plate stuck to the small apartment's table, and sight of it all sent a sudden flood of rage through the Sergeant that had nowhere to go but into the fists he didn't know he was clenching. With a huff of grief and disgust, Tano took one final look at the *human* cost of their war on Vendrick then backed out of the room with a lump in his throat and revenge on his mind.

Dex continued to lead them up-spin with caution as they weaved through the twisted wreckage toward their goal until they eventually came upon a large open courtyard surrounded by buildings with intricate facades that served as the small city's central square. At the far end of the space sat the bullet-riddled police station they were looking for, its doors blasted open and its windows all blown out from *internal* explosions. The two men carefully walked over to the quiet warzone, keeping their weapons at the ready just in case. "This was a pretty populated area," began Tano suspiciously, "so where the hell *is* everyone?" In silent response, Dex just pointed his index finger upward before turning and stepping through the door of the destroyed police station.

Tano cocked his head in confusion at the gesture, then slowly lifted the beam of his flashlight. He wished he hadn't. Floating against the glass ceiling above the city's central square, bobbing in a silently shifting mass within the vacuum, were hundreds upon hundreds of inert bodies. The old MDF sergeant had seen a lot in his day, but the sight of a whole city's population drifting in unceremonious heaps as far as his light would reach was too much for the man. He fixated on the mass, his true realization of the tragedy before him growing more and more with every face examined in the floating graveyard. Tano had seen death before, not of this scale but of the same concentration, while working salvage ops on destroyed battleships...But that had been different. Each of the corpses he had seen and been forced to work next to all donned military uniforms, be it that of his Navy or the other side's. That was easier for him to process, because each body came wrapped in its own tidy explanation as simply casualties of war. Soldiers who had gone into battle, of their own volition, and gave their lives for a cause they believed in. *This*, on the other hand... The faces in the dark above him were no soldiers. Innocent men, women, and most tragically the children were now nothing more than a silent monument to a single man's unspeakable cruelty. The war veteran had to wrestle a lump in his throat as his queasy stomach desperately urged him to vomit. Snapping his eyes shut, he stepped into the police station and mercifully away from the grisly sight. The Sergeant then promptly fell against the inner edge the doorway and dry heaved as he slammed a frustrated fist against the metal wall.

"Just try and keep your mind on those we can still save." Comforted Dex as he placed a reassuring hand on the older man's shoulder, "This wasn't us."

Tano nodded hesitantly and replied; "I know. I understand that logically, but it still gets to me. Whenever I think I've found the end-all-be-all example of the lowest mankind has to offer, our species goes off and surprises me again. I find it hard to believe that something like this can even happen in a just universe...Can't help but think it would've never happened if we hadn't started the ball rolling."

Dex stopped halfway up the stairs to the station's main floor and turned to face his comrade; "You know as well as I do, Mike, that there's nothing fair or just about this galaxy we call home. Every decency that we enjoy as a society has to be fought for and defended by decent folk such as yourself. Don't make the mistake of allowing the overwhelming weight of the *big* picture to drag you down. Just take solace in the fact that you're doing what you *can* to make the small picture, the one that you actually *live* in, a better place. It's not much, but it's something to hold onto when you've lost sight of the light. You're a good man, Sergeant Tano. Don't you ever allow the chaos of this existence of ours make you forget that."

Tano sighed heavily, visibly regathering himself, then quietly said; "Thanks Dex. You're right. I *can't* control the universe at large...but fuck me if it ain't depressing sometimes."

"Amen, brother." Replied Dex with a solemn nod before continuing his journey up the stairs. At the top of the burned-out stairwell they came across a dispatch control room, lined on either side with rows of discombobulated workstations and littered with charred debris. It was obvious that a protracted firefight had taken place in the small room, but it wasn't immediately evident who'd emerged from the bloodbath victorious. Bullet-riddled bodies silently bobbed against the ceiling, their long-clotted wounds emitting webs of frozen blood in the weightlessness.

"Looks like it was a hell of a fight." Commented the Sergeant as he sauntered deeper into the room to examine one of the corpses, "Mid-caliber weapons, too. Seems like our raiders had some military-grade gear on-hand."

"Well where in the hell did they get it?" asked Dex as he made his way toward a stack of crates that were mag-locked to the floor. After dropping to a knee in front of the nearest box, he clicked its latch and slowly lifted the lid. Sitting inside the foam lined crate were two Accia DL44 assault rifles, seemingly fresh from the factory. While the DL44's accuracy left much to be desired, its ease of use and legendary reliability had made it a household name and a go-to for police and militia forces galaxy-wide. Dex lifted the weapon from its container to inspect it, noting; "No markings, or serial number. These guns are hot and the work of someone who knows what they're doing. Nothing to trace, nothing to chase. Dead fuckin' end. All we *do* know is whoever brought these guys their toys was definitely a professional mover. The weapon crates over here are hardened with chromium sheeting and are outfitted with what looks like a small battery to run some sort of spoofer lining. This is some real deal shit."

"Let me see that." Said Tano as he stepped over to join his comrade. Squatting down by the black metal case, he poked at its pre-formed foam lining until he found a spot where it was loose. Tugging at the soft material, it began to come free; revealing the small square of metal beneath that featured a five by five-centimeter laser-etched image of a dolphin breaching an ocean wave. "It was that goddamn rat-dicked son of a bitch Becker." Spat the Sergeant, "I *knew* we couldn't trust him to use his fucking head when someone flashed some credits his way."

"Why *now* though?" pressed Dex with a level gaze at the offending picture, "From what it sounded like at our little VR summit, Drebbin has been itching to get his hands on some guns for quite a while. So why was he able to do it *now* and not then? What changed?"

"Funding, maybe?" replied the Sergeant with a defensive shrug, "How the hell should I know? All I *know* for sure here is that fucking fish is *always* found wherever Becker or his boys have been. Juvenile as shit, especially for a high-tier criminal like him, to intentionally leave evidence behind, but what else do you expect from a man whose ego could eclipse a freakin' star?"

With a sigh, Dex returned to his feet and started to scan the room until he found what he was looking for. An undamaged computer console sat on a desk at the edge of the room and the status lights were winking away diligently, oblivious to the catastrophic damage around it. "We may be able to use that console to scour what's left of the security feeds to see if we can locate any survivors." He suggested as he made his way toward the dimly glowing screen, "It's a long shot, I know, but we owe it to these people to at least try."

With a distracted nod, Tano returned to his feet and began to survey the bodies floating near the ceiling around him. "While you do that," said the Sergeant as he pulled one of the deceased over to him via the man's belt loop, "I'll start searching the stiffs for intel." As Tano made his way from one rigid form to another through the crimson-lit room, Dex let out sigh after frustrated sigh while flicking through the remaining active sensor feeds tied to Bengal city's fractured security network. With each *'Dead Connection'* report he came across, his heart sank a little more. After nearly five minutes, he reached the end of his list of connections and sighed one final sorrowful time as he powered the console down.

It was at this moment that Tano broke their momentary radio silence by saying in a pained hush, almost to himself; "Oh, girl, what have you gone and done now?" When he saw Dex looking over at him with a cocked head, the Sergeant continued; "Might want to get over here and take a look at this. Found Drebbin. He's dead as a fucking doornail without a scratch on him, but his tablet is still live. Looks like he had a pen pal we might know…"

The Sergeant slid the deceased man's forearm-mounted device out of its sleeve and flattened it out before handing it to his comrade. Dex retrieved the device and began to read the page it was displaying.

Mr. Drebbin,

You may not know me, but I was there at the VR summit last month and saw for myself that you were the only other soul in the room who had the resolve to do what needed to be done. Outsiders who simply don't understand what we've been through, and those who have been suffocated into inaction cannot be the ones to led us into the next phase of our liberation. They are content to simply record atrocity after atrocity, gathering evidence of our daily struggle as if our occupiers were ever going to see the inside of a court room. If we want Saiph to return to its former prosperity, we're going to have to take the system back from the criminal scourge ourselves. I thoroughly believe that fight starts with you and Bengal City. Attached to this message is an unaddressed credit voucher that should be enough for you to arm at least a dozen men. I know it isn't enough to fight a war, but maybe you can use it to end Bengal's fight quickly and without further suffering. I have also included the contact information of one of Saiph's best smugglers as well as the comm codes you'll need to make an order with his outfit. Good luck and may your actions to come be the beacon of hope this system has needed for so very long.

-Mirtana Ozimova

The instant that their shuttle's magnetic landing gear engaged upon the flightdeck of Hearth's docking bay, Tano was already at the back door jamming the button to lower the boarding ramp with seething impatience. As the Sergeant stood captive to the slow-motion process, Dex placed a hand on his shoulder to say; "Look, Mike, I don't wanna get in the way of your *told you so* moment or anything, but I think you need to spool it down a bit before you tell her what happened."

The Sergeant turned on the younger man and spat; "You think I should go easy on your girlfriend, is that it? She betrayed my...no, *our* trust and it ended up getting an entire goddamn *city* killed. So I think my approach will be more than adequate, thank you very much." With that, the shuttle's ramp had touched the ground and he was off faster than Dex had ever seen the hefty gentleman move before. He followed the lumbering older man out of the hangar and watched him make a beeline down the hall toward the cafeteria. Mirta was in the kitchen, throwing knives into her now well-worn cutting board she had mounted to the wall, and was so startled by the Sergeant's sudden arrival that she almost hurled one his way. When she saw that they had returned, she smiled and didn't have time to get a read on their mood before saying; "Well, how was it? What happened?"

Tano, containing his boiling anger, took a breath and replied; "Well, we met with your new friend Drebbin..."

Maintaining her mask of ignorant innocence, Mirta casually asked; "Oh? And how is he doing these days?"

"He's dead these days." Growled the Sergeant as he retrieved Drebbin's tablet from his vac-suit's back pouch and thrust it her way, "Along with twenty-two thousand four-hundred and sixty-six others."

With a look of horrified confusion, Mirta blurted; "Wait, what do you mean?!" while she retrieved the tablet from Tano.

As she read the contents on-screen, her own note to the wannabe freedom fighter, and recognition began to dawn across her face, the Sergeant raged; "Your little friend received your email and put *our* money to *your* intended use for it. Got thirty-one bystanders killed on his way into the police station, fourteen more during their fight to keep it...then the rest of everybody else when Vendrick heard what was happening and decided to stop by. You may have been too young to remember the Yakima fiasco for what it was, but I'm not...and I remember all too well. Had you heeded my *advice*, the people of Bengal station would be sitting down to dinner right about now. Instead, they are getting ready to burn up in Fūjin's atmosphere. And that's on **you**."

When the Sergeant accentuated his final word with a poke into her chest, she promptly vomited on his hand and stumbled backward in a daze until her heels found a bench at the table to fall onto. As she sat there, clutching at her hair with her face in her lap, she began to shake convulsively. When Dex moved to sit next to her, he could immediately tell that her violent spasming wasn't her crying; It was her body desperately trying to puke again. When he placed his hand on her shoulder in what he intended to be a comforting gesture, she shot upright as if she were hit with a bolt of electricity then shooed him away as she turned to retreat in a quick but mindless stupor out of the kitchen and down the hall out of sight.

"You went a little hard on her there, Sergeant…" chided Dex with a sigh as he returned to his feet, "I know you're mad, but you didn't need to dump it all on her doorstep like that. That wasn't fair."

"What isn't fair," burst Tano in a rage, "was the fact that *little shit* got to make a decision that effected the lives of thousands of people without consulting a single one of them first. We both know she's got the bloodlust and its obvious now that she can't be trusted to keep it in her pants."

"C'mon, Mike," contested Dex in a placating tone, "You know Mirta wasn't running the OP itself. This all just boils down to a disagreement in political strategy and she just so happens to have backed the wrong horse. There's no need to crucify her for it."

"Okay, Romeo," huffed the Sergeant with disgust, "You go off and lick your woman's wounds for her. *I'll* concern *myself* with trying to figure out where we even go from here…"

It was the third time Dex had gone up to knock on her door, and the third time he was met without a response from within. She went into isolation the week before and had not been seen since. The only signs of life from within the locked room were Mirta's occasional requests for food and for Vette to top off the whiskey in her room's beverage dispenser. Descending the stairs with his shoulders slumped in defeat, Dex made his way to the briefing room where Tano awaited him.

"She want any food this time?" asked the Sergeant as he looked up from the briefing room table's central holographic computer display, "Or is she still on a liquid diet?"

"Still burning her way through our supply of good whiskey." Replied Dex with a shrug as he took a seat across from the older man, "But I can't say I wouldn't do the same in her position."

"If this is going to turn into another lecture on how I was too hard on the lass, you can shove it!" spat Tano with a dismissive swipe of his hand through the tabletop hologram, "She heard what she needed to hear and now she's gotta deal with it in her own headspace."

"You know…It is what it is at this point, Mike." Retorted Dex with a shrug, "I can't fix her any faster than she wants to be fixed, but that doesn't mean I'm not going to be supportive wherever possible. You can go on ahead and keep playing bad-cop all you want if it makes you feel better. I'll worry about keeping her sane while *you* work through *your* response to all this, whether you *think* you're having one or not. In the meantime, we can't let Vendrick's actions go unanswered. We *have* to do something to limit his capabilities and we have to do it *now,* while he still feels like he has Saiph on the ropes."

"Haven't you been paying attention here, kid?" asked the old Sergeant with a sour grimace, "Vendrick has no more weak spots today than he had yesterday. What makes you seem to think he's grown a soft spot somewhere overnight?"

"What if I'm not interested in a *soft* spot?" asked Dex as he leaned forward with a hint of swelling excitement to his tone, "What if we hit him where he's *strong*? Give Governor Vinny a black eye and challenge his power in the region in a *real* way with our papier-mâché pirate lord... What do we know about that dirtside compound of Vendrick's that those Baylor folks have been visiting? Vette grabbed their nav data and we have their logs to reference if we want to plan an assault."

"If you aim to do that," retorted Tano as he leaned back in his chair with crossed arms, "all you're asking for is to have that shitstick show right back up at Meclan's doorstep with the same fate he brought for Yakima and Bengal. While it *may* be a tantalizing target, you'd never make it to the ground in one piece. The embedded AA that we *know about* would tear you to bits in *orbit*, let alone the hidden defenses they've surely got online. I mean, you *could* try to send Scalpel after them on a low bombing pass, but your odds there *still* aren't great."

"A bombing run on those guns is the *last* thing I'd want." scoffed Dex with a swelling smile, "Because those guns are exactly what I *want*."

The Sergeant cocked his head to the side, asking; "What do you mean? Kinda paradoxical if you ask me, because you can't really do one without first doing the other. Also, what in the hell would you even *do* with a turret that size if you *did* manage to snatch it? I hate to break it to you, but it's not like you can mount one of those things to the Hammer or anything...If that's what you were thinking."

"No, sir," answered the younger man with a shake of his head, "that's not what I had planned. The Hammer's got *plenty* onboard to get her by, trust me. What I was *more* interested in was getting *Meclan* set up with a nice little home defense system for when unwanted solicitors come a-knocking. So, that way, when the day comes to free Meclan from the ass-sacks currently in management, we're ready for Vendrick's favorite tantrum response. We'll draw him in close, then spank his bitch ass."

Tano sat back and sighed wearily as he said; "I like the concept, Dex, I do. But it's a moot point if you can't take that base, and you can't *take* that base without taking out its guns. Total catch twenty-two situation."

"You don't necessarily have to destroy an AA gun to take it out of action." countered Dex thoughtfully, "You can either kill its targeting system via the command computer, effectively rendering it blind, or cut its power to take it out of the fight entirely. The only problem would be actually *getting* there in the first place. Maybe, I dunno, slip into a vac-suit and hoof it in from a few clicks out?"

"No can-do on the ground approach, I'm afraid." Replied Tano as he pulled up a new figure on the table's central holographic display that showed a three-dimensional representation of the ground facility as well as a thousand or so yellow dots surrounding it in an intricate spiral pattern reaching outward, "When they made their recon pass, our orbital satellites picked up signs of a pretty tightly dispersed seismic spike array that stretches for approximately ten kilometers on all sides of the compound. Active-pulse and high power, so they aren't shy about announcing the existence of their digital moat. You can assume, as well, that those sensors are going to be paired with a pretty nasty network of mines and other smart munitions. If anything so much as displaces a rock within that zone, it's going to light that base up like a Christmas tree."

With a thoughtful stroke to his chin, Dex looked to the ceiling and asked; "Hey Vette? You've got the intel from that trader fleet Tano bamboozled the other week, right? Didn't you manage to scrape a bunch of deleted shipping manifests from their drives?"

"Yes, Commander," replied the AI dutifully, "I was able to collect seventy-one delivery records with partial cargo manifest information for twenty-four of those entries."

"Splendid." Replied Dex with a nod, "Do you think you have enough data within the available set to extrapolate an…eh…algorithm or something that can convincingly imitate a legitimate shipment order? Furthermore, would you be able to inject said phony scheduled delivery into their systems so they *let* us land?"

After a second and a half of silence, an eternity in A.I.-land, Vette answered his inquiry; "Yes, however not directly. I cannot access their internal computer network, but I can inject whatever delivery orders you require into the ground facility's nearest burst array. It will then sit in a queue and be delivered via standard and perfectly legitimate channels to our intended recipient."

"Bingo!" exclaimed Dex with two finger-guns aimed at the speaker in the ceiling, "That's our way in, then. We let them think they're receiving more supplies or some such, then bust out an entry team once landed."

"I feel obligated to mention, Commander," interjected the A.I. to set a frost over the man's budding celebration, "that if this supply manifest and nutritional schedule is accurate, the facility in question likely houses a contingent of nearly three-hundred personnel."

Dex allowed his shoulders to slump in momentary defeat before pumping them upwards again in a sudden shrug as he concluded; "Well, we'll just have to be quiet about it, then, I suppose. I *will* have those guns…One way or another."

Tano laughed, saying; "And how exactly are you fixing to do that? Skitter your way around the base under an upturned box? *Solid* plan."

"I'm not going in alone." Retorted the younger man as he leaned forward to study the holographic representation of the ground facility, "I'll need someone with me to help hold the control tower once we start locking doors and shutting things down. Someone small and compact. Someone who can fit inside a standard two by one cargo crate along with me and a few weapons."

"Absolutely not!" spat the Sergeant, "There's no way you're getting Mirta attached to another one of your half-baked schemes. She's in no state to be doing anything of the sort."

"I beg to differ." Argued the younger man in a patient measured tone, "She's in the exact kind of state that calls for this very sort of thing. She's in a spiral right now, Mike, and we need to give her something productive to do with her hands. Don't you think she'd want to do whatever she can to prevent Meclan from meeting the same fate as Bengal and Yakima?"

"I think she'll do whatever she can to prevent *herself* from being the cause of it," retorted Tano gruffly with a dismissive wave of his hand, "Which means I'm thinking her fight is over, Dex. She can't take it. Not after Bengal. Shit, I don't know if *I* can even still take it. Maybe the best option *is* to get out of Saiph. Move on...somewhere. Hell, could bring decent folk out *here* and keep em safe."

"And, like Noah, the noble Sergeant was forced to choose whom among the abandoned he would grant his salvation to." Began Dex prophetically with an outstretched sweep of his arms that morphed into a shrug, "Instead of, you know, finding himself a bigger fuckin' boat. How many people do you think Hearth could support, *realistically*? Two-hundred and fifty? Three-hundred, *max*. That's just science, mayte. Wouldn't you rather save *everyone* if you could? We're talkin' *thousands* here."

"We could fit thousands *here* if we really wanted to." Reasoned the Sergeant as he sat back in his chair with another stroke of his chin, "That's what the original design for the base called for, anyway. Hearth as it exists today was originally only supposed to house the maintenance workers and defense personnel for the facility. It was the valley *outside* that was supposed to be pressurized and populated. With the whole area being basically a giant impact crater with a frozen-over ceiling, Hearth's original designers came up with a way to embed airshield control nodes within the ice along the roof to project an air-tight dome that wouldn't erode the glacier above. Stable, air-tight, rad-shielded and, most importantly, hidden. It could be a solid plan B is all I'm saying..."

"While that *does* sound cool as shit," remarked Dex with an acknowledging nod, "It would be no replacement for the two-hundred-thousand or so folks in Saiph as a *whole* that need our help. I know its counterintuitive to take such decisive action so quickly after a tragedy on the scale of Bengal, but we have to hit back *now*... Or else you're going to see another ten years of subjugation that is just going to get worse. A man like Vendrick knows what he's doing when he does something like kill a city. There's a loss assessment that goes into making a decision like that, and he's already decided to place his bet on that math on two separate occasions now. What makes you think there wont be a third...or *fourth*? We need to change that calculation for him, rebalance that math, so it will never happen again."

"And if it doesn't work?" asked Tano pointedly, "What if the guns malfunction? Or if that ship of his, whatever it is, is able to shrug our attack off? We'd lose Meclan just as senselessly as Bengal went down. That'd be a hard sell to make..."

Dex just shrugged, saying; "Well if the choice were between living on my knees or dying on my feet, I know what I'd choose."

"Oh?" asked the Sergeant, beginning to get annoyed, "And what would you choose for your three-year-old daughter? What about your eighty-six-year-old mother who needs her daily meds to survive? Would you risk starting a civil war that could interrupt that supply? Even if it were for the *good of the system*? These fearful people that you have such a hard time identifying with are not cowardly for bowing to these fears. They are doing their duty to *their* loved ones the best way they know how. So, unless you can present them a plan that will allay those fears enough to have them agree to risk the lives of themselves and everyone they hold dear, you're not going to get the people of Meclan to agree to this."

"I may be of some assistance in this matter." interjected Vette from the ceiling speaker, "After reviewing the data gathered from the wreckage of Bengal Station, I have been able to identify several anomalies that call for further review. Much of the sensor data from the main arrays during the time of the attack has been scrubbed, but I was able to ascertain a sequence of events via Bengal's uncorrupted traffic management network. The readings I have found are...odd."

"Odd?" asked Dex with genuine concern at the A.I.'s seemingly uncertain tone, "Odd like how? Like the data was corrupted or altered somehow?"

"Nothing like that, Commander." Assured the A.I. with careful reserve, "I merely mean that the sequence of events does not make sense, scientifically. The only data available to draw from was the traffic system's array of Inaki radiation sensors for inbound ship detection, gravity sensors to monitor traffic flow, and a simple optical guidance feed for remote operator use. Via these tools, I was able to determine that a ship with a mass of just under fifty-thousand tons jumped in at six-seventeen AM, local time, and lingered for thirteen minutes before a second, outbound, jump signature was detected."

"Alright." Said Dex, nodding as he heard the info, "That about matches our sequence of assumed events. Vendrick hops in uninvited, drops his proverbial shit in the coat-check, then leaves without a trace. Like the worst party guest in history. So, beyond the whole death and suffering thing, what has you bugged about it? Sounds pretty straightforward to me..."

"Assuming a ship of that size were able to make a second transition into zerospace that quickly after jumping in, which it isn't," began Vette with her infinite well of patience, "the odd aspect of the situation is the fact that the ship's mass remained in-place after the outbound jump had run its course. The ship itself vanished off of the traffic control system's IR, EM, and RAD sensors, but its gravitational footprint remained."

Dex scratched his head, searching for an explanation before shrugging to say; "So he's using some fancy new drive tech that screws with gravity, or what? Kinda an odd thing for a pirate to be using, if you ask me."

"Actually, Commander," replied Vette cheerily, "I believe it was in fact fancy *old* tech at play here. His mass didn't go anywhere because *he* didn't go anywhere. His ship *faked* an outbound jump and activated some fashion of active sensor cloaking to coast away and complete their real-space getaway."

"You're telling me this guy has an *invisible* ship?" asked Dex incredulously, "You gotta be shitting me. And you're sure there's nothing fucky with those readings?"

"Nothing fucky, Commander." Answered the A.I. with flat certainty, "And the ship in question is rendered only *functionally* invisible, not literally invisible. While sophisticated sensors will struggle to pick it up, its mass will still blot out pinpoints of starlight if you know where to look."

"You said that the ship falls off of EM as well, correct?" Asked Dex as he leaned on the table and stroked his chin in thought, "Does that mean he has to take his shields down to do that little disappearing act of his?"

"That is correct, Commander." replied Vette with delight at the revelation, "Bengal's accessible EM sensors detected plasma encapsulation collapse around the attacking ship fifteen nanoseconds before the ensuing Inaki flash temporarily blinded Bengal station's traffic control array."

Dex slapped a palm onto the table and declared; "That's how we'll do it, then. We'll draw him in by sweeping the filth from Meclan, then we'll *'scare him off'* once he sees what we're packing. But we'll know better when he up and disappears and we'll send everything we have in his projected path...see what sticks to his invisible ass."

Five minutes later, Dex was already upstairs wrapping excitedly on Mirta's door. So persistently, in fact, that she finally peeled herself away from whatever important wallowing business she was attending to and answered the incessant banging; "Oh for fuck's sake! What?! What do you want?!"

"Open the door, please." Replied Dex calmly, "I have news and something to discuss. Don't worry, the Sergeant is in the kitchen at the moment, so you know we'll have about six hours to talk without him chiming in."

"He's right, though, Dex." countered Mirta softly as the door silently slid open to reveal the disheveled ruin of her room beyond. The silver foil sleeves of empty ration packets littered the ground, along with their half-eaten contents, and the display screen at the far end of the bedroom had several bloody impact cracks in its glass surface as if boxed bare fisted.

As Dex rounded the corner into her destroyed room, he was forced to suppress a gasp as he saw the state that Mirta *herself* was in. She was laying sprawled out on her bed in a days-old flightsuit with her head hanging over the bottom edge of the bed, looking back at Dex in the doorway without any life behind her eyes. Dried blood had caked up around her nose, upper lip, and forehead; Instantly making it clear that the destroyed screen had not been punched at all. "Jesus, Mirta." sighed Dex with deep concern, "What in the hell did you *do* to yourself?"

"Not nearly enough." She replied with a drunken slur, "Not even a percent of it. But don't you worry, I'mma have another go at it as soon as I find me legs..."

"You *do* realize that nothing that happened at Bengal was *your* fault, right?" asked Dex as he stepped over to sit on the bed next to her, "That was Drebbin and *his* piss-poor planning that did that. Even if Vendrick *hadn't* shown up, the redneck assault squad had already severely damaged Bengal's air recycling system. They'd all have suffocated before Tano and I even got there *anyways*."

"His planning, shitty or not, was always just theorycrafting until I provided him the means." She argued as she turned to face away from him, "I'm every bit as guilty as he is."

"The only thing you're guilty of is aggressively pursuing what *you* felt was right," soothed Dex as he wet a clump of his shirt in a nearby half-drank water glass and began to gently wipe the blood from her face, "I'd have done the same thing if I felt the way you did about the situation. Besides, you were far from his only benefactor. He must've had over thirty guys geared up to the gills. By the sounds of it, you only gave him enough to outfit...what? Ten guys? A dozen, tops?"

Mirta sighed and pushed Dex's hand away as she retorted; "You don't get it, Dex. You never will. Not until you've screwed up as royally as I have."

Dex gave up trying to clean her off and said; "Everyone makes mistakes, Mirta. Big and small. The only thing that really matters is your original intent and how you proceed from that point of failure. You fucked up last round, sure, but that doesn't mean you need to quit playing the game altogether."

"That's the problem, Dex!" spat Mirta as she sat back up to face him with an accusatory stare, "It's *not* a game, and sometimes *not playing* means that *fewer* people will die in the end."

"The *game* is already perpetually going on around you whether you choose to participate in it or not." Reasoned Dex as he plopped himself over to lay on the bed, "Best thing you can do is learn from your mistakes and move on. Binding yourself up with inaction does nothing but benefit the enemy while your own situation worsens."

"Learn from it and move on?" repeated Mirta incredulously with anger beginning to boil beneath her voice, "And what did we learn from this whole thing *besides* the fact that fighting back, once again, leads to tragedy? What's the takeaway *there*?"

"Meclan station, for example, could use a set of external defensive armament." He suggested with a simple shrug, "Wouldn't you agree? So, let's get a big-ass gun and strap it onto that badboy. Shoved under a dummy comms array or something like that to keep it hidden until we need it. That way, if the Governor ever swings by on the campaign trail, we can crack open a can of whoop-ass on whatever it is he's flying."

Mirta scoffed and rolled her eyes, saying; "While you're out shopping for these mythical free guns, could you pick me up a time machine? Had a bully in fourth grade that I'd like to kick out an airlock... While we're on the subject of dream acquisitions."

"Glazing over your urge to space a ten-year-old," began Dex with a chuckle, "I actually *do* know where we can get the gun Meclan will require. Only hitch is that I'll need *your* help to lift it."

Mirta rose an eyebrow and said; "Lift? What do you mean, lift?"

With an innocent smile to go with his shrug, Dex asked; "Do you wanna sneak into Vendrick's secret groundside facility, steal its AA turret for Meclan, maybe shoot a few bad-guys, then blow the whole damn place to high hell on our way out?"

Mirta just nodded once and laughed; "That's all you had to say."

Chapter 34

"I can*not* believe you talked me into getting inside yet *another* tiny-ass box." Complained Mirta as she shifted her elbow into Dex's ribs while readjusting herself within the cramped confines of their shared cargo crate, "Not to mention the fact that *this* time I have to deal with the smell of your...*eugh*... *everything*. When is the last time you even showered, for god's sake?!"

"You should know..." replied Dex with an unseen smirk, "You were there to help me get all the hard to reach bits."

After emitting what could only be described as a low gurgle of disgust, Mirta retorted; "Dex, that was *four days ago*. You've been, like, working out and shit. How have you not driven *yourself* nuts from the smell?"

"The secret," said Dex as he tapped an index finger to his forehead, "is that my nuts *don't* smell yet."

"As someone who currently has a vastly different vantage point on the issue," began Mirta while she struggled against her confines, "Let me assure you that you lack the requisite flexibility to make an educated judgement on that front."

"To be fair," began Dex with a lighthearted chuckle, "Your current *vantage point* is *waaay* closer tha-" He was cut off mid-sentence as the ship bucked suddenly beneath him, sending him smacking with quite some force into the lid of their metal box. "Are you actually trying to land this thing, or are you crashing into shit just for the hell of it at this point?" he asked with sarcastic bite into his comm as he rubbed the already-forming knot at the back of his head.

"Sorry for the bumpy ride, folks." replied Tano with the stress of a difficult flight coating his transmitted voice, "There's a hell of a sandstorm circling the upper atmosphere at the moment, and she's throwing me around something nasty. So, I suggest you hold onto something in there because it's not getting any better until we land. The good news on *that* front, by the way, is that our landing request has been approved and the bogus delivery order that Vette injected into their last data-burst was accepted. We've been cleared for landing near the central structure and the cargo drones will come to offload you into warehouse six. That is the closest I could get you to the command building without a human signing off on the delivery. Good luck, you two." Tano then abruptly closed his comm channel to focus on landing the unruly craft.

Mirta shifted uncomfortably and looked across the cramped box at Dex, a lone LED bathing his face in an unnatural red light. He squeezed her knee in a gesture of reassurance, and she simply replied with a quick nod that seemed distracted or half-hearted in some way. She hadn't spoken much since they were sealed into the box nearly an hour before. Instead, she chose to spend the duration of their long ride on her tablet studying a crude layout of the facility that Vette was able to cook up from the satellite data. Dex took her silence as nerves, at first. Then, as he watched her repeatedly dip her chin in a rhythmic fashion that slowed as her eyes began to scour the image before her, he quickly realized that she wasn't performing some repetitive prayer or nervous tick; She was counting off paces and distances quietly to herself, planning escape routes and alternate paths to their objective. Once again, he was impressed by the scrappy woman's professionalism and focus in the calm before the storm. Dex had known bad-ass veteran soldiers that showed more nerves on the way to their hundredth mission than Mirta exhibited on her third outing.

Then, like a knife through his thoughts, Dex could hear the sound of the ship's landing struts groaning as its thrusters powered down and surrendered the craft's weight over to them. There was a short moment of silence after touchdown, followed quickly by the telltale sound of the shuttle-craft's rear ramp lowering. Mirta squeezed her eyes shut in concentration, pressing her ear against the wall of the crate until the treads of a loader drone could be heard clicking up the ramp toward the shuttle's cramped cargo hold. The treads stopped in front of their nondescript grey box and paused for several seconds, the whirring of something mechanical ticking away internally with no other movement or action audibly evident. Dex and Mirta then both exhaled in relief when the small robot's arms could finally be heard locking their magnetic clamps onto the box. Shortly afterward, they both felt the sensation of movement as their little *Trojan crate* was lifted into the air and driven down the ramp.

They bounced along for about a minute and a half over gravel and dirt in no particularly discernable path or direction, listening to the roar of Tano's shuttle lifting off the pad to return to orbit. As soon as they felt the surface beneath the drone's treads transition them onto smooth concrete, they both let out a sigh of relief and loosened their death grips on the small handles they had installed within the crate. After heading up an incline and over a bump into what Dex assumed was warehouse six, their box was lifted and slid neatly into place on top of a similar stack of crates somewhere in what felt like the far corner of the cavernous storage space. The pit of Dex's stomach then lurched in dismay when he heard the scrape of a cargo box being stacked upon their own before the dutiful little cargo drone clacked away on further pressing business.

When he was sure that the loader drone had moved on, Dex let out a long slow breath and punctuated it with a small chuckle, saying; "Hey, at least they didn't set us upside down, right?" as he secured his positive-pressure breathing mask to his face.

The small planet orbited a backwater star that sat nearly ten lightyears outside the populated bubble and featured a class three, hydrogen-rich, atmosphere that was within the projected green band of its local star. This meant that any humans who wished to venture out in the open would need an oxygen mask, but not necessarily pressurized or protective clothing, to survive. The unnamed planet featured forty percent the gravity of Earth, contained no flora or macrobiological fauna, and its incessant winds were merciless by all observed accounts. Armed only with warm outer wear and their small rebreather units, the harsh nature of the planet could be held back for only so long. They'd need to limit their exterior exposure wherever possible and hurry their way to the protective pressurization of the control tower.

Dex wriggled his way up onto a knee and braced his back against the lid of their container. He first checked to make sure that Mirta had her mask secured, then he punched the small internal control panel to disengage the seal of their box. With a powerful hiss that quickly lowered in pitch as the pressure within the box equalized, a rubber seal along the inner edge fell away to reveal a large seam along the lid.

With a grunt of exertion, Dex heaved his back against the roof of their little box. The slab of thin metal only budged slightly at first, but, as he continued to strain, the opening slowly began to widen. After regathering himself, Dex thrust the stubborn lid open with one final muted growl that sent the crate on top of theirs sliding off to crash loudly to the floor and scatter its contents across the neat warehouse isle.

Mirta shot a scowl at her boxmate, shaking her head, and seethed; "Subtle." with borderline contempt while stepping out of the box to the corn-laden ground below.

"Did you have any better ideas?" Asked Dex sarcastically as he stepped out after her, nearly losing his footing after slipping on a runaway corn cob. Mirta didn't say anything, choosing instead to simply walk over to their box and unlatch a small door concealed into the front of it. As its hinge swung open, squeaking quietly into the silence, Mirta's unamused stare bore into Dex.

"Ah." he remarked as he scratched his head and examined the crate's new passage, "I did not know that they did that." Mirta just rolled her eyes and shook her head as she turned to retrieve their gear. Due to the tight confines of their entry method, Dex was unable to wear his combat armor and they were each only permitted one equipment backpack. The assault packs were of a military design that they had plundered from their raid on Baylor Company. They worked by storing items between a sandwich of micro-articulating bristles that would catalog, organize, and dispense any item that could fit through its aperture at the bottom of the bag. While Dex's backpack contained your standard wetwork staples such as explosive charges and a plethora of tools to choose from, Mirta's bag contained only a combat shotgun and several miniature remote-command reconnaissance drones that she and Vette had built together.

"You wanna take one of those things up and get us a read on who might be in the neighborhood?" Asked Dex as he gestured to the black case on her backpack, "The drone can feed us live tactical data in a space this big. Just fire it up and set it to orbit mode at ten meters or so. It'll do its thing on its own and mark any contacts it spots on our mask's overlay."

With professionalism instantly returning to her demeanor, she nodded and crouched to retrieve the automated device from the dispenser at the bottom of her bag. She withdrew a six-centimeter-wide doughnut comprised of two counter-rotating discs sandwiching the tiny components of an onboard flux-pin drive. With a few taps on her tablet, the small device leapt into the air and quickly disappeared into the lights overhead without a sound. "Eyes are up and running." She reported as she re-slung the backpack and hefted her shotgun.

Dex quickly brushed past Mirta and began to make his way for the door at the front of the storage building. Based on what he could tell from the base's layout, that would lead them out to the open-air courtyard that connected to the control center. He was staying low, cautiously following the rows of boxes toward the front of the building when he heard the click and whirr of a door's locking mechanism from up ahead. The entrance he was headed for then slowly began to slide open, so Dex quickly ducked behind a pallet of barrels and melted into its shadow. As the man at the far end of the warehouse stepped through the threshold of the doorway, Dex saw a faint red outline of his enemy, as well as the man's distance and armament information, displayed overtop the real world around him. The breather mask equipped newcomer was lazily slinging what appeared to be a military issue assault rifle and was making his way for an outlet panel on the wall near the door. When he reached it, he touched a command on its interface and a few rows of bright lighting swelled to life overhead.

In a panic at the sudden flood of illumination, Dex looked back toward where he saw Mirta last but found nothing where she had been. After a few moments of frantic searching, he was forced to return his attention to the man who was now making his way up the isle toward Dex and his unseen companion. The guard was wearing a black military flightsuit with a notably bare patch of Velcro at his shoulder and had a high quality sidearm to go along with his primary weapon. He donned no combat armor, but his military-issue ammunition belt and accompanying utility pouches spoke volumes as to the man's combat effectiveness if push came to shove. Nobody would spend the credits required to outfit an employee with that kind of hardware if they didn't know how to use it. As the guard approached his hidden isle along the row, Dex slinked around the far side of his chosen bundle of barrels to remain out of sight while the man passed. It was obvious that the guard had zeroed in on the spilled corn when he increased his pace as well as his rifle's readiness while nearing the disturbance. In a drawn-out series of heartbeats, Dex was torn on what to do. Then, as he rounded into the long row in silent pursuit of the guard, he watched as a dark figure leapt from its high perch that sat opposite the destroyed crate. The armed man was immediately flattened to the ground in the unexpected assault, and he could do little to stop his attacker as she wildly jabbed something into his chest over and over again with an animalistic ferocity.

"Woah, woah there..." soothed Dex as he approached the now blood-soaked Mirta who was still stabbing away, "I think you got him, dear. You, uh, wanna take a breather? I promise I'll let you stab him some more if you still feel like it a minute from now..."

As Dex's voice got through to her, Mirta ceased her onslaught and slumped to the side completely drained of energy. After gulping in several desperate ragged breaths, she rasped; "I'm sorry. I...I've never *killed* without a gun before. It's...it's *different*. It was *so* scary to be so close, Dex, and I could think of nothing but making sure...making sure it were done."

With a nod of understanding, Dex quietly said; "I get it...I do. It can be tough to get a job like that done with a blade as short as the one you've got there. If you want less of a workout next time, focus on the neck, brain stem, and eye sockets."

Silently gagging at the suggestion, Mirta returned to her feet and sputtered; "That's not...*ugh*. Never mind. I'll drink about this all later. For now, we need to clean this mess up before someone else happens along. Help me get him into *our* crate, then we can chuck the corn in after him."

They made quick work of concealing the body and did their best to use the sickly yellow corn husks to mop up as much of the spilled blood as possible before hiding the broken box pieces and sealing up the crate they had arrived in. Satisfied that their coverup would last as long as it needed to, Dex led Mirta out the front of the building and silently slipped onto the facility's campus beyond. The structure they were looking for had a stout two-story rectangular base with a two-hundred-meter-tall flight tower jutting up from its middle, and it sat as the central hub of the large, mainly subterranean, compound. Warehouse six, its label displayed in bright yellow above their heads, sat on the northeastern end of the base's outer ring of supporting buildings, leaving several hundred meters of barren open ground between the intruders and their goal.

"Alright," began Dex calmly as he crouched and turned to Mirta within the small recess of the warehouse's entryway, "we need to move fast across that open ground to the door of the central building that I marked on our overlay, but we're going to want to...Hey, are you okay?"

Mirta's eyes were wide as she stood with her mouth agape in the doorway of the warehouse, staring solidly over his shoulder as a lone tear traced its way down her cheek. After a moment of verbal floundering, she finally managed to say; "It's...It's so *big* out here. I never thought...."

"Oh, shit, I totally forgot!" he exclaimed with a slap to the side of his helmet, "Welcome to real gravity! Sorry your first planet had to be such a shithole...Anyways, shall we?"

Mirta nodded slowly, then held up her hand in a *stop* gesture, saying; "Hang on. Before we step out, let me take a look around with this." She then made a fist with her left glove, drawing a circle in the air above her head. This prompted the small drone that had been orbiting the inside of the warehouse to come shooting out the doorway and up into the sky where it disappeared from sight. After a few moments, the automated device's reconnaissance scan started to return red indicators that began flaring into existence on Dex's overlay. The drone had managed to identify a sphere-eye camera, two laser trip-gates, and an armed guard making his rounds around the outer catwalk that circled the exterior of the flight control tower.

With a frustrated sigh at sight of the unexpected layer of surveillance, Dex turned to Mirta and said; "Well, this will make things more interesting. Looks like the main airlock, the one we can count on being unlocked, is rigged with a proximity sensor. That means if we go through there, it's going to announce to the world that we've arrived. Furthermore, I am betting that system is tied to a personnel tracking system that would surely flag us for not being on the roster. Do you mind telling that thing to swing around the far side of the tower to see if there are any additional entrances we could use?"

With a nod, Mirta punched something into her tablet and then turned her attention to the sky. Though it were essentially invisible to the naked eye at its current altitude, the overlay in their masks tracked the tiny aerial gizmo as it ascended and proceeded to make a long swinging arc around the other end of the compound. As it completed its pass, another two cameras popped into view along with the faint yellow outline of a ladder that snaked its way up the far side of the control tower.

"Bingo." Stated Dex as he tagged the ladder in their shared overlay, "That's our way in. Only problem is getting to that emergency escape platform without being seen by the trio of cameras between here and there. Any ideas?"

"My drones could mate with the cameras and replace their video feed with an uneventful loop." Suggested Mirta with a shrug, "But that would mean fusing their transmission harness to the camera itself. So, we'd be down three fliers."

"That leaves us with what? Five?" asked Dex with a slow nod, "That sounds like a fair trade to me. Go ahead and make it happen. Just be sure that all your drones sync their takeover so any automated surveillance programs running on their end will pick up on only a single anomaly instead of three separate events."

"Good idea." Agreed Mirta as she withdrew two drones and set them in the dirt before her. Then, after tapping at her tablet for a few moments, the two little devices leapt into the air and noiselessly darted away. Several seconds later, the red icons representing all three cameras winked to green and she reported; "Alright, feeds are stable and battery life will keep them active and supplying the base's systems with a computer generated loop variation of a whole lot of nothing for the next three weeks if they need to."

"Good work." Commended Dex with a nod as he moved past her to crouch at the edge of their recessed entryway and lean around the corner. Seeing nothing with his naked eyes that the drones hadn't already reported, he turned back to Mirta and urged; "C'mon. Let's get moving before Rapunzel up there comes around again and spots us."

Both infiltrators then stayed low as they bounded across the open courtyard to the relative concealment against the vertical steel of the control tower building. Once at its base, they quickly made their way around to the far side of the structure and found the ladder that had been highlighted for them, discovering its lower dozen rungs blocked off by a security grate that was draped across them. Without missing a beat, Dex accessed his backpack's menu on his tablet and scrolled to the device he was looking for. After pressing *dispense* on the menu screen, he heard a mechanical whirr at his shoulder and received the familiar bulk of a thermogel puck in his awaiting hand at the lower end of the bag.

Dex placed the sticky backing of the miniature puck of thermite composite directly onto the power node that fed the security grate's electromagnetic lock and depressed the device's central activation button. The thermogel munition lit up with an embedded blue LED, then proceeded to blink a simple five second countdown sequence. When the count reached its climax, the external housing of the munition began to glow a brilliant orange-white and sparks started to spew forth from the failing power node. Then, before the chemical reaction could play itself out to its end, the magnetic lock failed and the security grate swung open on its spring-loaded hinge.

"Let me go up first." Warned Dex as he drew the ancient combustion-driven pistol from his thigh holster and affixed its accompanying suppressor, "I'm going to try and deal with this guy quietly, but in case it goes sideways; Use your active drone feeds to get a target lock on the lookout and prep a kinetic kill shell in your shotty. If I drop the ball, you take him down."

With a nod, Mirta drew her shotgun and thumbed the command to switch its fire mode, saying; "Be my guest. If you need me to step in, your safeword is *pineapples*." With a wink, she then affectionately swatted at Dex's derriere as he mounted the ladder to begin his ascent. His progress was slow, considering he had only a single hand to grasp the ladder with while training his pistol upward with the other, but he managed to reach the top before the roving guard had made his way back around again.

Cautiously pulling himself up onto the circular catwalk, Dex stayed low to remain out of sight of the ring of windows built into the control tower's command center. From what he could tell from his quick glance inside, there was only a single man at the controls within the room; And his head was down, concentrating on something glowing across his console's display screen. Tracking the roving guard via the red outline on his overlay, Dex made his way around to meet his foe.

The guard had his rifle slung across his back and was leaning casually against the railing while he scanned the landscape before him in a practiced yet repetition-dulled sweep. As the man straightened up to saunter to his next spot on the rail, Dex dashed forward and slammed his boot into the back of the guard's leg. The man buckled and dropped to a knee as a pair of hammer-fists came down on his wrists, rending his grip from the rail entirely. Before he could factor out what was happening to him, the guard's skull was then bounced off the very rail he had lost grip of and his world had gone hazy. In that daze, Dex positioned his body behind the kneeling man and used the entire weight of his torso to repeatedly crush his foe's windpipe against the railing. He thrust himself forward, driving the chest buckle of his backpack into the back of the man's head until he felt a sickening slackening of tension as something important broke lose within the man's upper spine. Allowing the guard to droop limply to the ground, Dex keyed his comm to say; "Our boy on the catwalk has been put to bed, so you're clear to climb on up. Looks like we only have one in there manning the control center, so I'm going to try and get him dealt with without blowing any holes in any of the consoles up here."

Then, without waiting for her response, Dex pulled open the door that led into the tower's single-man airlock and hit the cycle command on its input panel. A whooshing of air could briefly be heard, then the inner doorway blinked green along its edge as the hatch clicked itself unlocked. With nonchalant ease, the intruder pushed onto the control deck and immediately started for the technician buried into his console at the other end of the room. When the busy man had registered the sound of the airlock opening, he turned to complain; "Fair is fair. I'll go out when yo-"

His sentence was cut short, however, by the brutal spinning heel kick that Dex delivered to the side of the seated man's head, sending him spilling to the floor with stars dancing through his vision. To his credit, the technician struggled through his disorientation to seize a utility knife from his belt and began to swing it wildly in his attacker's direction. In an effort to pin down the weapon, Dex dropped himself atop the man on the ground and seized his knife hand. As the technician struggled, his attacker brought down a hail of elbows onto his temple that weakened his grip on the handle of the blade. Then, with one final elbow to the orbital bone, the man released his knife as his occipital lobe bounced off the deckplating. Dex quickly gained positive control of the knife and began to lean his weight behind it when he heard the deep rumble of an angry male voice boom from above; "Stop, *now*! Get off of him and drop your weapon *immediately*!"

The intruder slowly pulled himself upright, still straddling the technician, and looked up at the man who was training a pistol at his head as he let the knife clatter to the floor. "What are you doing here?!" demanded the armed newcomer as he took a step closer to his new prisoner, "Who *are* you?!"

"Uh...*Pineapples*?" replied Dex with an uncertain shrug. The armed man's face then only had the smallest fraction of a second to register confusion before a lance of metal sprouted out from his Adam's apple. Confusion instantly gave way to shock and fear as the man emitted his first gurgle, prompting him to drop his weapon and grasp instinctively at his throat. When the man had finally breathlessly stumbled backwards and fell onto an inactive console, he revealed Mirta standing with her hand on her hip in the threshold of the airlock. As the confusing set of events began to set in, Dex was the first to act by darting for the knife on the ground and heaving it toward the enemy underneath him. The technician caught the incoming weapon hand and had displayed an impressive show of strength in muscling it to a stop before the blade could reach him. Dex leaned forward, putting all of his weight and might into plunging the knife downward, but the blade barely moved a millimeter. With a frustrated sigh, Dex sat upright and brought a heavy palm-strike down onto the hilt of the knife with sufficient force to pierce the technician's upper torso by a centimeter or so. In his reaction to the pain, the technician's strength waivered for a split-second; Affording the intruder all the opportunity he required to heave himself forward and sink the entirety of the blade into his foe's chest.

Exhausted and breathing heavily from the exchange, Dex rolled off the dying technician and flopped to the floor. As he lay there, staring at the ceiling while he caught his breath, Mirta stepped into view and said; "Dumbass. Why didn't you wait for me? I'm getting tired of saving your sorry ass like that."

"Nice throw." he replied, ignoring her rebuke, "Didn't see contestant number three there on my way in, so he must've come from the lift in the hallway." Dex looked over at the man lying next to him on the ground, his blood-soaked chest no longer heaving in distress, and couldn't help but feel ...*off* about their brief encounter. That was when something occurred to him; "Shit. Mirta, do you remember seeing facial tats, or really any tats for that matter, on any of the blokes we've come across so far today? Something doesn't feel right."

With a cock of her head, Mirta narrowed her eyes in thought and answered; "No, not up here, and I don't believe the guy we stuffed into the crate had any ink either. Why? What're you thinking?"

"Like I said," insisted Dex with a shrug as he sat up, "Something doesn't *feel* right about it. How can we be sure these guys are for-sure tied up with Vendrick's evil-doing? They sure as shit don't fit the description of any of your lovely Governor's *other* employees on the payroll..."

"How should *I* know?" she retorted while helping him to his feet, "But the fact that Vendrick's spoils from squeezing *my* home system dry are all finding their way to this facility?...Yeah, that doesn't endear the staff here to me very much. If you really want to know what we're dealing with, you just need to get on with it and install the intrusion software that Vette cooked up for us. Main console is behind you to the left, so be my guest."

"Alright, I'll get the ball rolling." agreed Dex with a nod before pointing at her to warn, "But until we know more about the staff here, we're going *minimally* lethal. *Both* of us. For all we know, these poor shmucks are just a security firm that Vendrick hired to act as a bridge to legitimize Saiph's goods and move them out to market. Four down, while regrettable if their hands are clean, is better than kicking off the tinder box and getting *everyone* killed."

Dex spied the chair the technician had left vacant and stepped over to claim it for himself. Withdrawing a small fiber optic cable from his tablet, he slotted its glowing green end into the desktop interface and began tapping away on the secure workstation's keyboard. Shortly after, a chirp could be heard emanating from his tablet and a familiar progress bar materialized. Once it reached one hundred percent, the large display screen built into the console before him came to life with a gridwork of different surveillance feeds and a map of the facility with glowing icons representing each bulkhead and subsystem that could be controlled from the workstation.

"Woah!" marveled Mirta as more and more information glowed to life across the control center, "This place goes *way* deeper than Vette thought. It's an inverted cone, as we had predicted, but that's gotta have...what? Twenty sub-levels? What *is* this place?"

"I would very much like to find out." Replied Dex, distracted as he analyzed the data flowing before him, "Can you hop on that console over there and get started on trying to shut those AA cannons down? I'm going to lock down the control tower and start getting the lay of the land here." After shutting down the main elevator to the tower and adding his and Mirta's biometric data to the in-house security system, Dex decided to investigate the layout of the facility's lowest levels. Most labeling on the map stopped at around level twelve, but the few labels that *did* persist below that all referenced laboratories or various support infrastructure for lab equipment such as distilled water lines and bundles of various gas or chemical feeds. At the very bottom of the stack, on sub-level twenty-two, sat the base's defense control center wreathed in the black and red border of a lockdown indicator.

Upon discovering the personnel tracking option on the overlay, he activated it and noticed with chagrin that the warehouses and courtyard were luckily *not* included in its coverage area. The overlay did, however, include nearly two-thirds of the central cone of the facility, stretching to sub-level fifteen and manifesting each individual person as an orange-red dot upon the three-dimensional map on his screen. Below that point, the heatmap seemed greyed out and no data beyond the structural layout itself was available. To the left of the holographic structure was a series of stats, including the number of tracked entities. One-hundred and sixty-seven is the number that Dex found himself reading over and over again, trying to make sense of what he had gotten himself into.

With the specter of panic starting to claw at the back of his neck, Dex returned his attention to the facility map to try and locate where all these enemies were held up. After scrolling through page after page of floor layouts, he finally found a large cluster of orange on sub-level thirteen. The group of dots contained about ninety people in what appeared to be a wing of individual rooms lined in a long double row. Dex's first thought of how lucky they had been to show up while the bulk of Vendrick's forces slept quickly gave way to a nagging feeling in his gut. With a frustrated sigh, he zoomed in on one of the rooms and stared at it closer and more intensely to try and spark whatever it was that triggered his hindbrain. As he scanned the layout for something, anything out of the ordinary, the momentary monotony of the task became the trigger he had been looking for.

On the whole, it wasn't uncommon for someone to lock their door as they slept. In fact, quite the opposite was true. But when Dex noticed that every *single* door icon in the wing was showing as red, he finally saw with his conscious mind that which had caught his eye subconsciously. In any system where freedom of choice existed, variation would always be present. Even if it were the middle of the night from their perspective, one would expect to at least see *someone* up using the loo or even a pair of dots *overlapping* deep into the wee hours of any morning. Yet there was none of that to be seen here. Such rigid structure, Dex knew, could only really be found in three systems; Imprisonment, enslavement, or enlistment. Which were *they*, he wondered? With a new odd feeling twisting at his guts, he looked to Mirta and prompted; "You having any luck on neutering those guns? This place is starting to feel less like a cargo depot and more...I don't know. Something else."

Chapter 35

"God *damnit*!" cursed Mirta with yet another slam of her fist into the console, "That makes it the targeting system, capacitor banks, hydraulics, *and* fire control that are *all* inaccessible from here. Whoever designed this facility was thinking of this exact scenario, it seems, when they were drawing up the blueprints. All of the systems that functionally run the guns can be found on sub-level twenty-two, which means the defense command center is hard-wired to the AA platform via blast-reinforced conduits that *we* can't get at."

"Alright," began Dex with a stroke of his chin, "But what about the *power source* for the guns? If I cut the feed, their capacitor banks won't be able to recharge."

Shaking her head, Mirta retorted; "You know as well as I do, Dex, that they probably keep those guns fully juiced when on standby. Even if you cut their power, they'll still have enough onboard to do all the damage they need to."

"Very true," he conceded, "but if one were to mimic an overload coming down the line from the generator, it would trigger an emergency discharge of the AA gun's capacitor system to prevent any potential explosive reactions. All I'd need to know in that scenario is which generator is feeding the juice."

"Unfortunately," explained Mirta as she worked to change the display on her console, "there is no dedicated power generation for the AA. It is redundantly fed by three different generators in three separate areas of the facility. Again, whoever built this place knew what they were doing."

"So, I'll just have to rig em *all* to blow." Suggested Dex with a shrug, "Once I've faked the overload and all the Caps have been flushed, I can touch off all the explosives at once. Base might be left without power, but we're not really here looking for real estate."

"That works in theory and all," she returned with a pained expression, "but how do you plan on making your way through the hangar deck to the generator there, on to the main generator on sub-level fifteen, then down into the defense command center itself...all without being spotted or causing any trouble?"

"Simple." He retorted with another shrug, "I'll have you up here watching all the blinky dots and telling me where to go. You get to be my *guy in the van* on this one."

"What's a van?" asked Mirta, the confusion evident in her expression.

"What I *mean*" he explained, "is that you'll stay up here, apart from the crossfire and combat, to provide me ongoing technical support."

Mirta huffed at the thought, saying; "Oh, so you want to keep your woman safe in a box up here so you can go do the *real* work, is that it?"

Dex raised an eyebrow at that accusation and fumed; "I don't care what's in your pants or whether I've been in them or not, if that's what you're insinuating. So you can go ahead and put that one back in the deck, because I need an *asset* on the ground, that's *you*, to maintain control of this highly *strategic* position and provide support as I attempt to fulfil our mission's main objective. Not everyone can be the quarterback, Mirta, but that doesn't mean that everyone else on the field is useless."

Mirta rolled her eyes, saying; "The most useless thing around here is your habit for terrasider analogies, Dex, but I *do* get what you're saying...Despite your *own* best efforts. I'll be good and do my job, I promise. And I trust that *you'll* use my abilities wherever advantageous for the *mission* and not just when it's *safe* for me to do so."

"Deal." agreed Dex as he drew her in close for a kiss on the cheek, "Now you keep an eye on those generators and see if you can't subtly lock down the areas around them, or at least try to redirect some traffic away using the inconvenient placement of sanitation drones or something. I'll head for the one tucked at the rear of the hangar bay first, then we can decide where I go from there."

———————————————

Instead of using the elevator that was still locked down into maintenance mode, Dex descended the control tower's internal stairwell until he stopped to kneel at a landing with a locked set of doors that led into the lower, more secure, subterranean section of the base. He pulled his sleeve back and consulted his forearm mounted tablet for a map of the facility, seeing that he only had six more flights to descend before he reached the level he was looking for. Reaching up to his ear, Dex activated his comm to say; "Alright, I'm ready. Pop the lock on the stairwell and zip it up behind me." Without a verbal response from his counterpart, the LED indicator on the door in front of him winked green and a light click could be heard in the door jam. He then pushed it open without resistance and stepped through to continue his journey downward with his pistol at the ready.

Reaching the desired level without incident, Dex stopped at the doorway and consulted his tablet again. Pulling up the map of his current location, he studied the layout waiting for him beyond the door. A hallway featuring a pair of elevators would lead to a T intersection, with left taking him to the hangar deck and right leading to what appeared to be a locker or ready room of some sort that seemed empty according to the personnel heatmap overlay. Deciding he were as ready as he ever would be to face the path ahead, Dex snapped his pistol up and pushed through the door.

Finding the intersection indeed empty, he ducked left and hugged himself to the wall beside the door labeled 'Hangar' at the end of the short hallway. Swiping his palm against its locking mechanism prompted the grey bulk of the heavy door to slide away, revealing the cavernous space beyond. As Dex peeked in for a discreet look, the first thing he noticed set his blood frosty. "Mirta," he called on his comm after ducking back into the hall and closing the door behind him, "We have a problem. They have six fighters down here on a MALAS rail. Even if we take out the AA guns, the pilots of these craft could still bloody up the folks we've got coming in after us."

"I feel like this is another analogy here…" began Mirta uncertainly, "What is a Malsa rail? Is that like a salad bar?"

"MALAS." Corrected Dex with a pinch to the bridge of his nose, "As in Magnetically Accelerated Launch Assist Sys…Look, you don't care what the hell the acronym means. All you need to know is that it will launch six fighters *at* orbital velocity to reach out and spank the shit out of anything they catch the scent of on their scopes. If we don't deal with them *preemptively*, the Hammer and her escort are going to have a *really* bad day when they try to come back down to scoop us up."

"What happened to your benevolent non-violent streak you were just trying to lecture me about?" asked Mirta pointedly, amusement at the fringes of her tone.

"What I was *lecturing* you about" retorted Dex with a sigh, "was non-*lethality*. Not all violence is lethal. Those are R-Seventy-Ones on the rail out there, and I sorta know my way around that particular airframe. If I can get a charge on the main wiring harness, it'll just take out their flight control system and they'll still have a chance to live if they're smart enough to punch out."

"And how do you suppose you'll manage that?" challenged Mirta skeptically, "You think they'll just let you wander up and fiddle with their fighter craft? I count fifteen people in that hangar. What are the chances that *none* of them see you?"

Dex shot a glance to the door at the opposite end of the short hallway, labeled *Crew Prep*, and replied; "That would depend on how you define the word *see*." Then the edge of his lip tugged upward in an almost imperceptible smile as he crossed the hall and stepped past the automatically-opening doors. After a few minutes of searching through lockers, finding a few Naval challenge coins and entirely too much porn, Dex finally discovered an unlocked cubby that contained one of the jumpsuits that he had seen the workers in the hangar bay wearing. It was the muted burnt orange of all standard industrial safety gear with a stripe of dark grey running down each extremity, and each jumpsuit included a full hood with attached breather mask. The hood would be a blessing, he knew, because the base would undoubtedly be a fairly tight community and an unfamiliar face may be enough to raise suspicion.

Dex shed his backpack, placing it into the locker for safe keeping, and donned the utility jumpsuit. Before zipping up his disguise, he dispensed eight explosive pucks from his pack and stowed them in an internal pocket where they wouldn't bulge conspicuously. After securing his bulky breather mask in place, he straightened his commandeered tool belt and keyed his comm; "Alright, I'm headed for the MALAS rail first, then I'll b-line it for the rear of the hangar to get at generator number one. How clear are we looking on that front? Have you managed to steer folks away from it?"

Mirta's voice was quick to return in his ear; "The door at the far back end of the hangar, labeled B-Seventeen, is what will take you to the generator. Your cleaning drone idea is a no-go here, it would seem, because we have what I assume is an armed guard milling around outside the doorway. Hard to tell from looking at an orange dot, but he hasn't moved in the few minutes I've been watching."

"Sounds like we could use a distraction." Suggested Dex as he started for the exit of the locker room, "Any thoughts on that front? As long as they aren't *too* overt. We want them to perceive anything that goes down as an accident and not an attack."

Mirta scanned her control board, looking for anything and everything she could interact with remotely from her lofty perch. She could control the crane, but it wasn't currently carrying anything to drop. Opening the hangar doors was an option, but she doubted she would be able to deactivate the airshield quickly enough to do any real damage from decompression. That was when her eyes found the little yellow icon moving around on her screen, labeled 'Frgt_Drn_021'. Selecting the little dot as it creeped along, she was greeted with an options screen for the cargo drone. While she had the option to assume direct control of the device to cause some havoc, she elected instead to dig into the automated machine's safety-stop settings. She bumped the max appendage articulation speed, increased limb mobility arcs, disabled proximity sensors, and set it to *combat hustle* mode. With a smirk, she keyed the comm to warn; "Distraction inbound, get ready to move." as she uploaded the drone's new settings.

Dex heard a thunderous crash from the hangar and took that as his cue. Slipping out onto the flight deck, he made straight for the rearmost fighter on the rail system. As he did his best to nonchalantly stroll to his objective, he couldn't help but be distracted by the spectacle unfolding at the other end of the hangar. A yellow and black loader drone had seemingly downed a kilo-and-a-half of robo-cocaine and was zooming with reckless abandon between a stack of pallets and an awaiting shipping container, flinging its precious cargo to its final destination as if it were on fire. A handful of men in jumpsuits matching Dex's own were trying to both stop what was happening and stay outside the wrath of the automated madness, with one of the workers having already been run down by the eager machine's rampage.

Stifling a laugh as he ducked under the rearmost R-71 fighter, Dex ran his fingers along the smooth white underbelly of the craft until he discovered the seam he had been searching for. With a light bit of pressure on the recessed panel, he began to twist and the protective covering withdrew itself into the body of the fighter to reveal an electronics-laden compartment beyond. Finding the wiring junction he had been looking for, Dex withdrew a puck from his jumpsuit and affixed it to the smooth metal outer casing of the craft's main wiring harness. He then paired the explosive to his tablet, setting it to its thermogel detonation profile, and closed the underbelly compartment back up before moving up to the next fighter.

He worked his way forward, repeating the process four more times and setting each charge to detonate when it had traveled one-hundred meters from its initial point of arming. Before long, he noticed that the workers at the other end of the bay had finally managed to subdue the manic lifter drone with a repurposed net and lots of manpower. Setting to his task with as much haste as he could muster, Dex opened the underbelly panel of the final fighter and got to work. After he had placed his puck and was turning its base to activate the explosive device, he heard a sharp bark emanating from the front of the craft; "What the hell are you doing?! These birds are in full combat-standby! You looking to get your ass roasted down here?"

Dex mentally braced himself, then made a conscious effort to loosen his shoulders and expression as he closed the access hatch and answered; "Relax. I know the pilots aren't getting ready to take to the black, cuz *they're* the ones who sent me down here. They were bitching about some wobble on launch and asked me to take a look at it."

"Bullshit." Spat the man with agitation, "If there were a problem, *my* guys would've heard about it. This rail aint *your* job. It's mine."

"Yeah, no shit, guy." Riposted Dex with some agitation of his own, "You think I want to be down here doing *your* job? Like I don't have four-thousand *better* things to be doing with my goddamn time. *They* claim they've mentioned it to your folks before with no results, so they got the boss breathin' down *my* asscrack about it now. That *makes* it my problem. Or *made* it mine, till I fixed it for you. Y'all had the timing on the launch system's inertial dampening a few milliseconds off. Tracked it down to a failing relay that was slowing the initiation signal...You're welcome by the way."

Then, without waiting for a response from the other man, Dex just offered his hand to him in an unspoken request for help to his feet. The man automatically reached down and obliged without much thought, unconsciously recategorizing the unknown mechanic from stranger to co-worker in his mind. Dex hoisted himself up and quietly thanked the man, giving him a friendly clap on the shoulder as he started for the door labeled *B-seventeen*. To Dex, the feeling of the man confusedly gazing at the back of his head as he walked away was almost tangible, and he began to grind his teeth as he started to feel the hangar tech's stare burrowing into his back; Manifesting itself as a knot in his stomach. Dex knew he had to assertively continue to walk like he owned the place, or his gambit wouldn't pay off. Confidence *was* his camouflage and if it faltered now, he would surely perish.

With a stroke of luck, Dex found that the guard who had been outside B-seventeen was now busy surveying the aftermath of the drone malfunction. His path unimpeded, Dex slipped through the door without incident and locked it behind himself with a muted click. Beyond the door, his objective was obvious and loomed large in the middle of the room as a hemispherical mass of glowing lights and neatly bundled cabling that stretched into the ceiling above. Removing the final pair of explosive pucks from his hidden pocket, Dex stepped around the back side of the two-meter-tall device to find a place to put them; Deciding to affix the duo of explosive charges to the underside of a lip that ran along the half-sphere. After setting the discs to maximum yield and dropping them into the proper fire group, he returned to the door and slipped back out into the hangar.

As Dex was making his B-line back to the door that would take him into the locker room, he heard a voice raise from somewhere off to his left calling toward him; "Hey, guy, c'mere for a minute, will yah? Hey, I'm talking to you!" Dex did his best to act oblivious, rolling his head subtly back and forth to suggest he were engrossed in some music instead of desperately trying to ignore the increasingly frustrated man that was closing in on him. With a sigh of relief, he reached the door and breezed his way on through to the locker room. As soon as the door had closed behind him, Dex began to sprint for the rear of the tiled room while clawing at the seals of his utility suit.

The MALAS mechanic came thundering into the locker room moments later, yelling; "Alright, asshole, you and I are about to have a chat. Where the fuck did you skitter off to?" He then proceeded to systematically make his way down the rows of lockers, flaring his nostrils wider and with more evident fury with each empty bench he was met with. Finally noticing a pair of orange and grey boots under the bathroom stall in the far corner of the locker room, the man stormed his way over and proceeded to bang on its bolted door. With swelling frustration at the silence from the other side of the stall, the mechanic stepped back and threw a mighty kick at the barrier; Flinging it open with a thunderous crash.

"What the f-" was all he managed to say upon seeing the empty jumpsuit that was propped onto the toilet, before an arm was tightening around his neck from behind to quickly rob him of his consciousness.

_____

As Dex placed the final strip of tape across his snoring prisoner's mouth, he keyed his comm to say; "Alright, our employee of the month has been tucked in and I'm ready to move on to objective numero dos."

"You sure it's a good idea to leave that guy breathing?" asked Mirta skeptically, "Because he could screw us both if he wakes up early."

"The dude is gagged and hog-tied to a toilet." argued Dex as he hefted his backpack onto his shoulders, "He's about as much threat to us now as your standard Sunday-morning frat bro. We'll be fine."

Mirta sighed, saying; "If you think so, then I've got no complaints. For generator number two, you're going to want to return to the stairwell and keep pushing downward to sub-level fifteen. Here, I'll mark it on your overlay. That's going to be the main generator there, so make sure you pack enough of a punch to bring it down."

Spotting the new purple arrow at the lower edge of his vision, Dex followed it downward to find a diamond of the same color floating beneath his feet. Groaning at the _600m_ displayed above the icon, he turned for the locker room's exit and started for the stairwell. His ensuing descent into the facility was uneventful, thanks to Mirta's forethought of locking down all entrances to the stairs; Citing an ongoing gas leak as the cause on each door's status readout. As he approached the hatchway onto sub-level fifteen, Dex took a knee and consulted his comm; "Alright. Before I go after the generator, I need to lift some utility-grade battery packs off of something beefy if I'm gonna pull off my overload bit. Any janitorial drones or something nearby that you can see for me to cannibalize?"

"Nothing on this level," Replied Mirta in a concentration-edged tone, "But it looks like there are a couple automated cargo dollies stored on the floor above yours."

"Alright, mark it for me." Stated Dex with an internal groan as he checked the heatmap readout of sub-level _fourteen_ on his tablet. It was the floor that showed over ninety heat signatures, all neatly lined up in two rows. With an exasperated scoff, he reactivated his comm to complain; "Are you _shitting_ me? There are _no_ other batteries for me to use except for the ones that just _happen_ to be in the midst of, like, a _hundred_ bad-guys? Or are you just looking to cash in on my life insurance policy?"

"You're more than welcome to head back up to the hangar deck and see if they're willing to share a battery with you," suggested Mirta, "But they don't look too happy from where I'm sitting."

Seeing the new blue square glowing on his overlay with a small _64m_ above it, Dex drew his pistol and checked its attached suppressor as he began to ascend the stairs. Pushing out onto sub-level fourteen and into a long hallway lined with irregularly spaced doors, he moved silently across the smooth concrete floor until he reached an intersection. Taking a quick moment to consult the map, he saw that the hallway stretched out to either side of him and looped around to meet again on the far side of what appeared to be a large chamber in the center. The central chamber was lined on either side by a row of about forty heat-blips, each corresponding to their own small room on the blueprint, and two additional blips appeared to be posted outside the single door that seemed to lead into the space.

Noticing that the little blue square on the map was in a small utility closet at the far end of the central chamber, Dex rolled his eyes and keyed his comm; "Any idea on how I can get at those batteries without waking the friggin' marching band? Because it would get *real* loud if I went through the front door."

"I actually think I've already worked this one out for you." Offered Mirta excitedly, "If you take a left and follow the hallway for about a hundred meters or so, you should see a grate in the wall on your right side. This is the air-return for the recyclers. That particular return line originates at that grate and travels through the utility room we're looking for."

"On it." Replied Dex as he brought his pistol back into position and turned the indicated direction down the hallway. A few moments later, he came upon a metal grate inset into the white concrete wall right where Mirta had predicted it'd be. After inspecting its dimensions, however, he keyed his comm to incredulously ask; "Are you *kidding* me? Can you see from your end how small this damn thing is?!"

"…Said countless wives to their ever-ballooning husbands." Remarked Mirta with a snicker in Dex's ear.

"Can you take this shit seriously for like two-point-five seconds?" hissed Dex furiously through his teeth, "If I can't get this done, we're both very likely to die down here."

"Oh, quit being dramatic." Huffed the woman in the control tower with nonconcern, "It looked roughly human-sized from here...*you're* roughly human-sized. I don't see why you can't make it work."

With another pained roll of his eyes, Dex sighed and remarked; "And that's what *he* said." As he retrieved the knife from his belt and activated a button set within its handle. Seconds later, the cutting edge of the blade had glowed to a dull orange and it was plunged into the metal of the grate. The red-hot knife met very little resistance from the flimsy material and a tidy square had been cut within moments. Then, after shrugging off his backpack with a weary sigh, Dex returned the knife to his belt and pulled himself into the tight confines of the air-return duct. It was a squeeze, but he managed to shimmy his way fully inside and propel himself in short scoots along the dusty sheet-metal. "Now I actually *do* know what a TV dinner feels like..." he remarked idly as he struggled to bring his right arm forward.

"TV Dinner?" asked Mirta, caught off guard by the comment and beginning to worry, "Are you overheating? I swear it says here that it's supposed to be an air-return duct! I'm sorry!"

"No, no. You're alright." Assured Dex with a wince, "It's just an expression. Can you just keep an eye on my position and let me know when I am where I need to be?"

"I mean...now is good." Offered Mirta with an unseen shrug, "Anywhere in the next ten meters, really."

"What do you mean?" he asked, confused, "There're no grates in sight anywhere…Where do you expect me to get in from?"

"Grates?" said Mirta with surprise, "Ah. Grates. Umm…there's one about twenty meters on. Only problem is it pops out into one of those little rooms there."

"Screw that." Replied Dex with a shake of his head as he pulled his knife from its sheath and reactivated the hot cutting edge, "I'll just make my *own* way in." He then dipped his blade into the metal of the ducting in front of him, first cutting a pair of parallel lines away from himself then drawing his knife across to connect the two gashes at the far end. As a result, the sheet metal of the ducting folded down and revealed a darkened room beyond.

Dex activated the floodlight function on his tablet then gently lowered himself into the utility closet, paying close attention to avoid knocking anything off the shelf poised beneath his duct. Landing silently in the cluttered room, Dex quickly got to work identifying the stored dolly drones and pulling them out into the open. After he had cracked its external case and was elbow-deep in the machine, he heard what sounded like a soft whimper emanating from the duct. Once the disturbance had failed to repeat itself after several silent seconds of staring at the vent above, Dex continued his delicate task. By the time he was working on extracting the second battery from the butchered drone, the weak sound rose again, but sustained itself into a gentle wail that rang disturbingly childlike. Unable to ignore the possible auditory hallucinations any longer, Dex tucked the second scavenged battery blade into his jumpsuit and zipped it back up. He then pulled himself back into the duct and began his unplanned journey *deeper* into the air-return system. As he pulled himself along, the muffled echoes of a crying child grew louder and more distinct. Finally, he came across the grate that Mirta had mentioned and pressed his ear against it. He could see nothing but darkness on the other side, but the sounds of distress were definitely coming from beyond the thin metal barrier.

Dex drew the knife from its sheath once more and activated its red-hot blade to plunge it into the metal before him in a smooth but powerful downward stroke. He then complimented his central vertical slash with a pair of horizontal ones that stretched across both the top and the bottom of the grate. As he pushed the thin metal of the resulting flaps aside, Dex noticed belatedly that the whimpering had gone silent. Cautiously, he crawled out into the darkened space and whispered; "Hello? Is anyone in here? I mean you no har-"

His words were cut short when a tiny pair of feet came from out of the shadows above to slam themselves into the side of his neck. The unexpected onslaught was then sustained with a hailstorm of miniature bites and elbows when Dex reflexively caught his attacker mid-air. The diminutive assailant tried its best to squirm free, but the much larger and stronger adult was quickly able to quell the rebellion by holding his attacker tightly to his chest. "Hey!" hissed Dex with frustration as he fought the little boy in his grip, "Settle down for a minute, will you?! I'm not here to hurt you! I'm here to help! If you calm down and work with me here, we can get you hoOOOH!"

His negotiations were again cut short, this time by a well-aimed kick to his crotch that allowed Dex's pint-sized captive to skitter free. As the ex-navy Lieutenant regathered himself on the floor, his prepubescent quarry crouched on a bed in the far corner of the room; The little boy's terror clear to see even in the deeply shadowed light cast by Dex's tablet. "If I were a bad-guy," reasoned the kneeling stranger with pained drawn out patience, "Wouldn't I have used the *door* instead of cutting my way in? I'm *here* to help you, kid. I promise"

Still looking uncertain, the boy in the corner asked; "W-Where is my mom?" as tears began to well in his eyes, "I want my mom! Where did she go?"

"That's what I'm here to help you find out." Assured the strange man in a gentle tone, "I want to get you back to your mom and maybe learn a little bit about the bad men that took you. Do you think you can help me with that?" When the boy nodded hesitantly, Dex lowered himself to the floor to sit cross-legged before continuing; "My name is Dex. What's yours?"

The boy looked away for a moment, unsure of whether to answer, before he turned back to reply; "Luke."

"It's nice to meet you, Luke" greeted Dex with a slight bow of his head toward the young one, "And where do you hail from, Sir Luke? I'm an Earth man, myself."

"Beethree?...I think." Answered the boy with a tiny tentative squeak, "That's what my dad made me remember so I wouldn't forget."

"Beethrea?" repeated Dex with visible confusion, "Is that a planet or the name of a station?"

"That's *not* my station." Protested the little one with instantaneously boiled over impatience, "*My* station is the *tiger*. Dad said I could tell *anyone* and they would know where to take me. I *want* to see my mom!"

Dex threw up his palms in a placating gesture and soothed; "Alright, little man. Alright. We're gonna make that happen, okay? Do you know how you got here? How long have you been kept in this room for?"

The line of questioning visibly upset the child, his eyes spilling tears as he replied; "I don't know. I was ju-just playing CrushDojo then someone took my hood off and my mom was crying then they did something to my arm that made me sleep. Where's my mom? I want to see her. Is she okay? I want to go home!"

"Okay, bud, we're gonna get you there." Assured Dex through an ever-tightening knot in his chest, "Maybe we can look your ma up on Hūnet? What's her first and last name?"

"Patricia Patel." Recited the little one with a dutiful nod, his lip beginning to quiver again at thought of his missing mother.

With a reassuring nod of his own, Dex turned to his tablet and opened the Hūnet console that Vette had programmed for him. It would search not only the public records, but files kept on secured servers within the stations themselves such as police reports, medical information, and bank data. Traveling to Saiph's directory, he was forced to search by station. After scouring Meclan, Matsuoka, and Heldrin for signs of the boy's mother; There she was. Listed as sharing her apartment with two other cohabitants on Ring three, section B, in the main residence complex on Bengal station.

Chapter 36

"Mirta, do you read?" began Dex's hushed but urgent call over the comm, "Because we have a massive shift in the scope of our mission here."

"What?" asked Mirta, surprised by the intensity of the sudden transmission, "What do you mean, *shift in the scope of the mission*?...What did you *do*?"

"It's not about what I did," corrected Dex with a distracted glance toward the curious boy, "It's about what *they're* doing *here*. I found a survivor from Bengal station, Mirta, and he's just a kid. Plus, the facility map shows *another* floor just like this one on the untracked lower levels, so God only knows who else is locked up down here. We're not just onsite to lift guns and supplies anymore. This is a rescue mission."

Mirta, taken aback by the revelation, stuttered a bit as she replied; "A-are you s-sure he's really from Bengal? How can that be? It was utterly destroyed...we *both* saw what was left."

"Maybe the reason everything got so shot to shit was to conceal whatever it was they were doing beforehand?" offered Dex quietly with a shrug, "There *was* a lot of data on Bengal's central server that appeared to be pretty deliberately scrubbed. Maybe they were trying to hide a few kidnappings?"

"To what end though?" she demanded with frustration, "He's never done it before, and it makes no sense for him to start something like that now..."

"Who says he's never done this before?" challenged Dex with an unseen lifting of his brow, "Data suggests that the heavy-duty hauling outfit Tano nabbed is just one of many in a long line of shipment records that stretch back for years. What are the chances that all these rooms have been empty all that time?"

"*Are* there others?" asked Mirta pointedly, "Because it sounds like you found one so far. Who's to say the bloke next door isn't a baddie?"

"Well then, why don't I just check?" he asked as he rose to his feet, "Go ahead and unlock the door and I'll go introduce myself."

"No need." Remarked Mirta with a yawn, "Your biometrics have already been added to the system and you've got director-level access to all areas of the facility. Scanner is built into the door's input panel. *Literally* couldn't be easier."

Choosing to ignore her obvious undertones of frustration and boredom, Dex keyed his comm and replied; "Thanks for the tip." as he rose and approached the boy to say; "Alright, Sir Luke, I'm going to need you to hold down the fort here for a little while longer so I can go have a chat with the bad-guys. Can you do that for me?"

With a sheepish nod of permission from the little one, Dex proceeded to key the cell's door open with a silent whoosh; Rushing through its threshold with his pistol at the ready. Finding nothing but a dimly lit, high-ceilinged, hallway lined in twin rows of identical doors, he lowered his weapon and poked his head back into the child's cell to shoot the boy a friendly wink before keying the door shut again. Making sure to return his pistol to its holster, Dex walked to the next cell in the line and depressed its keypad. When the metal of the door withdrew, it left in its place the image of a cowering woman who looked up at the newcomer with profound terror in her eyes. She scurried backward in an awkward crab walk, trying to tuck herself as tightly into the corner of her little room as she could, then the young woman began to sob uncontrollably. As Dex stepped forward to comfort her, every muscle in her body went rigid and her expression went blank as she did her best to focus all her attention onto the wall in front of her in an effort to mentally flee from the situation. Reading the room and recognizing his presence for the catalyst it was, Dex held his hands up in a placating gesture and slowly backed out of the door as he said; "No need to fear, alright? We're here to get you and everyone else home. Just hang tight. The cavalry is here and we'll get you sorted out soon."

As the door closed on the poor woman's cell, Dex struggled to stifle an involuntary growl as he snatched his suppressed pistol from its holster. Checking the heatmap on his tablet one last time, he still only saw the pair of orange spots flanking either side of the prison block's main entrance. Wearing his jaw like so many kilos of hardened cement, he stormed off toward said reinforced door with his weapon swaying nonchalant at his side. When he reached the doorway, he took no time in casually pressing the door's release button and calmly watching it withdraw into the wall.

When the guard on the left had turned to investigate the sudden whooshing behind him, he spun to find himself looking down the end of a metal tube with just enough time to furrow his brow in confusion before a bright flash of light and heat winked him out of existence. As the first of the two guards snapped his head back in reaction to the point-blank shot, Dex lashed out with a front kick that pounded into the hip of the second man. The guard went down, being forced to instinctively divert his movement for the pistol on his hip into an action to break his fall. Then, before the bulk of the second doorman even had an opportunity to hit the concrete floor, Dex had already loosed three rounds into his unarmored chest.

As he withdrew his ancient pistol's custom-printed magazine to swap it out with a fresh one from the ammunition pouch on his belt, Dex keyed his comm to report; "Sentries on this level have all been put to bed. I want you to send a burst transmission to Vette and Tano, telling them to bring the Hammer down on their next unpowered orbit. It'll push our timetable a bit, but we need to get these folks out of here as soon as we can."

"So, did you *actually* tuck those guards into bed?" Replied Mirta with split attention as she focused on her screen, "Or are we back to killing folks again? Cuz, you see, it's funny how it's okay when *you* decide it is, but you keep me in this damn tower like a cursed princess because Tano's convinced you that I'm *inches away* from flying off the handle and killing like a *madman*."

"To be fair," began Dex with an unseen shrug, "You *did*, like twenty minutes ago, go flying off a *box* and proceed to ventilate some dude in what could be considered an angry-ish male-like manor..."

"Don't judge me for that, you ass!" spat Mirta with some unexpected venom to her tone, "What the hell else was I *supposed* to do? *I* was just trying to make sure that *your* dumb ass spilling all the corn didn't result in an alarm signal. You know...*Preserving the mission*? Something you'd get more of a chance to see me doing if I weren't up here all day riding the damn bench."

"Fair enough." Conceded Dex with a chuckle, "I'll let my deadly ninja-princess from her tower to once again rein her terror upon the townsfolk."

"*Excuse* me?" she challenged in response, "I'm my *OWN* goddamn ninja-princess, and I will reign whatever the hell I please over whoever I feel deserves it. Try that one again, but this time with less dickhead stuck in your throat."

"Okaaay," began Dex slowly, a bit confused by the sudden heat of her anger, "how about *would the free-agent of inconsequential gender and unquestionable mental fortitude like an opportunity to lead some people to safety in one of the pressurized warehouses and wait for extraction, all whilst possibly shooting several **different** people who deserve it along the way?*"

"Not a bad idea," Acknowledged Mirta with a reluctant chuckle of her own, "but you're still an asshole."

By the time Mirta locked up the control tower and descended to sub-level fourteen, Dex had already keyed open all the cell doors and was in the middle of shepherding all the cautious prisoners out into the block's shared atrium. Though he was having a hard time getting them to listen to what he had to say at first, it appeared that the sight of their dispatched abductors on the floor at the threshold of the doorway warmed their drug-hazed demeanor quite rapidly. Some of the captives were adults of middle age, but a great majority of them appeared under twenty and all of them donned the same tan colored pants and what appeared to be the grey cut of surgical scrub tops. They were all disoriented and none of them seemed to have much of a feel for how long they had been in their cells, but they all reported frequent instances of consciousness loss during their stay.

When Dex saw Mirta approaching, he broke from his quiet conversation with an older looking bearded man and asked her; "We all sealed up with our bus on the way?"

Mirta nodded, saying; "Yep. Hammer is finishing its current orbit, then will begin descent at the pre-arranged window. Stairwell is still sealed too, though I'm not sure how long the whole gas leak story will stand up to the collective impatience of everyone who wound up stuck on each floor. If we want to utilize that particular route *safely,* we're going to need to do it soon."

"Agreed." Said Dex as he pulled up his tablet and stepped over to present the map on its screen to her, "That's why I want you to take these folks and led them to hangar one. It's on Sub-level two and has an airshielded blast door that is large enough for the Hammer to set down in. Doesn't look like there's much traffic between here and there as long as everything stays locked down, but there *will* be a few folks to deal with on the Hangar deck itself. Can't really tell from the heatmap, but I doubt that all of them are armed security folks. You should be able to handle it if you get the drop on em."

"I have five drones and twenty-four micromissiles." Stated Mirta confidently, "I'd be able to *handle* those chumps if I brought the marching band along to play my entrance music. Oh, we *good*."

"I'm smarter than the guy who would argue with you on that." He remarked in return with a small smile, "And while you take these fine folks topside, I'm going to keep pressing downward. Saw a floor with a similar layout to this one on sub-level nineteen, but I've got no heatmap data for anything past fifteen. Might be abandoned, might not be. But it's worth a check if there's even the glimmer of hope that more survivors are down there. It's on the way to the turret control room anyways, so there's no real harm in it. Alright, you be careful and just remember to stay quicker than the other guy" Then, with a final wink and a squeeze of her shoulder, he was off down the hallway toward the central stairs.

After a short detour onto an unpopulated floor to set up his bomb slash overload gimmick on the main generator, his descent into the facility was abruptly cut short two levels down by a locked blast-rated door that bisected the subterranean stairwell. When he presented his palm to the doorway's biometric reader, its embedded indicator light winked yellow and chirped two low tones in the negative. With a frustrated sigh, he popped the fiber optic data cable from his tablet and paired it to the interface, allowing Vette's intrusion program to do its magic. After the customary handful of seconds of holding his tablet aloft for the program to run its course, Dex began to automatically withdraw his arm again when he noticed with surprise that the program was still at work. In the many years that he had been using one version or another of the intrusion software, he'd never seen it take more than the span of two full breaths to get the job done. Now, well into breath six, Dex was starting to get nervous. Just as he was about to give up and try a different angle, the door finally clicked and slid inward to reveal stark-white walls and stainless-steel handrails beyond. The stairwell continued downward, but it felt like he were stepping into another facility entirely; With even the lighting seeming more sterile and clinical in nature. With confusion still plastered across his face, he keyed his comm to say; "I ran into a door at Sub-level fifteen that apparently had some *super* hefty security algorithms running on a completely separate system than the one managing levels fourteen and above. Not sure what the deal is, but it explains the blank-out in our heatmap. I do *not* like the looks of it. How close are we to getting those folks ready to move?"

"One of the older women appears to have a broken leg," replied Mirta with a weary sigh, "So we're getting her splinted up and I am assigning a pair of guys to act as crutches and help her along. Stairwell is still locked down from here to the tower, so I will get them moving topward within five minutes or so."

"Make it two." Ordered Dex as he peeked around the corner to scout out the next landing, "The Hammer will be breaking orbit in less than twenty minutes, which puts them in transmission range right as they come into targeting range. We can't affor-"

Suddenly, his comment was cut off by a blaring alarm that was accompanied by the pulsing Red and Blue lightshow of a standard Federal Navy Combat Intrusion Alert. Momentarily panicked by the sudden flood of adrenaline hitting his bloodstream, Dex quickly stifled the evolutionary reaction and addressed his tablet for more information. After switching to the data feed for the facility above, the first thing Dex noticed was the loss of all heatmap tracking information. The second thing he noticed, other than the sudden pit that had formed in his stomach, was the red and blue glowing dot on the hangar level. "God damnit, Dex!" cut Mirta's voice into his earpiece, "You just *had* to grow a conscience and duct tape that guy to a toilet instead of just slitting the nosey bastard's throat and shoving his ass into a locker to be done with it. *Now* look where we're at. System is locking down and purging *all* biometric data, *including ours*. While, yay, *their* existing admin backups were purged and will not be able to override anything, *We* are also going to have to hack, burn, or blow through every door we come across from here on out."

"Well shit, now they've Deactivated one of my bombs on the MALAS rail." Declared Dex with a sigh as he tapped through his tablet, increasing the remaining charges in the hangar-level to maximum yield before manually detonating the firegroup. After a deep rumble of both primary and secondary explosions could be felt throughout the facility, Dex opened his comm to continue; "That won't help us much in the form of stealth, but it doesn't really change our objective or how we aim on getting there. Just keep those folks moving and seal up what you can behind you using Vette's intrusion doohickey. It replaces the software for the locking mechanism entirely, so anyone who's looking to come after you will have to put a torch to work. That should at least buy you enough time to hear them coming and prepare a proper response."

With a stress-strained voice, Mirta returned; "Decent idea, but this stairwell has a whole hell of a lot of doors. What are you going to do?"

"What I came here to do." he answered with a shrug as he descended yet another flight of stainless-steel steps, "The fact that the scumbags who run the place now know we're slinking around doesn't change a thing. More innocent people who got swept into this mess may very well still need our help down here. I can't ignore that."

"I understand." Replied Mirta quietly as she waved people out into the stairwell and instructed them to climb, "Just be careful, okay Dex?"

"I always am, love." Said Dex with a warm smile that she could hear as he spoke it, "It just doesn't always *look* that way from the outside."

When he arrived at the landing for sub-level nineteen, Dex began to hear the low thump of a rifle on single-fire, lazily cycling again and again, somewhere beyond the locked door he found himself staring at. With a fervor that caused him to fumble, Dex accessed his tablet and began running the intrusion program. As each additional shot rang out, he could tangibly feel a weight gathering on his back that threatened to shred his patience and send him hammering at the door with his fists. Luckily for the door *and* the bones in his hands, the program finally chirped, and the heavy slab of metal began to slide away. On the other side, he found what seemed like a locker room that led to some form of suitlock system constructed of frosted glass.

At either side of a central equipment exchange box that was built into the structural glass ahead of him sat a trio of rear-entry hazmat suit mounts. Wearers would step into the baggy suits, which clung securely to the *other* side of the glass via an airtight magnetic seal, then the docking system would zip them up before releasing its clamps on the back. It was a low-hassle and easily maintainable hazmat solution, but Dex had rarely seen such a sophisticated model in use anywhere outside government-funded labs and universities. With a sinking feeling in his gut, Dex once again shrugged his backpack off and stepped over to place his pistol and three extra magazines into the equipment exchange slot. Eyeing the four bare hazmat suit mounts surrounding his chosen suit in the row with a grind in his teeth, Dex slipped into the awkwardly oversized garment and allowed it to seal behind him.

Activating the hazmat suit's HUD with an eye gesture, he navigated to the initiation command and triggered it. Then, without much concern for the wearer's comfort, the suit contracted around his body; Save for a wide margin around his upper chest and head to account for the thick corrosive-resistant sheet of engineered plastic that hung suspended in front of his face. Uncomfortably shifting the crotch of his suit, he stepped toward the equipment box and reached in to retrieve his items. After a quick puff of sterilizing gas and a flash of blue light, the inner door opened and presented him his weapon. Seizing the pistol and its three spare magazines, he tucked the extra ammunition into the suit's front utility pouch and pushed forward at a jog in search of the source of the gunfire.

The room he found himself in was lined on both sides with a series of sinks and what appeared to be scientific equipment of varying disciplines. At the end of the lab sat a pair of frosted glass double-doors that suddenly flashed with blueish-green light from beyond as another report of gunfire rang in Dex's ears. With a swelling fury fueling his charge, he raised his weapon and stormed through the breech. As he emerged from the doorway, he found a chamber that very closely resembled the cell block above, but it was strewn with a series of boxes and other equipment that seemed to be in flux. Those details were secondary, however, to the three men who were about thirty meters away down the isle and all pointing their guns into a cell they had just opened.

Without much thought for accuracy, Dex loosed three rounds downrange. None of them hit their target, but they did come close enough to attract the attention of the trio of executioners. Turning from their grisly task, the gunmen began to return fire with their automatic weapons. In a scramble, Dex dove for cover behind a pallet of metal crates and watched as the objects stacked all around him erupted into a torrent of colored confetti. Finding a short lull in the rhythm of the incoming fire, Dex leaned himself out as low as he could and took aim at one of his clean-suited foes. Squeezing off two rounds, he watched in dismay as they both ultimately ended up as a pair of smudges on his target's hefty faceplate; Merely sending the man stumbling backward off balance.

With frustration, Dex sucked himself back into cover and began to scan his immediate area for anything useful. A couple meters to his rear was a rolling cabinet that appeared to be stocked with laboratory supplies. Along with the jugs of solvents and other scientific fluids that he tore through frantically, he found a canister of powderized zinc-oxide. With the swelling gunfire beginning to steal more and more of his mental bandwidth with each passing round, he lunged for the cabinet and retrieved the grey powder and a handful of empty laboratory flasks before retreating back into cover.

Combating the effects of his degrading dexterity as the whizz-snap of the incoming bullets tore deeper and deeper into his cover, Dex struggled to pour the fine powder into the thin neck of each delicate piece of glassware. With his task finally complete, he switched his pistol over to his right hand and hefted one of the flasks in his left. Waiting for another lull in the incoming fire, Dex leaned back and hurled the powder-filled glassware at the ceiling as hard as he could. The flask struck the roof at the mid-point between Dex and his assailants, raining the fine grey dust in a diluted mist that obscured the air. As the occluding effect crescendoed, Dex retrieved the remaining two flasks and ran as hard as he could toward the trio. While running and trying to see through the moisture that had built up on his faceplate's inner surface, he loosed three rounds toward the source of the most recent flash of gunfire. As his pistol locked back to signify it was empty, he could hear a yelp of pain from beyond the powdered veil.

When his concealment began to fade, Dex dove back behind another pallet of crates that sat just under ten meters from his foe's position and hunkered down to weather their angry torrent of incoming fire. Returning his pistol to his dominant left hand, Dex seized the second of his glass flasks and proceeded to heave it as hard as he could into the ceiling above. Once again, the glass shattered and resulted in a spectacular shower of grey dust. As the choking cloud settled over the cell block's central walkway, Dex got on his knees and cautiously peeked low around the corner of the box with his pistol at the ready. Two of his opponents were in cover and appeared to be discussing tactics with one another while the third in the gang was kneeling in pain in the middle of the isle, trying to regather himself despite the expanding patch of red across the left side of his hazmat suit. Choosing his target, Dex lined up a shot and squeezed his trigger three times in a rapid succession. The first of his rounds went wide, missing the knelt man by half a meter, but the follow-up pair landed where intended. The first of his two effective shots bit into the man's left shoulder, trailed closely by a second that tore its way through the side of the executioner's neck at the base of his skull. Instantly seeing the lethality of his volley, Dex whipped himself back into cover just as the fallen gunman's comrades returned fire with their rage evident in the eccentricity of their spray patterns.

When the dust began to die down again, Dex decided to press on the urgency that anger had flooded into his foe's bloodstream by raising his weapon over his cover and blind firing until the slide locked back. As he ejected the weapon's spent magazine, he hurled the last of his dust-filled flasks toward the ceiling at the mid-point between him and his enemy. While sliding a new magazine home, Dex stayed low and scrambled back toward an open cell three doors down to his left. Just as Dex had suspected, the adrenaline of being shot at paired with the anger of losing a teammate forced the gunmen into an aggressive posture that resulted in them charging at the third instance of their unknown enemy's homemade smoke bomb. Both men surged forward, firing blindly through the haze until they rounded on the box their opponent *had* been hiding behind. Before they recognized their mistake, Dex had already popped out from his new hiding spot in the open cell's doorway and sent four rounds at them. The first two shots found the upper chest of the closer gunman, while shots three and four went high to miss entirely.

With the final surviving gunman immediately returning fire, Dex was forced back into cover as chips of concrete began to blast away from the doorframe. Crouching low, further inside the ever-deteriorating doorway, he quickly leaned back out to send a round toward his now-advancing foe. The bullet bit into the man's hip, forcing him to the ground with a mighty *thwap* from his face shield as it smacked the cement floor. When Dex tried to lean back out to finish the job, he was almost caught by a hail of incoming rounds from the injured man who fired an unbalanced burst from his awkward prone position. Then, as Dex was quietly contemplating how to proceed, he heard the click-whine of a grenade's activation sequence rise from the walkway outside. Without thinking about it, he stepped out the doorway and squared up to the man on the ground; Who was already in the process of hurling the explosive device in his direction. The injured gunman's eyes then went wide when he watched the small black object being swatted back in his direction as the intruder bellowed; *"Nope!"*

When the explosion had finally stopped ringing in his ears, Dex stepped back out into the carnage of the walkway. The Detonation had obliterated the shiny white of the hallway's walls for a good five-meter radius and tore to shreds everything within its sphere of destruction, including the mangled remains of his final attacker. Then, as Dex knelt to briefly search the departed for equipment, he saw a flicker of movement in his peripheral from the far end of the cell block. Snapping his pistol to the ready, he started down the walkway at a full sprint.

Rounding the doorway he thought he had seen the shape moving into, he found another laboratory filled primarily with computer equipment. As he moved through the threshold, a Central Computer Farm came into view to his right and there was a single man quickly working his way down the server stacks turning the valves to trigger each individual machine's purge cycle. The action caused a small reservoir of specially formulated acid to flush through each server's main control board, rendering the entire machine void of all physical and electronic evidence; And he was nearly done working his way down the stack. With urgency, Dex rushed in to tear the saboteur away from the final valve and heaved him to the deck. The diminutive man hit the concrete floor with a mighty *oof* that manifested a crack across his plastic faceplate and he struggled to right himself after the impact. With unchecked rage, Dex seized the man by the scruff of his hazmat suit and drug him over to plop him into a nearby chair with unceremonious vigor while demanding; "What are you sick fuckin' assholes up to out here? Why have you taken these people? Why are we wearing goddamn marshmallow-man suits? *Talk*, nerd, or I'm gonna take that syringe on the table over there to give you a little jab to find out for myself. And if that one does nothing fun, I'll move on to that one..."

As Dex nodded to an auto-injector that was sitting next to a nearby sink, the man showed panic in his eyes and suddenly moved to kick at his captor's weapon. Dex was quick enough to yank his gun hand out of the way, but he was unable to prevent the man's other foot from slamming into his gut; sending the captive's chair bowling over backward. As Dex recovered and was bringing his gun back to bear on the man on the floor, the scientist had already drawn a concealed pistol from his chest pouch and was preparing to fire. His aim wasn't leveled at the intruder, however. Instead, the frantic man had chosen to set the muzzle of his pistol against the side of his own head before proceeding to depress its trigger.

"Sweet *Jesus*!" shouted Dex as he took in the aftermath of the desperate scientist's final act. His stunned investigation of the scene soon led his gaze back up to the sink and the auto-injector that sat perched at its edge. Eyeing it with newfound awe and fear, he keyed his comm to say; "Mirta, we've got another *huge* problem down here."

"Oh, for the *love* of...*ugh*, do you ever have any *good* news to report?" fumed Mirta in a hushed tone, "What did you do this time?"

"Mirta, listen carefully because this is important." Demanded Dex soberly, "I have very good reason to believe that this facility is producing or researching *some* fashion of biological weaponry, and I think the prisoners are intended to serve as the test subjects. I encountered a sweeper squad rocking hazmat suits in a medicalized cell block down here, and they were executing prisoners along the row in response to the base-wide alarm. Furthermore, they had some egg-head with them that purged all but one of the server blades on the stack down here before I got to him. One is better than none, though, so I'll throw it in my bag for Vette to have a look at."

"What about prisoners?" asked Mirta in a worried whisper, "Were you able to save any of them? What if they're infected?"

"I haven't had a chance to take stock of that yet," admitted Dex as he returned to his feet from extracting the lone functional server blade from the now-defunct stack, "but it looks like the suitlock system down here has seals on either end of the glass. If I find anyone down here who can be moved, I'll zip em up in a suit and send em your way. We can clear out the forward hold on the Hammer for them and Vette can do a full quarantine lockdown on that section. We need to get this data back to Hearth and get our wonderful A.I. chewing on it with all her newfound horsepower ASAP."

"This isn't good, Dex." She breathed quietly, "What have we stumbled across here? What are we getting involved with?"

"The truth, it would seem." is all he replied, delivered with an ever-present confidence she found ever-maddening.

After investigating the medicalized cell block, Dex was only able to find three prisoners, all of whom were female, still breathing but heavily drugged. Of the trio, one appeared in much worse shape than the others. While two of the captives appeared to be healthy, other than their patchwork of deep bruises and scars running across their faces, their third surviving companion was in dire straits. The woman in question was equally as bruised, but she was also running a high fever and had begun developing boils on her upper chest and neck. Her raspy breathing constantly sent her into fits of painful coughing and she nearly couldn't make the journey with Dex back to the Suitlocks. After getting her zipped up and putting the desperately sick woman in the care of the other two, he sent them up the stairwell to Mirta as he turned to finish his investigation.

Among the bullet-riddled corpses that filled the row, there were other bodies that appeared to have found a more nefarious end. Because he knew it would be relevant to Vette's research to come, he spent a few moments cataloging one of the infected bodies with a series of photographs. The departed was a middle-aged male covered in angry looking boils from head to toe. He appeared to have lost his hair in clumps, his fingernails had sloughed off, and there were dried tracks of crimson-black blood flowing from his eyes nose and ears over a grotesquely swollen face. He had no medical scanner with him, but it looked to Dex as if the man had broken several fingers as well as his ankle in some fit of convulsions before he expired. With a chill running down his spine, Dex toggled the door to the man's cell behind him and did his best to forget the sight as he turned to press deeper into the facility.

Chapter 37

Mirta's caravan of liberated prisoners had proceeded up the empty stairwell in an orderly and unimpeded fashion, Vette-locking every door they passed, until they reached sub-level eight. When Mirta had rounded the corner onto the landing, she was met with a shower of sparks that spilled from the sealed bulkhead. It appeared that someone was attempting to use a plasma torch to cut through the thick metal near the locking mechanism, and they were nearly complete. Seeing the small pilot hole at the center of the half-circle they were cutting, Mirta stepped closer to perform some mental arithmetic.

Deciding that her plan would work, she stepped up to the door and pressed her weapon's muzzle against the hole. After selecting a rocket load and disabling the minimum arming distance for its internal fragmentation charge, she pulled her trigger. The micromissile whizzed out of the weapon's lower barrel, directly through the crudely cut keyhole, and detonated with an impressive thump on the other side that managed to slightly bow the steel of the bulkhead outward. Then, satisfied that the enemy cutting operation had ceased for good, she continued to lead her flock up the stairs.

Upon arriving to the landing for sub-deck two, Mirta turned to the others and announced; "Alright, everyone, we're here. Just sit tight and do your best to stay quiet while I take a look around." She then stepped up to the door and reached behind her back to receive a drone from the dispenser mounted at the bottom of her backpack. Setting the automated device into scout mode, she released it and instructed the little bugger to find its way into the hangar beyond the locked door. The drone leapt from her hand and came to just as sudden of a stop about a meter above her head. It bobbed for a moment, lightly chirping, then proceeded to scan the area with its wide array of embedded sensors. Satisfied that it had found a route, the dutiful machine zipped off to follow a set of pipes up the wall before coming to another sudden stop in front of a dimpled metal grate in the wall that appeared to be an element of the facility's air-return system. Without hesitation, the busy little bot started its slow process of creating a hole for itself through the hardened steel using an articulating utility claw armed with a cutting laser. After a small disc of dull grey metal finally came tumbling from above, almost taking out one of the liberated prisoners, the drone disappeared into the air return. Mirta followed its progress on her tablet, mentally urging it to go faster through the winding innards of the ventilation system.

Then, as if the channel had been changed on her display, the cramped interior on the video feed transformed into a wide-open chamber as the drone slipped its way out a large intake vent. With its recon mode instantly activated, the drone immediately began to send live data on the conditions beyond the door. From its twenty-meter orbit near the roof at the center of the space, the drone counted twelve individuals moving about the hangar. Most of them were armed and patrolling the area, but some appeared to be preoccupied with moving freight into awaiting cargo containers. Mirta reviewed the data on her tablet, then proceeded to prioritize the enemy combatants by the threat they posed paired with their distance from the entrance to the stairwell. Once that task was complete, she opened a three-dimensional rendering of the hangar beyond and scrolled through to identify guards who were clumped close together in cliques or conversation. Identifying three such groups and tagging each huddle for a pair of airburst fragmentation rounds, she synced the requested operation to her shotgun and watched on its embedded display as the weapon armed all six of the loaded micromissiles.

Turning to the crowd of concerned faces that were crammed into the stairwell beneath her, Mirta held up a hand and said; "Okay guys, hang on while I go take care of a few of your gracious hosts. If I'm not back in five…keep waiting, I guess." And with that, she jabbed the door's control panel and surged through the threshold as it slid open. The moment she crossed into the hangar, she aimed her weapon toward the ceiling and held its trigger down. Mirta's shotgun sang out and emptied its entire payload of micromissiles in three staccato bursts, resulting in a flurry of red-orange rocket trails that swept through the air on great intentional arcs like fireflies on meth. Then, almost simultaneously, the hail of explosive devices streaked in with sub-millimeter precision to detonate within their chosen zones; Decimating seven of the enemy combatants with her opening volley.

Eager to capitalize on her shock and awe entrance, Mirta pressed her attack before the bad-guys had time to figure out what had even just happened to them. Via the upper three of her weapon's barrels, a cloud of self-splitting beads was magnetically accelerated toward an armed guard who had been attempting to seek cover behind a forklift drone just over ten meters away. The deadly spray bit into the man's upper torso and forced him viciously into the steel casing of the drone's outer hull with enough force to finish any job that the pellets themselves hadn't already achieved. When Mirta attempted to line up for a second shot, leveled at a nearby gunman who sat lurking behind an upturned sorting table, she was forced to duck back into cover when a muzzle flash rose in her peripheral vision from somewhere deeper into the hangar's interior. Narrowly escaping the enemy's volley of incoming fire by hunkering behind a metal crate, she decided to shift her focus toward replenishing her weapon's payload of micromissiles. First keying a customized button on her stock, she then reached to her backpack's dispenser to retrieve the bundle of micromissiles that was already waiting for her. With a quick and recently practiced motion, she slid each munition into her shotgun's reception port and listened with satisfaction as the shotgun's internal mechanism whirred to life while readying the first missile to fire.

Mirta first used the interface on her tablet to target the position of the guard behind the table, then loosed a single micromissile into the air to finish the job she had attempted to start earlier. The familiar red-orange streak took flight with an unpredictable flutter, then homed in on its intended recipient with the equivalent of a predatory pounce. The explosive charge whizzed up and hit the man directly in the shoulder, instantaneously ending his occupation of the improvised fortification in a messy display of overkill that took large chunks of the table and concrete with it. Of the three enemies that remained, only one of them appeared to be armed while the other two hunkered together behind the cargo container they had been working on before the fighting started. The man carrying a pistol was slowly making his way toward Mirta's position, confident that he remained undetected as he crept from box to box. "I see you, Dipshit." taunted Mirta to her stalker as she watched the man stop dead in his tracks on her tablet, "And if you don't want a missile to find its way into your rectal cavity, I'd suggest you drop the pistol and join your buddies over by the blue freight container. Your choice, hotshot, but I'm kinda getting bored with killing you assholes."

Mirta watched on her tablet's video feed as the man coyly tucked his pistol into his waistband while shouting; "Okay! I give up! Don't shoot, alright?"

"I can *literally* see you, genius." she yelled with exasperation, "Like, I *watched* you tuck that pistol back into your pants. Let's try that again, smartguy, only this time you can't be trusted with *pants* either. So, toss the gun and drop em, cheeks in the wind, or **you're** gonna be the next shade of red on the floor, walls, and ceiling. You dig?"

Visibly shaken by her descriptive threat, the man made a show of tossing his gun away over a stack of unlabeled boxes. Then, after looking around for the secret vantage point of his tormentor, he reluctantly unbuckled his trousers and dropped them to the ground. With a loud snort of laughter rising from behind Mirta's box, she teased; "Aww, no wonder you were so reluctant to get rid of that pea-shooter of yours. You just needed its frame to fill out the front of your pants, you poor devil. Now stop trying to shield that toddler dick of yours from the world and run along to join your little friends. Oh, and if you try anything dumb, I will not hesitate one *nanosecond* before wasting a rocket to turn you inside-out. Now **GO!**"

Upon arriving to sub-level twenty-two, which also happened to be the very bottom of the stairwell, Dex put the intrusion software to work on the hardened blast door he found set into a reinforced frame in the wall. As Vette's trusty software did its work, a small chime sounded from Dex's tablet that signified the completion of a timer. With a few taps across his screen, followed by a furrowing of his brow, he activated his comm to say; "Mirta, it looks like the Hammer is making its decent, but I can't ping her. I think all the ruckus in the MALAS hangar may have damaged some of the facility's comm equipment. I had hoped that I would have generator three rigged to blow by now, but my little series of detours screwed us. I'm going to run my overload gimmick now, then blow generators one and two. That should at least give us a few mi-"

"Why the hell are you wasting time telling me?" boomed Mirta to cut him off, "Just hurry up and blow the damn thing before they get a shot off!"

"Relax." Retorted Dex with a sigh, waiting for a small thump to play itself out through the walls before continuing, "I started the overload process before even opening my comm. I was getting to that part, actually. With a single generator working to recharge the gun's capacitors, I'll have a few minutes before they have enough juice for an effective shot. Layout is a bit labyrinthian by design, but I've got a path mapped out for myself. Only problem, really, will be all the damn doors between me and the defense command center."

"Famous last words." remarked Mirta pointedly, "Just don't rush your way into a pyre box, okay? I'm going to send down a few drones for some fire support."

"Fire support?" asked Dex as the odd statement distracted him from his fixation on the intrusion program's progress ticker, "How do you mean? You planning to high-speed bonk some motherfuckers or what?"

Mirta just shrugged as she continued to pull items out of her backpack for assembly and said; "That would work too, I suppose. But I think you'll like my original plan a bit better. You see, modularity is *key*, my young grassjumper. That's why the same micromissiles I carry in my shotgun can be attached as payload for *these* lil' guys. Two of them, each, to be exact. So just keep on going and my drones will catch up."

With a shrug, Dex watched the forty-centimeter-thick door retract into the wall in a slow methodical crawl. His patient silence was suddenly broken, however, by gunfire that had erupted from within the expanding doorway. Tucking himself to the edge of the doorframe, all Dex could do was grit his teeth and hope someone decided to reload soon. After the barrage had gone on long enough to display the enemy's sustained fire discipline, offsetting their reloading as to not interrupt the incoming hail of deadly ferroplastic, he chose extend the flexible probe from his tablet and poke it around the corner into the maelstrom for a look.

The hallway beyond the door was long and straight, lined with thick concrete columns to either side at an interval of roughly six meters. Four separate pockets of at least three individuals each had all tucked themselves into defensive positions along the route to the T intersection that sat at the far end of the fortified corridor, and they were all covering the advance of a team of four who were sprinting up the left-hand side. As Dex was considering sealing the door and Vette-locking his problems away on the other side, he was forced to duck when an object snapped by overhead with nearly no sound associated to it other than the mighty woosh of the air it displaced.

The little command-driven drone zipped into the defended hallway, scanning the position and weaponry of each enemy combatant within the span of a quarter second before the device obliterated itself against the far wall. The self-destruction was intentional, however, and its passing was followed almost immediately by a cluster of orange streaks that came following it out of the stairwell. With each of the eight rockets already having been told where it needed to go by the brave automated soul that had preceded them, they peeled off from the group to strike their chosen targets as the salvo made its way down the hall. The micromissiles all detonated within a quarter-second of one another and their combined blast sent a wave of pressure barreling out the doorway into the stairwell, knocking Dex to the ground and sending his ears into a ringing fit. As soon as he could shake his head clear, a trio of drones was already flying past him into the hallway beyond to inspect the damage they had wrought. "Holy hell, Mirta." He growled into his radio with a pained cough against the dust in the air, "You coulda at least given me a heads up that the friggin' apocalypse was inbound."

"What part of the word *payload* did you fail to understand?" asked Mirta with an incredulous groan, "It got the job done, didn't it? Drones are reporting the hallway clear and I already have one of them working the intrusion software on the next doorway for you. You're on your own past that, though, because my control signal once I get down there is pretty sucky. Wouldn't do you much good, anyhow, seeing as we are out of rockets now. I'll try to keep an eye on your feed and help out as best as I can from here, but I need to get to work clearing out a space for the Hammer to set down."

By the time Dex was finally working Vette's intrusion software on the door of the command center, three minutes and thirty-one seconds had already elapsed since the generators had been blown. Knowing his time was running short, he ground his teeth and kept idly squeezing the grip of his pistol while each percentage point ticked away on his tablet's progress bar. Then, as the final door slid open to reveal the facility's defense control center, Dex was left facing a middle-aged man who bore a surprised expression under the telltale grey and red of his UFEN Lieutenant Commander's beret.

The mustachioed officer dropped the tablet he was holding and went for the pistol at his hip, all while Dex was still frozen at the sight of the gold and silver insignia that sat pinned and polished upon the man's breast. As the muzzle of the officer's pistol grazed the top edge of his holster, Dex was finally snapped out of his mental lockup by a cold splash of adrenaline. In a rush of fight or flight that overrode any lingering moral or duty-based quandaries, the intruder flattened himself to the left-hand side of the doorway before snapping his antique pistol to the ready. Dex was not the first to fire, however.

The Lieutenant Commander loosed a three round burst of ferroplastic darts from his standard issue sidearm half of a heartbeat before Dex managed to squeeze his own trigger. While Dex was mentally focused on determining the effect of his own shot, the officer's volley struck first. The leading round went wide to splash against the opposite wall of the hallway beyond the open door, but the following pair were not so poorly directed. The first of the two struck the upper right-hand corner of Dex's backpack, obliterating the engineered plastic of its exterior to shreds as the third and final round dug into his shoulder just above his right collar bone.

Through the searing pain from both his new bullet wound and the plastic shrapnel of his backpack that was now embedded into the side of his face, Dex watched as his own dispatched round struck home. The custom-made hunk of crude lead composite sailed across the gap at a much slower pace than his enemy's modern munition, but it still ended up exactly where he needed it to be. Dex's single bullet bit into the crisp line of buttons upon the front of the Officer's uniform, right below the man's sternum, then blossomed into a micro-engineered mandala of destructive energy within his chest cavity. Then, with an intermittent gurgle to his voice as he fell to a knee, the Lieutenant Commander bellowed his final order; "*Fire!*" before succumbing to a painful cough that sent him sagging all the way to the deck.

The lights in the room suddenly dimmed and a faint thump could be felt underfoot, sending an icy fist tightening around Dex's heart as the large readout at the front of the command center confirmed with a simple graphic that the shot had gone out. With a blind rage overcoming him, the intruder stormed through the doorway with his pistol readied in a pained one-handed grip. Two men sat at consoles in the center of the room while a third stood flanking the door to his left. Recognizing the lone combatant who was already on his feet as the greatest and most immediate threat to him, Dex ducked low and heaved his undamaged shoulder into the flanking man who was belatedly beginning to draw his own weapon. The guard then let out a pained grunt as he was lifted by the much larger intruder and slammed into a console on the far wall, sending his weapon clattering to the floor. After cracking the sturdy glass of the viewscreen with their bodies in a painful crash, the two men both went tumbling to the ground tangled in a desperate grapple. The guard wrenched on the pistol in the intruder's grip with all of his might and it popped free to tumble to the floor nearby. But as the guard scrambled for it, Dex seized the man's outstretched arm and twisted with a sudden jerk to bring his foe's body into line for an arm bar.

With an ever-tightening squeeze that forced him to arch his whole body as hard as he could against the natural direction of his opponent's arm, Dex eventually felt the sickening pop he'd been waiting for. As the man underneath him roared with pain, the outnumbered intruder realized with a start that the seated technicians had already risen to their feet and were drawing their weapons on him. Without much of an alternative, Dex tugged the man toward him in an adrenaline-driven heave then hugged the squirming guard close to his body as the others opened fire. The incoming pistol rounds peppered Dex's human shield several times before his own luck finally ran out, culminating in what felt like a kick in the hip by a professional footballer. Knowing he could not withstand the barrage much longer, he frantically curled himself behind the now-limp guard as he struggled to reacquire his pistol in the scramble. Just as a round struck his exposed right elbow, Dex gained purchase on the lost weapon with his left hand and fought through the sudden agony to swing its muzzle into line. Even through his pain-blurred vision, it was a simple matter of muscle memory for him to accurately fire the ensuing quartet of lead-composite projectiles into the twin blurs of black and beige that stood less than three meters away.

Dex hadn't seen where his rounds struck the enemy, he just knew that they had both suddenly stopped shooting and fell to the floor in a wheezy twitching heap. Without a moment to waste, the intruder forced himself to a knee so he could see the control surface of the damaged console. With the cold specter of panic beginning to creep up his spine, Dex fiddled through sub-menus within sub-menus trying to find a control that would disable the defense cannon or cancel its pre-programmed fire-mission. Then he, with as much his body language as through his voice, said; *"Fuck it"* and began to draw puck after explosive puck out of his backpack. He armed them as he hastily made his way around the room to place them in every important looking nook and cranny he could find.

After setting a total of sixteen of the highly destructive devices, Dex glanced at the shot timer and saw that the automated cannon would fire its next volley in thirty-four seconds. Grouping all of the placed explosives into the same virtual fuse and arming them for detonation in *thirty* seconds, Dex sent the command and surged out the doorway with all the haste his battered body could muster. At a high-speed hobble, he was able to round a corner and had just began to hear the whirring of the intersection's heavy bulkheads sliding closed behind him when a crash of thunder came rolling down the tight hallway. The deafening roar was accompanied by an overwhelming blast of heat and pressure that spilled out through the remaining gap in the closing doorway, sending Dex tumbling across the metal deckplate until his world went black.

Chapter 38

"Any transmissions from the surface yet?" asked Tano frantically to his disembodied co-pilot as he studied the satellite footage of an explosion at the base nearly a half-hour before, "It's been ages since we've heard from them."

"Additional long-range communications are not likely at this time, Sergeant." explained Vette patiently, "This is due to the fact that the facility's only onsite hardware for such a signal has evidently been damaged beyond repair. We will have no new information available until we are in our final approach and the facility comes within reach of our short-range transmitters."

With a frustrated sigh, the Sergeant leaned back and complained; "Can't this bucket go any faster? At this point, I don't think we need to follow the designated appro-" Suddenly, Tano's griping was cut short when the significant weight of his body was jarringly yanked up out of his seat and hard to his left as the Hammer descended in a high-G roll. "What the hell?!" boomed the portly man once the blood had all rushed back out of his head, "Are you trying to give me an aneurysm or what? That's not what I meant by faster, you scientifically engineered psychopath!"

"Apologies, Sergeant." Stated the A.I. simply as it corrected and resumed their course, "Our sensors had detected a spike in EM output at the facility below, which prompted me to initiate evasive maneuvers."

"Evasive maneuvers?" asked Tano as he sourly rubbed against the newly forming bruise where his restraint belt had been, "Like, you can dodge rail darts now? When were you planning on sharing *that* little nugget with the class?"

"To be perfectly candid, Sergeant Tano," She admitted in a slightly reluctant tone, "we shouldn't have been able to dodge a round fired from that model of defense cannon from this close in the first place, or any *other* distance within its effective range for that matter. Which must mean that the dart fired at *us* was not utilizing the emplacement's full power potential."

"So, don't count on that working twice." said the Sergeant with an understanding nod as he winced beneath the grip of his restraint, "Gotchya. Alright, how long do we have before they shoot at us again? Do I need to find an escape pod or something?"

Vette's reply was immediate and came with a confident disconnection that could only be donned by an artificial soul; "You need not worry, Sergeant. If they manage to fire again, your death would certainly be instant and painless. Utilizing an escape cylinder at this atmospheric density, however, is ill-advised and would likely result in a very traumatic, fatal, journey into the surface of the moon. Touchdown in thirty-one seconds."

Wondering why her assurance had somehow made him feel better, Tano just gripped the arms of his chair and muttered a silent curse-ridden prayer as licks of de-orbiting flame began to dance across the front viewscreen. The Hammer's approach took a forty-five-degree angle from orbit toward a spot around five kilometers away from the facility, then abruptly flattened out to follow the terrain at a tight altitude of one-hundred meters. The hardest part of the whole process for the old Sergeant wasn't the uncertainty of whether or not the cannon would fire and apparently kill him instantly, but fighting his urge to take the sticks from his ship's artificial pilot as wind-swept dunes flashed by below.

"Handshake with Mirta's tablet has been established." Reported the A.I. out of the tense silence, "Request for landing has been confirmed and we are inbound for hangar number two. You may want to inform the ground team that now is the time to prepare for departure."

Chapter 39

Scent was the first thing to return to him from the void; An acrid, sterile, stench of iodine and medical gel that seemed to coat his nostrils in the terrible odor more and more with every breath he drew. Then, as his body stirred in protest to the newfound torture, Dex discovered another sensation; Pain. The sizzling-hot electric fire of nerve regrowth serum leapt from his entire right side, radiating mainly from an otherwise numbly pulsing hip and a stiff, tightly wrapped, shoulder. He must have made a face or sound without realizing it, because he was surprised and descended into a bit of a hazy panic when he began to hear a frantic patter of footsteps approaching.

"You're finally awake!" came an excited female voice that some corner of Dex's brain was telling him sounded familiar. As her shadow loomed overhead to block out the light, he forced his eyes open in an attempt to see her face. With a bit of alarm, Dex realized that only his left lid had complied while the other remained shrouded in darkness. "Hey, Vette," the voice continued, "he's ready to get up now. Let's hit him with a bit of that wake-up juice, please."

Suddenly, Dex felt a rush of warmth radiate up his left arm that quickly spread through his chest to engulf his entire body. As the flooding heat reached his neck and entered his skull, the haze around his monoscope vision melted away like frost off a windshield to leave Mirta standing over him with a worried expression plastered across her face. "H-...How long was I out?" he stuttered through a flare of sharp pain from his left side that was starting to come back into focus along with his vision.

"It has been three days, six hours, and twenty-two minutes since you were deposited into the Hammer's emergency medical support pod, Commander." Replied the ever-soothing yet not-quite-so empathetic voice of his stolen A.I., "I regret to inform you that your body has sustained significant damage during the operation and has required extensive repair while you were safely within a medically induced coma."

"It felt like you might say that." He grunted as he attempted to experimentally shift his weight in the cool green gel of the medical bed, "What kinda damage are we talkin' here, doc? Fender bender or full rebuild?"

Dex then detected the hint of a digital sigh before Vette began to list the extent of his injuries; "You sustained a fractured pelvis with accompanying nerve damage, two cracked ribs, a concussion with supplementary brain bleed, two burst eardrums, I was required to print you a completely new right clavicle, and I had to grow over fifty meters of biofiber to replace your shredded right trapezius. I am still in the process of conditioning your newly anchored muscle group and will have a replacement right eye to implant by tomorrow."

"Can you toss the eye and fab me up a bitchin' eye*patch* instead?" asked Dex hopefully, "Something in leather that already looks like it's already been worn down by the hot Australian sun for years... You know? Something *dusty* and apocalyptic..."

"What?" spat Mirta incredulously, "No, you idiot, you don't get to leave yourself crippled for the sake of a fashion accessory. What the hell is wrong with you?"

"It is a well-known fact that eyepatches are cool as *shit*." Argued Dex with an accusatory finger, "And anyone who gets to wear one automatically gets, like, forty percent more unfuckwithable. Lateral move at the *very* least."

Mirta slapped a palm to her face and groaned; "You can have two good eyes and still wear an eyepatch if you want, Dex. It *is* a free galaxy, you know…"

"*Is it though?*" challenged the injured in a suddenly humorless tone, "I've been off of my feet for too long. I need you to get me up to speed with what's been going down since I've been napping. Did we get our new cannon loaded up and moved to Meclan?"

"Yep." confirmed Mirta with a nod, "Had Vette use the admin login that Tano created for himself to cook up a phony work order requesting a new *'communications array'* be installed ASAP. Gun went up yesterday underneath the protective outer shell that Vette constructed for us and our people on-site have been running their printers around the clock ever since to crank out ammunition for it."

"How did our extraction go?" he asked as he tried to sit up straighter, "Did we lose anyone when we stormed the facility?"

Mirta shook her head, saying; "No losses. Resistance was pretty light because of the lockdown, so our people only exchanged fire once on their initial push into the courtyard to start unhooking the cannon. Carted a few warheads from the Hammer's racks down to the lab and set them on proxy-lock to blow. After sending through some drones to document everything we could inside the lab within the thirty-minute window we gave ourselves, we watched that god-forsaken place sink into the dirt on our way out. We *had* three prisoners boxed up on the Hammer and ready to interrogate, but Vette is saying they were outfitted with some sort of biological failsafe, surgically implanted into their brain stems, that prompted their tickers to stop beating once we jumped out of transmission range of the facility."

"That's pretty slick." Remarked Dex with what looked like an impressed nod, "*Too* slick for some knuckle-dragging pirate outfit to think of doing. I don't like it."

"Be that as it may," acknowledged Mirta with a simple shrug as she stepped forward to sit on the edge of the bed, "We *do* now know for sure that the facility itself was one-hundred-percent tied to and run by Vendrick's people."

Dex eyed her with a cautionary look, then inquired; "What makes us so sure? Have we gathered physical evidence?"

"We have." She remarked with a nod of certainty, "And as it turns out, Mike *doesn't* have some weird porn addiction." When she saw Dex's disgusted confusion rising across his face, she was quick to throw up her hands to explain; "What I mean is that when he was helping get the infected survivors settled into their quarantine, he recognized one of them from an old case that the young woman's grandmother had paid him to take on. The girl went missing over a decade ago and Mike's best lead put her on Yakima station about eight hours before it was attacked by Vendrick when he first arrived in Saiph."

Dex furrowed his brow with frustrated realization as he fumed; "So Bengal wasn't the first time he took prisoners en masse?!"

"He's *always* been taking us *en masse*." Seethed Mirta as she punched the gel of the medical bed, "After debriefing those poor folks, we've learned a lot about what's been going on around Saiph as a whole. They never, or rather *didn't always*, actually space everyone they dragged off to the airlock over the years. Instead, they brought them to that god-forsaken lab where the unfortunate souls were then systematically poisoned and observed until they died."

Dex sat a little straighter in bed and subtly bowed his head before somberly replying; "My god…*so* many people. To what end, damnit? And why are the women we found still alive and well if Vendrick was running such an efficient kill-factory down there? What makes *them* so special?"

"I believe I can answer that one, Commander." Interjected Vette a little too cheerily, "The women we recovered were from what I believe to be an immunity control group. After analyzing their blood and tissue samples, I have discovered a resistance to the main biological component of the weapon in both surviving women. One of them, the young woman who has confirmed that she was taken from Yakima station, possesses what appears to be a natural immunity to the pathogen. The other woman, whom has not been verbally responsive since her rescue, appears to have an artificially induced resistance to the weapon. It is my working theory that the women were exposed to iteration after iteration of the biological agent while the site's virologists worked to hone an inoculation to the weapon."

Dex pinched the bridge of his nose and rubbed it with swelling frustration as he grumbled; "So, it's pretty obvious at this point that everything Vendrick is doing out here is for the sake of making the sick-juice. Before I even have the mental bandwidth to *contemplate* what a pirate like Vendrick would do with *years'* worth of biological weapons research, we need to think about the aspect of the issue that we can actually respond to. What did we learn, exactly, about the weapon, and how does it work?"

"The results are troubling, Commander." Offered Vette somberly, "The main reason the engineered agent you discovered is so very effective is the multifaceted nature of its attack mechanism. From the data you collected on-site, paired with the blood samples taken from the deceased infected woman, I have cultivated a list of the biological threat's detectable symptoms. These indicators include hair loss, boils, muscular spasms, paralyzing seizures, and severe coagulopathy that eventually culminates into blood flow from the body's orifices. In addition to the biological element of the agent, there is also a radiological component to the delivery device."

"Radiological component?" asked Dex with sudden piqued concern, "What kind of radiological component?"

"Traces of a polonium nanocomposite were found within the blood stream of all cataloged victims." Explained the AI, "While the composite form of the isotope is less immediately lethal than its pure cousin, I believe it is intended to act as a dampening factor on the body's immune response to the introduced pathogen."

"How in the hell would they make something like that way out here in the sticks?" retorted Dex with the cold grip of fear filling his gut, "Doesn't an operation like that require massive backend support and robust supply lines? And why would someone like Vendrick be cooking it in the first place?"

"The *why*, I cannot determine, Commander," she replied apologetically, "but I believe I can shed light onto *how* it was done. I have compared samples of Meclan corn recovered from the facility's warehouse to samples of the contagion and have found common RNA markers that suggest the former was used to produce the latter. Furthermore, other supplies required for production of the bioweapon were also being delivered to the facility in the form of uraninite from the Verdigan mining outpost and trigger proteins from Matsuoka's pharmaceutical facilities."

"So, my home system has been a secret goddamn *weapon's factory* for the last ten years?!" spat Mirta with renewed outrage, "*How* many people, over the brutal course of that horrible decade, have died as sacrifice to this fucking science experiment? And more importantly, who gave Vendrick the money to do it in the first place?"

Dex nodded with equal agitation and added; "You might be onto something there, Mirta. This whole thing stinks of large entity involvement. First off, you have the theatrics of a false power structure. This comes in the form of the street trash that he's tatted up and set loose on the poor folks of Saiph. They keep everyone nice and distracted while Vendrick's *real* jackboots do the dirty work in the background. Then you have this whole business with *someone* going to the trouble of not only cutting off the system from Hūnet, but setting up a sophisticated backup relay pointed off to god knows where. It all seems very top-down calculated, you know? Super game-theorized and over-analyzed by gold-leaves and silver stars sorta plan. A very precise and calculated machine that is designed to produce a product with maximum possible concealment. Well, I think it's time we crush that production line and beat its designers to death with the scraps...And it all starts with Meclan."

As they all sat gathered around Hearth's grand conference table, the members of the fledgling resistance all studied an image of Meclan station. As its orange holo-representation sat suspended above the tabletop, slowly spinning in its familiar counter-rotating dance for gravity, a new lump was shown in blue adorning the inner crest of ring number one. "This is our secret weapon that will buy the freedom of Meclan and hopefully the rest of Saiph." Said Dex as he pointed to the now-blossoming petals of the blue addition, "This cannon, paired with the element of surprise, will be what we need to take out Vendrick and the capital ship he's used to murder over fifty-thousand people. Until now, that asshole has been out here like a kid with a goddamn magnifying glass, burning ants with impunity, and it's time for that little shit to have a run-in with the stinging variety."

When looks of confusion began to play across the faces of those around the table, instead of the expressions of inspired resolve Dex had been shooting for, Mirta sighed and began to explain for him; "It's kinda like killing grademites with a coolant canister. Analogies, Dex...Come on, man."

"Fine." Sighed the frustrated terrasider, "*Analogies aside,* we need to draw Vendrick's ship in, but we have to do so while Meclan is in a state to receive him. What I mean by that is we need to ensure that we have full control over Meclan's entire subsystem hierarchy before the wonderful Governor comes a-knockin'. This is because he has a nasty habit, it seems, for venting stations he disagrees with. And it can be assumed that he has some wireless option for achieving this due to the fact that one of those tattooed freak-jobs is not very likely to willingly sacrifice themselves for the sake of their pay-me-in-drugs sorta setup they've got going. So, to prevent his intrusion into the station's systems, our attack will have to be dual pronged. While the Hammer is dropping off our guys in the docks to make a whole hell of a lot of noise and draw all the baddies out into the fight, Mirta and I are going to already be on-site and ready to infiltrate Meclan's Operations Control Center to get Vette plugged in and running defense. From there, hopefully Vendrick catches wind of our takeover and jumps in to do his thing. Then, we can pin him down with Scalpel and Becker's folks, if he'll even agree to meet with Tano after the whole Bengal incident, for long enough to score some major hits with Meclan's new gun and maybe take Vendrick out before he runs away."

That was when one of the men on the docking drum assault team raised his hand to speak; "Apologies, sir, but there's only eight of us and about *eighty* of them on the ground in the docks, give or take. I understand that our combat armor will give us an edge, but I fail to see how that edge translates into victory over an enemy with a ten-to-one advantage in numbers."

"That's why we're going to *manufacture* you an advantage in numbers." Offered Mirta with a sly grin, "We will do this through the use of some drones that Vette and I have been developing that utilize photoreactive smokescreens to project phantom combatants onto the battlefield. These avatars will be controlled individually by Vette and can be tactically coordinated with on the fly via a software HUD package that we cooked up to go along with the system. The limitations of the technology include an inability to leave the occluding smoke, a maximum of four projected phantoms per drone, and a bit of an uncanny valley effect if an observer is too close to either the projector or one of the projections."

"And in addition to that," added Dex with a raised finger, "will be the fact that *you* will be able to communicate while *they* cannot. On that note, Vette, could you please queue up track number three on my *Rumbly bits* playlist to start pumping through the station's PA as the Hammer makes its entrance? *That* should do the trick."

As Mirta watched the newly added note appear on the meetings minutes that were displayed on the conference room's far wall, she tilted her head in confusion and asked; "What in the living hell is a *Bangarang*?"

Chapter 40

"Is it a Federal holiday today, or what?" lamented Zentril Feiadlo to his underling, Jeff, while both men sat alone in one of the docking drum's unusually empty cafés. Normally one flash of their ink was all it took to get the pathetic creatures working the joint to scurry at his whim, but the old man who ran the place had actually been so bold as to make *eye contact* with him through the glass porthole of the kitchen's bulkhead door as he locked it in his tattooed face.

"We could always borrow the drill from Bennie." Suggested Jeff hopefully, the colors across his face shifting from a cool blue to a muted purple, "Then we could get at that old bastard in time for him to make us lunch before we kill his stupid ass."

"You sure you know how to use that damn thing?" asked Zentril skeptically, "Because the last time you *borrowed* some shit you didn't know fuck-all about, we all almost died in a decom blast you dipshit."

"This will be nothing like last time, Zen," assured the suddenly anxious subordinate, "We're nowhere near an airlock an-" Suddenly, what sounded like a simple repeating guitar riff began flowing at max volume from every speaker in the area. Then the simple melody was joined by a repeating thump that came from above with enough bass to rattle one's chest cavity as a loud voice, unintelligible and seemingly glitchy, joined the swelling accompaniment. *'What the fuck'* mouthed the senior of the two gangsters beneath the auditory onslaught as a loud series of pops outside cut through the noise. Alarmed, both men shot to their feet and ran out of the dockside café to see a large trapezoidal freighter, black as space, coming through the rotating slot of the Dock's entrance airshield trailing a massive wave of thick grey smoke behind it. As the ashen billows rolled across the volume of the drum like an angry stormfront, swirling ominously in the dock's internal air currents, both men felt a primal dread setting in like a cement block at the pit of their stomachs. Rushing back to the table, both thugs retrieved their rifles and reluctantly shambled toward the smoke.

As they reached the docking platform, Zentril saw a knot of friendlies, about two-hundred meters down-spin, beginning to form over near a collection of cargo pods that sat strewn across an unused landing pad. As one of the gathering men noticed the pair of newcomers, he began to gesture them over frantically to join the throng of glowing faces who were all looking to their leader for guidance. Standing on a box at the center of the knot of gangsters was Rollo, the largest and meanest of the terrasiders on Meclan, and he seemed to be yelling at everyone about being sure to leave some survivors for him to play with. As Rollo's sermon was reaching its crescendo, the approaching grey cloud was almost upon them. Then, as the edges of the angry stormfront began to envelope the crowd, a tiny trail orange flame came zipping out of the fog to swirl in an intricate loop that terminated at the enthusiastic speaker's chest. After winking out momentarily when the guided round dug into the man's torso, the orange glow suddenly returned as a bright detonation that tore its victim asunder. After a heartbeat's worth of silent shock, the smoke slowly rolled in to swallow the landing pad as it burst into panic and chaos. The pirates opened fire on the fog, spraying wildly in every direction as if it would hold the oncoming tendrils of mist at bay. In response, a collection of muzzle flashes lashed out from seemingly all angles, High and low, to silence the report of the thug's weapons.

The fierce ambush lasted a matter of seconds, producing a rush of gunfire and the haunting sound of screams cut short, before the dock fell back into the relative calm of the numbing bassline. As he began to hyperventilate with his wide eyes glued on the approaching fog, Zentril started to see what appeared to be shadowy figures that were darting impossibly fast from cover to cover as the smoke advanced on them. With terror, Jeff lowered his rifle and unconsciously began to backpedal as he squealed; "Shit, man, it's the Feds or somethin'! We gotta get outta he-"

Zentril's loyal underling never finished his sentence, however, on account of his skull spontaneously blossoming into an expanding teardrop of blood, bone, and brain matter. As the tattooed gangster watched the body of his oldest friend fall limp to the deckplate, a shudder of fear ran through his spine that threatened to glue him in place. In an automatic reflex of self-preservation, the man ducked low and ran for cover behind a nearby one-by-one-meter cargo box while the choking grey stormfront rolled in and threatened to swallow him. Gripping his rifle with all of his terrified might, as if the universe itself were aiming to tear it from his hands, the man burst from his cover and made a mad low dash for the small stack of cargo he saw sitting on the next pad over.

As the thug bobbed and weaved across the open deck of the landing platform, the smoke slowly began to catch up to him. When the mist was finally nipping at his heels, he began to see shapes moving impossibly fast through his periphery in unnatural flips and bounds as their glowing red eyes tracked his progress. With a deeper terror now fueling his legs, the tattooed man abandoned his weave and began sprinting a straight course away from the oncoming artificial stormfront. Reaching the stack of boxes he had set out for, the hyperventilating man rounded their edge and turned to set his rifle on top before opening fire at nothing in particular. As his wild firing continued to stab at the fog in random sweeps, the tattooed man suddenly felt a spray of searing hot metal coat the side of his face when the box next to him burst apart and tumbled *toward* the fog.

Realizing quickly that the shot had come from behind, the thug spun to find a group of armed residents moving in on him from the other end of the docking drum. Leading the charge at the center, carting an outdated assault rifle with a cruel smile, was the owner of the dockside café who continued to fire his weapon with ill-skilled deadly intent at his former tormentor. As an incoming round bit into the heel of the thug's boot, he decided that facing the oncoming fog was his only option if he wanted to stay alive. With a gulp of air that he unconsciously held, he vaulted the damaged box and ran into the smoke with his rifle at the ready. Finding a nearby cargo drone that looked sturdy enough, the man rushed over and huddled himself behind its low bulk. With his heartbeat pounding in his ear, he scanned the occluded landing pad around him. As his vision swept past a nearby transport pod, he saw a figure moving at blinding speed that leaped and disappeared into the fog above.

Trying to track the entity with the muzzle of his rifle, the thug caught sight of it again leaping between tall stacks of cargo off to his left. The moment he managed to get the dark shape in his rifle sights, the tattooed man pulled his trigger and sent a long burst toward his unseen enemy. From what he could tell the shots should have landed, but the figure continued to move across the landing pad unfazed. With frustration, the thug waited until the shape returned to ground level and then he charged it with his shoulder down and his jaw clenched. Timing it perfectly for when his acrobatic enemy would be passing through a gap in some boxes, the man surged forward and plowed right into the figure...only to pass right through his foe and come crashing head-first into a fuel drum. Concussed and incredibly woozy, the man looked up from his haze to find a figure hovering over him. It was somehow more solid than before, calmly swaying as it stood there breathing heavily from exertion. Then, when the tattooed man cocked his head to speak, a belch of emerald flame rose from somewhere in front of him and his universe went blank.

When the overwhelming blast of the bumping music within the docking drum began to vibrate the structure of the station itself in a rhythmic thump, Dex and Mirta watched with malevolent delight as Vendrick's men started to pour out of the heavily protected primary control center on Meclan's central ring. They all seemed to be armed and were making a beeline for the elevator banks on a mission to head down to the docking drum to join in on the developing firefight. Once a majority of the on-site security had vacated the blast-hardened tower of concrete and glass, Dex began his descent from their perch upon the catwalk that ran along the central spine of the ring's ceiling. Using a bit of nanofiber line and a high-powered winch unit built into the waist of his newly painted red and black combat armor, Dex leapt from the catwalk and allowed the device to automatically slow his fall to a stop above the roadway.

With Mirta and her trusty Lancaster JL-97 on overwatch, Dex moved low from cover to cover behind unpowered transport pods and piles of junk as he continued up the deserted street toward the front entrance of the imposing structure. His advance was quickly noticed, however, and muzzle flashes began to illuminate several of the building's upper windows in rapid pops of blue-white. When the incoming rounds started to pepper the roadway, Dex lunged left and right in an artificially augmented serpentine as he dashed across wide swaths of open street toward his target. Little red tags automatically began to populate across the overlay in his faceplate, signifying enemy positions within the control center's windows, then disappeared almost as quickly with each thundering report from Mirta's rifle above.

The devastating effect of the unseen marksman was quick to drive Vendrick's men further into the structure for refuge, but they were quick to return as they poured out onto the street from the fortified building's main entrance. Dex opened fire on the handful of gunmen who were dashing for cover from the doorway and had managed to drop one then wing another before return fire began pouring in, forcing him to duck back behind the sturdy taxi pod he had chosen for cover. When the boom of Mirta's rifle rang out again, the sound of enemy rifles ceased almost immediately as they all ducked with terror that the distant specter of death had chosen *them* this time. Using the momentary silence, Dex vaulted over his protective taxi with the augmented strength of his armor and began sprinting as hard as he could for a stack of cargo boxes he had seen a pair of thugs hunker behind.

One of the tattooed men had mustered the courage to peek his head over their cover to investigate the source of the rapidly approaching thudding sounds, only to be met with the mirrored faceplate of an armored juggernaut in the midst of its final mighty stride before plowing into the stack of metal containers with the force of a charging bull. Crates went flying in every direction, toppling both men behind them to the ground amidst a torrent of batteries and ammunition that came spilling out. Dex was quick to regain his balance after the impact and was equally efficient at sweeping his assault rifle on full-auto across the dazed forms that lay at his feet.

The dispatched duo's colleagues were quick to respond to the armored attacker's aggression, using grenades in an effort to flush him out into the open. The electronically assisted hearing within Dex's helmet noted the distinct hum-whirr of several hand-tossed explosives being activated, giving him a precious handful of seconds to retreat into cover behind a nearby transport pod before the ensuing blast shook the roadway. As dust hung in the air, a pair of small trails materialized within the haze that were accompanied by the twin report of Mirta's Lancaster. Taking her covering fire as yet another opportunity to advance, Dex pushed forward with his assault rifle shouldered. When he burst forth from the smoke, he instantly spotted a gunman who had all his attention focused on his scope as he swept the ceiling for the unseen enemy sniper. By the time the man had registered the sound of Dex's approaching footfalls, a trio of burst-fire rounds were already making their way through his chest cavity.

As the armored attacker reached the cover of his newest dispatched foe, another man burst up from behind it and attempted to run for the safety of the building's entrance. Dex was quicker, however, and managed to seize the thug by the back of his neck in an augmented iron grip and lift him from the ground. Turning the man to face his own reflection within the soulless glare of an armored faceplate, Dex balled his hand into a tight fist and surged it forward with all of his might into the man's sternum shouting; "Kali-*fucking*-Ma!" accentuating each word with a new crushing blow to the man's increasingly concave chest. With his path finally unimpeded, Dex was able to cover the final remaining ground to the front entrance of the control center within a matter of seconds.

Finding the inner set of doors unlocked, Dex Rushed into the control center's lobby with his assault rifle at the ready. Instantly identifying a man who was attempting to hunker behind the reception desk, he swung his rifle into line and directed a pair of three-round-bursts in the defender's direction. His ferroplastic rounds bit straight through the carbon composite of the desk like butter, sinking themselves into the tattooed man with a wet thud that sent him to the ground and out of sight. Without stopping to check on his foe, Dex surged forward toward the bank of elevators at the far end of the lobby. As he was reaching to press the call button, however, the pair of doors directly in front of him began to part on their own to reveal the barrel chest of a massive man flanked by a pair of armed comrades to either side.

After thrusting his rifle between the expanding gap of the doors, Dex's shots were wrenched into the ceiling as the large man grabbed his muzzle and thrust it upward. Releasing his grip from the weapon's trigger assembly, Dex darted his hand to his thigh and withdrew his pistol in a flash. Whipping the ancient firearm out of its holster, he squeezed off two rounds from the hip that tore into the hulking man's gut. Dex then proceeded to wrench his rifle out of the pain-shocked man's grip to slam its butt against the temple of the gangster to the right who was already in the middle of drawing his pistol on the intruder. As the rifle struck the man with a devastating and supremely effective crunch across his jaw, player number three decided to enter the game with a series of hastily aimed pistol rounds that splashed across the articulating slats of Dex's abdominal armoring. With a wince of pain as the ferroplastic darts impacted against the ballistic composite fabric over his ribs, Dex ducked low to avoid the man's follow-up shot and braced his foot against the doorjamb of the elevator as he lunged at his enemy with technologically amplified ferocity. Connecting first with his armored shoulder, Dex heard a pained wheeze and felt a crackling pop as the third gunman released every atom of oxygen from his lungs upon being slammed into the elevator's back wall. Then, as the battered form of the third and final man slithered limply to the floor, the elevator doors slid closed amid the wild flash of Dex's assault rifle.

Upon reaching the top floor that was represented on the elevator's neat row of buttons, labeled *control room*, Dex stepped out amid an auditorium of display screens with a single man who was distractedly scurrying around between them. When the tattooed face of that man swung in the newcomer's direction, he instantly registered an expression of fear and panic as his hand shot to his holster. With a shaky grip, the control center's lone operator loosed an entire magazine from his pistol at the armored intruder, managing to strike his attacker only twice as the seemingly invulnerable demon continued its approach unfazed. Dex shrugged off the shots, re-mounting his assault rifle to the magnetic ring on his back as he confidently strode forward with a cool rage. The tattooed man threw his hands up as the faceless invader approached, pleading; "C'mon man. You got me, alright? I'm not-" Interrupting the man's panic-stricken rambling, the control tower operator was seized by the throat and lifted from his feet in a crushing grip.

As the man kicked and struggled against the mechanical grasp of his gauntlets, Dex scanned the room for the least important looking workstation he could find. Identifying one that seemed innocuous enough, with the words *PA System* lit up above its main interface, he stepped in front of it and proceeded to drive the man's head through the glass of its control surface in three mighty, fatal, heaves. "Control center is ours, Vette." Reported Dex calmly over the comm as his final adversary fell lifelessly to the deck, "Plugging in now... I'm ready when you are."

"Transfer complete." responded Vette via the room's built-in speakers, "The station and all of her subsystems are now fully under *my* direction. While a few injuries have been reported, I am pleased to report that combat operations within the docking drum have come to a close without a single friendly casualty. Vendrick's forces are splintered and many are surrendering to the local militia across all decks. Congratulations, Commander. Meclan is yours."

Dex shook his head with a weary sigh as he watched the swelling celebration in the docks unfolding on a nearby display screen, saying; "No, Vette. Meclan belongs to her *people* again. And *now* we get to embark on the much *more* difficult task of helping them *keep* it that way."

Chapter 41

The fabric of space boiled and spat and sparked with exotic energy as it was torn asunder along a rippling gash of heat, light, and Inaki radiation at a point just under ninety kilometers from Meclan station. Then, through the chaotic wound in spacetime, slipped the massive void-black hull of Vendrick's bulbous flagship. After waiting a handful of seconds for the local disturbance from their inbound jump to clear, the kilometer-long starship reached out to Meclan with a tight-beam communications array. Shortly after that initial contact, Vette's voice poured from the speakers of the Hammer to report; "The enemy ship has just attempted to vent all atmosphere on rings one two and three, but promptly withdrew their active connection when they realized that Meclan's systems were not responding."

"Were you able to get any bits of yourself upstream and onboard before they pulled the plug?" asked Dex hopefully as he eyed the gargantuan blot of nothingness centered in his viewscreen's magnified image.

"Connection was withdrawn too quickly for me to transfer any subroutines, Commander," Replied the A.I. regretfully, "but I *was* able to extract a basic system information report for the enemy ship. This should provide excellent data for my upcoming targeting solutions and allow me to more accurately bracket the critical areas we wish to disable. Targeting forward rail assembly now, Commander, and the cannon is primed for delivery of three rounds on your order. Please keep in mind, however, that each follow-up volley will subsequently require a one-minute thirty-nine second recharge cycle."

"As soon as you have a good shot on that railgun turret, Vette, you take it." Ordered Dex as he stabbed a finger toward his bridge's thruminum viewport. He then watched with a catch in his breath as the behemoth in the dark slowly began to yaw toward the station, its forty-meter-long railgun lowering into firing position from a divot set along the belly of the capital ship's impossibly black hull. Then, before Dex could verbally urge her to do so, Vette popped the disposable shell of Meclan's newly acquired defense cannon and let loose with a rapid triple burst of angry purple from its auto-tracking muzzle. The three-hundred-gram projectiles reached across the relatively short gap and slammed one after another into their target. The first round was mainly absorbed and deflected by the ship's robust plasma shielding, but round two was able to reach through the weakened envelope of protective energy to dig into the hull and destroy a trio of plasma projectors. With no shielding left to contend with in the area, round three ripped all the way into the bow's armor plating and obliterated the articulating gimbal mount that held the station-killing railgun in place. Then, with a magnificent secondary detonation from within the gun assembly's cooling system, the main body of the weapon went tumbling into space amid a hail of sparks and dying flame.

With a yelp of celebration, Dex keyed his comm to cheer; "That's a hit! We have *damn* good effect on target! The tiger's teeth have been pulled, Scalpel, and you are free to make your attack run. I want you hitting plasma relays and point defense along the rear of the hull as hard as you can. Go! Go!

Go!" His order was acknowledged by flashes of green confirmation lights across his control board, then Dex watched the twelve fighters of Scalpel squadron detach, one by one, from their hidden perches among the outer rings of the station to descend upon the enemy.

The Eagles screamed out to meet their target with liberal use of their chemical boosters, then fought to remain conscious as their crafts flipped and burned to decelerate into a practiced frenzy of orbits around the enemy ship. As they settled into their chaotic loops, each pilot of the squadron proceeded to individually jink and juke their craft through enemy's point defense fire in a decoupled and erratic tumble around the massive capital ship. Using their newly plundered and repurposed plasma repeaters, Scalpel worked as a group to whittle down four chosen strike points around the hull hopping from target to target in a constant barrage that managed to outpace the shield's plasma regeneration rate. After a dozen orbits beneath the calculated onslaught, the first of these targets, a point defense turret positioned near the ship's portside engine housing, burst into a violent blowtorch of green and blue. The flame that leapt forth disrupted the shield in the area and tore away armored plating around it in flecks of superheated composite until a secondary explosion from within ripped a three-meter-wide chunk of the outer hull away.

In response to the sudden catastrophic damage, the capital ship opened a compartment along its belly and released a cloud that looked like a plague of locusts as they spilled over the void-black hull toward the orbiting threat. The swarm of unshielded little flux drive devices had their attackers outnumbered a thousand to one and their kamikaze strategy quickly proved too effective for Scalpel to handle, consuming three of their pilots within the first fifteen seconds of their engagement. The squadron of Eagles was quick to break away from its collective orbit of the enemy capital ship, maneuvering into a burn together on an intercept course with Meclan. As Scalpel approached the station and their pursuers came into range, the Hammer opened up on the swarm with its impressive array of forward-facing weaponry from the comfort of its perch above the entrance to the docking bay. The swarm reacted instantly to the new threat, spreading out to avoid clump-targeting and moving into a three-dimensional pincer maneuver aimed at the besieged station.

With a sudden panic, Dex realized that the enemy swarm was moving not toward himself or the fleeing members of Scalpel, but for Meclan's newly installed defense turret. "All ships, protect that cannon!" he bellowed into the comm, "Arm EMP missiles and set them for proxy-burst to maximize your effective splash damage across the swarm, then I need you to get them off the racks and downrange as quickly as possible."

"There are too many of them!" shouted one of Scalpels pilots, "I can't break away enough to get a good lock and my shields can't take another hit! They are closing in and I am bingo on booster juice."

"Hold on, Three!" urged Dex as he wrenched on his control sticks, "I'm moving the Hammer into blocking position! Get behind me!" Disengaging the ship from its magnetic grip on the station, he lurched the war-freighter into motion with grim determination. Burping his ascent boosters just right, Dex was able to swing the Hammer up into position between the retreating Eagles and the automated swarm that pursued them. Then, in another display of delicate timing, Vette allowed the first wave of self-detonating drones to get within ten meters of the Hammer's hull plating before discharging the upper shield capacitors in a massive directional EM burst that scrambled a large swath of the remote devices, disarming their detonation mechanisms before momentum carried the majority of them slamming into the Hammer's unshielded hull. After enduring a rumble that chattered teeth and sent countless items throughout the bridge tumbling to the floor, the Hammer began to yaw of its own accord to port as thrusters along its starboard side started to fail. "Vette, damage report!" shouted Dex as he tried to make sense of the data flowing across his screen for himself, "How bad did they get us?"

"Plasma relays in zones three through five are damaged and containment is at twenty-nine percent, Commander." Replied Vette as if she were delivering the weather, "Fire suppression systems are at work in the engineering compartment and I have been required to shut reactor number two down for repair."

Dex winced at news of the damage, then pursed his lips to ask; "Do we at least have any weapons still online?"

"Negative, Commander." Reported Vette with what sounded like a disappointed sigh, "Weapon system coolant loop has been compromised. Maintenance diagnostic is underway now."

As Dex was frantically going through a list looking for something he *did* have left, his heart sank with each red *inactive* flag he ran across. Missiles *Hatch Obstructed* Railgun *Power-feed failure* Plasma repeaters *Coolant system compromised* Tractor array *Guidance loss* Smokescreen *Depleted* Flares *Ready* Dex threw his head back and sighed in frustration, asking "I don't suppose you can think of a way for me to kill a few hundred drones with a handful of flares?"

"Negative, Commander." Replied the A.I. with disappointment, "I may be able to bring a single plasma repeater online, but your rate of fire would depend heavily on the effectiveness of any repairs I am able to conjure up. Enemy drones will make impact in twenty-seven seconds."

Then, as Dex was about to unleash a creative string of expletives, a sudden flicker of pseudomotion rose in the space between the station and Vendrick's capital ship that quickly burst into a flash of dazzling color, dissolving into a tight bundle of six large ships that sat floating motionless in the void. After three seconds had ticked away, the heavily armored freighters burst apart in a practiced array and started to burn hard for Meclan. Before Dex could target the incoming ships and attempt to force a launch of his obstructed missile batteries in a newfound panic, he heard the voice of Sergeant Michael Tano playing out over his bridge's speakers; "Sorry I'm late. Since Becker was giving us the cold shoulder, I figured I'd invite my new friends from Baylor Company to the party instead. We are on-site and guns hot, mister Sloan. Captain Ingram has the helm and his fleet is at your command."

"We're glad you could drop in!" boomed Dex with a flood of relief over the radio channel, "You think you guys could swing in and help out with our little drone problem?"

"Say no more." Came the voice of what Dex assumed was Captain Ingram as his six Atlas I3s began to spread out and orient their bellies toward the station, "We've got ourselves a brand new E-war package that I'm eager to play with." As the radio channel fell quiet, a massive directional burst of electromagnetic energy washed over the Hammer and blinded her sensors completely for a full nine seconds. Suddenly, as the lumbering beasts simultaneously came into range, all six lower turrets on all six of the heavily armed haulers opened fire on the severely disoriented enemy drones, boiling the space in front of the defense cannon into a stitchwork of electric-blue fire. The incoming hail of plasma was chaotic, but it was expertly aimed and Vendrick's drones began to fall in wave after wave of miniature detonations while they continued to throw themselves across the dark.

As it grew obvious that the tide of the battle had officially turned against them, Vendrick's capital ship began to yaw away from Meclan and started a hard acceleration burn away from the abbreviated battle. Then, with a bright flash and a burst of powerful Inaki radiation, the massive vessel instantly disappeared from all sensors. "We got good trajectory data and a firing solution dialed up, Vette?" asked Dex with a quiet calm.

"Vector is calculated, and I am prepared to fire." Reported the A.I. dutifully, "On your order, Commander."

"Send it." Replied Dex with a gentle nod. The defense cannon then burped a bright flash of purple and its heavy projectile reached across the dark to manifest a blossom of crimson flame just under one-hundred and fifty kilometers away. As the damaged ship leaked radiation from its destroyed main reactor into the void, the stealth effect began to fail and the lumbering hulk became visible again to the group's sensors.

"Gear up and get ready to roll." Ordered Dex over the ship's intercom to the boarding team below as he watched the disabled behemoth slowly start to tumble in the distance, "I'd like to take a stroll on over to Vendrick's boat and introduce myself...Maybe have a friendly *chat*. Whaddaya say, guys? Care for a spot of tea with the Governor?"

As the Hammer neared the dark and drifting capital ship, its kilometer-long bulbous void-black hull gently turning end over end, Vette expertly piloted the damaged freighter to latch onto the larger vessel at its relatively stable midpoint using the mighty magnetic grip of their landing struts. Deploying with their magboots engaged, the boarding team followed Dex's lead across the impossibly black enemy hull until they found the outer hatch that Vette had identified for them on their overlay. Breaching the door without incident using the timeless duo of a cutting torch and a pair of crowbars, they moved into the artificial gravity of the enemy ship and squeezed themselves to fit within the tight confines of its destroyed airlock. Manually pulling the outer door closed behind himself, Dex made a hand gesture with his thumb and pinky finger. This action prompted two of the men in his group to step forward and each present a heavily rubberized loop of fabric that they then began applying to the inner edge of the compromised doorway. Once the placement operation was complete and the seal was confirmed solid, Dex cycled the enemy airlock with his fingers secretly crossed.

A pulsing red glow engulfed the nine tightly packed men as ambient sound slowly began to return to the world. After nearly thirty seconds of the constant hiss, a steady green light glowed to life within the interior of the space and the inner door proceeded to swing open. Their chosen airlock had led into what appeared to be an unpopulated maintenance shop, and they all swept the space expertly as they spread out to fill it in a matter of seconds. Taking a knee, Dex pulled open a map of the vessel on his tablet to double check his route to the bridge. They were currently on the Starboard side at the very aft of the vessel, in a section that sat across the central corridor from what appeared to be an access hatch to the engineering deck. Once in that main corridor, they would be heading straight for nearly six-hundred meters before they would reach the entrance to the Capital ship's protected bridge within the armored heart of the vessel. Confident that he had memorized the simple handful of turns and intersections that he would have to traverse, he lowered the tablet and opened a comm to Vette within the Hammer; "Alright, Vee, is there anything you can do to lock the crew down a bit as we make our push for the bridge?"

"Unfortunately, Commander," explained the A.I. as a new objective marker winked to life on his HUD, "I will have no control over local systems until you find me a terminal with access to the ship's central computer, and all such terminals are present only on the bridge of this vessel."

"Well, it looks like we're running the gauntlet then, gentlemen." Declared Dex with a determined exhale as he returned to his feet, "I want three on rear guard with no more than a twenty-meter lag, and a fourth with them on tech sealing up what they can behind us. To those of you with micromissiles, I want you to set those puppies to directional airburst and wait until you have an opening to splash more than one per pop. Stagger the hallway, stay cool, and watch your slice. Let's *move*." The boarding team burst from the machine shop in an angry rush with Dex in the lead, sweeping their weapons over every square inch of the area beyond, only to be met with an empty and sparsely lit hallway. Emboldened by the utter lack of resistance, they surged forward to the next intersection in their journey, finding yet *another* unimpeded stretch of corridor. With an uneasy feeling starting to swell at the back of his mind, Dex pushed ahead using an extra helping of patience and caution. Their unnervingly silent journey through the enemy capital ship took two more uneventful turns before their path led them to the vessel's main corridor that ran along its spine.

Then, as the boarders entered the last stretch before the command deck's heavy blast-hardened door, they were finally blessed with the suspense-shattering sound of gunfire when several men leaned out from recessed doorways along the hall ahead to spring their awaiting trap. "Multiple contacts!" shouted Dex as the rest of his companions followed his lead by ducking into the hallway's recessed series of doorways, "Thirty-two meters, front! Boomers, you're up! Then we push *hard. Go!*"

In acknowledgement of his order, Dex heard three pops and saw a trio of angry fireflies shoot past him down the corridor. Two heartbeats later, a rattling series of detonations could be heard that immediately ceased the incoming fire of their enemy. In a rush of adrenaline, Dex rolled out of cover and charged down the hall toward the settling smoke and debris with his weapon at the ready. As he ran, he kept his attention trained not only on the path ahead but on the handful of recessed doorways that stood between him and the sealed bridge. In the end, his assault was unnecessary, however. Three men, armed with assault rifles but not armored, lie dead at the foot of the bridge's sealed double-slabs of blast-hardened steel. The deceased appeared to be donning the same simple unmarked black uniforms that their counterparts from the weapons lab had worn and by the looks of it they were entirely unprepared to repel a boarding action of *any* kind.

Quickly setting to work on the door with Vette's intrusion software, Dex turned his attention to the others and said; "Alright, I want four of you to stay out here and watch our six. Rest of you are on me. If any of you see a cocky motherfucker in there wearing some kinda goofy-ass hat, that sonofabitch is *mine*... The evilest of dickbags, no matter *where* you run into them, always seem to be drawn to overly elaborate headgear for some stupid reason, and I bet our lovely Governor is no different." As Dex made his claim on the day's biggest catch, the door to the bridge finally chirped in the affirmative and its massive slabs of metal began to withdraw into the wall. The armored men rushed through the gap together, sweeping their weapons high and low to cover every nook and cranny of the bridge's amphitheater of steel and glass as they poured in to cover the space. They found themselves surrounded on all sides by men and women in black uniforms, one crewman for each console that sat along the twin double rows that faced the center of the room, but not a single shot rang out from the intruders. Their quiet muzzles were no product of mercy or surrender, however, but of awe at the twenty-six motionless bodies that were draped limply across their control boards.

The first to tear himself away from the spectacle, Dex automatically shot a hand up to point toward the floating icon on his HUD as he barked; "Tech! Get Vette plugged in ASAP! I need her up and running so she can get to the bottom of whatever the hell just happened in here." The *Aye* that rose in response to his order fell across deaf ears, though, as Dex kept his weapon at the ready and pressed further into the bridge to examine the elevated and display-screen-laden command couch that sat perched to a swivel mount at the far end of the room. The elaborate chair was facing toward the far wall, which was covered from floor to ceiling in display screens that showed a live external camera feed as Meclan slowly passed through its field of view while the unpowered Capital ship continued its unpowered tumble.

Rushing forward with his finger already feeling heavy as it sat on his trigger, he rounded the front of the command chair and was met with a surge of frustration as he found the seat empty. According to his thermal readings, the command couch was still warm and showed other signs of recent life in the form of freshly shelled pistachios filling the cup holder alongside a still-smoldering cigar. When he plucked the sweetly scented roll of tobacco out of the makeshift trash, its glowing tip released a trail of thick grey smoke that crawled up his hand to diffuse into the air and danced as intricate swirls in the harsh lighting above. As he turned the brown bundle in his fingers, he noticed with private delight that the unignited end of the old-fashioned relaxation device had been chewed to bits by the frustrated enemy Captain.

"Shit, Commander." Broke Vette's voice suddenly from the speakers overhead in a matter-of-fact tone that nearly made the line humorous.

With a sudden look of confusion, Dex shot his gaze to the ceiling and asked; "What was that, Vette? Shit?"

"Yes, Commander." Responded the A.I. frankly, "This vessel was in the process of its self-destruct sequence when I loaded onboard, and the detonation countdown had already reached three-hundred and fifty milliseconds before I managed to disable the sequence."

"Shit." Repeated Dex with a shudder of primal awareness at his near-miss, "So where the hell is Vendrick, then? And what in the hell happened to the crew here?"

After the slightest hint of a pause, an infinity in her accelerated mindspace, Vette replied; "Unknown. Both internal and external sensor records before my occupation of the vessel's systems are unavailable. While I cannot locate the ship's former Captain, I can confirm that the only remaining lifesigns aboard are those of yourself and your team. The ship is yours, Commander."

Chapter 42

"Where are we going?" asked Mirta with a giggle as Dex led her into a taxi pod that had its windows blanked out, "If this is some ploy to get me naked in a public place, you can forget about it, buddy…"

"Nothing like that." Laughed Dex with an easy smile, "At least not *this* time, anyways." He added with a mischievous glint.

She punched his arm as she scooted into her seat next to him and huffed; "Fine, I'll play along. Do we at least have time to discuss Vette's findings while we're on the way? It's been nearly a *week* and she's combed over all the debris and data under the sun fifty times over. I *know* she's a bit of a perfectionist and doesn't want to speak of anything she's not certain, but I *need* to know what happened out there, Dex. We all do."

Dex sighed, leaning back into the taxi's soft couch as he replied; "She found a whole lot of nothing, it seems. Vendrick's big bad capital ship was mostly automated and running on a skeleton crew. Based on supplies and other materials found onboard, it is obvious that the vessel was connected to the ground facility that we scrubbed. So we know that much at least. No clues as to who these jokers actually are, but one thing we do know is that they were not prepared at *all* for a protracted naval battle *or* an internal fight to repel boarders. We absolutely caught them with their pants down when we exerted control over the encounter and forced them to fight on our terms, there's no doubt about that."

"What about Vendrick?" pressed Mirta with a little bit too much urgency, betraying her turbulent mood on the subject, "Where the fuck is *that* asshole?"

"That's the bit that has had Vette chewing on so much data the past few days." explained Dex with a nod, "Can't be sure, but as best as we can tell it went down like this… Once it was clear to the brave Governor that a boarding team had made entry and was coming for his ass, that pussy flipped the kill switch on his bridge crew, activated the ship's scuttle command, then made a bee line for some sort of stealth-tech escape craft. We found the empty moorings for it on the deck beneath the bridge and Meclan's sensors confirmed an outward jump from the area about twelve hours after combat had ceased. Coward wanted to fake his own death and get away Scott-free, but the joke's on him. Now we have a space station, three years worth of food, and fifty-five percent of a bad-ass warship for Vette to trick out. And at this point. I'd wager, all *he's* got is a handful of angry investors that may be looking to shorten his lifespan a bit."

Mirta, in her bitterness over Vendrick's escape, refused to smile at the news, but she did nod gravely and managed to say; "With his ability to kill a station in one shot off the table, it's going to be easier to get people around here on their feet and fighting. Reports are already coming in, from Heldrin, Matsuoka, and Verdigan alike that Vendrick's guys are starting to close ranks and circle the wagons a bit. They know they're cut off and it scares them, Dex. For the first time in ten years, *they* fear *us*. Thank you.

Thank you for coming into my bar that day and deciding on a whim to take it upon yourself to return Saiph its soul. I...*We* could never repay you for what you've given us an opportunity to build here. We finally have a future again."

Dex smiled and replied with a laugh as the taxi pod came to a stop and he lifted its door; "Don't thank me until you've seen my craftsmanship. Alright, close your eyes and take my hand. C'mon, trust me. I won't bite..."

Mirta narrowed her eyes with suspicion at him before shutting them fully and providing her hand. He then led her out of the vehicle and guided her down a short path over what felt like uneven cobblestone. When he stopped her, he stepped behind her and held his hands over her eyes to say; "I did nothing when I got here but give you and the folks of Meclan a little push. Y'all did the rest to get where you are today. To illustrate that, I wanted to do a little something to help remind you that life can always get better if you're willing to sow the seeds of that better life. If you're ready to not only fight for it, but to tend to it once it's bloomed..."

With that, he removed his hands and Mirta was suddenly looking up at a gleaming marble Adonis, its white stone and rich veins of gold shining in Saiph's natural blue light as water slowly trickled from the tip of its lightning bolt down to its base. At the foot of the restored fountain sat a ring of freshly tilled dirt in place of the ratty nest of weeds that *had* populated the space the night before. "I wanted you to help me replant the flowers here." He explained with a simple gesture toward a bucket filled with gardening tools, "Because I wanted *you* to be the first to bring new life to Meclan...And I was kinda looking forward to sticking around to see how it grows..."

With tears in her eyes, Mirta turned to him and buried her face in his chest while he silently held her tight, looking out the domed glass ceiling above at the long line of ships who were all patiently waiting to enter Meclan's docks under the watchful eye of the newly-rebranded *Free Saiph Ship* (*F.S.S.*) *Yakima,* which had been towed into place for its first official duty. They had all come for the same reason, groups large and small, all responding to the same radio message that was now blasting itself on repeat to every corner of Saiph in Dex's confident and unwavering voice;

"*Bring me your tired, your poor, your huddled masses yearning to breathe free; And on Meclan, they shall. People of Saiph, the shadow of your occupation is lifting and there is nothing your oppressors can do to reverse the coming tide of your freedom. So join not just me, but your neighbor, your teacher, your barber, and that guy you see on the shuttle every morning in our universally held goal to provide a decent life for ourselves and our families. The doors here on Meclan are always open to those who can get to us, and we have plenty of empty apartments from which you can have your go at that dream. We've claimed sizable food reserves from our occupiers and can support many, but will also be working to recover our food production capabilities over the next few months. As our crops here start to yield, we will begin sharing our bounty to feed the rest of Saiph... Just as Meclan's harvests always used to. And to those who cannot find their way to our halls, hold tightly to your hope and burn bright the flame of your resistance. For we are not just here, but hiding in plain sight among you...because we are you... Your neighbor, your teacher, your barber...Hunting the beasts who saw fit to brand themselves for our retribution. The tide is shifting, brothers and sisters, and the fear is now theirs...*"

TO BE CONTINUED IN BOOK II...

Stranger's War

(Coming whenever it's done)

www.ingramcontent.com/pod-product-compliance
Lightning Source LLC
Chambersburg PA
CBHW030156200626
46812CB00017B/2180